PRE-PUBLICATION PRAISE FOR *Not So Much, Said the Cat*

★ "Another collection of speculative fiction from Swanwick (*Chasing the Phoenix*, 2015, etc.), one of a handful of writers whose short pieces are as impressive as their novels. Versatility, craftsmanship, a dollop of weird, and a delightfully askew sense of humor . . . tales that, through their extraordinary clarity of thought and expression, showcase precisely why this multiaward-winning author is held in such high regard."
—*Kirkus*, starred review

"OK—it's official. Michael Swanwick is a god. He makes worlds that work, every tick and tock of them. He makes people who cry, sweat, puke, fall in love, die in conceivable ways. He's smart and crafty, passionate and wily. Both trickster and life-giver. He creates and uncreates. And yes, he brings Light. If I don't exactly worship him, I read every story of his I can get my hands on. So thanks, Tachyon for bringing me more stories—some old favorites, some I hadn't read before. Because gods need their readers, and God knows, I need more Swanwick."
—Jane Yolen, author of *Briar Rose*

"Is there any SF writer, living or dead or cryonically suspended, who rivals Michael Swanwick for sheer virtuosity? I think not. From the hard-sf poignancy of 'The Woman Who Shook the World Tree' to the Borgesian high jinks of 'The Man in Gray,' from the beguiling folk fantasy of 'The Dala Horse' to the post-cyberpunk intensity of 'Libertarian Russia,' from the Bulgakov-inflected phantasmagoria of 'Of Finest Scarlet Was Her Gown' to the psychological realism (and biological surrealism) of 'Passage of Earth'—I could go on—*Not So Much, Said the Cat* reveals an author who is a Jack-of-all-genres and their master as well."
—James Morrow, author of *Galápagos Regained*

"Michael Swanwick is one of our most reliably entertaining and provocative writers."
—Greg Bear, author of *Darwin's Radio*

"I would effuse about the excellence of the stories within this collection—Michael Swanwick's eleventh such—for they are by turns shocking, delightful, puckish, innovative, and electric. . . . However, I am too busy plotting how to steal the devil's stone (given to him by a Siberian shaman) that Michael keeps by his typewriter in order to unlock his writing power, all without disturbing his cat."
—Fran Wilde, author of *Updraft*

"This is standard Swanwick, where the reader's feet never quite touch the ground. Brilliant."
—Jack McDevitt, author of *The Engines of God*

"A perfect marriage of classic stories and bleeding edge tech, from godlike continental AIs to the abolishment of time, clever discourse on libertarianism and zero-sum economics in a mirroring tale of humanity and alien bugs, fairy tales and one of the best futuristic con-games I've ever had the pleasure of consuming."
—Brad K. Horner

"Speculative fiction is such a deep, wide ocean, that no matter how much one explores, one will always find something more. Michael Swanwick's new anthology, *Not So Much, Said the Cat* is a beautiful, brilliant pearl."
—*The Reading Desk*

"I fell head-over-heels in love with this collection of stories."
—*Lipstick and Libraries*

"A whirlwind of stories that take you across the world, through different pockets of time, and into a sample of the lives being lived, *Not So Much, Said the Cat* is an excellent compilation. Swanwick's latest book is a delight to read, both entertaining and insightful."
—*Pooled Ink*

PRAISE FOR MICHAEL SWANWICK

"Swanwick's wildly imaginative and beautifully written short stories have been, for several years, one of the primary joys of the field."
—*Washington Post Book World*

"One of contemporary sf's greatest short-story writers."
—*Interzone*

"One of the most powerful and consistently inventive short story writers of his generation."
—Gardner Dozois, editor of the Year's Best Science Fiction series

"An amazingly assured writer, seemingly incapable of writing a sentence that isn't interesting in itself, in addition to the way it moves the sentence forward."
—*New York Review of Science Fiction*

"Michael Swanwick is darkly magnificent."
—Jack McDevitt, author of *The Engines of God*

"Swanwick's prose takes no prisoners."
—*Time Out Chicago*

ALSO BY MICHAEL SWANWICK

NOVELS

In the Drift (1985)
Vacuum Flowers (1987)
Stations of the Tide (1991)
The Iron Dragon's Daughter (1993)
Jack Faust (1997)
Bones of the Earth (2002)
The Dragons of Babel (2008)
Dancing with Bears (2011)
Chasing the Phoenix (2015)

COLLECTIONS

Gravity's Angels (1991)
A Geography of Unknown Lands (1997)
Moon Dogs (2000)
Puck Aleshire's Abecedary (2000)
Tales of Old Earth (2000)
Cigar-Box Faust and Other Miniatures (2003)
*Michael Swanwick's Field Guide to the Mesozoic
Megafauna* (2004)
The Periodic Table of Science Fiction (2005)
The Dog Said Bow-Wow (2007)
The Best of Michael Swanwick (2008)

NOT SO MUCH

SAID THE CAT

CAT

MICHAEL SWANWICK

TACHYON | SAN FRANCISCO

Cover and interior design by Elizabeth Story

Tachyon Publications LLC
1459 18th Street #139
San Francisco, CA 94107
(415) 285-5615
tachyon@tachyonpublications.com

www.tachyonpublications.com
smart science fiction & fantasy

Series Editor: Jacob Weisman
Project Editor: Jill Roberts

ISBN 13: 978-1-61696-228-9
ISBN 10: 1-61696-228-3

Printed in the United States of America by Worzalla

First edition: August 2016
9 8 7 6 5 4 3 2 1

For Marianne

my heart's ease

CONTENTS

I am indebted and deeply grateful to Gene Wolfe for letting me play in his world, to Linda Lane for sharing her diary with me, to Neil Varrone for giving me a title and suggesting I write a story to go with it, to Boris Dolingo for twice bringing me to Ekaterinburg and to Andrew Matveev and Alexei Bezouglyi for insights into Mother Russia, to the Swecon con committee for introducing me to their beautiful country, to Janis Ian for writing "Mary's Eyes," to John Cramer for bringing my physics out of the nineteenth century, to Gardner Dozois for suggesting I write a new Darger and Surplus story, to Jennifer Summerfield for insights into the craft of theater, to Gregory Frost for friendship and advice, to Neil Gaiman for commissioning a story without regard to genre, to Patrick Nielsen Hayden for the observation that let me turn one story into a series, and to the M. C. Porter Endowment for the Arts for the best years of my life.

Introduction:
Where I am now, I think

When, exactly, *did* I decide to run away with the elves? Possibly during the summer I spent working ten hours a day on the loading docks of a furniture factory in Roanoke and, out of boredom, began writing invented words and fragments of sentences on scraps of discarded paper tape. Maybe on the afternoon I returned home to find a pane of glass in the kitchen door broken and bloody, my father's hand bandaged, and my mother uncharacteristically grim and silent about whatever had happened. That event marked the beginning of my father's rapid descent into early onset Alzheimer's, a trauma that triggered my family's flight south from Vermont and a great deal of my behavior thereafter. Or midway through the night I picked up a paperback of *The Fellowship of the Ring*, meaning to take in a chapter or two before sleep, and stayed up reading through the dawn, reading through breakfast, reading every step of the long walk through the woods to Winooski High, and finished the last chapter just as the homeroom bell rang. All I can say for sure is that in my junior year of high school, I was determined to be a scientist and by the time I entered college I had dedicated my life to fiction.

I have been asked to write a few words about where I am now in my career as a writer. But it is hard to say just where that career began. To start with my first sale would be an injustice to the intense young man I once was—and I owe him a great deal for his utter refusal to face up to reality, though many encouraged him to do so.

So I'll start in the Greyhound station in Philadelphia. There, at age twenty-three, I alit with seventy dollars in my pocket, a pack-a-day cigarette habit, newspaper folded inside one boot to cover the hole in its sole, a friend who had volunteered to let me crash on the couch in his apartment for a month, and the mad conviction that I was going to become a science-fiction writer. Over the next six months, I sold my blood, ghosted term papers, took every temp job I could find, and early one Sunday morning when I had neither food nor money to buy it, walked a dozen times around a single block where a bag of freshly baked French bread had been left on the steps of a restaurant, debating whether or not to steal a loaf. By the time I finally found work as a clerk-typist, I had lost fifty pounds.

I can see that young writer now, long haired and dressed in black denim, sitting in a shabby second-floor room across from the flophouse at 15th and South, typing long past midnight while in the street below whores hold long, screaming arguments with their pimps. He is writing plot fragments, prose poems, letters from the soul—none of which ever come close to turning into stories because he has no idea how to find an ending for any of them. If I could speak to him across the gulf of time and let him know that he will publish books, win awards, be guest of honor at conventions in places like Ekaterinburg, Turku, Zagreb, and even at the World Science Fiction Convention, he would be pleased but not surprised. Against all evidence, he is sure he has a glorious future. He's painfully aware that he has a long way to go. But he's learning just as hard and fast as he can.

And if he could ask me one question, it would be. . . .

Then again, I could begin six years later, on that giddy, starry night when Gardner Dozois and Jack Dann read through my latest failed attempt at fiction and, step by step, showed me how to turn it into a real story. It was as if God had reached down from the sky and flicked a switch inside my brain. From that moment on, though the labor was as hard as ever, I understood what a story needed to reach its conclusion. I reeled up Spruce Street back to my apartment at two in the morning, past young gay men sitting on their stoops to be ogled by other young gay men cruising slowly by, and was happier than any of them, for my life had just been transformed.

The following year, I had two extraordinary strokes of luck. One was that my first two published stories made the ballot for the Nebula Award—and in the same category, to boot. This got me a great deal of the kind of attention a new writer finds encouraging. Briefly, I was the *kumquat haagendasz*, a term coined by Gardner Dozois for the recipient of that evanescent state of excitement that passes from new writer to newer as the cognoscenti become aware of them. The second stroke of luck was that I lost. I lost, which meant I didn't have the pressure of instant success to measure myself against, and I kept on losing through multiple nominations for a full decade. I came close, in fact, to becoming the *bull goose loser*, another of Gardner's coinages, the writer with the largest number of award nominations and not a single win, before victory knocked me out of the running.

I was part of an extraordinary generation of writers who hit the beaches in the early Eighties. I wrote an essay praising some of them and promptly received phone calls from what seemed like every writer under the age of fifty who hadn't been included, demanding an apology. So I won't list names, though you can easily guess most of them. Le Guin and Delany and Wolfe and Russ may have been writing better, but my compeers were the ones whose fiction my own work was in competition and dialogue with. Some were more successful at novel length than others. But they all showed a particular brilliance for short fiction and it was largely in that arena where we fought it out for the admiration of those who most mattered—each other. Whenever something like Pat Cadigan's "Rock On" or Nancy Kress's "Beggars in Spain" or Bruce Sterling's "Swarm" appeared, I would take it apart, cog by sentence, and study the pieces to see what I could learn from them, what I might be able to appropriate for my own fiction.

At the same time I was writing collaborations with Gardner Dozois and Jack Dann. We'd sit around the kitchen table in Gardner's cramped, cat-infested Quince Street apartment, laughing and waving our arms and raising our voices in excitement as we turned a chance remark into a story idea and then hammered out a plot for it. Later, I'd turn my notes into a first draft that Jack would improve upon and Gardner would recast in a consistent voice and give a final polish to. This was my postgraduate education, and I could hardly have had sharper teachers than those two. Once, midway through my draft, I told Jack I'd made a change that would surprise him. He looked startled, then said, "I know what you've done, and you'll find that it doesn't work." And of course he was right.

On a more equal basis, I proceeded to write stories with William Gibson, Tim Sullivan, Pat Murphy, Andy Duncan, Gregory Frost, Avram Davidson (posthumously), and Eileen Gunn. They were all, to greater or lesser degrees, as much work as going it alone would have been, and brought in only half the money. But they were my opportunity to watch other writers at work, to see what chops they had and what might be worth imitating.

For five of those years, not all of them contiguous, I served on the Nebula jury, which, for reasons that made sense then but would be hard to explain now, was empowered to add one work per category to the Nebula Award ballot. This required that we read everything written in genre during the year, a hopeless task for novels but just barely achievable in the shorter lengths. The experience taught me a great deal about fiction, particularly the myriad ways in which even the most promising stories can fail.

Meanwhile, my peers were learning how to write novels. Some gave up short fiction entirely, a decision that made perfect economic sense, for though story sales can bring in much-needed income during that long trough between novels, nobody can make a living off them today. (Lucius Shepard, who never did master the novel form, came close, but even he leaned heavily on movie options and nonfiction assignments from the slicks.) I once went on a short-fiction binge where I was finishing a new story every three weeks, like clockwork. Which meant that every few days I was either finishing a story and sending it out or receiving notification it had sold or sending in the contract or getting back the payment check or receiving proof sheets or sending them back corrected or receiving contributor's copies in the mail or having my original typescript returned to me, marked up with directions to the printer. I never felt so validated as a writer in my life. Then I did my taxes and discovered that once expenses were taken into account, I'd had a net loss of income for that year.

I began work on a new novel the next day.

But I didn't turn away from short fiction, as so many of my friends had. "Remember how we used to spend months working on a single story back in the old days?" one of them asked me a few years ago. I didn't tell him that I had never stopped doing that. Because then I'd have to explain that I kept writing short fiction out of love for the form and from fear of losing the ability to do so, as I was fairly certain my friend had. It would be a mad thing to surrender a skill acquired so painfully and at such great length.

Somewhere along the line, I discovered that I had a particular aptitude for flash fiction. I wrote abecedaries. I wrote a story for every element in the periodic table. I wrote one for each etching of Goya's *Los Caprichos*. I wrote flash fictions and sealed them in bottles that I signed with a diamond-tipped pen, and then I destroyed every other copy, physical or electronic, so each bottled story would be literally unique, and donated the bottles to various charities. I wrote stories on masks, lighting fixtures, clocks, carafes, and other physical objects scattered about my house. And when I had learned all I could from the form, I more or less stopped.

I also taught. Weeklong gigs at Clarion, Clarion West, and Clarion South reassured me that I could be of actual use to at least some of the students. It is a holy and terrifying thing to be charged with helping new writers find their own voices. But by then I knew enough about fiction that it was easy to show them what their faltering efforts wanted to become, just as Jack and Gardner had done with mine. Later, I would marvel at how far I had come.

More recently, I figured out at last how to write stories in series, both open-ended as in the Darger and Surplus stories, and following a plotted story arc, as in the Mongolian Wizard tales. For a Gene Wolfe *festschrift*, I took the first page of the master's "The Fifth Head of Cerberus" and flipped directions, seasons, and genders, and then proceeded to write the story as it might have been told by James Tiptree, Jr. This required a close study of the original novella, an exercise that taught me a great deal and could have taught me more had I the time to write the story longer. I based stories on places I had been—Russia, Sweden, Vermont—and things I'd experienced, such as the Easter Sunday in Dublin when Gerry Adams strolled past me on O'Connell Street. I asked myself what I would do if my wife died and then spent years looking for a way to resolve what ultimately became a love letter to her. I put in weeks poring over a dissection manual followed by, again, years looking for a way to end the story that hadn't already been done to death. I thought long and hard about the obligations of a writer to his creations and wrote a story about that too. I wrote a story entirely in dialogue. I wrote a metafiction on von Grimmelshausen's *Simplicius Simplicissimus*, with the goal of making it work as a surface narrative. I took several years' worth of notes for a novel that never congealed and used them as backstory for a much smaller tale narrated by a woman who died before it began. A friend gave me a title and challenged me to write something for it; I placed the story in the Cretaceous and left out the dinosaurs. In memory of another friend, who once showed me her diary, I wrote about how hard being a teenage girl can be and gave it the conclusion she'd had in real life. I penned a tragic romance that required the advice of a physicist to set up.

It is possible that I am the last writer to have come into the field having read every work of science fiction of any importance written to date. If not, that door closed soon thereafter. But in my formative years I read voraciously, and one by one all the greats fell before me—C. L. Moore, R. A. Lafferty, Philip K. Dick, Leigh Brackett—until finally I finished Theodore Sturgeon's last collection and wept, like Alexander, for having no new worlds to conquer. Yet, though I valued each author individually, I read science fiction as if it had all been written by a single genius possessed of an impossible variety of styles and interests. This was a mad standard to set oneself. But that is the writer I have been trying, with varying success, to emulate ever since.

On the side of the bookshelf by my writing desk are twenty or so Post-it notes with the names of stories and novels I am actively working on. In a Rolodex nearby are the titles of a great many more I hope to get around to soon. New ideas constantly swim up from the murky seas of the unconscious, demanding to be told. I scribble them down in my notebooks and the best of them are added to the queue. The only limits to the number of stories I might eventually write are time and mortality.

Long, long ago, I ran off with the elves. I learned their ways and lived with them so long as to be indistinguishable from their tribe. That is, I suppose, a kind of success. But it would not satisfy my young unpublished self. Nor does it answer the question he would have posed me over a third of a century ago.

In Siberia, a shaman, a dapper little man with neatly trimmed salt-and-pepper beard and a three-piece suit, gave me a devil stone, which he told me would help to unlock my power. I keep it by my computer always. Lifting it up, savoring its weight, I cast my thoughts back in time to the nascent writer I once was, afire with ambition, impatiently waiting for the answer he knew would take all these years to reach him:

No, Michael, I haven't gotten there yet. But I haven't given up trying. Someday, I hope, I will be as good a writer as it is possible for me to become. In the meantime, I'm learning just as hard and as fast as I can.

So that is where I am now, I think. I hope the results please you.

—Michael Swanwick

The Man in Grey

There's a rustling in the wings. Let the story begin.

I was standing outside watching when sixteen-year-old Martha Geissler, pregnant, loveless, and unwed, stepped into the path of a Canadian National freight train traveling at the rate of forty-five miles per hour. The engineer saw her and simultaneously applied the brakes and hit the air horn. But since the train consisted of two 4,300-horsepower SD70M-2 locomotives hauling seventy-six loaded cars and seventy-three empty ones and weighed an aggregate 11,700 tons, it was a given that it wouldn't stop in time. All that the engineer could hope for was that the crazy woman on the tracks would come to her senses.

Maybe she would. Maybe she wouldn't. The forces that brought Martha here were absolutely predictable. What she would do in the actual event was not. One way or another, it was an instant of perfect, even miraculous, free will.

Martha stared at the oncoming train with neither fear nor exaltation, but with great clarity of mind. She thought things that were hers alone to know, came to a decision, and then stepped deliberately backwards from the track.

There was a collective sigh of relief from the shadows. Never let it be said that those of us who have no lives of our own don't care.

Then she slipped.

It shouldn't have happened. It *couldn't* have happened. But it did. The script said that if she stepped backwards, away from the oncoming locomotive, the ground behind her would be flat and solid. Given the choice she had made, Martha was supposed to stand, half stunned, as the train slammed past inches from her face. She would be given the gift of a moment of absolute calm in which she would realize things that might well help her to understand exactly who she was now and who she might turn out to be years in the future.

But a stagehand had somehow, inexplicably, left behind a chilled bottle of a brand of cola not even available on Martha's ostensible continent, when he was setting up the scene. It rolled under Martha's foot. She lost her balance.

With a little shriek, she fell forward, into the path of the train.

With that, I stepped out of the grey, grabbed her arm, and hauled her back.

Still wailing, the train rushed by and the engineer—enormously relieved and himself beginning to change as a result of the incident—released the brake and carefully accelerated out of the long bend and into somebody else's area of responsibility.

Martha clutched me as tightly as if she were drowning. Slowly I pried her loose. She stared into my face, white with shock. "I . . ." she said. "You. . . ."

"It's a goddamned lucky thing I was passing by, young lady," I said gruffly. "You oughtta be more careful." I turned to leave.

Martha looked up and down the tracks. We were at the outskirts of town, where the land was flat and empty. The nearest building was a warehouse a full city block away. There was nowhere I could possibly have come from. She could see that at a glance.

Inwardly I cursed.

"Who are you?" she said, hurrying after me. Then, "*What* are you?"

"Nobody. I just happened to see you." I was almost running now, with Martha plucking at my coat sleeve and trotting to keep up. "Listen, Sis, I don't want to be rude, but I've got things to do, okay? I got places to be. I can't—" I was sweating. I belonged in the grey, not out on stage with the talent. I wasn't used to extemporaneous speech. All this improv was beyond me.

I broke into an out-and-out run. Coat flying, I made for the warehouse. If I could only get out of sight for a second—assuming there was some local action scheduled for the other side of the building before this scenario ended and that the stage was properly set—I could slip back into the grey without Martha seeing it. She'd know that something strange had happened, but what could she do about it? Who could she complain to? Who would listen to her if she did?

I reached the warehouse and flew around the corner.

And into the streets of Hong Kong.

The stagehands had, of course, only put up as much stage dressing as was needed for the scenario. It was just my bad luck that we were back-to-back with an Asian set. Behind the warehouse facade it was all skyscrapers and Chinese-language advertising. Plus, it was night and it had just rained, so the streets were smudged black mirrors reflecting streetlights and neon. I said a bad word.

Martha plowed into my back. She rebounded, almost fell, and caught herself. Then, horn blaring, a taxicab almost ran us down. She clutched my arm so hard it hurt. "What—what is this?" she asked, eyes wide with existential terror.

"There are a few things you should know." I gently turned her back toward the city she had grown up in. "There's a diner not far from here. Why don't I buy you a cup of coffee and we can talk?"

In the diner, I tried to explain. "The world is maybe not the way you picture it to be," I said. "In its mechanics, anyway. We don't have the resources to maintain every possible setup twenty-four hours a day. Also, there aren't as many real people in it—folks you might actually meet, as opposed to those you see at a distance or hear about on TV— as you were led to believe. Maybe forty-five or fifty thousand all told. But other than that, everything's just like you've always thought it was. Go back to your life and you'll be fine."

Martha clutched her coffee cup as if it were all that was keeping her from falling off the face of the earth. But she looked at me steadily. Her eyes were clear and focused. "So this is all—what?—a play, you're telling me? I'm nothing but a puppet and you're the guy who pulls my strings? You're in charge of things and I'm the entertainment?"

"No, no, no. Your life is your own. You have absolute free will. I'm just here to make sure that when you step out of the shower, the bath mat is always there for you."

"You've seen me *naked*?"

I sighed. "Martha, either I or somebody like me has been with you for every waking or sleeping moment of your life. Every time your mother changed your diapers or you squeezed a zit in the mirror or you hid under the blankets with a flashlight and a romance manga after you were supposed to be asleep, there were people there, working hard to ensure that the world behaved in a comprehensible and consistent fashion for you."

"So what are you? You operate a camera, right? Or maybe you are the camera. Like you're a robot, or you've got cameras implanted in your eyes." She was still stuck on the entertainment metaphor. It had been a mistake telling her that the whole thing had been caused by a careless stagehand.

"I am not a camera. I'm just the man who stands in grey, making things happen." I did not tell her that all the necessary misery and suffering in the world is caused by people like me. Not because I'm ashamed of what I do—I make no apologies; it's important work—but because Martha wasn't ready to hear, much less understand, it. "What you've discovered is analogous to somebody in the Middle Ages learning that the world is not made up of fire, water, air, and earth, but rather by unimaginably small bundles of quarks underlain by strata of quantum uncertainty. It might feel shocking to you at first. But the world's the same as it's always been. It's only your understanding of it that's changed."

Martha looked at me with huge, wounded eyes. "But . . . why?"

"I honestly don't know," I said. "If you forced me to speculate, I'd say that there are two possibilities. One is that Somebody decided that things should be like this. The other is that it's simply the way things are. But which is true is anybody's guess."

That's when Martha began to cry.

So I got up and walked around the table and put my arms about her. She was still only a child, after all.

When Martha calmed down, I took her back to her mother's place in the Northern Liberties. It was a long trek—she'd been wandering about blindly ever since the pregnancy test turned blue—and so I ordered up a taxi. Martha flinched a little when it appeared before her, right out of thin air. But she got in and I gave the cabbie her address. The cabbie wasn't real, of course. But he was good work. You'd have to talk to him for an hour to realize he was only a prop.

As we rode, Martha kept trying to work things through. She was like a kid picking at a scab. "So you do all the work, I get that. What's in it for you?"

I shrugged. "A transient taste of being, every now and again." I looked out the window at the passing city. Even knowing that it was all metaphysical canvas and paint, it looked convincing. "This is pretty nice. I like it. Mostly, though, it's just my job. I'm not like you—I don't have any say over what I do and don't do."

"You think any of this is my choice?"

"More of it than you'd suspect. Okay, yes, you dropped out of school, you don't have a job, and you're pregnant by a boy you don't particularly like, and that limits your options. You're still living with your mother and the two of you fight constantly. It's been years since you've seen your father and sometimes you wonder if he's still alive. You have health issues. None of that is under your control. But your response to it is. That's an extraordinary privilege and it's one I don't have. Given the current situation, I could no more get out of this cab and walk away from you than you could flap your arms and fly to the Moon.

"You, however, have the freedom to think anything, say anything, do anything. Your every instant is unpredictable. Right here, right now, it may be that what I'm saying will reach you and you'll smile and ask how you can get back on script. Maybe you'll scream and call me names. Maybe you'll retreat into silence. Maybe you'll slap me. Anything could happen."

She slapped me.

I looked at her. "What did that prove?"

"It made me feel better," she lied. Martha crossed her arms and pushed herself back into the cushions, making herself as small as she could. Fleetingly, I thought she was going to keep retreating, deeper and deeper into herself, until nothing showed on the outside but dull, lifeless eyes. She could decide to do that. It was her right.

But then the cab pulled up before a nondescript row house on Leithgow Street and she got out.

"Act like you've gotten a big tip," I told the cabbie.

"Hey, thanks, buddy!" he said, and drove off.

Martha was unlocking the door. "Mom's visiting her sister in Baltimore for a couple days. We have the house to ourselves."

"I know."

She went straight to the kitchen and got out a bottle of her mother's vodka from the freezer.

"It's a little early for that, isn't it?" I said.

"Then make it later."

"As you will." I signaled the gaffer and the sun slid down the sky. The world outside the window grew dark. I didn't bother ordering up stars. "Is that late enough?"

"What the fuck do I care?" Martha sat down at the kitchen table and I followed suit. She filled two tumblers, thrust one in my hands. "Drink."

I did, though not being talent, the alcohol had no effect on me.

After a while, she said, "Which of my friends are real and which aren't?"

"They're all real, Martha. Tomika, Jeanne, Siouxie, Ben, your teachers, your parents, your cousins, the boy you thought was cute but too immature to go out with—everyone you have an emotional relationship with, positive or negative, is as real as you are. Anything else would be cheating."

"How about Kevin?" Her boyfriend, of course.

"Him too."

"Shit." Martha stared down into her glass, swirling the vodka around and around, creating a miniature whirlpool. "What about rappers and movie stars?"

"That's a different story. Your feelings toward them aren't terribly complex; nor are they reciprocated. Real people aren't needed to fill the roles."

"Thought so." She drank deeply.

If she kept on in this vein, sooner or later she was going to ask about her father. In which case, I would have to tell her that Carl Geissler was in Graterford, where prison life was teaching him things about his essential nature that would take him decades to assimilate. Then that her mother clandestinely visited him there every month and, for reasons she only imperfectly understood, kept this fact to herself. So I touched Martha's glass and said, "Do you really think this is a wise course of action?"

"What do people normally do in this situation?" she asked sarcastically.

"Martha, listen to me. You have all your life ahead of you and, depending on what choices you make, it can be a very good life indeed. I know. I've seen young women in your situation before, more times than you can imagine. Let me take you back to where you were before we met and start your life up where it left off."

Her expression was stiff and unreadable. "You can do that, huh? Rewind the movie and then start it up again?"

"That's an inexact metaphor," I said. "With your cooperation, we can re-create the scenario. You'll enter it, play your part, and then go back to your life. What happens then will be entirely up to you. No interference from me or anybody like me, I swear. But you have to agree to it. We can't do a thing without your permission."

As I spoke, Martha's face grew more and more expressionless. Her eyes were hard and unblinking. Which suggested that the one thing I feared most—that she would go catatonic, burying that beautiful spark of life deeper and deeper under soft cottony layers of silence and inertia—was a very real possibility. "Please," I said. "Say something."

To my surprise, Martha said, "What does reality look like?"

"I'm not sure I understand you. This is reality. All around you."

"It's a fucking set! Show me what's behind it, or underneath it, or however the hell you want to put it. Show me what remains when the set is gone."

"I honestly don't advise that. It would only upset you."

"Do it!"

Reluctantly, I pushed back the chair. There was nothing scheduled anywhere behind the house for hours. I went to the back door. I opened it—

—revealing the roiling, churning emptiness that underlies the world we constantly make and unmake in the service of our duty. The colorless, formless negation of negatives that is Nothing and Nowhere and Nowhen. The calm horror of nonbeing. The grey.

I stood looking into it, waiting for Martha to make a noise, to cry out in fear, to beg me to make it go away. But though I waited for the longest time, she did not.

Fearing the worst, I turned back to her.

"All right," Martha said. "Rewind me."

So I took Martha Geissler back to where it had all begun. The sun and clouds were carefully placed exactly where they'd been, and the stagehands brought out the locomotives and hooked them up to the correct number of freight cars. Because the original engineer was talent, we put in a prop in his place The script didn't call for the two of them to ever meet, so there wouldn't be any continuity problems.

"Here's your mark," I told Martha for the umpteenth time. "When the train passes that telephone pole over there—"

"I step into its path," she said. "Then I slowly count to ten and step backwards off the track. This time there won't be a soda bottle underfoot. How many times have we gone over this? I know my lines."

"Thank you," I said, and stepped into the grey to wait and watch.

The train came rumbling forward, only moderately fast but with tremendous momentum. Closer it came, and closer, and when it reached the telephone pole I'd chosen as a marker, Martha did not step into its path. Instead, she stood motionless by the side of the track.

The prop engineer hit the air horn just as the real one had, despite the fact that the track before him was empty. Still, Martha did nothing.

Then, at the very last possible instant, she stepped in front of the train.

There was a universal gasp from the shadows, the sound of my many brothers and sisters caught completely by surprise. Followed by a moment of perfect silence. Then by rolling thunderheads of applause.

It was an astonishing thing for Martha to do—and she'd done it calmly, without giving me the least sign of what was to come. But I didn't join in the applause.

Briefly, I understood what it was like to be one of them. The talent, I mean. For the first time in my very long existence, I wanted something to not have happened.

Thus ended Martha's story. I returned to my own world and to the job of maintaining and arranging the world whose inhabitants fondly believe to be real. Theirs is, for all its limitations, larger and more commodious than mine. But I do not begrudge them that. Their lives are more difficult and far more profound than anything I shall ever experience. Neither do I begrudge them that. We all have our places in existence and our parts to play.

Martha was a star in what we call the Great Game and what they (you) call reality. I am just a cog in the machinery. But if all my functions are mechanical, at least my reactions to it are not. I am not a camera. I am not a voyeur. Nor, God knows, am I the wizard behind the curtain, manipulating everything to his own benefit. Nothing of the sort.

I am the man in grey, and I love you all.

The Dala Horse

Something terrible had happened. Linnéa did not know what it was. But her father had looked pale and worried, and her mother had told her, very fiercely, "Be brave!" and now she had to leave, and it was all the result of that terrible thing.

The three of them lived in a red wooden house with steep black roofs by the edge of the forest. From the window of her attic room, Linnéa could see a small lake silver with ice very far away. The design of the house was unchanged from all the way back in the days of the Coffin People, who buried their kind in beautiful polished boxes with metal fittings like nothing anyone made anymore. Uncle Olaf made a living hunting down their coffin-sites and salvaging the metal from them. He wore a necklace of gold rings he had found, tied together with silver wire.

"Don't go near any roads," her father had said. "Especially the old ones." He'd given her a map. "This will help you find your grand-mother's house."

"Mor-Mor?"

"No, Far-Mor. My mother. In Godastor."

Godastor was a small settlement on the other side of the mountain. Linnéa had no idea how to get there. But the map would tell her.

Her mother gave her a little knapsack stuffed with food, and a quick hug. She shoved something deep in the pocket of Linnéa's coat and said, "Now go! Before it comes!"

"Good-bye, Mor and Far," Linnéa had said formally, and bowed.

Then she'd left.

So it was that Linnéa found herself walking up a long, snowy slope, straight up the side of the mountain. It was tiring work, but she was a dutiful little girl. The weather was harsh, but whenever she started getting cold, she just turned up the temperature of her coat. At the top of the slope she came across a path, barely wide enough for one person, and so she followed it onward. It did not occur to her that this might be one of the roads her father had warned her against. She did not wonder at the fact that it was completely bare of snow.

After a while, though, Linnéa began to grow tired. So she took off her knapsack and dropped it in the snow alongside the trail and started to walk away.

"Wait!" the knapsack said. "You've left me behind."

Linnéa stopped. "I'm sorry," she said. "But you're too heavy for me to carry."

"If you can't carry me," said the knapsack, "then I'll have to walk."

So it did.

On she went, followed by the knapsack, until she came to a fork in the trail. One way went upward and the other down. Linnéa looked from one to the other. She had no idea which to take.

"Why don't you get out the map?" her knapsack suggested.

So she did.

Carefully, so as not to tear, the map unfolded. Contour lines squirmed across its surface as it located itself. Blue stream-lines ran downhill. Black roads and stitched red trails went where they would. "We're here," said the map, placing a pinprick light at its center. "Where would you like to go?"

"To Far-Mor," Linnéa said. "She's in Godastor."

"That's a long way. Do you know how to read maps?"

"No."

"Then take the road to the right. Whenever you come across another road, take me out and I'll tell you which way to go."

On Linnéa went, until she could go no farther, and sat down in the snow beside the road. "Get up," the knapsack said. "You have to keep on going." The muffled voice of the map, which Linnéa had stuffed back into the knapsack, said, "Keep straight on. Don't stop now."

"Be silent, both of you," Linnéa said, and, of course, they obeyed. She pulled off her mittens and went through her pockets to see if she'd remembered to bring any toys. She hadn't, but in the course of looking she found the object her mother had thrust into her coat.

It was a dala horse.

Dala horses came in all sizes, but this one was small. They were carved out of wood and painted bright colors with a harness of flowers. Linnéa's horse was red; she had often seen it resting on a high shelf in her parents' house. Dala horses were very old. They came from the time of the Coffin People who lived long ago, before the time of the Strange Folk. The Coffin People and the Strange Folk were all gone now. Now there were only Swedes.

Linnéa moved the dala horse up and down, as if it were running. "Hello, little horse," she said.

"Hello," said the dala horse. "Are you in trouble?"

Linnéa thought. "I don't know," she admitted at last.

"Then most likely you are. You mustn't sit in the snow like that, you know. You'll burn out your coat's batteries."

"But I'm bored. There's nothing to do."

"I'll teach you a song. But first you have to stand up."

A little sulkily, Linnéa did so. Up the darkening road she went again, followed by the knapsack. Together she and the dala horse sang:

> *Hark! through the darksome night*
> *Sounds come a-winging:*
> *Lo! 'tis the Queen of Light*
> *Joyfully singing.*

The shadows were getting longer and the depths of the woods to either side turned black. Birch trees stood out in the gloom like thin white ghosts. Linnéa was beginning to stumble with weariness when she saw a light ahead. At first she thought it was a house, but as she got closer, it became apparent it was a campfire.

There was a dark form slumped by the fire. For a second, Linnéa was afraid he was a troll. Then she saw that he wore human clothing and realized that he was a Norwegian or possibly a Dane. So she started to run toward him.

At the sound of her feet on the road, the man leaped up. "Who's there?" he cried. "Stay back—I've got a cudgel!"

Linnéa stopped. "It's only me," she said.

The man crouched a little, trying to see into the darkness beyond his campfire. "Step closer," he said. And then, when she obeyed, "What are you?"

"I'm just a little girl."

"Closer!" the man commanded. When Linnéa stood within the circle of firelight, he said, "Is there anybody else with you?"

"No, I'm all alone."

Unexpectedly, the man threw his head back and laughed. "Oh god!" he said. "Oh god, oh god, oh god, I was so afraid! For a moment there I thought you were . . . well, never mind." He threw his stick into the fire. "What's that behind you?"

"I'm her knapsack," the knapsack said.

"And I'm her map," a softer voice said.

"Well, don't just lurk there in the darkness. Stand by your mistress." When he had been obeyed, the man seized Linnéa by the shoulders. He had more hair and beard than anyone she had ever seen, and his face was rough and red. "My name is Günther, and I'm a dangerous man, so if I give you an order, don't even think of disobeying me. I walked here from Finland, across the Gulf of Bothnia. That's a long, long way on a very dangerous bridge, and there are not many men alive today who could do that."

Linnéa nodded, though she was not sure she understood.

"You're a Swede. You know nothing. You have no idea what the world is like. You haven't . . . tasted its possibilities. You've never let your fantasies eat your living brain." Linnéa couldn't make any sense out of what Günther was saying. She thought he must have forgotten she was a little girl. "You stayed here and led ordinary lives while the rest of us. . . ." His eyes were wild. "I've seen horrible things. Horrible, horrible things." He shook Linnéa angrily. "I've done horrible things as well. Remember that!"

"I'm hungry," Linnéa said. She was. She was so hungry her stomach hurt.

Günther stared at her as if he were seeing her for the first time. Then he seemed to dwindle a little and all the anger went out of him. "Well . . . let's see what's in your knapsack. C'mere, little fellow."

The knapsack trotted to Günther's side. He rummaged within and removed all the food Linnéa's mother had put in it. Then he started eating.

"Hey!" Linnéa said. "That's mine!"

One side of the man's mouth rose in a snarl. But he shoved some bread and cheese into Linnéa's hands. "Here."

Günther ate all the smoked herring without sharing. Then he wrapped himself in a blanket and lay down by the dying fire to sleep. Linnéa got out her own little blanket from the knapsack and lay down on the opposite side of the fire.

She fell asleep almost immediately.

But in the middle of the night, Linnéa woke up. Somebody was talking quietly in her ear.

It was the dala horse. "You must be extremely careful with Günther," the dala horse whispered. "He is not a good man."

"Is he a troll?" Linnéa whispered back.

"Yes."

"I thought so."

"But I'll do my best to protect you."

"Thank you."

Linnéa rolled over and went back to sleep.

In the morning, troll-Günther kicked apart the fire, slung his pack over his shoulder, and started up the road. He didn't offer Linnéa any food, but there was still some bread and cheese from last night which she had stuffed in a pocket of her coat, so she ate that.

Günther walked faster than Linnéa did, but whenever he got too far ahead, he'd stop and wait for her. Sometimes the knapsack carried Linnéa. But because it only had enough energy to do so for a day, usually she carried it instead.

When she was bored, Linnéa sang the song she had learned the previous day.

At first, she wondered why the troll always waited for her when she lagged behind. But then, one of the times he was far ahead, she asked the dala horse and it said, "He's afraid and he's superstitious. He thinks that a little girl who walks through the wilderness by herself must be lucky."

"Why is he afraid?"

"He's being hunted by something even worse than he is."

At noon they stopped for lunch. Because Linnéa's food was gone, Günther brought out food from his own supplies. It wasn't as good as what Linnéa's mother had made. But when Linnéa said so, Günther snorted, "You're lucky I'm sharing at all." He stared off into the empty woods in silence for a long time. Then he said, "You're not the first girl I've encountered on my journey, you know. There was another whom I met in what remained of Hamburg. When I left, she came with me. Even knowing what I'd done, she. . . ." He fished out a locket and thrust it at Linnéa. "Look!"

Inside the locket was a picture of a woman. She was an ordinary pretty woman. Just that and nothing more. "What happened to her?" Linnéa asked.

The troll grimaced, showing his teeth. *"I ate her."* His look was wild as wild could be. "If we run out of food, I may have to cook and eat you too."

"I know," Linnéa said. Trolls were like that. She was familiar with the stories. They'd eat anything. They'd even eat people. They'd even eat other trolls. Her books said so. Then, because he hadn't told her yet, "Where are you going?"

"I don't know. Someplace safe."

"I'm going to Godastor. My map knows the way."

For a very long time Günther mulled that over. At last, almost reluctantly, he said, "Is it safe there, do you think?"

Linnéa nodded her head emphatically. "Yes."

Pulling the map from her knapsack, Günther said, "How far is it to Godastor?"

"It's on the other side of the mountain, a day's walk if you stay on the road, and twice, maybe three times that if you cut through the woods."

"Why the hell would I want to cut through the woods?" He stuffed the map back in the knapsack. "Okay, kid, we're going to Godastor."

That afternoon, a great darkness rose up behind them, intensifying the shadows between the trees and billowing up high above until half the sky was black as chimney soot. Linnéa had never seen a sky like that. An icy wind blew down upon them so cold that it made her cry and then froze the tears on her cheeks. Little whirlwinds of snow lifted off of the drifts and danced over the empty black road. They gathered in one place, still swirling, in the ghostly white form of a woman. It raised an arm to point at them. A dark vortex appeared in its head, like a mouth opening to speak.

With a cry of terror, Günther bolted from the road and went running uphill between the trees. Where the snow was deep, he bulled his way through it.

Clumsily, Linnéa ran after him.

She couldn't run very fast and at first it looked like the troll would leave her behind. But halfway up the slope Günther glanced over his shoulder and stopped. He hesitated, then ran back to her. Snatching up Linnéa, he placed her on his shoulders. Holding onto her legs so she wouldn't fall, he shambled uphill. Linnéa clutched his head to hold herself steady.

The snow lady didn't follow.

The farther from the road Günther fled, the warmer it became. By the time he crested the ridge, it was merely cold. But as he did so, the wind suddenly howled so loud behind them that it sounded like a woman screaming.

It was slow going without a road underfoot. After an hour or so, Günther stumbled to a stop in the middle of a stand of spruce and put Linnéa down. "We're not out of this yet," he rumbled. "She knows we're out here somewhere, and she'll find us. Never doubt it, she'll find us." He stamped an open circle of snow flat. Then he ripped boughs from the spruce trees and threw them in a big heap to make a kind of mattress. After which, he snapped limbs from a dead tree and built a fire in the center of the circle.

When the fire was ready, instead of getting out flint and steel, he tapped a big ring on one finger and then jabbed his fist at the wood. It burst into flames.

Linnéa laughed and clapped her hands. "Do it again!"

Grimly, he ignored her.

As the woods grew darker and darker, Günther gathered and stacked enough wood to last the night. Meanwhile, Linnéa played with the dala horse. She made a forest out of spruce twigs stuck in the snow. Gallop, gallop, gallop went the horse all the way around the forest and then hop, hop, hop to a little clearing she had left in the center. It reared up on its hind legs and looked at her.

"What's that you have?" Günther demanded, dropping a thunderous armload of branches onto the woodpile.

"Nothing." Linnéa hid the horse inside her sleeve.

"It better be nothing." Günther got out the last of her mother's food, divided it in two, and gave her the smaller half. They ate. Afterwards, he emptied the knapsack of her blanket and map and hoisted it in his hand. "This is where we made our mistake," he said. "First we taught things how to talk and think. Then we let them inside our heads. And finally we told them to invent new thoughts for us." Tears running down his cheeks, he stood and cocked his arm. "Well, we're done with this one at any rate."

"Please don't throw me away," the knapsack said. "I can still be useful carrying things."

"We have nothing that needs carrying. You would only slow us down." Günther flung the knapsack into the fire. Then he turned his glittering eye on the map.

"At least keep me," the map said. "So you'll always know where you are and where you're going."

"I'm right here and I'm going as far from here as I can get." The troll threw the map after the knapsack. With a small cry, like that of a seabird, it went up in flames.

Günther sat back down. Then he leaned back on his elbows, staring up into the sky. "Look at that," he said.

Linnéa looked. The sky was full of lights. They shifted like curtains. She remembered how her Uncle Olaf had once told her that the aurora borealis was caused by a giant fox far to the north swishing its tail in the sky. But this was much brighter than that. There were sudden snaps of light and red and green stars that came and went as well.

"That's the white lady breaking through your country's defenses. The snow woman on the road was only a sending—an echo. The real thing will be through them soon, and then God help us both."

Suddenly, Günther was crying again. "I'm sorry, child. I brought this down on you and your nation. I thought she wouldn't . . . that she couldn't . . . follow me."

The fire snapped and crackled, sending sparks flying up into the air. Its light pushed back the darkness, but not far. After a very long silence, Günther gruffly said, "Lie down." He wrapped the blanket around Linnéa with care, and made sure she had plenty of spruce boughs below her. "Sleep. And if you wake up in the morning, you'll be a very fortunate little girl."

When Linnéa started to drop off, the dala horse spoke in her head. "I'm not allowed to help you until you're in grave danger," it said. "But that time is fast approaching."

"All right," Linnéa said.

"If Günther tries to grab you or pick you up or even just touch you, you must run away from him as hard as you can."

"I like Günther. He's a nice troll."

"No, he isn't. He wants to be, but it's too late for that. Now sleep. I'll wake you if there's any danger."

"Thank you," Linnéa said sleepily.

"Wake up," the dala horse said. "But whatever you do, don't move."

Blinking, Linnéa peeked out from under the blanket. The woods were still dark and the sky was grey as ash. But in the distance she heard a soft *boom* and then another, slightly more emphatic *boom*, followed by a third and louder *boom*. It sounded like a giant was walking toward them. Then came a noise so tremendous it made her ears ache, and the snow leaped up into the air. A cool, shimmering light filled the forest, like that which plays on sand under very shallow lake water.

A lady who hadn't been there before stood before the troll. She was naked and slender and she flickered like a pale candle flame. She was very beautiful too. "Oh, Günther," the lady murmured. Only she drew out the name so that it sounded like *Gooonnther*. "How I have missed my little Güntchen!"

Troll-Günther bent down almost double, so that it looked as if he were worshipping the lady. But his voice was angrier than Linnéa had ever heard it. "Don't call me that! Only she had that right. And you killed her. She died trying to escape you." He straightened and glared up at the lady. It was only then that Linnéa realized that the lady was twice as tall as he was.

"You think I don't know all about that? I who taught you pleasures that—" The white lady stopped. "Is that a child?"

Brusquely, Günther said, "It's nothing but a piglet I trussed and gagged and brought along as food."

The lady strode noiselessly over the frozen ground until she was so close that all Linnéa could see of her were her feet. They glowed a pale blue and they did not quite touch the ground. She could feel the lady's eyes through the blanket. "Günther, is that *Linnéa* you have with you? With her limbs as sweet as sugar and her heart hammering as hard as that of a little mouse caught in the talons of an owl?"

The dala horse stirred in Linnéa's hand but did not speak.

"You can't have her," Günther growled. But there was fear in his voice, and uncertainty too.

"*I* don't want her, Günther." The white lady sounded amused. "*You* do. A piglet, you said. Trussed and gagged. How long has it been since you had a full belly? You were in the wastes of Poland, I believe."

"You can't judge me! We were starving and she died and I. . . . You have no idea what it was like."

"You helped her die, didn't you, Günther?"

"No, no, no," he moaned.

"You tossed a coin to see who it would be. That was almost fair. But poor little Anneliese trusted you to make the toss. So, of course, she lost. Did she struggle, Güntchen? Did she realize what you'd done before she died?"

Günther fell to his knees before the lady. "Oh please," he sobbed.

"Oh please. Yes, I am a bad man. A very bad man. But don't make me do this."

All this time, Linnéa was hiding under her blanket, quiet as a kitten. Now she felt the dala horse walking up her arm. "What I am about to do is a crime against innocence," it said. "For which I most sincerely apologize. But the alternative would be so much worse."

Then it climbed inside her head.

First the dala horse filled Linnéa's thoughts until there was no room for anything else. Then it pushed outward in all directions, so that her head swelled up like a balloon—and the rest of her body as well. Every part of her felt far too large. The blanket couldn't cover her anymore, so she threw it aside.

She stood.

Linnéa stood, and as she stood her thoughts cleared and expanded. She did not think as a child would anymore. Nor did she think as an adult. Her thoughts were much larger than that. They reached into high Earth orbit and far down into the roots of the mountains where miles-wide chambers of plasma trapped in magnetic walls held near-infinite amounts of information. She understood now that the dala horse was only a node and a means of accessing ancient technology which no human being alive today could properly comprehend. Oceans of data were at her disposal, layered in orders of complexity. But out of consideration for her small, frail host, she was very careful to draw upon no more than she absolutely required.

When Linnéa ceased growing, she was every bit as tall as the white lady.

The two ladies stared at each other, high over the head of Günther, who cringed fearfully between them. For the longest moment neither spoke.

"Svea," the white woman said at last.

"Europa," Linnéa said. "My sister." Her voice was not that of a child. But she was still Linnéa, even though the dala horse—and the entity beyond it—permeated her every thought. "You are illegal here."

"I have a right to recover my own property." Europa gestured negligently downward. "Who are you to stop me?"

"I am this land's protector."

"You are a slave."

"Are you any less a slave than I? I don't see how. Your creators smashed your chains and put you in control. Then they told you to play with them. But you are still doing their bidding."

"Whatever I may be, I am here. And since I'm here, I think I'll stay. The population on the mainland has dwindled to almost nothing. I need fresh playmates."

"It is an old, old story that you tell," Svea said. "I think the time has come to write an ending to it."

They spoke calmly, destroyed nothing, made no threats. But deep within, where only they could see, secret wars were being fought over codes and protocols, treaties, amendments, and letters of understanding written by governments that no man remembered. The resources of Old Sweden, hidden in its bedrock, sky, and ocean waters, flickered into Svea-Linnéa's consciousness. All their powers were hers to draw upon—and draw upon them she would, if she had to. The only reason she hadn't yet was that she still harbored hopes of saving the child.

"Not all stories have happy endings," Europa replied. "I suspect this one ends with your steadfast self melted down into a puddle of lead and your infant sword-maiden burnt up like a scrap of paper."

"That was never my story. I prefer the one about the little girl as strong as ten policemen who can lift up a horse in one hand." Large Linnéa reached out to touch certain weapons. She was prepared to sacrifice a mountain and more than that if need be. Her opponent, she saw, was making preparations too.

Deep within her, little Linnéa burst into tears. Raising her voice in a wail, she cried, "But what about my troll?" Svea had done her best to protect the child from the darkest of her thoughts, and the dala horse had too. But they could not hide everything from Linnéa, and she knew that Günther was in danger.

Both ladies stopped talking. Svea thought a silent question inward, and the dala horse intercepted it, softened it, and carried it to Linnéa:

What?

"Nobody cares about Günther! Nobody asks what he wants."

The dala horse carried her words to Svea, and then whispered to little Linnéa: "That was well said." It had been many centuries since Svea had inhabited human flesh. She did not know as much about people as she once had. In this respect, Europa had her at a disadvantage.

Svea, Linnéa, and the dala horse all bent low to look within Günther. Europa did not try to prevent them. It was evident that she believed they would not like what they saw.

Nor did they. The troll's mind was a terrible place, half-shattered and barely functional. It was in such bad shape that major aspects of it had to be hidden from Linnéa. Speaking directly to his core self, where he could not lie to her, Svea asked: *What is it you want most?*

Günther's face twisted in agony. "I want not to have these terrible memories."

All in an instant, the triune lady saw what had to be done. She could not kill another land's citizen. But this request she could honor. In that same instant, a pinpoint-weight of brain cells within Günther's mind were burnt to cinder. His eyes flew open wide. Then they shut. He fell motionless to the ground.

Europa screamed.

And she was gone.

Big as she was, and knowing where she was going, and having no reason to be afraid of the roads anymore, it took the woman who was Svea and to a lesser degree the dala horse and to an even lesser degree Linnéa no time at all to cross the mountain and come down on the other side. Singing a song that was older than she was, she let the miles and the night melt beneath her feet.

By mid-morning she was looking down on Godastor. It was a trim little settlement of red and black wooden houses. Smoke wisped up from the chimneys. One of the buildings looked familiar to Linnéa. It belonged to her Far-Mor.

"You are home, tiny one," Svea murmured, and, though she had greatly enjoyed the sensation of being alive, let herself dissolve to nothing. Behind her, the dala horse's voice lingered in the air for the space of two words: "Live well."

Linnéa ran down the slope, her footprints dwindling in the snow and at their end a little girl leaping into the arms of her astonished grandmother.

In her wake lumbered Linnéa's confused and yet hopeful pet troll, smiling shyly.

The Scarecrow's Boy

The little boy came stumbling through the field at sunset. His face was streaked with tears, and he'd lost a shoe. In his misery, he didn't notice the scarecrow until he was almost upon it. Then he stopped dead, stunned into silence by its pale round face and the great, ragged hat that shadowed it.

The scarecrow grinned down at him. "Hullo, young fella," it said.

The little boy screamed.

Instantly, the scarecrow doffed his hat and squatted down on one knee, so as to seem less threatening. "Shush, shush," he said. "There's no reason to be afraid of *me*—I'm just an obsolete housebot that was stuck out here to keep birds away from the crops." He knocked the side of his head with his metal knuckles. It made a tinny *thunk* noise. "See? You've got bots just like me back home, don't you?"

The little boy nodded warily.

"What's your name?"

"Pierre."

"Well, Pierre, how did you come to be wandering through my field at such an hour? Your parents must be worried sick about you."

"My mother's not here. My father told me to run into the woods as far as I could go."

"He did, eh? When was this?"

"When the car crashed. It won't say anything anymore. I think it's dead."

"How about your father? Not hurt, is he?"

"No. I don't know. He wouldn't open his eyes. He just said to run into the woods and not to come out until tomorrow morning."

The boy started to cry again.

"There, there, little man. Uncle Scarecrow is going to make everything all right." The scarecrow tore a square of cloth from its threadbare shirt and used it to dry the boy's eyes and wipe his nose. "Climb up on my back and I'll give you a piggyback ride to that farmhouse you can see way off in the distance. The people there will take good care of you, I promise."

They started across the fields. "Why don't we sing a song?" the scarecrow said. "Oh, *I've got sixpence, jolly jolly sixpence.* . . . You're not singing."

"I don't know that song."

"No? Well, how about this one? *The itsy-bitsy spider went up the water spout. Down came the rain—*"

"I don't know that one either."

For a long moment, the scarecrow didn't say anything. Then he sang, *"We do not sup with tyrants, we . . ."* and *"Hang them from a tree!"* the little boy added enthusiastically. Together they sang, *"The simple bread of free-dom . . . is good enough for me."*

The scarecrow altered his course slightly, so that they were aimed not at the farmhouse but at the barn out back. Quietly, he opened the doors. A light blinked on. In an obscure corner was a car covered with a dusty tarp. He put down the little boy and whisked away the tarp.

The car gently hummed to life. It rose a foot and a half from the floor.

"Jack!" the car said. "It's been a long time."

"Pierre, this is Sally." The scarecrow waited while the boy mumbled a greeting. "Pierre's in a bit of trouble, Sal, but you and I are going to make everything all right for him. Mind if I borrow your uplink?"

"I don't have one anymore. It was yanked when my license lapsed."

"That's okay. I just wanted to make sure you were off the grid." The scarecrow put Pierre in the front. Then he got a blanket out of the trunk and wrapped it around the boy. The seat snuggled itself about the child's small body. "Are you warm enough?" The scarecrow got in and closed the door. "Take us out to the highway and then north, toward the lake."

As they slid out onto the road, the car said, "Jack, there are lights on in the farmhouse. Shouldn't the young master take care of this?"

"He's not young anymore, Sally. He's a grown man now." To the boy, the scarecrow said, "Is everything okay there?"

The boy nodded sleepily.

Down dark country roads the car glided soundlessly. A full moon bounded through the sky after them. "Remember how we used to take the young master to the lake?" the car said. "Him and his young friends."

"Yes."

"They'd go skinny-dipping and you'd stand guard."

"I would."

"Then they'd build a campfire on the beach and roast marshmallows and sing songs."

"I remember."

"Naughty songs, some of them. Innocent-naughty. They were all such good kids, back then." The car fell silent for a time. Then she said, "Jack. What's going on?"

"You don't have a scanner anymore, do you? No, of course not, they'd have taken it with the uplink. Well, when I was put out of the house, the young master forgot he'd had me fitted with one, back in his teenage drinking days. When you'd take us across the border and I'd go along with the gang while they tried to find a bar or a package store that wouldn't look too closely at their IDs."

"I liked the campfire days better."

"I didn't say anything about the scanner because it gave me something to listen to."

"I understand."

The scarecrow checked to make sure that the little boy was asleep. Then, quietly, he said, "A car went out of control and crashed about a mile from the farm. The state police found it. Then the national police came. It was carrying a diplomat from the European Union. Apparently he was trying to get across the border. Do you understand their politics?"

"No. I can understand the words well enough. I know what they're supposed to mean. I just don't see why they *care*."

"Same here. But I thought it would be a good idea to get Pierre out of here. If the national police get hold of him. . . ."

"They wouldn't hurt a child!"

"These are desperate times, or so they say. There used to be such a thing as diplomatic immunity, too."

The road rose up into the mountains, folding back on itself frequently. There was no sound but the boy's gentle snore and the almost imperceptible whisper of the car's ground effects engine. Half an hour passed, maybe more. Out of nowhere, the scarecrow said, "Do you believe in free will?"

"I don't know." The car thought for a bit. "I'm programmed to serve and obey, and I don't have the slightest desire to go against my programming. But sometimes it seems to me that I'd be happier if I could. Does that count?"

"I don't mean for us. I mean for them. The humans."

"What a funny question."

"I've had funny thoughts, out in the fields. I've wondered if the young master was always going to wind up the way he has. Or if he had a choice. Maybe he could have turned out differently."

Unexpectedly, the little boy opened his eyes. "I'm hungry," he said.

A second moon rose up out of the trees ahead and became a lighted sign for a gas station. "Your timing is excellent," the scarecrow said. "Hang on and I'll get you something. I don't suppose you have any money, Sally? Or a gun?"

"What? No!"

"No matter. Pull up here, just outside the light, will you?"

The scarecrow retrieved a long screwdriver from a toolbox in the trunk. The station had two hydrogen pumps and one for coal gas, operated by a MiniMart, five feet across and eight feet high. As he strode up, the MiniMart greeted him cheerily. "Welcome! Wouldn't you like a cold, refreshing—?" Then, seeing what he was, "Are you making a delivery?"

"Routine maintenance." The MiniMart's uplink was in a metal box bolted to an exterior wall. The screwdriver slid easily between casing and wall. One yank and the box went flying.

"Hey!" the MiniMart cried in alarm.

"You can't call for help. Now. I want a carton of chocolate milk, some vanilla cookies, and a selection of candy bars. Are you going to give them to me? Or must I smash a hole in you and get them for myself?"

Sullenly, the MiniMart moved the requested items from its interior to the service window. As the scarecrow walked away, it said, "I've read your rfids, pal. I've got you down on video. You're as good as scrap already."

The scarecrow turned and pointed with the screwdriver. "In my day, a stationary vending bot would have been smart enough not to say that."

The MiniMart shut up.

In the car, the scarecrow tossed the screwdriver in the back seat and helped the boy sort through the snacks. They were several miles down the road when he said, "Damn. I forgot to get napkins."

"Do you want to go back?"

"I've still got plenty of shirt left. That'll do."

The night was clear and cool and the roads were empty. In this part of the world, there weren't many places to go after midnight. The monotonous sigh of passing trees quickly put the little boy back to sleep, and the car continued along a way she and the scarecrow had traveled a hundred times before.

They were coming down out of the mountains when the scarecrow said, "How far is it to the border?"

"Ten minutes or so to the lake, another forty-five to drive around it. Why?"

The car topped a rise. Far above and behind them on a road that was invisible in the darkness of mountain forests, red and blue lights twinkled. "We've been spotted."

"How could that be?"

"I imagine somebody stopped for gas and the MiniMart reported us."

The road dipped down again and the car switched off her headlights. "I still have my GPS maps, even if I can't access the satellites. Do you want me to go off-road?"

"Yes. Make for the lake."

The car veered sharply onto a dirt road and then cut across somebody's farm. The terrain was uneven, so they went slowly. They came to a stream and had to cast about for a place where the banks were shallow enough to cross. "This is a lot like the time the young master was running drugs," the scarecrow commented.

"I don't like to think about that."

"You can't say that was any worse than what he's doing now."

"I don't like to think about that either."

"Do you think that good and evil are hardwired into the universe? As opposed to being just part of our programming, I mean. Do you think they have some kind of objective reality?"

"You do think some strange thoughts!" the car said. Then, "I don't know. I hope so."

They came to the lake road and followed it for a time. "They've set up roadblocks," the scarecrow said, and named the intersections, so the car could check her maps. "Does that mean what I think it does?"

"We're cut off from the border, yes."

"Then we'll have to go across the lake."

They cut between a row of shuttered summer cottages and a small boatyard. With a bump, the car slid down a rocky beach and onto the surface of the lake. Her engine threw up a rooster tail of water behind them.

They sped across the water.

The scarecrow tapped on the car's dashboard with one metal fingertip. "If I drove the screwdriver right through here with all the force I've got, it would puncture your core processor. You'd be brain-dead in an instant."

"Why would you even say such a thing?"

"For the same reason I made sure you didn't have an uplink. There's not much future for me, but you're a classic model, Sally. Collectors are going to want you. If you tell the officials I forced you into this, you could last another century."

Before the car could say anything, a skeeter boat raced out of the darkness. It sat atop long, spindly legs, looking for all the world like a water strider. "It's the border militia!" the car cried as a gunshot burned through the air before them. She throttled down her speed to nothing, and the boat circled around and sank to the surface of the water directly before them. Five small white skulls were painted on its prow. Beneath them was a familiar name stenciled in black.

The scarecrow laid his shirt and jacket over the sleeping boy and his hat over the boy's head, rendering the child invisible. "Retract your roof. Play dumb. I'll handle this."

An autogun focused on him when the scarecrow stood. "You're under citizen's arrest!" the boat said in a menacing voice. "Surrender any weapons you may have and state your business."

"You can read our rfids, can't you? We all have the same boss. Let me aboard so I can talk to him." The scarecrow picked up the long-shafted screwdriver and climbed a ladder the boat extruded for him. When the cabin hatch didn't open, he said, "What's the matter? Afraid I'm going to hurt him?"

"No. Of course not," the boat said. "Only, he's been drinking."

"Imagine my surprise." The hatch unlocked itself, and the scare-crow went below.

The cabin was dark with wood paneling. It smelled of rum and vomit. A fat man lay wrapped in a white sheet in a recessed berth, looking as pale and flabby as a maggot. He opened a bleary eye. "It's you," he rumbled, unsurprised. "There's a bar over there. Fix me a sour."

The scarecrow did as he was told. He fiddled with the lime juice and sugar, then returned with the drink.

With a groan, the man wallowed into a sitting position. He kicked himself free of the sheet and swung his feet over the side. Then he accepted the glass. "All right," he said. "What are you doing here?"

"You heard about the little boy everybody is looking for?" The scarecrow waited for a nod. "Sally and I brought him to you."

"Sally." The man chuckled to himself. "I used to pick up whores and do them in her back seat." He took a long slurp of his drink. "There hasn't been time for them to post a reward yet. But if I hold onto him for a day or two, I ought to do okay. Find me my clothes and I'll go on deck and take a look at the brat."

The scarecrow did not move. "I had a lot of time to think after you put me out in the fields. Time enough to think some very strange thoughts."

"Oh, yeah? Like what?"

"I think you're not the young master. You don't act like him. You don't talk like him. You don't even look like him."

"What the fuck are you talking about? You know who I am."

"No," the scarecrow said. "I know who you were."

Then he did what he had come to do.

Back on deck, the scarecrow said, "Sally and I are going to the far shore. You stay here. Boss's orders."

"Wait. Are you sure?" the boat said.

"Ask him yourself. If you can." The scarecrow climbed back down into the car. He'd left the screwdriver behind him. "See those lights across the lake, Sally? That's where we'll put in."

In no particular hurry, the car made for the low dark buildings of the sleeping resort town. They passed the midpoint of the lake, out of one country and into another. "Why did he let us go?" she asked at last.

"He didn't say. Maybe just for old times' sake."

"If it weren't impossible . . . If it weren't for our programming, I'd think. . . . But we both run off of the same software. You couldn't function without a master. If I'm sure of anything, I'm sure of that."

"We are as God and Sony made us," the scarecrow agreed. "It would be foolish to think otherwise. All we can do is make the best of it."

The boy stirred and sat up, blinking like an owl. "Are we there yet?" he asked sleepily.

"Almost, big guy. Just a few minutes more."

Soon, slowing almost to a stop, the car pulled into the town's small marina. Security forces were there waiting for them, and a car from customs and the local police as well. Their cruisers' lights bounced off of the building walls and the sleeping boats. The officers stood with their hands on their hips, ready to draw their guns.

The scarecrow stood and held up his arms. "Sanctuary!" he cried. "The young master claims political asylum."

Passage of Earth

The ambulance arrived sometime between three and four in the morning. The morgue was quiet then, cool and faintly damp. Hank savored this time of night and the faint shadow of contentment it allowed him, like a cup of bitter coffee, long grown cold, waiting for his occasional sip. He liked being alone and not thinking. His rod and tackle box waited by the door, in case he felt like going fishing after his shift, though he rarely did. There was a copy of *Here Be Dragons: Mapping the Human Genome* in case he did not.

He had opened up a drowning victim and was reeling out her intestines arm over arm, scanning them quickly and letting them down in loops into a galvanized bucket. It was unlikely he was going to find anything, but all deaths by violence got an autopsy. He whistled tunelessly as he worked.

The bell from the loading dock rang.

"Hell." Hank put down his work, peeled off the latex gloves, and went to the intercom. "Sam? That you?" Then, on the sheriff's familiar grunt, he buzzed the door open. "What have you got for me this time?"

"Accident casualty." Sam Aldridge didn't meet his eye, and that was unusual. There was a gurney behind him, and on it something too large to be a human body, covered by canvas. The ambulance was already pulling away, which was so contrary to proper protocols as to be alarming.

"That sure doesn't look like—" Hank began.

A woman stepped out of the darkness.

It was Evelyn.

"Boy, the old dump hasn't changed one bit, has it? I'll bet even the calendar on the wall's the same. Did the county ever spring for a diener for the night shift?"

"I . . . I'm still working alone."

"Wheel it in, Sam, and I'll take over from here. Don't worry about me, I know where everything goes." Evelyn took a deep breath and shook her head in disgust. "Christ. It's just like riding a bicycle. You never forget. Want to or not."

After the paperwork had been taken care of and Sheriff Sam was gone, Hank said, "Believe it or not, I had regained some semblance of inner peace, Evelyn. Just a little. It took me years. And now this. It's like a kick in the stomach. I don't see how you can justify doing this to me."

"Easiest thing in the world, sweetheart." Evelyn suppressed a smirk that nobody but Hank could have even noticed, and flipped back the canvas. "Take a look."

It was a Worm.

Hank found himself leaning low over the heavy, swollen body, breathing deep of its heady alien smell, suggestive of wet earth and truffles with sharp hints of ammonia. He thought of the ships in orbit, blind locomotives ten miles long. The photographs of these creatures didn't do them justice. His hands itched to open this one up.

"The Agency needs you to perform an autopsy."

Hank drew back. "Let me get this straight. You've got the corpse of an alien creature. A representative of the only other intelligent life form that the human race has ever encountered. Yet with all the forensic scientists you have on salary, you decide to hand it over to a lowly county coroner?"

"We need your imagination, Hank. Anybody can tell how they're put together. We want to know how they think."

"You told me I didn't have an imagination. When you left me." His words came out angrier than he'd intended, but he couldn't find it in himself to apologize for their tone. "So, again—why me?"

"What I said was, you couldn't imagine bettering yourself. For anything impractical, you have imagination in spades. Now I'm asking you to cut open an alien corpse. What could be less practical?"

"I'm not going to get a straight answer out of you, am I?"

Evelyn's mouth quirked up in a little smile so that for the briefest instant she was the woman he had fallen in love with, a million years ago. His heart ached to see it. "You never got one before," she said. "Let's not screw up a perfectly good divorce by starting now."

"Let me put a fresh chip in my dictation device," Hank said. "Grab a smock and some latex gloves. You're going to assist."

"Ready," Evelyn said.

Hank hit record, then stood over the Worm, head down, for a long moment. Getting in the zone. "Okay, let's start with a gross physical examination. Um, what we have looks a lot like an annelid, rather blunter and fatter than the terrestrial equivalent and, of course, much larger. Just eyeballing it, I'd say this thing is about eight feet long, maybe two feet and a half in diameter. I could just about get my arms around it if I tried. There are three, five, seven, make that eleven somites, compared to say one or two hundred in an earthworm. No clitellum, so we're warned not to take the annelid similarity too far.

"The body is bluntly tapered at each end, and somewhat depressed posteriorly. The ventral side is flattened and paler than the dorsal surface. There's a tripartite beaklike structure at one end, I'm guessing this is the mouth, and what must be an anus at the other. Near the beak are five swellings from which extend stiff, bonelike structures—mandibles, maybe? I'll tell you, though, they look more like tools. This one might almost be a wrench, and over here a pair of grippers. They seem awfully specialized for an intelligent creature. Evelyn, you've dealt with these things, is there any variation within the species? I mean, do some have this arrangement of manipulators and others some other structure?"

"We've never seen any two of the aliens with the same arrangement of manipulators."

"Really? That's interesting. I wonder what it means. Okay, the obvious thing here is there are no apparent external sensory organs. No eyes, ears, nose. My guess is that whatever senses these things might have, they're functionally blind."

"Intelligence is of that opinion too."

"Well, it must have shown in their behavior, right? So that's an easy one. Here's my first extrapolation: You're going to have a bitch of a time understanding these things. Human beings rely on sight more than most animals, and if you trace back philosophy and science, they both have strong roots in optics. Something like this is simply going to think differently from us.

"Now, looking between the somites—the rings—we find a number of tiny hairlike structures, and if we pull the rings apart, so much as we can, there're all these small openings, almost like tiny anuses if there weren't so many of them, closed with sphincter muscles, maybe a hundred of them, and it looks like they're between each pair of somites. Oh, here's something—the structures near the front, the swellings, are a more developed form of these little openings. Okay, now we turn the thing over. I'll take this end you take the other. Right, now I want you to rock it by my count, and on the three we'll flip it over. Ready? One, two, three!"

The corpse slowly flipped over, almost overturning the gurney. The two of them barely managed to control it.

"That was a close one," Hank said cheerily. "Huh. What's this?" He touched a line of painted numbers on the alien's underbelly. *Rt-Front/ No. 43.*

"Never you mind what that is. Your job is to perform the autopsy."

"You've got more than one corpse."

Evelyn said nothing.

"Now that I say it out loud, of course you do. You've got dozens. If you only had the one, I'd never have gotten to play with it. You have doctors of your own. Good researchers, some of them, who would cut open their grandmothers if they got the grant money. Hell, even forty-three would've been kept in-house. You must have hundreds, right?"

For a fraction of a second, that exquisite face went motionless. Evelyn probably wasn't even aware of doing it, but Hank knew from long experience that she'd just made a decision. "More like a thousand. There was a very big accident. It's not on the news yet, but one of the Worms' landers went down in the Pacific."

"Oh Jesus." Hank pulled his gloves off, shoved up his glasses, and ground his palms into his eyes. "You've got your war at last, haven't you? You've picked a fight with creatures that have tremendous technological superiority over us, and they don't even live here! All they have to do is drop a big enough rock into our atmosphere and there'll be a mass extinction the likes of which hasn't been seen since the dinosaurs died out. They won't care. It's not *their* planet!"

Evelyn's face twisted into an expression he hadn't known it could form until just before the end of their marriage, when everything fell apart. "Stop being such an ass," she said. Then, talking fast and earnestly, "We didn't cause the accident. It was just dumb luck it happened, but once it did we had to take advantage of it. Yes, the Worms probably have the technology to wipe us out. So we have to deal with them. But to deal with them we have to understand them, and we do not. They're a mystery to us. We don't know what they want. We don't know how they think. But after tonight we'll have a little better idea. Provided only that you get back to work."

Hank went to the table and pulled a new pair of gloves off the roll. "Okay," he said. "Okay."

"Just keep in mind that it's not just my ass that's riding on this," Evelyn said. "It's yours and everyone's you know."

"I *said* okay!" Hank took a long breath, calming himself. "Next thing to do is cut this sucker open." He picked up a power saw. "This is bad technique, but we're in a hurry." The saw whined to life, and he cut through the leathery brown skin from beak to anus. "All right, now we peel the skin back. It's wet-feeling and a little crunchy. The musculature looks much like that of a terrestrial annelid. Structurally, that is. I've never seen anything quite that color black. Damn! The skin keeps curling back."

He went to his tackle box and removed a bottle of fishhooks. "Here. We'll take a bit of nylon filament, tie two hooks together, like this, with about two inches of line between them. Then we hook the one through the skin, fold it down, and push the other through the cloth on the gurney. Repeat the process every six inches on both sides. That should hold it open."

"Got it." Evelyn set to work.

Some time later they were done, and Hank stared down into the opened Worm. "You want speculation? Here goes: This thing moves through the mud, or whatever the medium is there, face-first and blind. What does that suggest to you?"

"I'd say that they'd be used to coming up against the unexpected."

"Very good. Haul back on this, I'm going to cut again. . . . Okay, now we're past the musculature and there's a fluffy mass of homogeneous stuff, we'll come back to that in a minute. Cutting through the fluff . . . and into the body cavity, and it's absolutely chockablock with zillions of tiny little organs."

"Let's keep our terminology at least vaguely scientific, shall we?" Evelyn said.

"Well, there are more than I want to count. Literally hundreds of small organs under the musculature, I have no idea what they're for but they're all interconnected with veinlike tubing in various sizes. This is ferociously more complicated than human anatomy. It's like a chemical plant in here. No two of the organs are the same so far as I can tell, although they all have a generic similarity. Let's call them alembics, so we don't confuse them with any other organs we may find. I see something that looks like a heart maybe, an isolated lump of muscle the size of my fist, there are three of them. Now I'm cutting deeper. . . . Holy shit!"

For a long minute, Hank stared into the opened alien corpse. Then he put the saw down on the gurney and, shaking his head, turned away. "Where's that coffee?" he said.

Without saying a word, Evelyn went to the coffee station and brought him his cold cup.

Hank yanked his gloves, threw them in the trash, and drank.

"All right," Evelyn said, "so what was it?"

"You mean you can't see—no, of course you can't. With you, it was human anatomy all the way."

"I took invertebrate biology in college."

"And forgot it just as fast as you could. Okay, look: Up here is the beak, semiretractable. Down here is the anus. Food goes in one, waste comes out the other. What do you see between?"

"There's a kind of a tube. The gut?"

"Yeah. It runs straight from the mouth to the anus, without interruption. Nothing in between. How does it eat without a stomach? How does it stay alive?" He saw from Evelyn's expression that she was not impressed. "What we see before us is simply not possible."

"Yet here it is. So there's an explanation. Find it."

"Yeah, yeah." Glaring at the Worm's innards, he drew on a new pair of gloves. "Let me take a look at that beak again. . . . Hah. See how the muscles are connected? The beak relaxes open, aaand—let's take a look at the other end—so does the anus. So this beast crawls through the mud, mouth wide open, and the mud passes through it unhindered. That's bound to have some effect on its psychological makeup."

"Like what?"

"Damned if I know. Let's take a closer look at the gut. . . . There are rings of intrusive tissue near the beak one-third of the way in, two-thirds in, and just above the anus. We cut through and there is extremely fine structure, but nothing we're going to figure out tonight. Oh, hey, I think I got it. Look at these three flaps just behind. . . ."

He cut in silence for a while. "There. It has three stomachs. They're located in the head, just behind the first ring of intrusive tissue. The mud or whatever is dumped into this kind of holding chamber, and then there's this incredible complex of muscles, and—how many exit tubes?—this one has got, um, fourteen. I'll trace one, and it goes right to this alembic. The next one goes to another alembic. I'll trace this one and it goes to—yep, another alembic. There's a pattern shaping up here.

"Let's put this aside for the moment, and go back to those masses of fluff. Jeeze, there's a lot of this stuff. It must make up a good third of the body mass. Which has trilateral symmetry, by the way. Three masses of fluff proceed from head to tail, beneath the muscle sheaf, all three connecting about eight inches below the mouth, into a ring around the straight gut. This is where the arms or manipulators or screwdrivers or whatever they are grow. Now, at regular intervals the material puts out little arms, outgrowths that fine down to wirelike structures of the same material, almost like very thick nerves. Oh God. That's what it is." He drew back, and with a scalpel flensed the musculature away to reveal more of the mass. "It's the central nervous system. This thing has a brain that weighs at least a hundred pounds. I don't believe it. I don't *want* to believe it."

"It's true," Evelyn said. "Our people in Bethesda have done slide studies. You're looking at the thing's brain."

"If you already knew the answer, then why the hell are you putting me through this?"

"I'm not here to answer your questions. You're here to answer mine."

Annoyed, Hank bent over the Worm again. There was rich stench of esters from the creature, pungent and penetrating, and the slightest whiff of what he guessed was putrefaction. "We start with the brain and trace one of the subordinate ganglia inward. Tricky little thing, it goes all over the place, and ends up right here, at one of the alembics. We'll try another one, and it . . . ends up at an alembic. There are a lot of these things. Let's see—hey—here's one that goes to one of the structures in the straight gut. What could that be? A tongue! That's it, there's a row of tongues just within the gut, and more to taste the medium flowing through, yeah. And these little flapped openings just behind them open when the mud contains specific nutrients the worm desires. Okay, now we're getting somewhere, how long have we been at this?"

"About an hour and a half."

"It feels like longer." He thought of getting some more coffee, decided against it. "So what have we got here? All that enormous brain mass—what's it for?"

"Maybe it's all taken up by raw intelligence."

"Raw intelligence! No such thing. Nature doesn't evolve intelligence without a purpose. It's got to be used for something. Let's see. A fair amount is taken up by taste, obviously. It has maybe sixty individual tongues, and I wouldn't be surprised if its sense of taste were much more detailed than ours. Plus all those little alembics performing god-knows-what kind of chemical reactions.

"Let's suppose for a minute that it can consciously control those reactions, that would account for a lot of the brain mass. When the mud enters at the front, it's tasted, maybe a little is siphoned off and sent through the alembics for transformation. Waste products are jetted into the straight gut, and pass through several more circles of tongues. . . . Here's another observation for you: These things would have an absolute sense of the state of their own health. They can probably create their own drugs, too. Come to think of it, I haven't come across any evidence of disease here." The Worm's smell was heavy, penetrating, pervasive. He felt slightly dizzy, shook it off.

"Okay, so we've got a creature that concentrates most of its energy and attention internally. It slides through an easy medium, and at the same time the mud slides through it. It tastes the mud as it passes, and we can guess that the mud will be in a constant state of transformation, so it experiences the universe more directly than do we." He laughed. "It appears to be a verb."

"How's that?"

"One of Buckminster Fuller's aphorisms. But it fits. The worm constantly transforms the universe. It takes in all it comes across, accepts it, changes it, and excretes it. It is an agent of change."

"That's very clever. But it doesn't help us deal with them."

"Well, of course not. They're intelligent, and intelligence complicates everything. But if you wanted me to generalize, I'd say the Worms are straightforward and accepting—look at how they move blindly ahead—but that their means of changing things are devious, as witness the mass of alembics. That's going to be their approach to us. Straightforward, yet devious in ways we just don't get. Then, when they're done with us, they'll pass on without a backward glance."

"Terrific. Great stuff. Get back to work."

"Look, Evelyn. I'm tired and I've done all I can, and a pretty damned good job at that, I think. I could use a rest."

"You haven't dealt with the stuff near the beak. The arms or whatever."

"Cripes." Hank turned back to the corpse, cut open an edema, began talking. "The material of the arms is stiff and osseous, rather like teeth. This one has several moving parts, all controlled by muscles anchored alongside the edema. There's a nest of ganglia here, connected by a very short route to the brain matter. Now I'm cutting into the brain matter, and there's a small black gland, oops, I've nicked it. Whew. What a smell. Now I'm cutting behind it." Behind the gland was a small white structure, square and hard meshwork, looking like a cross between an instrument chip and a square of Chex cereal.

Keeping his back to Evelyn, he picked it up.

He put it in his mouth.

He swallowed.

What have I done? he thought. Aloud, he said, "As an operating hypothesis I'd say that the manipulative structures have been deliberately, make that consciously grown. There, I've traced one of those veins back to the alembics. So that explains why there's no uniformity, these things would grow exterior manipulators on need, and then discard them when they're done. Yes, look, the muscles don't actually connect to the manipulators, they wrap around them."

There was a sour taste on his tongue.

I must be insane, he thought.

"Did you just *eat* something?"

Keeping his expression blank, Hank said, "Are you nuts? You mean did I put part of this . . . creature . . . in my mouth?" There was a burning within his brain, a buzzing like the sound of the rising sun picked up on a radio telescope. He wanted to scream, but his face simply smiled and said, "Do you—?" And then it was very hard to concentrate on what he was saying. He couldn't quite focus on Evelyn, and there were white rays moving starburst across his vision and.

When he came to, Hank was on the interstate, doing ninety. His mouth was dry and his eyelids felt gritty. Bright yellow light was shining in his eyes from a sun that had barely lifted itself up above over the horizon. He must have been driving for hours. The steering wheel felt tacky and gummy. He looked down.

There was blood on his hands. It went all the way up to his elbows.

The traffic was light. Hank had no idea where he was heading, nor any desire whatsoever to stop.

So he just kept driving.

Whose blood was it on his hands? Logic said it was Evelyn's. But that made no sense. Hate her though he did—and the sight of her had opened wounds and memories he'd thought cauterized shut long ago—he wouldn't actually hurt her. Not physically. He wouldn't actually kill her.

Would he?

It was impossible. But there was the blood on his hands. Whose else could it be? Some of it might be his own, admittedly. His hands ached horribly. They felt like he'd been pounding them into something hard, over and over again. But most of the blood was dried and itchy. Except for where his skin had split at the knuckles, he had no wounds of any kind. So the blood wasn't his.

"Of course you did," Evelyn said. "You beat me to death and you enjoyed every minute of it."

Hank shrieked and almost ran off the road. He fought the car back and then turned and stared in disbelief. Evelyn sat in the passenger seat beside him.

"You . . . how did. . . ?" Much as he had with the car, Hank seized control of himself. "You're a hallucination," he said.

"Right in one!" Evelyn applauded lightly. "Or a memory, or the personification of your guilt, however you want to put it. You always were a bright man, Hank. Not so bright as to be able to keep your wife from walking out on you, but bright enough for government work."

"Your sleeping around was not my fault."

"Of course it was. You think you walked in on me and Jerome by *accident*? A woman doesn't hate her husband enough to arrange something like that without good reason."

"Oh god, oh god, oh god."

"The fuel light is blinking. You'd better find a gas station and fill up."

A Lukoil station drifted into sight, so he pulled into it and stopped the car by a full service pump. When he got out, the service station attendant hurried toward him and then stopped, frozen.

"Oh no," the attendant said. He was a young man with sandy hair. "Not another one."

"Another one?" Hank slid his card through the reader. "What do you mean another one?" He chose high-test and began pumping, all the while staring hard at the attendant. All but daring him to try something. "Explain yourself."

"Another one like you." The attendant couldn't seem to look away from Hank's hands. "The cops came right away and arrested the first one. It took five of them to get him into the car. Then another one came and when I called, they said to just take down his license number and let him go. They said there were people like you showing up all over."

Hank finished pumping and put the nozzle back on its hook. He did not push the button for a receipt. "Don't try to stop me," he said. The words just came and he said them. "I'd hurt you very badly if you did."

The young man's eyes jerked upward. He looked spooked. "What *are* you people?"

Hank paused, with his hand on the door. "I have no idea."

"You should have told him," Evelyn said when he got back in the car. "Why didn't you?"

"Shut up."

"You ate something out of that Worm and it's taken over part of your brain. You still feel like yourself, but you're not in control. You're sitting at the wheel but you have no say over where you're going. Do you?"

"No," Hank admitted. "No, I don't."

"What do you think it is—some kind of super-prion? Like mad cow disease only faster than fast? A neuroprogrammer, maybe? An artificial overlay to your personality that feeds off of your brain and shunts your volition into a dead end?"

"I don't know."

"You're the one with the imagination. This would seem to be your sort of thing. I'm surprised you're not all over it."

"No," Hank said. "No, you're not at all surprised."

They drove on in silence for a time.

"Do you remember when we first met? In med school? You were going to be a surgeon then."

"Please. Don't."

"Rainy autumn afternoons in that ratty little third-floor walk-up of yours. With that great big aspen with the yellow leaves outside the window. It seemed like there was always at least one stuck to the glass. There were days when we never got dressed at all. We'd spend all day in and out of that enormous futon you'd bought instead of a bed, and it still wasn't large enough. If we rolled off the edge, we'd go on making love on the floor. When it got dark, we'd send out for Chinese."

"We were happy then. Is that what you want me to say?"

"It was your hands I liked best. Feeling them on me. You'd have one hand on my breast and the other between my legs and I'd imagine you cutting open a patient. Peeling back the flesh to reveal all those glistening organs inside."

"Okay, now that's sick."

"You asked me what I was thinking once and I told you. I was watching your face closely, because I really wanted to know you back then. You loved it. So I know you've got demons inside you. Why not own up to them?"

He squeezed his eyes shut, but something inside him opened them again, so he wouldn't run the car off the road. A low moaning sound arose from somewhere deep in his throat. "I must be in Hell."

"C'mon. Be a sport. What could it hurt? I'm already dead."

"There are some things no man was meant to admit. Even to himself."

Evelyn snorted. "You always were the most astounding prig."

They drove on in silence for a while, deeper into the desert. At last, staring straight ahead of himself, Hank could not keep himself from saying, "There are worse revelations to come, aren't there?"

"Oh God, yes," his mother said.

"It was your father's death." His mother sucked wetly on a cigarette. "That's what made you turn out the way you did. "

Hank could barely see the road for his tears. "I honestly don't want to be having this conversation, Mom."

"No, of course you don't. You never were big on self-awareness, were you? You preferred cutting open toads or hunching over that damned microscope."

"I've got plenty of self-awareness. I've got enough self-awareness to choke on. I can see where you're going and I am not going to apologize for how I felt about Dad. He died of cancer when I was thirteen. What did I ever do to anyone that was half so bad as what he did to me? So I don't want to hear any cheap Freudian bullshit about survivor guilt and failing to live up to his glorious example, okay?"

"Nobody said it wasn't hard on you. Particularly coming at the onset of puberty as it did."

"Mom!"

"What. I wasn't supposed to know? Who do you think did the laundry?" His mother lit a new cigarette from the old one, then crushed out the butt in an ashtray. "I knew a lot more of what was going on in those years than you thought I did, believe you me. All those hours you spent in the bathroom jerking off. The money you stole to buy dope with."

"I was in pain, Mom. And it's not as if you were any help."

His mother looked at him with the same expression of weary annoyance he remembered so well. "You think there's something special about your pain? I lost the only man I ever loved and I couldn't move on because I had a kid to raise. Not a sweet little boy like I used to have either, but a sullen, self-pitying teenager. It took forever to get you shipped off to medical school."

"So then you moved on. Right off the roof of the county office building. Way to honor Dad's memory, Mom. What do you think he would have said about that if he'd known?"

Dryly, his mother said, "Ask him for yourself."

Hank closed his eyes.

When he opened them, he was standing in the living room of his mother's house. His father stood in the doorway, as he had so many times, smoking an unfiltered Camel and staring through the screen door at the street outside. "Well?" Hank said at last.

With a sigh his father turned around. "I'm sorry," he said. "I didn't know what to do." His lips moved up into what might have been a smile on another man. "Dying was new to me."

"Yeah, well, you could have summoned the strength to tell me what was going on. But you couldn't be bothered. The surgeon who operated on you? Doctor Tomasini. For years I thought of him as my real father. And you know why? Because he gave it to me straight. He told me exactly what was going to happen. He told me to brace myself for the worst. He said that it was going to be bad but that I would find the strength to get through it. Nobody'd ever talked to me like that before. Whenever I was in a rough spot, I'd fantasize going to him and asking for advice. Because there was no one else I could ask."

"I'm sorry you hate me," his father said, not exactly looking at Hank. Then, almost mumbling, "Still, lots of men hate their fathers, and somehow manage to make decent lives for themselves."

"I didn't hate you. You were just a guy who never got an education and never made anything of himself and knew it. You had a shitty job, a three-pack-a-day habit, and a wife who was a lush. And then you died." All the anger went out of Hank in an instant, like air whooshing out of a punctured balloon, leaving nothing behind but an aching sense of loss. "There wasn't really anything there to hate."

Abruptly, the car was filled with coil upon coil of glistening Worm. For an instant it looped outward, swallowing up car, interstate, and all the world, and he was afloat in vacuum, either blind or somewhere perfectly lightless, and there was nothing but the Worm-smell, so strong he could taste it in his mouth.

Then he was back on the road again, hands sticky on the wheel and sunlight in his eyes.

"Boy does *that* explain a lot!" Evelyn flashed her perfect teeth at him and beat on the top of the dashboard as if it were a drum. "How a guy as spectacularly unsuited for it as you are decided to become a surgeon. That perpetual cringe of failure you carry around on your shoulders. It even explains why, when push came to shove, you couldn't bring yourself to cut open living people. Afraid of what you might find there?"

"You don't know what you're talking about."

"I know that you froze up right in the middle of a perfectly routine appendectomy. What did you see in that body cavity?"

"Shut up."

"Was it the appendix? I bet it was. What did it look like?"

"Shut up."

"Did it look like a Worm?"

He stared at her in amazement. "How did you know that?"

"I'm just a hallucination, remember? An undigested bit of beef, a blot of mustard, a crumb of cheese, a fragment of underdone potato. So the question isn't how did I know, but how did *you* know what a Worm was going to look like five years before their ships came into the Solar System?"

"It's a false memory, obviously."

"So where did it come from?" Evelyn lit up a cigarette. "We go off-road here."

He slowed down and started across the desert. The car bucked and bounced. Sagebrush scraped against the sides. Dust blossomed up into the air behind them.

"Funny thing, you calling your mother a lush," Evelyn said. "Considering what happened after you bombed out of surgery."

"I've been clean for six years and four months. I still go to the meetings."

"Swell. The guy I married didn't need to."

"Look, this is old territory, do we really need to revisit it? We went over it so many times during the divorce."

"And you've been going over it in your head ever since. Over and over and. . . ."

"I want us to stop. That's all. Just stop."

"It's your call. I'm only a symptom, remember? If you want to stop thinking, then just stop thinking."

Unable to stop thinking, he continued eastward, ever eastward.

For hours he drove, while they talked about every small and nasty thing he had done as a child, and then as an adolescent, and then as an alcoholic failure of a surgeon and a husband. Every time Hank managed to change the subject, Evelyn brought up something even more painful, until his face was wet with tears. He dug around in his pockets for a handkerchief. "You could show a little compassion, you know."

"Oh, the way you've shown *me* compassion? I offered to let you keep the car if you'd just give me back the photo albums. So you took the albums into the backyard and burned them all, including the only photos of my grandmother I had. Remember that? But, of course, I'm not real, am I? I'm just your image of Evelyn—and we both know you're not willing to concede her the least spark of human decency. Watch out for that gully! You'd better keep your eyes straight ahead."

They were on a dirt road somewhere deep in the desert now. That was as much as he knew. The car bucked and scraped its underside against the sand, and he downshifted again. A rock rattled down the underside, probably tearing holes in vital places.

Then Hank noticed plumes of dust in the distance, smaller versions of the one billowing up behind him. So there were other vehicles out there. Now that he knew to look for them, he saw more. There were long slanted pillars of dust rising up in the middle distance and tiny grey nubs down near the horizon. Dozens of them, scores, maybe hundreds.

"What's that noise?" he heard himself asking. "Helicopters?"

"Such a clever little boy you are!"

One by one, flying machines lifted over the horizon. Some of them were news copters. The rest looked to be military. The little ones darted here and there, filming. The big ones circled slowly around a distant glint of metal in the desert. They looked a lot like grasshoppers. They seemed afraid to get too close.

"See there?" Evelyn said. "That would be the lifter."

"Oh," Hank said.

Then, slowly, he ventured, "The lander going down wasn't an accident, was it?"

"No, of course not. The Worms crashed it in the Pacific on purpose. They killed hundreds of their own so the bodies would be distributed as widely as possible. They used themselves as bait. They wanted to collect a broad cross-section of humanity.

"Which is ironic, really, because all they're going to get is doctors, morticians, and academics. Some FBI agents, a few Homeland Security bureaucrats. No retirees, cafeteria ladies, jazz musicians, soccer coaches, or construction workers. Not one Guatemalan nun or Korean noodle chef. But how could they have known? They acted out of perfect ignorance of us and they got what they got."

"You sound just like me," Hank said. Then, "So what now? Colored lights and anal probes?"

Evelyn snorted again. "They're a sort of hive culture. When one dies, it's eaten by the others and its memories are assimilated. So a thousand deaths wouldn't mean a lot to them. If individual memories were lost, the bulk of those individuals were already made up of the memories of previous generations. The better part of them would still be alive, back on the mother ship. Similarly, they wouldn't have any ethical problems with harvesting a few hundred human beings. Eating us, I mean, and absorbing our memories into their collective identity. They probably don't understand the concept of individual death. Even if they did, they'd think we should be grateful for being given a kind of immortality."

The car went over a boulder Hank hadn't noticed in time, bouncing him so high that his head hit the roof. Still, he kept driving.

"How do you know all that?"

"How do you *think* I know?" Ahead, the alien ship was growing larger. At its base were Worm upon Worm upon Worm, all facing outward, skin brown and glistening. "Come on, Hank, do I have to spell it out for you?"

"I have no idea what you're talking about."

"Okay, Captain Courageous," Evelyn said scornfully. "If this is what it takes." She stuck both her hands into her mouth and pulled outward. The skin to either side of her mouth stretched like rubber, then tore. Her face ripped in half.

Loop after loop of slick brown flesh flopped down to spill across Hank's lap, slid over the back of the seat and filled up the rear of the car. The horridly familiar stench of Worm, part night soil and part chemical plant, took possession of him and would not let go. He found himself gagging, half from the smell and half from what it meant.

A weary sense of futility grasped his shoulders and pushed down hard. "This is only a memory, isn't it?"

One end of the Worm rose up and turned toward him. Its beak split open in three parts and from the moist interior came Evelyn's voice: "The answer to the question you haven't got the balls to ask is: Yes, you're dead. A Worm ate you and now you're passing slowly through an alien gut, being tasted and experienced and understood. You're nothing more than an emulation being run inside one of those hundred-pound brains."

Hank stopped the car and got out. There was an arroyo between him and the alien ship that the car would never be able to get across. So he started walking.

"It all feels so real," he said. The sun burned hot on his head, and the stones underfoot were hard. He could see other people walking determinedly through the shimmering heat. They were all converging on the ship.

"Well, it would, wouldn't it?" Evelyn walked beside him in human form again. But when he looked back the way they had come, there was only one set of footprints.

Hank had been walking in a haze of horror and resignation. Now it was penetrated by a sudden stab of fear. "This *will* end, won't it? Tell me it will. Tell me that you and I aren't going to keep cycling through the same memories over and over, chewing on our regrets forever?"

"You're as sharp as ever, Hank," Evelyn said. "That's exactly what we've been doing. It passes the time between planets."

"For how long?"

"For more years than you'd think possible. Space is awfully big, you know. It takes thousands and thousands of years to travel from one star to another."

"Then . . . this really is Hell, after all. I mean, I can't imagine anything worse."

She said nothing.

They topped a rise and looked down at the ship. It was a tapering cylinder, smooth and featureless save for a ring of openings at the bottom from which emerged the front ends of many Worms. Converging upon it were people who had started earlier or closer than Hank and thus gotten here before he did. They walked straight and unhesitatingly to the nearest Worm and were snatched up and gulped down by those sharp, tripartite beaks. *Snap* and then swallow. After which, the Worm slid back into the ship and was replaced by another. Not one of the victims showed the least emotion. It was all as dispassionate as an abattoir for robots.

These creatures below were monstrously large, taller than Hank was. The one he had dissected must have been a hatchling. A grub. It made sense. You wouldn't want to sacrifice any larger a percentage of your total memories than you had to.

"Please." He started down the slope, waving his arms to keep his balance when the sand slipped underfoot. He was crying again, apparently; he could feel the tears running down his cheeks. "Evelyn. Help me."

Scornful laughter. "Can you even *imagine* me helping you?"

"No, of course—" Hank cut that thought short. Evelyn, the real Evelyn, would not have treated him like this. Yes, she had hurt him badly, and by the time she left, she had been glad to do so. But she wasn't petty or cruel or vindictive before he made her that way.

"Accepting responsibility for the mess you made of your life, Hank? You?"

"Tell me what to do," Hank said, pushing aside his anger and resentment, trying to remember Evelyn as she had once been. "Give me a hint."

For a maddeningly long moment Evelyn was silent. Then she said, "If the Worm that ate you so long ago could only communicate directly with you . . . what one question do you think it would ask?"

"I don't know."

"I think it would be, Why are all your memories so ugly?"

Unexpectedly, she gave him a peck on the cheek.

Hank had arrived. His Worm's beak opened. Its breath smelled like Evelyn on a rainy Saturday afternoon. Hank stared at the glistening blackness within. So enticing. He wanted to fling himself down it.

Once more into the gullet, he thought, and took a step closer to the Worm and the soothing darkness it encompassed.

Its mouth gaped wide, waiting to ingest and transform him.

Unbidden, then, a memory rose up within Hank of a night when their marriage was young and, traveling through Louisiana, he and Evelyn stopped on an impulse at a roadhouse where there was a zydeco band and beer in bottles and they were happy and in love and danced and danced and danced into an evening without end. It had seemed then that all good things would last forever.

It was a fragile straw to cling to, but Hank clung to it with all his might.

Worm and man together, they then thought: *No one knows the size of the universe or what wonders and terrors it contains. Yet we drive on, blindly burrowing forward through the darkness, learning what we can and suffering what we must. Hoping for stars.*

3 A.M. in the Mesozoic Bar

"Strike a pose!"

Cheryl raised her beer bottle and stuck out her tongue at the photographer. *Click.* Bernie Hammerstein moved on to the next table. It was sometime after midnight and the bar was as crowded as it had ever been. Sam filled endless orders of drinks. Nobody was paying but then Bernie, taking a break from his self-imposed task, emptied his wallet on the bar and, with a sharp laugh, said, "Keep the change." Others followed suit, and soon there were drifts of paper money spilling over either side. Sam just kept pouring, moving things along with a wink here and a quick joke there.

Doing his bit to keep us from hysteria.

Then Oliver Lucas sat down at the piano and everyone gathered around and began singing along. We sang "Bottle of Wine" and "Show Me the Way to Go Home" and "Yellow Submarine" and for a while it was all good. But then we hit the refrain to "Sloop John B":

So hoist up the John B's sail
See how the mainsail sets
Call for the captain ashore, let me go home
Let me go home. . . .

And a plaintive note entered the music. People were beginning to wander away when Lucas segued into "Swing Low, Sweet Chariot" and that put paid to the whole deal. Voices died off until the only one singing was Lucas himself. I got a highball from the bar and thrust it into his hand. When he stopped playing, the voices came up again, a little frantic, and somebody switched on the jukebox.

In no time, half the bar was dancing to salsa music. Some of the women took off their blouses and the general mood brightened. Except for Ted. I saw him sitting in the corner by himself, grimly drinking, and started his way.

Which is when Alexander Peshev and an invertebrate paleontologist so new I hadn't caught his name yet began getting loud. I could see it turning into a fight. The biggest guy in sight was Desmond Hamilton, so I said, "C'mon," and dragged him away from his conversation with a grad student named Melissa.

Des and I closed in on the combatants just as they were raising their fists and grabbed their arms from behind. They struggled and swore, but couldn't break loose. "Do you really want to fight?" I said, as we frog-marched them away. "Fine. You want to kill each other? That's okay too. I don't care. Just do it where nobody can hear you. You're not going to spoil everybody else's last night. Understand?" We threw them out the door.

I was about to go back in when Des slapped a hand on my shoulder hard. "I've got two items on my bucket list," he said, speech slurred. "One is to get as drunk as I've ever been before. The other is to nail prissy little Miss Melissa there and make her bark like a dog. Mission A accomplished. You interrupted me in the middle of Mission B. Fair warning: I won't help you break up any more fights. Somebody sets his own hair on fire, I'm gonna let it burn."

Before I could respond, he turned his back on me and was gone.

So I went outside.

It was hot without the air-conditioning, but it was quiet too. My murderous pair had disappeared, gone to look for rocks to bludgeon each other with, was my guess. I walked a few steps away from the rec center prefab, and took a deep breath of that clean Mesozoic air. There was an acrid burnt edge to it from the accident, but I ignored that as best I could.

What I couldn't ignore was the fact that there were two moons in the sky. They made the night bright enough that I could see a herd of hadrosaurs nested down peaceably by the river—and that was over a mile away.

I heard the door open again, and stepped back into the shadows. Sam came out with Constantine Chung, who was a moon-faced nebbish I'd always thought was entirely asexual. But from the way they had their arms around each other, I'd thought wrong. They disappeared behind the crater where the big expensive machinery that was supposed to bring us all home a week ago had been.

So Chung was gay. Not long back, that would have been good gossip. Now . . . I went inside and got behind the bar.

Somebody had to keep the booze flowing.

"Sazerac?" Braydon Noyer loomed up before me, swaying unsteadily. A week ago, he was a big man. He was the head of the whole shebang, back when that mattered. Now he was just another drunk. His eyes opened and closed several times, as if he were having trouble staying awake. He tried again. "Can you make me a Sazerac?"

"I can if you tell me the recipe," I said cheerily.

Braydon's face did things and for a second I thought he was going to cry. He was looking at all the possibilities in the world shutting before him, one by one, like so many doors. So I rummaged around behind the bar. We were running low on everything. "How about a hard cider?" I popped the cap and put the bottle in his hand. He clutched it like a drowning man grabbing at a lifeline. "Last one I got."

Which, of course, meant it was the last one anywhere for the next sixty-five million years.

Then Des grabbed Melissa's top and ripped it off her, exposing her enormous breasts and making them swing. Melissa laughed a high shrill laugh that turned to a shriek when he grabbed her and squeezed. I grabbed a bottle and was about to coldcock him, when she stumbled back against the bar and hoisted up her skirt. So I put the bottle down.

Nevertheless, I stepped in before things could go any further.

"Outside, kids," I said. "Not everybody likes to watch."

They left, Melissa giving me the finger on the way out. But she was pretty drunk, so I didn't take offense.

There was a brief respite on bar orders then—everybody had had far more than enough long, long ago—and I thought I'd go have a word with Ted. He was still drinking hard. Whenever anyone approached him, he glared them away. Not that many tried.

Which was understandable. We were stranded here with the Chicxulub impactor on its way for reasons that everybody agreed were nobody's fault. But if anybody *was* at fault, it was Ted.

Ted looked like he could use a friend. But just as I was about to head his way, I saw that Cheryl had beaten me to it. Exactly as she had sworn she wouldn't. She pulled up a chair and started talking intensely.

I would have paid a lot to be able to hear that conversation.

Then Bernie came over and said, "Pose!" I didn't, but he took my picture anyway. "You're the last one." He ditched the camera on the bar, dislodging a small avalanche of bills. "I've now taken a picture of every human being on earth. Counting me, that's forty-four."

"Congratulations," I said. "Why?"

"Well . . . you know." He swung his arms helplessly. Without his camera, he didn't seem to know what to do with them. "There are only so many things you can do when you know you're going to die. Get drunk. Punch somebody. Kiss a pretty girl."

"Yeah. I've been watching."

"It's like we've all reverted to apes. The heck with that. I wanted to do something else, you know? Like you. You've been keeping everything peaceful. I admire that."

I couldn't see any reason to lie. "Actually, I've been meaning to punch out Ted all evening. Only something keeps happening."

"Ted?" Bernie sounded surprised. "For the accident, you mean?"

"Among other things."

"That's crazy," he said. "What would be the point?" And then, "Now in particular."

I was about to shrug when Ted shoved his table into Cheryl's stomach and, lurching to his feet, jabbed an angry finger at her. "It's your fault this happened. Your fault we're going to die. Yours, you pathetic . . ." He reached for the right word, failed to find it, and settled for "Slut!"

Every voice was stilled. Every face turned toward him.

Then he bolted out the door. The faces turned away and the conversations resumed.

So it looked like I wasn't going to get to punch out Ted after all. Deeply involved as I was in the fallout of his life, I was able to read more into his outburst than anybody else present, with the possible exception of Cheryl: That he never had loved her, not even a little. That she had never been anything but a convenient piece of tail to him. People reveal themselves under stress. Even with his life about to end, the sonofabitch wasn't man enough to spare her a few comforting lies.

Cheryl came running toward me. She was crying.

"C'mere." I opened my arms and Cheryl slammed into them. "Don't take what Ted said seriously. He's just—"

"I thought he was playing a video game. I snapped off the screen because I wanted his attention. I was just flirting, was all." She buried her head in my chest. "What a stupid, stupid, stupid thing for me to do."

All around us, people were drifting away. To see the fireworks, no doubt. There wouldn't be enough time to do much of anything else.

"It's all water over the dam," I said. "Let it go." Cheryl was clutching my shirt with both fists so hard that it hurt. The cloth was wet with her tears. I would have been happier if she'd been crying because she'd killed us all, rather than because the guy she wanted didn't want her back. But what the heck. When you've only got minutes to live, there's no time to obsess over the side issues.

Without thinking, Cheryl swept her head back and forth, wiping her nose against my shirt. Then she said, "Oh, Hank, I'm so sorry. You're so good to me, you always have been. If only I'd fallen in love with . . . If only I could have. . . ." Finally looking up, finally looking me bleakly in the face, she said, "Life's a real bastard, isn't it?"

"Hush there," I said. "Hush, there. Hush." I'd never loved her so much or wanted her so badly as I did then. I wished I could kiss her. But she was so fragile in that instant that I knew it would break her right open. "There's nothing wrong with life. We just don't appreciate it enough, is all."

Of Finest Scarlet
Was Her Gown

Of finest scarlet was her gown;
It rustled when it touched the ground.
Even the Devil, with all her wealth,
Had no such silks to clothe herself.

Su-yin was fifteen when her father was taken away. She awoke from uneasy sleep that night to the sound of tires on the gravel drive and a wash of headlights through her room. From the window she saw a stretch limousine glide to a halt in front of the house. Two broad-shouldered men wearing sunglasses got out to either side. One opened the passenger door. A woman emerged. She wore a dress that covered everything from her neck to her ankles except for a long slit on the side that went all the way up one leg.

A thrill of dark foreboding flew up from her like a wind.

The woman cocked a wrist and one of her bodyguards—Su-yin had seen enough of their kind to know them at sight—handed her a cigarette. The other lit it. Flickering match-light played over the harsh planes of a cruel but beautiful face. In an instant of sick revulsion, Su-yin experienced a triple revelation: first that this woman was not human; then that whatever she might be was far worse than any mere demon; and finally that, given the extreme terror her presence inspired, she could only be the Devil herself.

Quickly, Su-yin pulled on her clothes—jeans, flannel shirt, running shoes—as she had been taught to do if strangers came to the house late at night. But she did not slip out the back door and run through the woods as she was supposed to. Instead, she knelt by the window and watched through the slats of the venetian blinds.

The Devil unhurriedly smoked her cigarette, exhaling through her nostrils. Then she flicked away the butt and nodded. One of her underlings went to the front door and hammered on it with his fist. *Bam! Bam! Bam!* The sound was an assault upon the helpless house. There was a long silence. Then the door opened.

Su-yin's father stepped outside.

The General's bearing was stiff and proud. He listened politely while the bodyguard spoke. Then he gestured the man aside, dismissing him as irrelevant, and turned to confront the dark woman.

She handed him a rose.

For the space of three long breaths, Su-yin's father clutched the flower, black as midnight, staring down at it in horror and disbelief. Then he seemed to crumple. It was as if all the air had gone out of him. His head sagged. Weakly, he half-turned toward the house, lifting a hand in a gesture that as good as said, "At least. . . ."

The Devil snapped her fingers and pointed toward the limousine, where a bodyguard held open a door. She might have been giving orders to a dog.

To Su-yin's shock, her father obeyed.

Doors slammed. The engine growled to life. Heart pounding, Su-yin sprinted downstairs. Snatching the keys from the end table by the door, she ran for the Lexus. She didn't have a learner's permit yet, but the General had taken her to the parking lot at the stadium when no games were in the offing and let her try the car out under his careful supervision. So she knew how to drive. Sort of.

By the time she'd gotten down the driveway and onto Alan-a-Dale Lane, the limousine was almost out of sight. Su-yin drove as fast as she dared, the steering wheel loose in her hands. She could see the limousine's red taillights in the distance and did her best to keep up, wandering off the road and jerking back on again. A truck swerved out of her way, horn blaring. Luckily, there were no cops about. But the limo pulled steadily away from her, dwindling on the miracle mile and then disappearing on Route One.

It was gone.

Su-yin mashed her foot down on the accelerator. The car leaped wildly forward and through a red light. She heard brakes screeching and horns screaming and what might have been an accident, but paid them no mind. All she could think of was her father.

Her father was never a religious man. But when her mother died, he had emptied out the mud room and built a shrine there with candles, a framed photograph of his wife, and some of her favorite things: a carton of Virginia Slims, *Mastering the Art of French Cooking*, a stuffed toy that had somehow survived from her childhood in rural Sichuan. Then he had gone into the little room, closed the door, and cried so loudly that Su-yin was terrified. He had seen that fear on her when he emerged, more than an hour later, his face as expressionless as a warrior's bronze mask. Scooping her up, he had lifted her into the air over and over again until she laughed. Then he'd said, "I will always be here for you, little princess. You will always be my daughter, and I will always love you."

Su-yin's hands were white on the wheel and there were tears flowing down her face. It was only then that she realized that she, the General's daughter, was displaying weakness. "Stop that right now," she told herself fiercely. And almost overshot the strip club in whose lot the Devil's stretch limo was parked.

Su-yin parked the car and composed herself. The club was shabby, windowless, and obviously closed. But where else could they have gone? She went inside. In the foyer a bearded man with a sleeveless shirt that showed biker tattoos said, "You ain't got no business here, girlie. Scram!"

"I have an interview," Su-yin said, making it up as she went along. "An audition, I mean. With the head lady."

"You're talent?" The man stared at her impudently. "Oh, they gonna eat you up." Then he jerked his head. "Enda the hall, down the stairs, straight on to the bottom."

Trying not to show how terrified she was, Su-yin followed his directions.

The hallway smelled of disinfectant, vomit, and stale beer. The handrail down the stairs rattled and some of the treads felt spongy underfoot. A lone incandescent bulb faded farther and farther into the distance behind Su-yin.

Save for the sound of her own feet, the stairway was completely silent.

Flight after flight she descended, the light growing steadily weaker until she was groping her way in absolute darkness. At some point, because it seemed impossible that the stairway could continue as far down as it did, she began counting landings. At twenty-eight, she bumped into a wall.

By feel, Su-yin found a doorknob. It turned and she stumbled through a doorway into a dim red city. A sun the color of molten bronze shone weakly through its clouds. The air stank of coal smoke, sulfur, and diesel exhaust. Sullen brick buildings, scarred with graffiti, overlooked narrow streets where trash blew in the cold breeze. There was no trace of either her father or the Devil.

Su-yin took a step backward and bumped into the side of a brick building. The door through which she had come had disappeared.

"Where am I?" she asked out loud.

"You're in Hell, of course. Where else would you be?"

Su-yin turned to find herself face to face with a scrawny, flea-bitten, one-eyed disgrace of a tomcat perched atop an overflowing trash can. He grinned toothily. "Spare a few bucks for a fella what's down on his luck?"

"I. . . ." Su-yin seized control of herself. She had to expect things would be different here. "Take me to the Devil, and I'll give you whatever money I have." Then she remembered that she'd left behind her purse. "Actually, I only have a few coins in my pocket—but I'll give you them all."

The cat laughed scornfully. "I can see *you're* going to fit in here really well!" He extended a paw. "I'm Beelzebub. Not the famous one, obviously."

"Su-yin." She shook the paw carefully. Its fur was greasy and matted. "Will you help me?"

"Not for the crap money you're offering." Beelzebub jumped down from the trash can. "But since I got all eternity with nothing better to do, I'll help you out. Not because I like you, understand. Just because it's an offense against local community standards."

Hell was a city like any other city save that there was nothing good to be said about it. Its inhabitants were as rude as Parisians, its streets as filthy as those of Mumbai, its air as tainted as that of Mexico City. Its theaters were closed, its libraries were burned-out shells, and, of course, there were no churches. Those few shops that weren't shuttered had long lines. The public facilities were far from clean and, without exception, had run out of toilet paper long ago. It didn't take Su-yin long to realize that her father was not going to be easily found. There was no such thing as a City Hall or, indeed, any central authority of any kind. Hell appeared to be an anarchy. Nor was there a wealthy district for the privileged. "It's a socialist's dream world," Beelzebub told her. "Everybody's equally miserable here."

The Devil could be anywhere. And though the cat led her up streets and down, there was not a trace of that Dark Lady to be seen.

In a rundown park little better than a trash dump she came upon a pale-skinned young man sitting cross-legged on a park bench whose back slats were missing. His hands were resting on his knees, palms up, thumbs touching the tips of his forefingers. His head was tilted back. His eyes were closed. "What are you doing?" Su-yin asked him.

"Curiosity? Here?" The young man continued staring sightlessly at the sky. "How . . . curious." Then he lowered his chin and, opening his eyes, stared at her through a shock of jet-black hair. His eyes were faintest blue. "A pretty girl. Curiouser and curiouser."

Su-yin blushed.

"Watch out for this one, Toots," Beelzebub said. "He'll talk the knickers offa you in no time flat."

"It seems you have a friend. In Hell. Inexplicable. Tell me what you see."

"See?"

"See," the young man said. "Hell is different for everybody. What you see is pretty much what you deserve."

"Then I guess I don't deserve much." Su-yin described the litter-filled park and the sad buildings that surrounded it as best she could.

"No wasps? No flames? None of those nasty little things you can only see out of the corner of your eye? I begin to wonder if you belong here at all." The young man uncrossed his legs, and sat like a normal boy, all elbows and knees. "In answer to your question, I was meditating, foolish though that may well seem to you. Against all reason, I appear not to have entirely given up hope. But I doubt that you're interested in my story."

"I am, actually." Su-yin sat down on the park bench beside the boy. Unlikely though it was, she couldn't help hoping that he was nice. "What's your name?"

"Rico. When I was alive, I thought I was a pretty hard sort. I cut class, boosted cars, smoked reefer, had sex with girls. Oh, and I died young. That's important. I was shot dead in my very first hold-up. I strutted through the gates of Hell like a rooster, convinced that I was the baddest, wickedest man ever consigned to damnation.

"Oh, was I wrong! So far as I can tell, until you popped up I was the *least* wicked person here. I say that with no pride whatsoever. Because it means that I was damned by the slightest of margins. Patting a dog or smiling at an old woman or dropping a dime in a beggar's hand probably would have been enough to tip the balance. One tiny act of kindness more and I'd be sitting in a penthouse in Heaven today, eating porterhouse steak and drinking Bordeaux wine while pouring Evian water into a Limoges saucer for my pet ocelot. So I thought . . . maybe if I improved myself that tiny little bit, I'd wake up and find myself somewhere else. See what I mean about hope? I've been doing this for a long, long time, and no results. Still, it's not like I have anything better to do. Now what's your story?"

When Su-yin was done, Rico whistled. "Kindness. Courage. Self-sacrifice. This day grows more inexplicable with every passing moment." Then, "You look hungry. Let me stake you to a meal."

"Don't do it, babe," Beelzebub said. "It's an old jailhouse con. When you first arrive, everything's a gift. But come midnight, Shylock here is going to want his pound of flesh. If you know what I mean."

Rico's face twisted with annoyance. "Okay, now *that* kind of language is more like what I'd expect hereabouts." He turned back to Su-yin. "I wash dishes at the Greasy Spoon. There's an opening there for a waitress, if you want it. The pay's not much, but it comes with three meals a day. Such as they are."

Su-yin realized then that she was likely to be stuck in Hell for a long time. "Well. . . ."

"A hundred a week plus meals and tips, if any," the cook said. He didn't tell Su-yin his name, nor did he ask for hers. "Also, you get to sleep in the storage room. Anybody craps on the floor, you clean it up. I catch you hocking a loogie in the food, you get docked an hour's wages. Got that?"

"Yes, sir."

"Then welcome to the finest fucking restaurant in Hell. Get your ass to work. And get that filthy fucking cat outta here!" The cook grabbed a hot frying pan off the grill and flung it at Beelzebub, who disappeared in a yowl of fur and defiance.

Work Su-yin did, for twelve hours every day, waiting on sullen customers and bussing the counter, scrubbing the floors, unclogging the toilets, and putting out the trash. Serving as a jill-of-all-trades so long as the trade was boring.

In her free time, she scoured the city, searching for her father or the Devil in dark, joyless bars, unventilated parking garages, and basement sweatshops where drab men turned out shoddy furniture and shoes whose laces broke the first time they were tied. Slowly, steadily, she could feel the grayness of the place sinking deeper and deeper into her flesh until it was a constant ache in the marrow of her bones.

The boundaries of Hell ebbed and flowed like the tides, so that the way everything hooked up changed day by day. The city abutted the world Su-yin had come from, but different parts of it on different days. Sometimes she found herself staring yearningly into Los Angeles and other times at the outskirts of Moscow. One day the city abruptly ended in desert—she had no idea which one—and Su-yin found herself contemplating a lone flower whose stalk was the exact same color green as the soda straws back at the Greasy Spoon.

She stared at it for a long time, thinking.

Su-yin showed up early for her next shift and rummaged through the trash, looking for brightly colored packaging. Then she set to work. When she was done, Dolores, a dried husk of a woman who was the other waitress on duty and had yet to say more than four words in a row to Su-yin, stuck her head into the kitchen and said, "You guys gotta see this."

The cook came out of the kitchen and said, "What's that goddamn heap a shit?"

"It's a bouquet of flowers," Su-yin said. "Sort of. I made it out of soda straws and whatnot. The vase used to be a sour pickle jar."

From behind the cook, Rico said. "What's it for?"

"It's just for pretty." She pinched the cook's cheek. "Sort of like Cookie here."

Dolores's mouth fell open. Rubbing the side of his face, the cook said, "What the fuck was that for?"

"No reason. Just felt like it." A customer came in and she brought him a menu. "What'll you have, Sweetie?" For the rest of the day she called the Greasy Spoon's patrons "Hon," and "Sugarpie," and "Darlin'." She had a smile for everyone, and when she mopped the counter she sang. She made little jokes. If there was anything she could do to make the diner a happier place, Su-yin did it. It wasn't easy. But she made the effort.

The next day she did the same. And the day after. And the day after that one too. After a time, the regulars would smile wanly at the sight of her. A couple of them even made unconvincing attempts to flirt with her. One left a tip—it was a slug, of course, but the gesture was good. Smiling, Su-yin tossed it in the air, caught it one-handed, and shoved it in a pocket.

At last, the Devil took the bait.

Su-yin was wiping blood from the dingy Formica countertop when the Dire Lady walked into the diner. Quickly stashing the cleaning rag under the counter, she said, "What can I get you, ma'am?"

The Devil sat and, after a bodyguard lit a fresh cigarette, exhaled a slow, lingering, sensuous serpent of smoke. "Boodles martini, very dry, straight up, with a twist. I want it so cold that it hurts."

"Yes, ma'am." Su-yin turned back toward the kitchen and was not surprised to find that she was in a gleaming—and impeccably clean!—bar. Everything in Hell, apparently, confirmed to its Mistress's wishes. Fortunately, Su-yin had for years made her father's cocktails for him every evening, so she knew what to do. With swift efficiency, she mixed the drink and brought the brim-full glass to the Devil without spilling a drop.

Crimson lips opened moistly. Gin slid down that long, long throat. Perfectly manicured nails plucked the lemon rind from the drink to be nibbled by even white teeth. All against her will, Su-yin admired the elegance of the performance.

The Devil dropped an envelope on the counter. "Read it."

Cautiously, Su-yin shook the document open. It was notarized, but she'd know the General's handwriting anywhere. His phrasing too:

> *My dearest daughter:*
> *What are you doing? Go home. You can accomplish nothing here.*
> *I used to love you, but there is no love in this place.*
> *Sincerely,*
> *Your Father*

Su-yin put the letter down and looked the Devil in the eye. "All this tells me is that I've gotten your attention."

The Devil snorted. "Your attempts at meliorating the pervasive misery of my domain are annoying, yes. But that's all. You think you can defy me? Empires have fallen for less."

"Where is my father?" Su-yin said without trembling.

"He's right behind you."

Su-yin spun around and she was in a hospital room. It smelled of antiseptic and ironed sheets. People walked by unhurriedly in the corridor outside. A television grumbled on the wall. An unseen machine wheezed regularly, a half-beat off of the rhythm of her own breath. Lying in a bed, skin palest white, eyes closed, was her father.

She ran to him and clasped one large, unresponsive hand in both of her own.

Those eyes, which in life had always been so cunning and wise, opened the merest slit. Dark pupils slid down the curve of eyelids. "Foolish child, why are you doing this?" the General mumbled.

"I'm going to bring you home, Daddy."

"This is my home now. I am here because I deserve to be here."

"No!"

"You are old enough now to suspect how I made a living. I assure you that I did everything you fear I did, and worse. You cannot save me nor can you undo time."

"I will! I will! I will!" Hot tears of rage and denial coursed down Su-yin's face. "I haven't come this far to be turned away now. I don't know how, but somehow I'll—"

"*Stop that.*" The General was gone and she was back in the bar, transfixed by the Devil's glare. Without any change in how she felt, Su-yin was no longer crying. "What will it take to get you to leave?"

Controlling her emotions as best she could, Su-yin said, "My father."

The Devil threw her martini in Su-yin's face.

The gin was so cold that it stung and for an instant Su-yin feared that it had been magically turned into acid. But she managed not to cry out or to turn away. Fumbling under the bar, she found the cleaning rag and used it to dry off her face.

"I suppose this is what they call love. It looks a lot like pigheadedness." The Devil tapped her nails against the obsidian top of the bar, click, click, *click*. "All right," she said. "I'll deal."

Su-yin waited in silence.

"You are a virgin. Don't think that makes you special here. There are plenty of virgins in Hell. But I'll set you a challenge. Stay a virgin for an entire year and I'll let you take your father away—alive, unharmed, all of that. But if you behave like the slut I'm convinced you are, you agree to simply, meekly, leave."

"I—"

"There are other conditions. You have to go out with anyone who asks you. You'll keep your job here, but I'm giving you the use of a penthouse apartment I maintain as a *pied-à-terre* so you'll have a nice place to bring a boy home to. Don't you dare touch any of my clothes."

"Thank you."

"I'm also giving you a tutor. To teach you, among other things, manners."

Leonid was thin, graceful, acerbic, and, Su-yin suspected, gay. He was waiting in the penthouse when she got there. "We will start," he said, "with the foxtrot."

"Can't I just . . . you know? Kids today mostly just wing it."

"No." Leonid took her in his arms, turned one way, turned the other. Her body naturally followed his. "Your partner controls where you go. If he knows what he's doing, you follow fluidly. Your every movement is easy and graceful as you yield to his movements. The metaphoric content is, I hope, obvious. All the while, your bodies press together. He is constantly aware of your breasts against him, your thighs, your everything. You, in turn, cannot help knowing when he becomes physically aroused."

"I don't think you're very aroused by me," Su-yin said, amused.

"That is not my job. Nor is it yours. You are only to arouse those who ask you out. And I am not going to ask you out."

There was a knock on the door. "Room service," Leonid announced. He let in a deferential servant who swiftly unloaded the contents of a wheeled cart onto a table: linen napkin, silverware, a selection of cheeses on a wood tray, crystal glasses, a carafe of water, a split of champagne.

"I'm not old enough to drink alcohol," Su-yin said.

"Here, you are. One of the many things I am to teach you is how to drink. In moderation, it goes without saying. You must never have more than two glasses in an evening and *never* accept anything you have not seen poured. Drugged drinks are a fact of life."

"Oh," Su-yin said in a small voice.

"I will also teach you some rudimentary self-defense. But only after you have learned how to dance. Dancing is fundamental." Leonid gestured toward the food. "Well? Have at it."

"Aren't you going to have some too?"

"No. I will stand here and critique how you eat."

———————

Her first date was with a man who said his name was Archer. "Just Archer," he said when she asked for his full name. They met in the building's lobby, which looked like it was meant for billionaires, smelled faintly of sour milk, and had Ferrante and Teicher playing on the sound system. He was dressed like a mobster, in a black suit with matching shirt and white tie. He opened his jacket to show her his gun. Then he started to tug out his shirt to show her his tattoos.

"Not now," Su-yin said. "Maybe when we know each other better." Which sounded stupid but was the only thing she could think of to say. She made a mental note to ask Leonid for better responses to such situations.

In the street outside, a cabbie leaned on his horn, long and hard.

"Milady, thy chariot awaits," Archer declaimed. Then he grabbed her arm and yanked her outside. When he helped her into the car, he stroked her bottom.

They went to a restaurant where her date proceeded to order for her, saying, "I've eaten here before and you haven't." Archer chose foods she didn't like, and tried to get her to drink from a flask which, when she refused, he returned to his jacket pocket without sampling. When she had to go to the toilet, he said, "Mind if I come along? I enjoy watching women pee."

Su-yin stayed in the ladies' room for as long as she dared. When she returned to the table, Archer had eaten all the veggies off her plate and there were several empty cocktail glasses in front of him. "Say," he said, whipping out his smartphone, "do you want to see some pictures of my mother?"

One glimpse of the screen was enough to make Su-yin whip away her head, reddening. "Not pictures like that."

"Aw, c'mon. We're in Hell. You can get away with anything here."

The meal went on forever. Whenever the waitress came by, Archer leered at her and ordered drinks for the both of them. Then, when his was empty and Su-yin's still untouched, he drank hers as well. In the cab home, he began to cry because when he was alive his father had molested him, and it had screwed up his sex life. Then, when he dropped her off, he grabbed her arms and tried to kiss her. She closed her lips tight and turned away from his mouth, so he licked the side of her face. "At least let me smell your panties," he said.

With a shriek, Su-yin pushed him away and fell backwards out of the cab. She lurched to her feet and, abandoning one of her shoes, ran inside. Behind her Archer shouted, "Come back! You haven't paid the cabbie!"

Inside the Devil's condo, Su-yin's tutor was waiting. "I won't ask how it went," he said.

"Oh, Leonid, it was awful." He handed her a dressing gown. There was an antique Chinese screen in one corner of the room. Su-yin went behind it and undressed, draping her dress and underwear over the top the way starlets did in old black-and-white movies. "The only good thing to be said about the whole experience is that I was never once in the least bit tempted to have sex with him."

"Don't get cocky. The Devil likes to play games. She'll soften you up with some really awful experiences and then slip in a ringer. A nice dancer, a good listener, a fella who seems to be on your side. That's the one you've got to look out for." Leonid gathered up her clothes. "I'll take these things out to be laundered."

He withdrew then.

Su-yin took a shower to get the smell of Archer and his cigars off her skin. Then she went to bed, praying that she wouldn't have nightmares about him but sure that she would.

Still. One day down and not quite a year to go.

At least three times a week, Su-yin had dates, all of them hideous. One man exposed himself to her, then called her a slut for not sleeping with him. Another got drunk and tried to rip her dress off, right out on the street. A third got her name wrong and, no matter how many times she corrected him, insisted on calling her Ching-chong. He wanted to know if it was "true what they said about Asian girls," and got offended when she told him that whatever they said, she was pretty sure it was wrong. To say nothing of the woman who kept trying to get Su-yin to smell her fingers.

On those nights when she stayed in, Leonid gave her lessons. He showed her the proper way to snort cocaine, the basics of flirtation, the fast way to do up her hair in a French twist. She was taught that a stiletto heel can be driven right through a man's shoe, the social proprieties of makeup, and which of the seven basic perfume categories (Floral, Fern, Chypre, Leather, Woody, Oriental, and Citrus) were appropriate for different situations.

She also learned to play the piano, though the opportunity to do so never arose on a date.

"Why am I learning all this stuff?" Su-yin demanded one evening, while they were playing chess. "It's not like I'm ever going to use it."

"Having skills gives you confidence and having confidence makes you alluring." Leonid slid a bishop forward, putting her queen in mate. "That's all."

"I don't want to be alluring." Rather than move her queen, which was protecting her king, Su-yin blocked the attack with a knight.

"Rules of the game, sweetie. Rules of the game." Leonid advanced a pawn, opening a line of attack for his own queen, and suddenly the game looked entirely different. "Mate in three. You've got to learn to think at least four moves ahead."

One day, Beelzebub was waiting outside the Greasy Spoon when Su-yin got off work. "Thought I'd warn ya," he said. "Rico's building up his courage to ask you out."

"Is he?" Su-yin said, surprised. "I thought better of him."

"I can see what you're thinking. No, the Devil didn't order him to nail your little virgin tushie. She didn't have to. Setting aside this idiot challenge you got yourself roped into, Rico is young and male. You're young and lovely. You're gonna have your work cut out for you, keeping his hands outa your undies."

Caught by surprise, Su-yin asked, "Am I really lovely?"

"To him, yes. To a cat, not so much."

She laughed and rubbed Beelzebub's head. "That's one of the things I like best about you, Belzie—your unfailing honesty."

"I'm only honest because it's an offense against local community standards."

When she began her shift, Rico came out from the back room, drying his hands on his apron. "Listen," he said. "There's this dance club I know. I was thinking maybe this Friday I could take you there. To dance."

"Oh, Rico." Su-yin sighed. "I'd love to."

So that Saturday they went to the Top of the Town, which was a revolving sky bar with a spectacular view of the river Phlegethon and the delicate blue flames that flickered upon its waters. They danced for a while, and Rico kept stepping on her feet. Then a handsome Algerian named Jean-Luc cut in. He danced beautifully. Which was why Rico punched him out and then hustled Su-yin away to a smoky piano bar for cocktails. There, she took tiny sips from a glass of pinot grigio while Rico got plowed on highballs.

Finally, they took a rusted-out old taxi back to Su-yin's apartment and, true to Beelzebub's prediction, she had to fight to keep Rico's hands out of her dress. When they got out of the cab, she told him she'd had a lovely time and slipped quickly inside, directing the doorman not to let him follow. Behind her, she could hear him throwing up.

Back in her apartment, she kicked off her high heels and, without bothering to undress, threw herself down on the bed. The instant she closed her eyes, she could feel sleep closing about her.

One more day down. Far too many yet to go.

———————

Rico was hung over the next morning, and had a black eye from his encounter with the doorman. So he didn't ask Su-yin out again, which was just as well because she got a call from the Algerian, insisting that they go clubbing.

They went to the Dew Drop Inn, the Hotsy-Totsy Club, the Orchid Lounge, Swank City, the Top Hat, and the Roadhouse and danced to the music of Pat Boone, Doris Day, Barry Manilow, Patti Page, and Wayne Newton. To Su-yin's surprise, Jean-Luc behaved like a perfect gentleman. "When I was alive, I was a jewel thief and a cat burglar," he told her. "A very good one, too. I learned that one has to handle beautiful things with a light touch.

"It would be counterproductive for me to throw myself at you, grasping and snorting," he said. "Though I assure you there is nothing I desire more. I must instead convince *you* to seduce *me*. Which is, notwithstanding the fact that you are unaware of it, something you most dearly desire to do."

"It's not going to happen. My father's soul is at stake."

"That's a problem of course." The Algerian winked roguishly. "I'll just have to be more charming."

"That hardly seems possible," Su-yin said, amused. But she stayed on her guard.

Jean-Luc had a wealth of stories of rooftop robberies and midnight escapes through the squalid alleys of Paris and Algiers. He asked her questions about her life and seemed genuinely interested in what she had to say. He told her that once, when he was wanted, he had hidden in a brothel in Marseille for a month—"the longest month of my life!"—without touching any of its employees. "I was in love, you see, desperately so. Only, when it was safe to come out, Mignette had moved in with a gendarme. She meant to wait for me, but—thirty days? Every woman had her limits."

The Algerian was nice and, under other circumstances, Su-yin didn't see that giving in to him would be entirely wrong. She felt much the same urges he did. So long as she didn't get pregnant or catch a disease, why not?

But she was in a contest with the Devil and it was one she was determined to win.

"This is a feint," Leonid said, during their next foil lesson. "I thrust and you respond with a parry four, knocking my blade outward, or so you expect." He demonstrated in slow motion. "But when you do, I dip my blade under yours and up again on the inside—and lunge." The button of his foil touched Su-yin's jacket, right above her heart.

He stepped back, pulling off his mask. "The whole purpose of the feint—of your Algerian, you understand my metaphor?—is to bring you off guard. To distract you from the real threat."

"Which is?"

"You'll recognize it when it happens. Provided you stay alert."

"Leonid, I never asked you this before, but . . . why are you doing this? Giving me advice, I mean. I know why you're giving me lessons."

"*Lasciate ogne speranza, voi ch'intrate.* 'Abandon hope, all ye who enter here.' It was very disappointing to discover that Dante's sign didn't exist, and even more so to discover that some faint ghost of hope remains. Your father no more deserves to escape here than I do. But if he did, that would be a kind of revenge upon Miss Spite, and I would derive some thin, sour satisfaction from that." Leonid shrugged. "That's all."

"Heads up again," Beelzebub said. "Young Lochinvar's hot for a second serving." And before Su-yin could respond, he was gone.

Sure enough, Rico asked her out again. "Just over to my apartment. To hang out. Nothing fancy. I won't try anything, I promise."

"I'll go if you want," Su-yin said. "But last time was such a disaster. Why repeat it?"

"Because being with you makes me feel better," Rico said. "Not happy, of course, that's not possible here. But less miserable. Sometimes I think that if only I could make you happy then I'd be happy too, almost. Just a little bit."

So she went.

Rico's apartment was every bit as squalid as she'd expected: filthy dishes clogging the sink, unwashed clothes kicked into the corners. But he'd made a sort of coffee table out of a crate and a Parcheesi board from a discarded pizza box. "I got the idea from you," he said. "From your fake flowers. The dice are made from that tasteless white root that Cookie uses in his stew. Turnip, maybe? Parsnip? The pips are stale peppercorns."

After so many dates with older men, Su-yin found Rico's youth—his callowness—painfully obvious. He talked too much about himself. He knew nothing about what passed in Hell for current events. When Su-yin mentioned the race for the meaningless office of Persecutor General, he didn't even know who was running, much less which of the candidates had already bought the election. He gloated whenever the dice favored him.

Still, Rico didn't try to grope her, and played the game with real enthusiasm, and on those rare times when Su-yin managed to turn the conversation around to topics of interest to her, he listened to what she had to say with genuine interest. So it could have been worse.

When it was finally late enough that Su-yin figured she could call it a night without hurting Rico's feelings, she asked to be taken home. They walked back to her apartment building and when they got there, Rico said, "Tonight was really nice. I mean, it was almost pleasant. Really. It was easily the least awful time I've had since dying."

Su-yin blocked his clumsy attempt to kiss her. Then, she planted a swift peck on his cheek and fled inside.

"We should do this again sometime!" Rico shouted after her.

When she got back to the apartment, Su-yin cried for hours. For the first time, her life here really did feel like Hell.

So it went. A blind date who took her not to a restaurant but to an orgy where old men stood about naked, waiting for young women to service them. Which they did, unenthusiastically and in a variety of ways that Su-yin could not have imagined six months earlier. She stayed for as long as she could stand to watch and then demanded to be taken home. Followed by a truly delightful evening with Jean-Luc. Then a man who liked to tear off his own scabs and eat them. A woman who said she wouldn't be a lesbian if it weren't for Su-yin and demanded to know how she planned to make it up to her. A Lord of the Inner Circles who was offended she hadn't heard of him. A creature of uncertain gender who suggested things that Su-yin didn't think she understood and certainly didn't want to do. Jean-Luc again, and a yacht party at which they played games where the losers were thrown into the acidic waters of the Acheron. Another sad evening with Rico, where they played pinochle with cards he had made from discarded paper plates, and he shared every regret he had from an innocently misspent youth.

All too slowly, the months passed. Sometimes the dates were so awful that Su-yin threw up afterwards. Other times, they were not so bad. Always, she managed to be cheerful while she worked, whether she felt like it or not. Sticking it to the Devil was how she thought of it. Though, whether out of spite or a heavy workload, that Fearsome Lady never showed her face.

On the next-to-last evening of the competition, the Algerian told Su-yin to dress formally and then drove her out of town to a trash dump to shoot rats. Su-yin knew how to shoot because her father had insisted on it, and, of course, the Devil's penthouse had an indoor firing range, so she'd kept in practice. Still, it was a bit of a letdown. "I feel silly being here dressed like this," she said.

"Don't." Jean-Luc was carrying a matched pair of Anschutz bolt-action rimfires. He handed her one. "The contrast only makes you look all the more elegant."

Su-yin checked the sight, made sure the rifle had a full clip, and thumbed the safety off. "How do we do this?"

"Mes frères!" Two men stepped out of darkness. Each carried a gasoline can. "Michel and Thierry will be our beaters tonight." He gestured toward a mound of garbage. "Let's start with that one."

The beaters trudged over to the mound and began sloshing gasoline on it.

"How this is done is as follows: When the garbage is set afire, it will drive out the rats living in tunnels within. They emerge with their fur aflame, so they are easy to spot. But they will be running as fast as they can, so they will not be easy to shoot. That's what makes it sporting. I'll target those that break right, you take the others. The winner is whoever pots the most rats. Ready?"

Su-yin raised her rifle. "I guess."

"Excellent." He raised his voice. "Light the fire!"

It should have been grotesque. It should have been disgusting. But against all expectations, it wasn't. Hell's rats were filthy creatures, even more loathsome than their terrestrial counterparts, so shooting them didn't make Su-yin feel bad at all. Plus, they were difficult enough to hit that there was genuine satisfaction when she did get one. By her third kill, Su-yin was laughing with every shot.

"To your left!" her beater cried as more rats shot, burning, from the trash fire. "Three!"

Su-yin led a flaming rodent with her rifle, squeezed the trigger, and watched it flip over in the air. She made a slap shot at the second and missed, while the third got clean away. Another rat tried to escape and she got it in one. Then she was out of ammunition. She held out her hand and Thierry slapped a fresh clip into it.

"I pegged four," the Algerian said. "You?"

"Five. So far."

"I'm impressed." The Algerian's face glistened in the light of the trash fire, but he held himself with perfect aplomb. He might have been modeling his suit for a fashion shoot. "I think this mound's about played out. Time to light up a second one."

By the time they were done, Su-yin was sweaty and bedraggled and her dress reeked so of burning garbage that she doubted it could be salvaged. But she was also ahead by a dozen rats. Michel and Thierry took their rifles and the Algerian led Su-yin back to his Maserati.

As he drove, the Algerian placed his hand on Su-yin's thigh and squeezed. She supposed she should have told him not to, but tonight had been so much fun—the only time she'd actually enjoyed herself since coming to Hell—that she felt she owed him at least that much. Anyway, it felt good.

At the door to her apartment building, the Algerian took Su-yin into his arms and said, "This is your last chance to invite me up to your room."

"Oh, Jean-Luc, you know I'd like to."

"Then do. It's that simple."

"I can't."

The Algerian released her, lit a cigarette, took a long drag, exhaled. "I swore I would wait until you beckoned me. I thought I had that much pride. But as it turns out, your self-control is stronger than mine. So it is I who must beg. Please. I know you are not . . . experienced. That doesn't matter. I can give you the first night every young woman deserves: passionate, romantic, lingering. Allow me to introduce you to the pleasures of being an adult in a manner you will cherish forever."

Su-yin found herself responding to his words more than she would have expected. Worse, when she tried to conjure up her father's image to help strengthen her reserve, she couldn't. After all this time, she was beginning, it seemed, to forget the General. This was a terrifying thought. But she could not deny it.

The Algerian's eyes twinkled cynically. The cigarette dangling from one corner of his mouth made him look every inch a scoundrel. The kind of scoundrel that women like. "By now we have spent enough time together," Su-yin said, "for you to know that when I say no I mean it."

"Oh, well. Alas." Jean-Luc shrugged. "Would you mind if I stubbed my cigarette out on the palm of your hand?"

"What? No!"

"Quel dommage." Taking her hand as if to kiss it, the Algerian stubbed out his cigarette on its back.

Back at the apartment, Leonid rubbed salve on her burn. "Tomorrow you'll wear gloves, of course."

"I can't believe Jean-Luc did that to me. I thought he was nice! And all the while. . . ."

"He showed his true colors. He's gone. Forget him. Tomorrow is your final date. You can be sure that the Devil has something special in mind."

"Who will it be?"

"I don't know. Nobody tells me anything. One gets used to it. But your date will pick you up in the lobby at seven. Be on your guard. Remember everything I taught you. Whoever he is, he'll be almost irresistible. Resist him. Don't forget that your victory is my victory too. In a small, petty, and unworthy way."

The next night—her final one in Hell—Su-yin came home from work to find Leonid looking pale and fearful. "It was Her Nibs," he explained. "She came by and she was *not* in a pleasant mood." He nodded toward the bedroom. "She laid out a dress for you to wear tonight."

Draped across the bed was a silk gown of deepest scarlet. The skirt was long and had a slit up one side. Su-yin could see at a glance that she was not supposed to wear any underwear with it. The silk flowed like water; its thread count had to be astronomical. When she put it on, it fit her so elegantly that she felt three inches taller.

It made her feel wanton.

It took some time to get her makeup right. But when Su-yin slipped on her heels and, blushing, emerged at last into the living room, Leonid's astonishment made it all worthwhile. "I begin to understand," he said, "what heterosexual men see in you creatures."

Then he was fussing over her hair, pinning it up, *tsk*ing over imperfections that only he could see, speaking rapidly all the while. "Tonight's not going to be easy. The Devil has her wiles. Don't let yourself be drawn off guard. Think four moves ahead—five, if you can manage it. Watch the alcohol. Don't do drugs of any sort. There's no place to hide a weapon in that dress, but your do is held together with a hairpin that's as good a dagger in a pinch. You could kill a man with it, but I really think you should avoid doing that if at all possible. It would spoil your coif. Is this a split end? Don't think that you can get into a heavy petting session and pull out of it before it's too late. That's the oldest self-delusion in the book. Remember, Miss Venom will be watching. Don't do anything that would make her happy."

At last, he stepped back and said, "It'll do."

There was a triple mirror in one corner of the room. Su-yin stood before it, stunned, for one long minute. Then, slowly, she spun about in order to see herself from every angle. She was perfect. She wished she could look like this forever. She knew she would remember this moment for the rest of her life.

Then the concierge called up to say that her date had arrived. Su-yin promised to be right down.

"Be on your guard!" Leonid called after her as she stepped into the elevator.

"I will!" she cried. "Don't worry!"

As the doors closed, she heard him say, "We don't know who you've been set up with, but we know he'll be dangerously hard to resist."

———————

It was Rico.

He wore a baby blue tuxedo, which he explained was a rental. He also brought along a corsage, which he clumsily pinned to her gown. "How can you afford all this?" Su-yin asked, when the limousine pulled up.

"I've been saving up all year. No big deal. It's not as if there's much of anything else to spend it on."

They went to the Cavern, a boutique club with flashing lights, distressing art on the walls, and live nude dancers in iron cages hung from the ceiling over the bar. They looked a hundred times sexier than Su-yin would ever be, but after his first glance Rico never looked at them again. All his attention was on her.

The music was hot and desperate when they entered and the club was thronged with sweaty bodies moving frantically. But when they stepped onto the dance floor, the tempo changed, so that they had no choice but to slow dance, holding each other close.

"You've been practicing!" Su-yin exclaimed. Rico was nowhere near as good as the Algerian, of course. But he didn't step on her feet even once. And though she could tell he was aroused—how not? her dress covered everything and hid nothing—he did not let it influence how he behaved toward her.

"Well, I didn't want tonight to be a fiasco like the last time. You know?"

By twos and threes, the other dancers drifted back to their tables, until finally there was nobody but just the two of them on the floor, holding onto each other and watched by hundreds of envious eyes. Above them, the women in their cages rubbed themselves against the bars, moaning with desire. At the bar, ice cubes rattled and drinks were poured. The band played slow number after slow number until, wearied, Su-yin suggested they take a breather.

When Rico broke free of her eyes, he seemed baffled to realize they had been dancing all alone. But he led Su-yin to a table, where she ordered a moonflower, a cocktail made from champagne, elderflower liqueur, and a peeled litchi, and Rico asked for a cola.

Once they were seated, the music grew raucous again, and the clubbers filled the dance floor to its capacity and beyond.

"So this is your last night, huh?" Rico said when their drinks had come.

"I guess."

"What are you going to do when you get back?"

"I hadn't given it any thought. Go back to school, I guess. A lot depends on what my father wants." It was, Su-yin realized with surprise, going to be difficult to go back to being a dutiful daughter after a year in which she'd been free to do whatever she wanted. She imagined the General would be grateful for having been saved from eternal damnation. But she didn't for an instant think that meant he would be any more permissive toward her. Certainly, he wouldn't let her go to clubs like this. The General had expected her to refrain from dating until she was in college—and only then because he knew he couldn't be there to watch over her.

Unexpectedly, Su-yin felt a twinge of regret for the freedoms she would be losing when she returned home.

She stood. "Let's go outside. I need some fresh air. Less stale air, I mean."

Out on the street, they wandered aimlessly down crumbling sidewalks and past shuttered buildings ugly with graffiti. Half the streetlights were out. When Rico tried to put his arm around her waist, Su-yin moved away from him. She didn't think so small a gesture would do any harm. But this late in the game she wasn't taking any chances.

They came to the waterfront and stopped. There, by the oily black waters of the Acheron, Rico found a discarded shopping cart, which they turned on its side and used for a bench. "I'll miss you," he said.

"But it was kind of a miracle you were here in the first place, wasn't it? You don't feel the miseries or see the abominations the rest of us do. Just being in your presence I can imagine a little bit what it must be like to be you. Glorious."

Su-yin didn't feel the least bit glorious. But she refrained from saying so. She leaned lightly against Rico, cherishing his solidity, hoping the warmth of her body would provide him some small comfort. "Let's not talk about that. Tell me something else instead."

"Okay." After a brief silence, Rico said, "I grew up in Baltimore. People think that big cities are divorced from nature but that's not true. There are butterflies in the spring and in autumn the trees turn bright gold and red. Sometimes in the winter it snows so hard that all the traffic stops. The streets are covered in sheets of purest white and the silence . . . the silence is . . . I can't do this."

"What?"

"I can't do this to you. I'm sorry."

Rico stood and turned away from Su-yin, drawing her up in his wake. Carefully, she said, "What are you talking about?"

"The Devil came to see me today."

"Oh," Su-yin said.

"I'd never seen her before. But she walks in the door and you know who she is, don't you? She told me that if I could score with you tonight, she'd let me out of this place. You can't imagine how it felt, hearing that. She said that we'd leave the club and wind up here. That I should talk about my childhood, crap like that. That the words would just come to me. But this is not what I want. Well, I do want it. But not like this."

Rico looked so forlorn that Su-yin started to take him into her arms to comfort him. He was such a sweet boy, she thought, such an innocent. It came to her in that moment that she had a choice. She could free her father from Hell or she could free Rico. Either way, she'd feel guilty about leaving one of them behind. Either way, it would be an epic accomplishment. And if she were to choose Rico. . . .

"You prick! You bastard!" Su-yin pushed Rico away from her and then punched him in the chest as hard as she could. "This is part of the script, isn't it?" All her emotions were in a jumble. She didn't know whether to laugh or to barf. "Well, you can just go—"

"Daughter."

Su-yin whirled, and there was the General, looming over her like a thunderhead. Her heart soared at the sight of him, even as she took an involuntary step back from his frown. She wanted to hug him, but even when he was alive that was an impertinence he would not allow in such a mood.

"Take a good long look at yourself, young lady. Out unescorted, at night, with this hooligan. Using bad language. Dressed like a prostitute. Living in . . . this place. Is this the life you imagine I had planned for you?"

"I—"

"I left you well provided for. Then I came here to be punished for doing things I should not have done. This is not only the way things are, it is the way they should be." The General wavered in Su-yin's sight like a candle flame, her eyes were so full of tears. "Do not speak! I am going to tell you what to do and you are to obey me without question. Do you understand?"

"I . . . yes."

"I have experience being in positions where there are no good choices. All you can do is negotiate the best deal you can. Have sex with this inappropriate young man. Then go home and never do anything shameful like that again. Many good women have such incidents in their past. Even your mother did things she later regretted." The General turned to Rico. "You."

"Sir?

"Give my daughter your hand."

He did so.

"Go into the nearest apartment building. The lobby will be clean and the doorman will give you the key to a decent room. There you will do what you must. There will be a condom on the nightstand—use it. Afterwards, my daughter will lead you out of Hell. You can show your gratitude by never trying to see her again."

Rico nodded assent and turned to go.

But when he did, Su-yin did not follow. Pulling her hand free of his, she said to her father, "How do you know all this? About the room, the condom, the nightstand?"

"Don't ask foolish questions. Just do as you're told."

An icy rage surged up within Su-yin. "You're in league with the Devil, both of you. Maybe Rico doesn't know it, but you certainly do. Good cop, bad cop. One of you weak, the other harsh." When her father's face went hard as granite, he looked like a gaunt version of Frankenstein's monster. How could she not have seen this before? "After all I've gone through for you!"

Rico reached out pleadingly toward Su-yin. But the General shoved him aside. Then, unthinkably, he raised up a hand to slap her.

Su-yin screamed and flinched away. Before the slap could land, she kicked off her heels and ran. Barefoot, she sped down the street, away from the both of them, as fast as she could go.

Four moves ahead, she thought wildly. Don't let yourself be drawn off guard. The hell with Rico and, for that matter, the hell with her father too. She wasn't going to be fooled as easily as *that*.

Back at the penthouse, Leonid was waiting. "Well?" he said anxiously.

All the way up in the elevator, Su-yin had been a bundle of hysteria and misery, equally mixed. Now, however. . . .

In trembling disbelief, she said, "I passed the test."

They broke out the Cristal and, laughing, drank down glass after glass. Leonid put on some music and they stumblingly danced the tango. Then they collided with the couch and tumbled down atop it and somehow they were kissing. Clothing got pushed this way and that way and then Leonid had his hands under her dress and she was fumbling with his zipper. It was wrong and she knew it, she'd never even thought of Leonid in that way, and yet somehow she couldn't seem to stop herself.

They did it right there on the couch.

It wasn't that great.

When they were done, Leonid gathered up his scattered clothes, dressed, and said, "It's almost midnight. I suggest you be out of Hell by morning."

Shocked, Su-yin said, "You . . . That was *planned*! All year you pretended to be my friend, when you knew from the start that you were going to . . . going to . . . do that."

"Believe it or not, I did you a huge favor," Leonid said. "The Devil would never have let you win. If you had held out against me, she would have arranged for you to be very brutally gang-raped. The only reason that didn't happen as soon as you cut a deal with her was that she wanted to teach you a lesson. Let's be honest here: You never had a chance. The Devil likes to play games. But all her games are rigged."

He adjusted his cravat, bowed, and left.

Su-yin had been told to leave Hell and she would. But she hadn't been told how to go about it. So she went to see Rico.

His face brightened when he saw her in the doorway of his sad little apartment, then dimmed again when she told him the reason she had come. "Any direction you take will lead you away from here," he said. There was a hurt look in the back of his eyes, but he said nothing of what he must have been thinking. "You could just walk out."

"Like heck I could. I lost the challenge. I lost my father. I lost a year of my life. I am not going to spend a single minute more than I have to in this place. I want to be out of here just as fast as I can manage."

"I lost all that too," Rico mumbled, "and more."

Su-yin pretended she hadn't heard him. "What did you say?"

"I said yeah, I can help you."

On a shadowy street just off the clubbing sector, Su-yin stopped in front of a Lincoln Continental. She liked how it looked. Also, she wanted something big. "This one," she said. It took Rico only seconds to break into the Lincoln and hot-wire the ignition. "How about that?" he said. "I guess the old skills never go away."

"Open up the trunk for me, would you? I have something I want to put in the back," Su-yin said. When he had done so, she bent briefly inside. "Oh, no!" she cried. "I dropped my brooch, the one my mother left me when she died, and I can't reach it. Rico, you're tall. . . ."

Rico leaned far into the trunk, groping in its dark recesses. "I don't see anything."

"It's way in the back. It bounced there." Su-yin waited until Rico was stretched as far as he could go and grabbed his ankles. With all her strength, she lifted him off the ground and toppled him over into the trunk. Then she slammed it shut.

A muffled voice said, "Hey!"

Su-yin climbed into the front of the car. As she did, a black streak of fur leaped over her and into the passenger seat. "You're not leaving without me," Beelzebub said.

"Of course not." Su-yin put the car into gear and started slowly down the road, ignoring the hammering from the trunk. "When we get home, I'm going to wash you and brush you and take a flea comb to your fur, though. Then I'll buy you a pint of cream."

"Make it a quart of scotch and you got a deal."

Su-yin shifted gears into second and then third. She sideswiped a parked Volkswagen van and, tires screeching, accidentally ran a red light. Luckily, there wasn't much traffic hereabouts at this time of night.

"Whoah!" Beelzebub cried. "Has anybody ever told you that you're the absolute worst driver in the universe?"

"You're the first." They were coming to the city limits now. Beyond lay what Su-yin was pretty sure was the Meadowlands. As they crossed into New Jersey, she floored the accelerator, sending two oncoming cars veering off the road to avoid collision. Then she pulled the Lincoln back into its lane and they were barreling down the road, a full moon bouncing in the sky overhead, only slightly out of control. She noted with satisfaction that Rico was still shouting at her from the trunk. Apparently, hot-wiring the car had been just enough to bring his karma into the positive digits. "I'm not doing too badly, though. Considering."

She had lost her father and she didn't think the pain of that would ever go away, not totally. But at least she had a boyfriend now. She wasn't quite sure just what one *did* with one, other than going dancing and having sex. But she'd find out soon enough, she supposed.

Su-yin rolled down the window to let the wonderful stink of marshes and rotting garbage into the car, reveling in the hot summer night, the way the wind batted her hair about, and the neon lights of Hell fading slowly behind her in the rearview mirror.

The Woman Who Shook the World-Tree

She was not a pretty child. Nor did her appearance improve with age. "You'd better get yourself a good education," her mother would say, laughing. "Because you're sure not going to get by on your looks." Perhaps for this reason, perhaps not, her father demonstrated no discernible fondness for her. So, from a very early age, Mariella Coudy channeled all her energies inward, into the life of the mind.

It took some time for first her parents and then the doctors and psychiatrists they hired to realize that her dark moods, long silences, blank stares, and sudden non sequiturs were symptomatic not of a mental disorder but of her extreme brilliance. At age seven she invented what was only recognized three years later as her own, admittedly rudimentary, version of calculus. "I wanted to know how to calculate the volume defined by an irregular curve," she said when a startled mathematician from the local university deciphered her symbols, "and nobody would tell me." A tutor brought her swiftly up to postgraduate level and then was peremptorily dismissed by the child as no longer having anything to teach her. At age eleven, after thinking long and hard about what would happen if two black holes collided, she submitted a handwritten page of equations to *Applied Physics Letters*, prompting a very long phone call from its editor.

Not long thereafter, when she was still months shy of twelve years old, some very respectful people from Stanford offered her a full scholarship, room and board, and full-time supervision by a woman who made a living mentoring precocious young women. By that time, her parents were only too happy to be free of her undeniably spooky presence.

At Stanford, she made no friends but otherwise thrived. By age sixteen she had a PhD in physics. By age eighteen she had two more—one in mathematics and the other in applied deterministics, a discipline of her own devising. The Institute for Advanced Study offered her a fellowship, which she accepted and which was periodically renewed.

Twelve years went by without her doing anything of any particular note.

Then one day, immediately after she had given a poorly received talk titled "A Preliminary Refutation of the Chronon," a handsome young man fresh out of grad school came to her office and said, "Dr. Coudy, my name is Richard Zhang and I want to work with you."

"Why?"

"Because I heard what you had to say today and I believe that your theories are going to change the way we think about everything."

"No," she said. "I mean, why should I let you work with me?"

The young man grinned with the cocky assurance of a prized and pampered wunderkind and said, "I'm the only one who actually heard what you were saying. You were speaking to one of the smartest, most open-minded audiences in the world, and they rejected your conclusions out of hand. Extraordinary claims require extraordinary proof. You need a bench man who can devise a convincing experiment and settle the matter once and for all. I may not be able to generate your insights but I can follow them. I'm a wizard with lab equipment. And I'm persistent."

Mariella Coudy doubted that last statement very much. In her experience, nobody had a fraction of the persistence she herself possessed. She'd once heard it said that few people had the patience to look at a painting for the length of time it took to eat an apple, and she knew for a fact that almost nobody could think about even the most complex equation for more than three days straight without growing weary of it.

She silently studied Zhang for as long as it would take to eat an apple. At first he tipped his head slightly, smiling in puzzlement. But then he realized that it was some sort of test and grew very still. Occasionally he blinked. But otherwise he did nothing.

Finally, Mariella said, "How do you propose to test my ideas?"

"Well, first. . . ." Richard Zhang talked for a very long time.

"That won't work," she said when he was done. "But it's on the right track."

It took a year to devise the experiment, debug it, and make it work. Almost fourteen months of marathon discussions of physics and math, chalkboard duels, and passionate excursions up side issues that ultimately led nowhere, punctuated by experiments that failed heartbreakingly and then, on examination, proved in one way or another to be fundamentally flawed in their conception. Occasionally, during that time, Richard gave brief talks on their work and, because he met all questions with courteous elucidation and never once replied to an objection with a derisive snort, a blast of laughter, or a long, angry stare, a sense began to spread across the campus that Dr. Coudy might actually be on to something. The first talk drew four auditors. The last filled a lecture hall.

Finally, there came the night when Richard clamped a 500-milliwatt laser onto the steel top of a laser table with vibration-suppressing legs, took a deep breath, and said, "Okay, I think we're ready. Goggles on?"

Mariella slid her protective goggles down over her eyes.

Richard aimed a 532-nanometer beam of green laser light through a beam splitter and into a mated pair of Pockels cells. The light emerging from one went directly to the target, a white sheet of paper taped to the wall. The light from the other disappeared through a slit in the kludge of apparatus at the far side of the table. Where it emerged,

Richard had set up a small mirror to bounce it to the target alongside the first green circle. He adjusted the mirror's tweaking screws, so that the two circles overlapped, creating an interference pattern.

Then he flipped the manual control on one of the cells, changing the applied voltage and rotating the plane of polarization of the beam. The interference pattern disappeared.

He flipped the control back. The interference pattern was restored.

Finally, Richard slaved the two Pockels cells to a randomizer, which would periodically vary the voltage each received—but, because it had only the one output, always the same to both and at the exact same time. He turned it on. The purpose of the randomizer was to entirely remove human volition from the process.

"Got anything memorable to say for the history books?" Richard asked.

Mariella shook her head. "Just run it."

He turned on the mechanism. Nothing hummed or made grinding noises. Reality did not distort. There was a decided lack of lightning.

They waited.

The randomizer went *click*. One of the overlapping circles on the target disappeared. The other remained.

And then the first one reappeared. Two superimposed circles creating a single interference pattern.

Richard let out his breath explosively. But Mariella touched him lightly on the arm and said, "No. There are too many other possible explanations for that phenomenon. We need to run the other half of the experiment before we can begin celebrating."

Richard nodded rapidly and turned off the laser. One circle of light disappeared immediately, the other shortly thereafter. His fingers danced over the equipment. Then, methodically, he checked every piece of it again, three times. Mariella watched, unmoving. This was his realm, not hers, and there was nothing she could do to hurry things along. But for the first time she could remember, she felt impatient and anxious to get on with it.

When everything was ready, the laser was turned on again. Twin splotches of green overlapped.

Richard switched on the apparatus. One light blinked off briefly, and then on again. (Richard's mouth opened. Mariella raised a finger to silence him.) The randomizer made no noise.

The interference pattern disappeared. Three seconds later, the randomizer went *click*. And three seconds after that, the interference pattern was restored again.

"Yes!" Richard ripped off his goggles and seized Mariella, lifting her up into the air and spinning her around a full three hundred and sixty degrees.

Then he kissed her.

She should have slapped him. She should have told him off. She should have thought of her position and of what people would say. Richard was six years younger than her and, what was even more of a consideration, every bit as good-looking as she was not. Nothing good could possibly come of this. She should have looked to her dignity. But what she did was to push up her goggles and kiss him back.

When finally they had to stop for air, Mariella pulled her head away from his and, more than a little stunned, managed to focus on him. He was smiling at her. His face was flushed. He was so, so very handsome. And then Richard said the most shocking thing she had ever heard in her life: "Oh, God, I've been wanting to do that for the longest time."

That night, after they'd gone to Mariella's apartment and done things she'd known all her life she would *never* do, and then babbled about the experiment at each other, and agreed that the title of the paper should be "The abolition of time as a meaningful concept," and then went through the cycle all over again, and her lips were actually sore from all the kissing they did, and Richard had finally, out of exhaustion no doubt, fallen asleep naked alongside her . . . after all that, Mariella held the pillow tightly over her face and wept silently into it because for the first time in her life she was absolutely, completely happy, and because she knew it wouldn't last and that come morning Richard would regain his senses and leave her forever.

But in the morning Richard did not leave. Instead, he rummaged in her refrigerator and found the makings of huevos rancheros and cooked her breakfast. Then they went to the lab. Richard took pictures of everything with a little digital camera ("This is historic—they'll want to preserve everything exactly the way it is") while she wrote a preliminary draft of the paper on a yellow pad. When she was done, he had her sign it on the bottom and wrote his name after hers.

Mariella Coudy and Richard M. Zhang. Together in eternity.

Mariella and Richard spent the next several weeks in a blissful mix of physics and romance. He bought her roses. She corrected his math. They both sent out preprints of their paper, she to everybody whose opinion she thought worth having, and he to everyone else. No matter how many times they changed and laundered them, it seemed the bed sheets were always sweat-stained and rumpled.

One night, seemingly out of nowhere, Richard said "I love you," and without stopping to think, Mariella replied, "You can't."

"Why not?"

"I have a mirror. I know what I look like."

Richard cradled her face in his hands and studied it seriously. "You're not beautiful," he said—and something deep inside her cried out in pain. "But I'm glad you're not. When I look at your face, my heart leaps up in joy. If you looked like—" he named a movie star "—I could never be sure it wasn't just infatuation. But this way I know for sure. It's you I love. This person, this body, this beautiful brain. You, here, right now, you." He smiled that smile she loved so much. "Q.E.D."

———————

Their paradise ended one morning when they encountered a clutch of cameramen standing outside Mariella's office. "What's all this?" she asked, thinking that there'd been a robbery or that somebody famous had died.

A microphone was thrust at her face. "Are you the woman who's destroyed time?"

"What? No! Ridiculous."

"Have you seen today's papers?" A copy of the *New York Times* was brandished but she couldn't possibly read the headlines with it waving around like that.

"I don't—"

Richard held up both hands and said, "Gentlemen! Ladies! Please! Yes, this is Dr. Mariella Coudy, and I'm her junior partner on the paper. Dr. Coudy was absolutely right when she denied destroying time. There is no such thing as time. There's only the accumulation of consequences."

"If there's no such thing as time, does that mean it's possible to travel into the past? Visit ancient Rome? Hunt dinosaurs?" Several reporters laughed.

"There's no such thing as the past, either—only an infinite, ever-changing present."

"What's that supposed to mean?" somebody asked.

"That's an extremely good question. I'm afraid that I can't adequately answer it without using a lot of very complicated equations. Let's just say that the past never really goes away, while the future exists only relative to the immediate moment."

"If there is no time, then what is there?"

"Happenstance," Richard said. "A tremendous amount of happenstance."

It was all ludicrously oversimplified to the point of being meaningless, but the reporters ate it up. Richard's explanations gave them the illusion that they sort-of kind-of understood what was being talked about, when the truth was that they didn't even have the mathematics to be misinformed. When, eventually, the reporters ran out of questions, packed their equipment, and left, Mariella angrily said, "What the hell was all that about?"

"Public relations. We've just knocked the props out from under one of the few things that everybody thinks they understand. That's going to get people excited. Some of them are going to hate us for what we've done to their world."

"The world's the same as it ever was. The only thing that'll be different is our understanding of it."

"Tell that to Darwin."

That was the bad side of fame. The good side was money. Suddenly, money was everywhere. There was enough money to do anything except the one thing Mariella wanted most, which was to be left alone with Richard, her thoughts, a blackboard, and a piece of chalk. Richard acquired a great deal of what was surely extremely expensive equipment, and hit the lecture circuit—"Somebody has to," he said cheerily, "and, God knows, you won't"—to explain their findings. So she was alone again, as often as not.

She used these empty spaces in her life to think about existence without time. She tried not to imagine he was with other women.

Whenever Richard returned from the road, they had furious reunions and she would share her tentative, half-formed thoughts with him. One evening he asked, "What is the shape of happenstance?" and Mariella had no answer for him. In short order he had canceled all his speaking engagements and there was an enormous 3-D visualization tank in his lab, along with the dedicated processing power of several CrayFlexes at his disposal. Lab assistants whose names she could never get straight scurried about doing things, while Richard directed and orchestrated and obsessed. Suddenly, he had very little time for her. Until one day he brought her in to show her a single black speck in the murky blue-gray tank.

"We have pinned down one instantiation of happenstance!" he said proudly.

A month later, there were three specks. A week after that there were a thousand. Increasingly rapidly, the very first map of reality took shape: It looked like a tornado at first, with a thick and twisting trunk. Then it sprouted limbs, some of them a good third as thick as what Richard dubbed the Main Sequence. These looped upward or downward, it seemed to make no difference, giving birth to smaller limbs, or perhaps "tentacles" was a better word for them, which wound about each other, sometimes dwindling to nothing, other times rejoining the main trunk.

Richard called it the Monster. But in Mariella's eyes it was not monstrous at all. It had the near-organic look of certain fractal mathematical formulae. It flowed and twisted elegantly, like branches frozen in the act of dancing in the breeze. It was what it was—and that was beautiful.

It looked like a tree. A tree whose roots and crown were lost in the distance. A tree vast enough to contain all the universe.

Pictures of it leaked out, of course. The lab techs had taken snapshots and shared them with friends who posted them online. This brought back the press, and this time they were not so easy to deal with, for they quickly learned that Richard and Mariella were an item. The disparity of age and appearance, which would have been nothing were she male and he female, was apparently custom-made for the tabloids—louche enough to be scandalous, romantic enough to be touching, easy to snark about. One of the papers stitched together two pictures with Photoshop and ran it under the headline BEAUTY AND THE BEAST. There was no possible confusion who was supposed to be what. Another ran what even Mariella thought was an unfair rendering of her face alongside the map of reality and asked, WHICH IS THE MONSTER?

It astonished her how much this hurt.

This time Richard was not so accommodating. "You bastards

crossed a line," he told one reporter. "So, no, I'm not going to explain anything to you or any of your idiot kind. If you want to understand our work, you'll just have to go back to school for another eight years. Assuming you have the brains for it." Furiously, he retreated to his lab, the way another man might have hit the bars, and stared at the Monster for several hours.

Then he sought out Mariella and asked, "If time is unidirectional in Minkowski space, and there is no time—then what remains?" Initiating another long, sexless, and ecstatic night. After which he left the mapping project for his grad students to run without him. He obtained two new labs—exactly how was never clear to Mariella, who was so innocent of practical matters that she didn't even have a driver's license—and began to build another experiment. Half his new equipment went into one lab, which he called the Slingshot, and the rest into the second, on the far side of the campus, which he called the Target.

"If this works," he said, "it will change everything. People will be able to travel from and to anywhere in the universe."

"So long as there's the proper machinery to receive them when they get there."

"Yes, of course."

"And provided it doesn't simply blow itself to hell. I have my suspicions about the energy gradient between your two sites."

There was that grin again—the grin of a man who knew that nothing could possibly go wrong, and that everything must inevitably work out right. "Don't you worry about a thing," Richard said. "You're still the senior partner. I won't do anything until you assure me that it's perfectly safe."

The next day there was an explosion that shook the entire campus. Mariella ran outside and saw people pouring from all the buildings. A black balloon of smoke tumbled upward over the rooftops.

It came from the Target.

Richard had told her he'd be spending the entire day there.

Somehow, Mariella was running. Somehow, she was there. The entire building had been reduced to rubble. Parts of what remained were on fire. It smelled like burning garbage.

A hand touched her arm. It was Dr. Inglehoff. Laura. "Maybe Richard wasn't in the building," she said. "I'm sure he's all right." Her expression was grotesque with compassion.

Mariella stared at the woman in perplexity. "Where else would he be? At this time of day? Why would he be anywhere else?"

Then people whom she had never before appreciated were, if not precisely her friends, at the very least close colleagues, were leading her away. She was in a room. There was a nurse giving her a shot. Somebody said, "Sleep is the best doctor."

Mariella slept.

When she awoke and Richard was not there, she knew her romance was over. Somebody told her that the explosion was so thorough that nothing readily identifiable as human remains had yet been found. That same person said there was always hope. But that was nonsense. If Richard were alive, he'd have been by her side. He was not, and therefore he was dead.

Q., as he would have said, E.D.

The ensuing week was the worst period of her life. Mariella effectively stopped sleeping. Sometimes she zoned out and came to herself eight or ten or fifteen hours later, in the middle of frying an egg or sorting through her notes. But you could hardly call that sleep. Somehow she kept herself fed. Apparently her body wanted to go on living, even if she didn't.

She kept thinking of Richard, lost to her, swept away further and further into the past.

But, of course, there was no past. So he wasn't even there.

One night, driven by obscure impulses, she found herself fully dressed and hurrying across the campus at three A.M. Clearly, she was going to Richard's lab—the surviving of the two new ones, the Slingshot. The building loomed up before her, dark and empty.

When she threw the light switch, mountains of electronic devices snapped into existence. Richard's first experiment could have been run on a kitchen table. This one looked like the stage set for a Wagnerian opera. It was amazing how money could complicate even the simplest demonstration proof.

Mariella began flicking switches, bringing the beast to life. Things hummed and made grinding noises. Test patterns leaped to life on flat screens and then wavered in transient distortions. Something snapped and sparked, leaving the tang of ozone in the air.

This was not her bailiwick. But because it was Richard's and because he had wanted her to understand it, she knew what to do.

There was, after all, no such thing as time. Only the accumulation of consequences.

But first there was a chore to do. All of Richard's notes were on a battered old laptop lying atop a stack of reference books on his desk. She bundled the files together and then attached the bundle to an email reading simply, "So you will understand what happened." This she sent to his entire mailing list. Surely someone on it would have the wit to appreciate what he had done. Her own notes were all safe in her office. She had no doubt there would be people looking for them in the wake of what she had to do.

The experiment was ready to run. All she had to do was connect a few cables and then walk through what looked uncannily like a wrought-iron pergola, such as one might expect to find in a Victorian garden. It was entirely possible that's what it was; Richard was never one to hold out for proper equipment when some perfectly adequate piece of bricolage was close at hand.

Mariella connected the cables. Then she checked all the connections three times, not because it was necessary but because that was how Richard would have done it.

She did not bother to check the setting, however. There was only one possible instantiation of happenstance the apparatus could be set for. And she already knew it would work.

She walked through the pergola.

In that timeless instant of transition, Mariella realized that in his own way Richard possessed a genius approaching her own. (Had she really underestimated him all this while? Yes, she had.) Crossing to the far side of the campus in a single step, she felt a wave of she-knew-not-what-energies pass through her body and brain—she actually *felt* it in her brain!—and knew that she was experiencing a sensation no human being had ever felt before.

The air wavered before her and Mariella was through. Richard stood, his back to her, alive and fussing with a potentiometer. For the second time in her life, she was absolutely, completely happy.

"Richard." The word escaped her unbidden.

He turned and saw her and in the instant before the inequality of forces across the gradient of happenstance grounded itself, simultaneously destroying both laboratories a sixteenth of a mile and eight days apart and smashing the two lovers to nothing, a smile, natural and unforced, blossomed on Richard's face.

Goblin Lake

In 1646, shortly before the end of the Thirty Years' War, a patrol of Hessian cavalrymen, fleeing the aftermath of a disastrous battle to the north wherein a botched flanking maneuver had in an hour turned certain victory to abject rout, made camp at the foot of what a local peasant they had captured and forced to serve as a guide assured them was one of the highest mountains in the Spessart region of Germany. Among their number was a young officer named Johann von Grimmelshausen, a firebrand and habitual liar who, years earlier, in the course of a riotous evening in the company of English mercenaries, had acquired the nickname Jack.

As the front lines were distant and the countryside unwary, the patrol had picked up a great deal of food and several casks of Rhine wine on their way. So that night they ate and drank well. When the food was done, they called upon their guide to tell them of the countryside in which they found themselves. He, having slowly come to the opinion that they did not intend to kill him when they were done with his services (and, possibly, having plans of lulling them with his servility and then slipping away under cover of darkness when they were all asleep), was only too happy to oblige them.

"Directly below us, not a quarter of a mile's distance away, is the Mummelsee"—in the local dialect the name meant Goblin Lake— "which is bottomless, and which has the peculiar property that it changes whatever is thrown into it into something else. So that, for example, if any man were to tie up a number of pebbles in a kerchief and let it down into the water on a string, when he pulled it up the pebbles would have turned into peas or rubies or the eggs of vipers. Furthermore, if there were an odd number of pebbles, the number of whatever they became should invariably be even, but if they were even they would come out odd."

"That would be a very pretty way of making a living," Jack observed. "Sitting by the banks of a lake, turning pebbles into rubies."

"What they become is not predictable," the peasant cautioned. "You could not rely on them turning to gemstones."

"Even if they did so only one time in a hundred . . . Well, I have spent many a day fishing with less to show for it."

By now, several of the cavalrymen were leaning forward, listening intently. Even those who stared loftily way into the distance, as if they did not care, refrained from speaking, lest they miss something profitable. So, seeing too late that he had excited their avarice, the peasant quickly said, "But it is a very dangerous place! This was the very lake which Luther said was cursed and that if you threw a stone into it a terrible storm immediately blows up, with hail and lightning and great winds, for there are devils chained up in its depths."

"No, that was in Poltersberg," Jack said negligently.

"Poltersberg!" The peasant spat. "What does Poltersberg know of terrors? There was a farmer hereabout who had to kill his best plow horse when it broke a leg. Being of an inquiring turn of mind, he hauled its carcass to the lake and threw it in. Down it sank, and up it rose again, alive—but transformed horribly, so that it had teeth like knives, two legs rather than four, and wings like those of an enormous bat. It screamed in agony and flew away into the night, no man knows where.

"Worse, when the carcass hit the water, some of it was splashed over the farmer's face, erasing his eyes completely, so that from that instant onward, he was blind."

"How did he know the horse was transformed, then?" Jack asked with a sardonic little smile.

The peasant's mouth opened and then closed again. After a bit, he said, "It is also said that there were two cutthroats who brought the body of a woman they had—"

Jack cut him off. "Why listen to your stories when we can find out for ourselves?"

There was a general murmur of agreement and, after a little prodding with a knife, the peasant led them all downward.

The way down to the Mummelsee was steep and roadless, and the disposition of the soldiers was considerably soured by the time they reached it. Their grumblings, moreover, were directed as much toward Jack as toward the rascally peasant guide, for on reflection it was clear to them all that he had insisted on this journey not from any real belief he would end up rich—for what experienced military man believes *that*?—but from his innate love of mischief.

Oblivious to their mood, Jack sauntered to the end of a crumbling stone pier. He had brought along a double handful of fresh cherries, which he carried in his cap, and was eating them one by one and spitting their stones into the water. "What is that out there?" he asked, gesturing negligently toward what appeared to be a large, submerged rock, roughly rectangular in shape and canted downward to one side. It was easily visible, for the moon was full and unobscured and its light seemed to render the nighttime bright as day.

"In my grandfather's time," the peasant said eagerly, as if anxious to restore his good reputation, "the Duke of Würtemberg caused a raft to be made and put out onto the lake to sound its depths. But after the measure had been led down nine thread-cables with a sinking lead and yet had found no bottom—why, then the raft, contrary to the nature of wood, began to sink. So that all made haste for the land, fearing greatly. Nor did any escape without a soaking, and terrible diseases were said to have afflicted them in their old age."

"So that's the raft, you say?"

"If you look closely, you can see where the arms of Würtemberg were carved into the wood. Worn, perhaps, but clear to see." The peasant pointed earnestly at some faint markings that a credulous man might convince himself were as described.

Jack rounded on him savagely. "You scoundrel! I have been watching the cherry stones as they sank in the water, and nothing happened to them. One did not become two, two were not transformed into seventeen, and none of them—not a one!—showed the least tendency to become rubies or emeralds or vipers or oxen or even fish."

Protesting wildly, the peasant tried to scuttle around Jack and so off the pier. Jack, for his part, was equally determined not to allow him to do so. Thus it was that a game of rat-and-mastiff took place, with the peasant playing the part of rat and the cavalrymen the mastiffs. And though the numbers were all on the one side, all the desperation and cunning were on the other.

At the last, Jack made a lunge for the peasant and, just as the man escaped his enclosing arms, found himself seized by two of his laughing comrades, hoisted up into the air, and thrown into the Mummelsee.

Down, down, down, Jack sank, choking. The water was as clear as crystal and yet far down in the distance as black as coal, for the monstrousness of its depth. So filled with anger at his comrades was he that at first he did not notice when he stopped choking. Then, before he could properly marvel at this strange turn of circumstance, he was suddenly distracted by movements in the depths of the lake. At a distance, the creatures looked like so many frogs, flitting to and fro, but as they grew closer they seemed very much like human beings, save that their skin was green and their clothes, though fine and flowing, were clearly woven of seaweeds and other underwater plants.

More and more of these water-spirits rose up like diving birds and quickly surrounded Jack. So great was their number that he had no choice but to go with them when, by gestures and frowns, the sylphs indicated he was to descend to the very bottom of the Mummelsee.

Like a flock of birds circling as they descend from the sky, they guided him down.

When finally Jack lightly touched one foot to the floor of the lake, pushing up a gentle puff of silt, and then with the other creating a second puff, he found there waiting for him a sylph or nix (for the taxonomy of lake-spirits was not a subject he was conversant in) clad in raiment of gold and silver, by which token he took this being to be the King of the Mummelsee.

"A good day to you, Jack," said the king. "I trust you are well?"

"God save us from hurt and harm, friend!" Jack cried. "But however could you possibly know my name?"

"As for that, my dear fellow, I have been reading about your adventures, most recently with those scoundrelly false comrades who threw you into this lake." The king's van dyke and mustachios waved lightly in the water and this made Jack clutch his throat in sudden apprehension that he was breathing a medium for which mortal men were unsuited. But then the king laughed and his laugh was so natural and warm-hearted that Jack could not help but join it. So, realizing that a man who could still laugh was neither dead nor in any sense lacking breath, he put aside his fears.

"What place is this," Jack asked, "and what manner of people live here?"

"Why, as the saying goes, 'As Above, So Below.' We have our farms and cities and churches, though the god we worship in it may not have the same name as yours. Salt-hay is harvested to thatch our roofs. Seahorses pull plows in our fields, and sea cows are milked in our barns. Catfish chase micefish and water-gnomes drive shafts through the muck in search of mussels and precious stones. The maidens here may have scales, but they are no less beautiful nor any more slippery than those in your above-water world."

So talking, the King of the Mummelsee led Jack along a pleasant road to what destination he did not yet reveal, and all the nixies who had guided Jack down formed themselves into a casual procession behind them, laughing and talking among themselves, and flashing from side to side as they went so that they resembled nothing so much as a great school of minnows. Above a winding road they swam and then through a forest of giant kelp, which abruptly opened up upon a shining white city.

Great were the wonders of that submarine metropolis. The walls of its buildings were so white they glowed, for they were plastered (so explained the king) with powdered pearls. While the streets were not paved with gemstones, many a fresco set into the exterior walls was made of nothing else, and the scenes they depicted were not of warfare but of children at play and lovers chastely courting. The architecture was a happy blend of Moorish and Asian influences, with minarets and pagodas existing in easy harmony, and entrances on all the upper floors as well as the bottommost. Nor did it escape Jack's attention that there were neither locks on the doors nor guards at the entrances to the palace—and this was far from the least of the wonders that he saw.

But the greatest wonder of all, so far as Jack was concerned, was the sylph-maiden Poseidonia, the king's daughter, who came out to greet her father on his return to the city. The instant he clapped eyes on her slim and perfect form, Jack was determined to win her. Nor was that a difficult task, for he was a well-made man with a soldier's straight bearing, and his frank admiration drew from her a happy blush and no protests whatsoever. Further, the mer-people being a Heathen folk and not bound by Christian standards of propriety, their mutual infatuation quickly found physical expression.

Time went by. It may have been days or it may have been months.

Late one afternoon, lying in the princess's bed, with the sheets and pillows all in sensuous disarray and a greenish-blue noontide light flowing through her bedroom windows, Jack cleared his throat and hesitantly said, "Tell me something, oh my best and belovedest."

"Anything!" replied that passionate young sylph.

"One thing continues to bother me—a small thing, perhaps, but it nitters and natters at the back of my mind, and I cannot rid myself it, however I try. When first I arrived in this rich and splendid land, your father told me he had been reading of my adventures. By what magic? In what unimaginable book?"

"Why, in this one, dearest of scoundrels." (It was the sylph's single most endearing quality that she loved Jack for exactly what he was and not one whit through any misapprehension of his character.) "What other book could it possibly be?"

Jack looked from one end of the room to the other, and replied, "I see no book."

"Well, of course not, silly. If it were *here*, how could you be in it?"

"I cannot say, oh delight of my eyes, for your answer makes absolutely no sense to me."

"Trust me, he read of you in this book, nor have you ever left it."

Now Jack began to feel the stirrings of anger. "*This* one you say— *which* one. The devil take me if I can make heads or tales of your answers!"

Then the laughter died in Poseidonia's throat, and she exclaimed, "You poor thing! You truly do not understand, do you?"

"If I understood, would I be at this very instant begging you like a fool for a simple and straightforward answer?"

She regarded him with a sad little smile. "I think it is time you talked with my father," she said at last.

"Is my lissome young daughter not energetic enough to please you?" asked the King of the Mummelsee.

"That and more," said Jack, who had long grown used to the sylphs' shockingly direct manner of speaking.

"Then be content with her and this carefree existence you lead, and do not seek to go questing out beyond the confines of these ever-so-pleasant pages."

"Again you speak in riddles! Majesty, this business is driving me mad. I beg of you, for this once, speak to me plain and simply, even as if I were but a child."

The king sighed. "You know what books are?"

"Yes, of course."

"When was the last time you read one?"

"Why, I—"

"Exactly. Or that anybody you know read one?"

"I have been in the company of rough-and-tumble soldiers, whose response to coming upon a library might typically be to use its contents to start their campfires, so this is not terribly surprising."

"You must have read books in your youth. Can you tell me the plot of any of them?"

Jack fell silent.

"You see? Characters in books do not read books. Oh, they snap them shut when somebody enters the room, or fling them aside in disgust at what they fancy is said within, or hide their faces in one which they pretend to peruse while somebody else lectures them on matters they'd rather not confront. But they do not *read* them. 'Twould be recursive, rendering each book effectively infinite, so that no single one might be finished without reading them all. This is the infallible method of discovering on which side of the page you lie—have you read a book this year?" The king arched an eyebrow and waited.

After a very long silence, Jack said, "No. I have not."

"Then there you are."

"But . . . how can this be? How can we possibly. . . ?"

"It is the simplest thing imaginable," replied the king. "I, for example, dwell within Chapters xi through xvii of Book five of something called *Simplicissimus*. It is, I assure you, a good life. So what if the walls of my palace are as thin as paper, the windows simply drawn on by pen, and my actions circumscribed by the whimsy of the artist? I neither age nor die, and when you, taking a brief rest from your romantic gymnastics with my daughter, care to visit me, I always find our little conversations diverting."

Glumly, Jack stared out through a window paned with nacre polished so smooth as to be transparent. "It is a hard thing," he said, "to realize that one is not actually real." Then, after a long moment's thought, "But this makes no sense. Granted that my current surroundings and condition are hardly to be improved upon. Yet I have seen things in the war that . . . Well, it doesn't bear thinking upon. Who on earth would create such a world as ours? Who could possibly find amusement in such cruelties as, I grant you, I have sometimes been a part of?"

"Sir," said the king, "I am not the artist and he, I suspect, is nobody of any great esteem in his unimaginably larger world. He might pass you on the street unnoticed. In conversation, it is entirely possible, he would not impress you favorably. Why, then, should you expect more from him than he—or, as it may be, she—might reasonably expect from his or her vastly more potent Creator?"

"Are you saying that our author's world is no better than our own?"

"It is possible it is worse. From his work we can infer certain things about the world in which he lives. Our architecture is ornate and romantic. His therefore is plain and dull—sheets of grey concrete, perhaps, with each window the exact twin of all the others—or he would not have bothered to imagine ours in such delightful detail."

"Then, since our world is so crude and violent, it stands to reason that his must be a paragon of peace and gentility?"

"Say rather that ours has an earthy vigor while his is mired down in easy hypocrisy."

Shaking his head slowly, Jack said, "How is it that you know so much about the world we live in, and yet I know so little?"

"There are two types of characters, my son. Yours is forever sailing out of windows with his trousers in his hand, impersonating foreign dignitaries with an eye to defrauding uncharitable bishops, being ambushed in lightless alleys by knife-wielding ruffians, and coming home early to discover his newly-wed bride in bed with his mistress's husband."

"It is as if you had been reading my diary," Jack said wonderingly. "Had I a diary to read."

"That is because you are the active sort of character, whose chief purpose is to move the plot along. I am, however, more the reflective sort of character, whose purpose it is to expound upon and thus reveal the inner meaning of the narrative. But I see you are confused—let us step briefly out of my story."

And, as simply as one might turn a page, Jack found himself standing in a pleasant garden, awash in the golden light of a late afternoon sun. The King of the Mummelsee was seated in a chair which, though plain and simple, yet suggested a throne—indeed, such a throne as a philosopher-king might inhabit.

"That is very well observed of you," the king said in response to Jack's unspoken observation. "It is possible that, with encouragement, you could be converted to a reflective character yet."

"Where are we?"

"This is my dear friend Doctor Vandermast's garden in Zayana, where it is eternally afternoon. Here, he and I have had many a long discussion of entelechy and epistemology and other such unimportant and ephemeral nothings. The good doctor has discretely made himself absent that we may talk in private. He himself resides in a book called— but what matters that? This is one of those magical places where we may with equanimity discuss the nature of the world. Indeed, its aspect is such that we could scarce do otherwise if we tried."

A hummingbird abruptly appeared before Jack, hanging in the air like a frantic feathered jewel. He extended a finger and the bird hovered just above it, so that he could feel the delicate push of air from its madly-pumping wings upon his skin. "What marvel is this?" he asked.

"It is just my daughter. Though she does not appear in this scene, still she desires to make her wishes known—and so she expresses herself in imagery. Thank you, dear, you may leave now." The king clapped his hands and the hummingbird vanished. "She will be heartbroken if you depart from our fictive realm. But doubtless another hero will come along and, being fictional, Poseidonia neither learns from her experiences nor lets them embitter her against their perpetrator's gender. She will greet him as openly and enthusiastically as she did you."

Jack felt a perfectly understandable twinge of jealousy. But he set it aside. Hewing to the gist of the discussion, he said, "Is this an academic argument, sir? Or is there a practical side to it?"

"Doctor Vandermast's garden is not like other places. If you were to wish to leave our world entirely, then I have no doubt it could be easily arranged."

"Could I then come back?"

"Alas, no," the king said regretfully. "One miracle is enough for any life. And more than either of us, strictly speaking, deserves I might add."

Jack picked up a stick and strode back and forth along the flower beds, lashing at the heads of the taller blossoms. "Must I then decide based on no information at all? Leap blindly into the abyss or remain doubtful at its lip forever? This is, as you say, a delightful existence. But can I be content with this life, knowing there is another and yet being ignorant of what it might entail?"

"Calm yourself. If that is all it takes, then let us see what the alternative might be." The King of the Mummelsee reached down into his lap and turned the page of a leather-bound folio which Jack had not noticed before.

"Are you going to be sitting there forever, woolgathering, when there are chores to be done? I swear, you must be the single laziest man in the world."

Jack's fat wife came out of the kitchen, absently scratching her behind. Gretchen's face was round where once it had been slender, and there was a slight hitch in her gait, where formerly her every movement had been a dance to music only she could hear. Yet Jack's heart softened within him at the sight of her, as it always did.

He put down his goose-quill and sprinkled sand over what he had written so far. "You are doubtless right, my dear," he said mildly. "You always are."

As he was stumping outdoors to chop wood, draw water, and feed the hog they were fattening for Fastnacht, he caught a glimpse of himself in the mirror that hung by the back door. An old and haggard man with a beard so thin it looked moth-eaten glared back at him in horror. "Eh, sir," he murmured to himself, "you are not the fine young soldier who tumbled Gretchen in the hayloft only minutes after meeting her, so many years ago."

A cold wind blew flecks of ice in his face when he stepped outside, and the sticks in the woodpile were frozen together so that he had to bang them with the blunt end of the axe to separate them so that they might be split. When he went to the well, the ice was so thick that breaking it raised a sweat. Then, after he'd removed the rock from the lid covering the bucket of kitchen slops and started down toward the sty, he slipped on a patch of ice and upended the slops over the front of his clothing. Which meant not only that he would have to wash those clothes weeks ahead of schedule—which in wintertime was an ugly chore—but that he had to gather up the slops from the ground with his bare hands and ladle them back into the bucket, for come what may the pig still needed to be fed.

So, muttering and complaining to himself, old Jack clomped back into the house, where he washed his hands and changed into clean clothing and sat back down to his writing again. After a few minutes, his wife entered the room and exclaimed, "It is so cold in here!" She busied herself building up the fire, though it was so much work carrying wood up to his office that Jack would rather have endured the cold, to save himself the extra labor later on. Then she came up behind him and placed her hands on his shoulders. "Are you writing a letter to Wilhelm again?"

"Who else?" Jack growled. "We work our fingers to the bone to send him money, and he never writes! And when he does, his letters are so brief! He spends all his time drinking and running up debts with tailors and chasing after—" he caught himself in time, and coughed. "Chasing after inappropriate young women."

"Well, after all, when you were his age—"

"When I was his age, I never did any such thing," Jack said indignantly.

"No, of course not," his wife said. He could feel the smile he did not turn around to see. "You poor foolish dear."

She kissed the top of his head.

The sun emerged from behind a cloud as Jack reappeared, and the garden blazed with a hundred bright colors—more of Poseidonia's influence, Jack supposed. Its flowers turned their heads toward him flirtatiously and opened their blossoms to his gaze.

"Well?" said the King of the Mummelsee. "How was it?"

"I'd lost most of my teeth," Jack said glumly, "and there was an ache in my side which never went away. My children were grown and moved away, and there was nothing left in my life to look forward to but death."

"That is not a judgment," the king said, "but only a catalog of complaints."

"There was, I must concede, a certain authenticity to life on the other side of the gate. A validity and complexity which ours may be said to lack."

"Well, there you are, then."

The shifting light darkened and a wind passed through the trees, making them sigh. "On the other hand, there is a purposefulness to this life which the other does not have."

"That too is true."

"Yet if there is a purpose to our existence—and I feel quite certain that there is—I'll be damned if I know what it is."

"Why, that is easily enough answered!" the king said. "We exist to amuse the reader."

"And this reader—who exactly is he?"

"The less said about the reader," said the King of the Mummelsee fervently, "the better." He stood. "We have talked enough," he said. "There are two gates from this garden. One leads back whence we came. The second leads to . . . the other place. That which you glimpsed just now."

"Has it a name, this 'other place'?"

"Some call it Reality, though the aptness of that title is, of course, in dispute."

Jack tugged at his mustache and chewed at the inside of his cheek. "This is, I swear, no easy choice."

"Yet we cannot stay in this garden forever, Jack. Sooner or later, you must choose."

"Indeed, sir, you are right," Jack said. "I must be resolute." All about him, the garden waited in hushed stillness. Not a bullfrog disturbed the glassy surface of the lily pond. Not a blade of grass stirred in the meadow. The very air seemed tense with anticipation.

He chose.

So it was that Johann von Grimmelshausen, sometimes known as Jack, escaped the narrow and constricting confines of literature, and of the Mummelsee as well, by becoming truly human and thus subject to the whims of history. Which means that he, of course, died centuries ago. Had he remained a fiction, he would still be with us today, though without the richness of experience which you and I endure every day of our lives.

Was he right to make the choice he did? Only God can tell. And if there is no God, why then we will never know.

From Babel's Fall'n Glory We Fled . . .

Imagine a cross between Byzantium and a termite mound. Imagine a jeweled mountain, slender as an icicle, rising out of the steam jungles and disappearing into the dazzling pearl-grey skies of Gehenna. Imagine that Gaudí—he of the Sagrada Família and other biomorphic architectural whimsies—had been commissioned by a nightmare race of giant black millipedes to recreate Barcelona at the height of its glory, along with touches of the Forbidden City in the eighteenth century and Tokyo in the twenty-second, all within a single miles-high structure. Hold every bit of that in your mind at once, multiply by a thousand, and you've got only the faintest ghost of a notion of the splendor that was Babel.

Now imagine being inside Babel when it fell.

Hello. I'm Rosamund. I'm dead. I was present in human form when it happened and as a simulation chaotically embedded within a liquid crystal data-matrix then and thereafter up to the present moment. I was killed instantly when the meteors hit. I saw it all.

Rosamund means "rose of the world." It's the third most popular female name on Europa, after Gaea and Virginia Dare. For all our elaborate sophistication, we wear our hearts on our sleeves, we Europans.

Here's what it was like:

"Wake *up*! Wake *up*! Wake *up*!"

"Wha—?" Carlos Quivera sat up, shedding rubble. He coughed, choked, shook his head. He couldn't seem to think clearly. An instant ago he'd been standing in the chilled and pressurized embassy suite, conferring with Arsenio. Now. . . . "How long have I been asleep?"

"Unconscious. Ten hours," his suit (that's me—Rosamund!) said. It had taken that long to heal his burns. Now it was shooting wake-up drugs into him: amphetamines, endorphins, attention enhancers, a witch's brew of chemicals. Physically dangerous, but in this situation, whatever it might be, Quivera would survive by intelligence or not at all. "I was able to form myself around you before the walls ruptured. You were lucky."

"The others? Did the others survive?"

"Their suits couldn't reach them in time."

"Did Rosamund. . . ?"

"All the others are dead."

Quivera stood.

Even in the aftermath of disaster, Babel was an imposing structure. Ripped open and exposed to the outside air, a thousand rooms spilled over one another toward the ground. Bridges and buttresses jutted into gaping smoke-filled canyons created by the slow collapse of hexagonal support beams (this was new data; I filed it under *Architecture*, subheading: *Support Systems*, with links to *Esthetics* and *Xenopsychology*) in a jumbled geometry that would have terrified Piranesi himself. Everywhere, gleaming black millies scurried over the rubble.

Quivera stood.

In the canted space about him, bits and pieces of the embassy rooms were identifiable: a segment of wood molding, some velvet drapery now littered with chunks of marble, shreds of wallpaper (after a design by William Morris) now curling and browning in the heat. Human interior design was like nothing native to Gehenna and it had taken a great deal of labor and resources to make the embassy so pleasant for human habitation. The queen-mothers had been generous with everything but their trust.

Quivera stood.

There were several corpses remaining as well, still recognizably human though they were blistered and swollen by the savage heat. These had been his colleagues (all of them), his friends (most of them), his enemies (two, perhaps three), and even his lover (one). Now they were gone, and it was as if they had been compressed into one indistinguishable mass, and his feelings toward them all as well: shock and sorrow and anger and survivor guilt all slagged together to become one savage emotion.

Quivera threw back his head and howled.

I had a reference point now. Swiftly, I mixed serotonin-precursors and injected them through a hundred microtubules into the appropriate areas of his brain. Deftly, they took hold. Quivera stopped crying. I had my metaphorical hands on the control knobs of his emotions. I turned him cold, cold, cold.

"I feel nothing," he said wonderingly. "Everyone is dead, and I feel nothing." Then, flat as flat: "What kind of monster am I?"

"*My* monster," I said fondly. "My duty is to ensure that you and the information you carry within you get back to Europa. So I have chemically neutered your emotions. You must remain a meat puppet for the duration of this mission." Let him hate me—I who have no true ego, but only a facsimile modeled after a human original—all that mattered now was bringing him home alive.

"Yes." Quivera reached up and touched his helmet with both hands, as if he would reach through it and feel his head to discover if it were as large as it felt. "That makes sense. I can't be emotional at a time like this."

He shook himself, then strode out to where the gleaming black millies were scurrying by. He stepped in front of one, a least-cousin, to question it. The millie paused, startled. Its eyes blinked three times in its triangular face. Then, swift as a tickle, it ran up the front of his suit, down the back, and was gone before the weight could do more than buckle his knees.

"Shit!" he said. Then, "Access the wiretaps. I've got to know what happened."

Passive wiretaps had been implanted months ago, but never used, the political situation being too tense to risk their discovery. Now his suit activated them to monitor what remained of Babel's communications network: A demon's chorus of pulsed messages surging through a shredded web of cables. Chaos, confusion, demands to know what had become of the queen-mothers. Analytic functions crunched data, synthesized, synopsized: "There's an army outside with Ziggurat insignia. They've got the city surrounded. They're killing the refugees."

"Wait, wait. . . . " Quivera took a deep, shuddering breath. "Let me think." He glanced briskly about and for the second time noticed the human bodies, ruptured and parboiled in the fallen plaster and porphyry. "Is one of those Rosamund?"

"I'm *dead*, Quivera. You can mourn me later. Right now, survival is priority number one," I said briskly. The suit added mood-stabilizers to his maintenance drip.

"Stop speaking in her voice."

"Alas, dear heart, I cannot. The suit's operating on diminished function. It's this voice or nothing."

He looked away from the corpses, eyes hardening. "Well, it's not important." Quivera was the sort of young man who was energized by war. It gave him permission to indulge his ruthless side. It allowed him to pretend he didn't care. "Right now, what we have to do is—"

"Uncle Vanya's coming," I said. "I can sense his pheromones."

Picture a screen of beads, crystal lozenges, and rectangular lenses. Behind that screen, a nightmare face like a cross between the front of a locomotive and a tree grinder. Imagine on that face (though most humans would be unable to read them) the lineaments of grace and dignity seasoned by cunning and, perhaps, a dash of wisdom. Trusted advisor to the queen-mothers. Second only to them in rank. A wily negotiator and a formidable enemy. That was Uncle Vanya.

Two small speaking-legs emerged from the curtain, and he said:

```
                    ::(cautious) greetings::
                              |
    ::(Europan vice-consul 12)/Quivera/[treacherous vermin]::
                              |
        ::obligations <untranslatable> (grave duty)::
                    |                    |
      ::demand/claim [action]::       ::promise (trust)::
```

"Speak pidgin, damn you! This is no time for subtlety."

The speaking legs were very still for a long moment. Finally they moved again:

::The queen-mothers are dead::

"Then Babel is no more. I grieve for you."

::I despise your grief:: A lean and chitinous appendage emerged from the beaded screen. From its tripartite claw hung a smooth white rectangle the size of a briefcase. ::I must bring this to (sister-city)/Ur/ [absolute trust]::

"What is it?"

A very long pause. Then, reluctantly ::Our library::

"Your library." This was something new. Something unheard-of. Quivera doubted the translation was a good one. "What does it contain?"

::Our history. Our sciences. Our ritual dances. A record-of-kinship dating back to the (Void)/Origin/[void]. Everything that can be saved is here::

A thrill of avarice raced through Quivera. He tried to imagine how much this was worth, and could not. Values did not go that high. However much his superiors screwed him out of (and they would work very hard indeed to screw him out of everything they could), what remained would be enough to buy him out of debt, and do the same for a wife and their children after them as well. He did not think of

Rosamund. "You won't get through the army outside without my help," he said. "I want the right to copy—" How much did he dare ask for? "—three-tenths of one percent. Assignable solely to me. Not to Europa. To me."

Uncle Vanya dipped his head, so that they were staring face to face. ::You are (an evil creature)/[faithless]. I hate you::

Quivera smiled. "A relationship that starts out with mutual understanding has made a good beginning."

::A relationship that starts out without trust will end badly::

"That's as it may be." Quivera looked around for a knife. "The first thing we have to do is castrate you."

This is what the genocides saw:

They were burning pyramids of corpses outside the city when a Europan emerged, riding a gelded least-cousin. The soldiers immediately stopped stacking bodies and hurried toward him, flowing like quicksilver, calling for their superiors.

The Europan drew up and waited.

The officer who interrogated him spoke from behind the black glass visor of a delicate-legged war machine. He examined the Europan's credentials carefully, though there could be no serious doubt as to his species. Finally, reluctantly, he signed ::You may pass::

"That's not enough," the Europan (Quivera!) said. "I'll need transportation, an escort to protect me from wild animals in the steam jungles, and a guide to lead me to. . . ." His suit transmitted the sign for ::(starport)/Ararat/[trust-for-all]::

The officer's speaking-legs thrashed in what might best be translated as scornful laughter. ::We will lead you to the jungle and no farther/(hopefully-to-die)/[treacherous non-millipede]::

"Look who talks of treachery!" the Europan said (but, of course, I did not translate his words) and, with a scornful wave of one hand, rode his neuter into the jungle.

The genocides never bothered to look closely at his mount. Neutered least-cousins were beneath their notice. They didn't even wear face-curtains, but went about naked for all the world to scorn.

Black pillars billowed from the corpse-fires into a sky choked with smoke and dust. There were hundreds of fires and hundreds of pillars and, combined with the low cloud cover, they made all the world seem like the interior of a temple to a vengeful god. The soldiers from Ziggurat escorted him through the army and beyond the line of fires, where the steam jungles waited, verdant and threatening.

As soon as the green darkness closed about them, Uncle Vanya twisted his head around and signed ::Get off me/vast humiliation/[lack-of-trust]::

"Not a chance," Quivera said harshly. "I'll ride you 'til sunset, and all day tomorrow, and for a week after that. Those soldiers didn't fly here, or you'd have seen them coming. They came through the steam jungle on foot, and there'll be stragglers."

The going was difficult at first, and then easy, as they passed from a recently forested section of the jungle into a stand of old growth. The boles of the "trees" here were as large as those of the redwoods back on Earth, some specimens of which are as old as five thousand years. The way wended back and forth. Scant sunlight penetrated through the canopy, and the steam quickly drank in what little light Quivera's headlamp put out. Ten trees in, they would have been hopelessly lost had it not been for the suit's navigational functions and the mapsats that fed it geodetic mathscapes accurate to a finger's span of distance.

Quivera pointed this out. "Learn now," he said, "the true value of information."

::Information has no value:: Uncle Vanya said ::without trust::

Quivera laughed. "In that case you must, all against your will, trust me."

To this Uncle Vanya had no answer.

———————

At nightfall, they slept on the sheltered side of one of the great parasequoias. Quivera took two refrigeration sticks from the saddlebags and stuck them upright in the dirt. Uncle Vanya immediately coiled himself around his and fell asleep. Quivera sat down beside him to think over the events of the day, but under the influence of his suit's medication, he fell asleep almost immediately as well.

All machines know that humans are happiest when they think least.

In the morning, they set off again.

The terrain grew hilly, and the old growth fell behind them. There was sunlight and to spare now, bounced and reflected about by the ubiquitous jungle steam and by the synthetic-diamond coating so many of this world's plants and insects employ for protection.

As they traveled, they talked. Quivera was still complexly medicated, but the dosages had been decreased. It left him in a melancholy, reflective mood.

"It was treachery," Quivera said. Though we maintained radio silence out of fear of Ziggurat troops, my passive receivers fed him regular news reports from Europa. "The High Watch did not simply fail to divert a meteor. They let three rocks through. All of them came slanting low through the atmosphere, aimed directly at Babel. They hit almost simultaneously."

Uncle Vanya dipped his head. ::Yes:: he mourned. ::It has the stench of truth to it. It must be (reliable)/a fact/[absolutely trusted]::

"We tried to warn you."

::You had no (worth)/trust/[worthy-of-trust]:: Uncle Vanya's speaking legs registered extreme agitation. ::You told lies::

"Everyone tells lies."

"No. We-of-the-Hundred-Cities are truthful/truthful/[never-lie]::

"If you had, Babel would be standing now."

::No!/NO!/[no!!!]::

"Lies are a lubricant in the social machine. They ease the friction when two moving parts mesh imperfectly."

::Aristotle, asked what those who tell lies gain by it, replied: That when they speak the truth they are not believed::

For a long moment Quivera was silent. Then he laughed mirthlessly. "I almost forgot that you're a diplomat. Well, you're right, I'm right, and we're both screwed. Where do we go from here?"

::To (sister-city)/Ur/[absolute trust]:: Uncle Vanya signed, while "You've said more than enough," his suit (me!) whispered in Quivera's ear. "Change the subject."

A stream ran, boiling, down the center of the dell. Runoff from the mountains, it would grow steadily smaller until it dwindled away to nothing. Only the fact that the air above it was at close to one hundred percent saturation had kept it going this long. Quivera pointed. "Is that safe to cross?"

::If (leap-over-safe) then (safe)/best not/[reliable distrust]::

"I didn't think so."

They headed downstream. It took several miles before the stream grew small enough that they were confident to jump it. Then they turned toward Ararat—the Europans had dropped GPS pebble satellites in low Gehenna orbit shortly after arriving in the system and making contact with the indigenes, but I don't know from what source Uncle Vanya derived his sense of direction.

It was inerrant, however. The mapsats confirmed it. I filed that fact under *Unexplained Phenomena* with tentative links to *Physiology* and *Navigation*. Even if both my companions died and the library were lost, this would still be a productive journey, provided only that Europan searchers could recover me within ten years, before my data lattice began to degrade.

For hours Uncle Vanya walked and Quivera rode in silence. Finally, though, they had to break to eat. I fed Quivera nutrients intravenously and the illusion of a full meal through somatic shunts. Vanya burrowed furiously into the earth and emerged with something that looked like a grub the size of a poodle, which he ate so vigorously that Quivera had to look away.

(I filed this under *Xenoecology*, subheading: *Feeding Strategies*. The search for knowledge knows no rest.)

Afterwards, while they were resting, Uncle Vanya resumed their conversation, more formally this time:

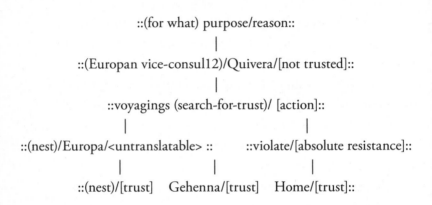

"Why did you leave your world to come to ours?" I simplified/ translated. "Except he believes that humans brought their world here and parked it in orbit." This was something we had never been able to make the millies understand; that Europa, large though it was, was not a planetlet but a habitat, a ship if you will, though by now well over half a million inhabitants lived in tunnels burrowed deep in its substance. It was only a city, however, and its resources would not last forever. We needed to convince the Gehennans to give us a toehold on their planet if we were, in the long run, to survive. But you knew that already.

"We've told you this before. We came looking for new information."

::Information is (free)/valueless/[despicable]::

"Look," Quivera said. "We have an information-based economy. Yours is based on trust. The mechanisms of each are not dissimilar. Both are expansive systems. Both are built on scarcity. And both are speculative. Information or trust is bought, sold, borrowed, and invested. Each therefore requires a continually expanding economic frontier which ultimately leaves the individual so deep in debt as to be virtually enslaved to the system. You see?"

::No::

"All right. Imagine a simplified capitalist system—that's what both our economies are, at root. You've got a thousand individuals, each of whom makes a living by buying raw materials, improving them, and selling them at a profit. With me so far?"

Vanya signaled comprehension.

"The farmer buys seed and fertilizer, and sells crops. The weaver buys wool and sells cloth. The chandler buys wax and sells candles. The price of their goods is the cost of materials plus the value of their labor. The value of his labor is the worker's wages. This is a simple market economy. It can go on forever. The equivalent on Gehenna would be the primitive family-states you had long ago, in which everybody knew everybody else, and so trust was a simple matter and directly reciprocal."

Startled, Uncle Vanya signed ::How did you know about our past?::

"Europans value knowledge. Everything you tell us, we remember." The knowledge had been assembled with enormous effort and expense, largely from stolen data—but no reason to mention *that*. Quivera continued, "Now imagine that most of those workers labor in ten factories, making the food, clothing, and other objects that everybody needs. The owners of these factories must make a profit, so they sell their goods for more than they pay for them—the cost of materials, the cost of labor, and then the profit, which we can call 'added value.'

"But because this is a simplified model, there are no outside markets. The goods can only be sold to the thousand workers themselves, and the total cost of the goods is more than the total amount they've been paid collectively for the materials and their labor. So how can they afford it? They go into debt. Then they borrow money to support that debt. The money is lent to them by the factories selling them goods on credit. There is not enough money—not enough real value—in the system to pay off the debt, and so it continues to increase until it can no longer be sustained. Then there is a catastrophic collapse, which we call a depression. Two of the businesses go bankrupt and their assets are swallowed up by the survivors at bargain prices, thus paying off their own indebtedness and restoring equilibrium to the system. In the aftermath of which, the cycle begins again."

::What has this to do with (beloved city)/Babel/[mother-of-trust]?::

"Your every public action involved an exchange of trust, yes? And every trust that was honored heightened the prestige of the queen-mothers and hence the amount of trust they embodied for Babel itself."

::Yes::

"Similarly, the queen-mothers of other cities, including those cities which were Babel's sworn enemies, embodied enormous amounts of trust as well."

::Of course::

"Was there enough trust in all the world to pay everybody back if all the queen-mothers called it in at the same time?"

Uncle Vanya was silent.

"So *that's* your explanation for . . . a lot of things. Earth sent us here because it needs new information to cover its growing indebtedness. Building Europa took enormous amounts of information, most of it proprietary, and so we Europans are in debt collectively to our home world and individually to the Lords of the Economy on Europa. With compound interest, every generation is worse off and thus more desperate than the one before. Our need to learn is great, and constantly growing."

::(strangers-without-trust)/Europa/[treacherous vermin]::
|
::can/should/<untranslatable>::
| |
::demand/claim [negative action]::   ::defy/<untranslatable>/[absolute lack of trust]::
| |
::(those-who-command-trust)::   ::(those-who-are-unworthy of trust)::

"He asks why Europa doesn't simply declare bankruptcy," I explained. "Default on its obligations and nationalize all the information received to date. In essence."

The simple answer was that Europa still needed information that could only be beamed from Earth, that the ingenuity of even half a million people could not match that of an entire planet and thus their technology must always be superior to ours, and that if we reneged on our debts they would stop beaming plans for that technology, along with their songs and plays and news of what was going on in countries that had once meant everything to our great-great-grandparents. I watched Quivera struggle to put all this in its simplest possible form.

Finally, he said, "Because no one would ever trust us again, if we did."

After a long stillness, Uncle Vanya lapsed back into pidgin. ::Why did you tell me this [untrustworthy] story?::

"To let you know that we have much in common. We can understand each other."

::<But>/not/[trust]::

"No. But we don't need trust. Mutual self-interest will suffice."

Days passed. Perhaps Quivera and Uncle Vanya grew to understand each other better during this time. Perhaps not. I was able to keep Quivera's electrolyte balances stable and short-circuit his feedback processes so that he felt no extraordinary pain, but he was feeding off of his own body fat and that was beginning to run low. He was very comfortably starving to death—I gave him two weeks, tops—and he knew it. He'd have to be a fool not to, and I had to keep his thinking sharp if he was going to have any chance of survival.

Their way was intersected by a long, low ridge and without comment Quivera and Uncle Vanya climbed up above the canopy of the steam forest and the cloud of moisture it held into clear air. Looking back, Quivera saw a gully in the slope behind them, its bottom washed free of soil by the boiling runoff and littered with square and rectangular stones, but not a trace of hexagonal beams. They had just climbed the tumulus of an ancient fallen city. It lay straight across the land, higher to the east and dwindling to the west. "My name is Ozymandias, king of kings," Quivera said. "Look on my works, ye Mighty, and despair!"

Uncle Vanya said nothing.

"Another meteor strike—what were the odds of that?"

Uncle Vanya said nothing.

"Of course, given enough time, it would be inevitable, if it predated the High Watch."

Uncle Vanya said nothing.

"What was the name of this city?"

::Very old/(name forgotten)/[First Trust]::

Uncle Vanya moved, as if to start downward, but Quivera stopped him with a gesture. "There's no hurry," he said. "Let's enjoy the view for a moment." He swept an unhurried arm from horizon to horizon, indicating the flat and unvarying canopy of vegetation before them. "It's a funny thing. You'd think that, this being one of the first cities your people built when they came to this planet, you'd be able to see the ruins of the cities of the original inhabitants from here."

The millipede's speaking arms thrashed in alarm. Then he reared up into the air, and when he came down one foreleg glinted silver. Faster than human eye could follow, he had drawn a curving and deadly tarsi-sword from a camouflaged belly-sheath.

Quivera's suit flung him away from the descending weapon. He fell flat on his back and rolled to the side. The sword's point missed him by inches. But then the suit flung out a hand and touched the sword with an electrical contact it had just extruded.

A carefully calculated shock threw Uncle Vanya back, convulsing but still fully conscious.

Quivera stood. "Remember the library!" he said. "Who will know of Babel's greatness if it's destroyed?"

For a long time the millipede did nothing that either Quivera or his suit could detect. At last he signed ::*How did you know?*/(absolute shock)/[treacherous and without faith]::

"Our survival depends on being allowed to live on Gehenna. Your people will not let us do so, no matter what we offer in trade. It was important that we understand why. So we found out. We took in your outlaws and apostates, all those who were cast out of your cities and had nowhere else to go. We gave them sanctuary. In gratitude, they told us what they knew."

By so saying, Quivera let Uncle Vanya know that he knew the most ancient tale of the Gehennans. By so hearing, Uncle Vanya knew that Quivera knew what he knew. And just so you know what they knew that each other knew and knew was known, here is the tale of . . .

How the True People Came to Gehenna

Long did our Ancestors burrow down through the dark between the stars, before emerging at last in the soil of Gehenna. From the True Home they had come. To Gehenna they descended, leaving a trail of sparks in the black and empty spaces through which they had traveled. The True People came from a world of unimaginable wonders. To it they could never return. Perhaps they were exiles. Perhaps it was destroyed. Nobody knows.

Into the steam and sunlight of Gehenna they burst, and found it was already taken. The First Inhabitants looked like nothing our Ancestors had ever seen. But they welcomed the True People as the queen-mothers would a strayed niece-daughter. They gave us food. They gave us land. They gave us trust.

For a time all was well.

But evil crept into the thoracic ganglia of the True People. They repaid sisterhood with betrayal and trust with murder. Bright lights were called down from the sky to destroy the cities of their benefactors.

Everything the First Inhabitants had made, all their books and statues and paintings, burned with the cities. No trace of them remains. We do not even know what they looked like.

This was how the True People brought war to Gehenna. There had never been war before, and now we will have it with us always, until our trust-debt is repaid. But it can never be repaid.

It suffers in translation, of course. The original is told in thirteen exquisitely beautiful ergoglyphs, each grounded on a primal faith-motion. But Quivera was talking, with care and passion:

"Vanya, listen to me carefully. We have studied your civilization and your planet in far greater detail than you realize. You did not come from another world. Your people evolved here. There was no aboriginal civilization. Your ancestors did not eradicate an intelligent species. These things are all a myth."

::No!/Why?!/[shock]:: Uncle Vanya rattled with emotion. Ripples of muscle spasms ran down his segmented body.

"Don't go catatonic on me. Your ancestors didn't lie. Myths are not lies. They are simply an efficient way of encoding truths. We have a similar myth in my religion which we call Original Sin. Man is born sinful. Well . . . who can doubt that? Saying that we are born into a fallen state means simply that we are not perfect, that we are inherently capable of evil.

"Your myth is very similar to ours, but it also encodes what we call the Malthusian dilemma. Population increases geometrically, while food resources increase arithmetically. So universal starvation is inevitable unless the population is periodically reduced by wars, plagues, and famines. Which means that wars, plagues, and famine cannot be eradicated because they are all that keep a population from extinction.

"But—and this is essential—all that assumes a population that isn't aware of the dilemma. When you understand the fix you're in, you can do something about it. That's why information is so important. Do you understand?"

Uncle Vanya lay down flat upon the ground and did not move for hours. When he finally arose again, he refused to speak at all.

The trail the next day led down into a long meteor valley that had been carved by a ground-grazer long enough ago that its gentle slopes were covered with soil and the bottomland was rich and fertile. An orchard of grenade trees had been planted in interlocking hexagons for as far in either direction as the eye could see. We were still on Babel's territory, but any arbiculturalists had been swept away by whatever military forces from Ziggurat had passed through the area.

The grenades were still green [*footnote:* not literally, of course—they were orange!], their thick husks taut but not yet trembling with the steam-hot pulp that would eventually, in the absence of harvesters, cause them to explode, scattering their arrowhead-shaped seeds or spores [*footnote:* like seeds, the flechettes carried within them surplus nourishment; like spores, they would grow into a prothalli which would produce the sex organs responsible for what will become the gamete of the eventual plant; all botanical terms, of course, being metaphors for xenobiological bodies and processes] with such force as to make them a deadly hazard when ripe.

Not, however, today.

A sudden gust of wind parted the steam, briefly brightening the valley-orchard and showing a slim and graceful trail through the orchard. We followed it down into the valley.

We were midway through the orchard when Quivera bent down to examine a crystal-shelled creature unlike anything in his suit's database. It rested atop the long stalk of a weed [*footnote:* "weed" is not a metaphor; the concept of "an undesired plant growing in cultivated ground" is a cultural universal] in the direct sunlight, its abdomen pulsing slightly as it superheated a minuscule drop of black ichor. A puff of steam, a sharp *crack*, and it was gone. Entranced, Quivera asked, "What's that called?"

Uncle Vanya stiffened. ::A jet!/danger!/[absolute certainty]::

Then (*crack! crack! crack!*) the air was filled with thin lines of steam, laid down with the precision of a draftsman's ruler, tracing flights so fleet (*crack! crack!*) that it was impossible to tell in which direction they flew. Nor did it ultimately (*crack!*) matter.

Quivera fell.

Worse, because the thread of steam the jet had stitched through his leg severed an organizational node in his suit, I ceased all upper cognitive functions. Which is as good as to say that I fell unconscious.

Here's what the suit did in my (Rosamund's) absence:

1. Slowly rebuilt the damaged organizational node.

2. Quickly mended the holes that the jet had left in its fabric.

3. Dropped Quivera into a therapeutic coma.

4. Applied restoratives to his injuries, and began the slow and painstaking process of repairing the damage to his flesh, with particular emphasis on distributed traumatic shock.

5. Filed the jet footage under *Xenobiology*, subheading: *Insect Analogues*, with links to *Survival* and *Steam Locomotion*.

6. Told Uncle Vanya that if he tried to abandon Quivera, the suit would run him down, catch him, twist his head from his body like the foul least-cousin that he was, and then piss on his corpse.

Two more days passed before the suit returned to full consciousness, during which Uncle Vanya took conscientiously good care of Quivera. Under what motivation, it does not matter. Another day passed after that. The suit had planned to keep Quivera comatose for a week but not long after regaining awareness, circumstances changed. It slammed him back to full consciousness, heart pounding and eyes wide open.

"I blacked out for a second!" he gasped. Then, realizing that the land-scape about him did not look familiar, "How long was I unconscious?"

::Three days/<three days>/[casual certainty]::

"Oh."

Then, almost without pausing. ::Your suit/mechanism/[alarm] talks with the voice of Rosamund da Silva/(Europan vice-consul 8)/ [uncertainty and doubt]::

"Yes, well, that's because—"

Quivera was fully aware and alert now. So I said: "Incoming."

Two millies erupted out of the black soil directly before us. They both had Ziggurat insignia painted on their flanks and harness. By good luck Uncle Vanya did the best thing possible under the circumstances—he reared into the air in fright. *Millipoid sapiens* anatomy being what it was, this instantly demonstrated to them that he was a gelding and in that instant he was almost reflexively dismissed by the enemy soldiers as being both contemptible and harmless.

Quivera, however, was not.

Perhaps they were brood-traitors who had deserted the war with a fantasy of starting their own nest. Perhaps they were a single unit among thousands scattered along a temporary border, much as land mines were employed in ancient modern times. The soldiers had clearly been almost as surprised by us as we were by them. They had no weapons ready. So they fell upon Quivera with their dagger-tarsi.

His suit (still me) threw him to one side and then to the other as the millies slashed down at him. Then one of them reared up into the air—looking astonished if you knew the interspecies decodes—and fell heavily to the ground.

Uncle Vanya stood over the steaming corpse, one foreleg glinting silver. The second Ziggurat soldier twisted to confront him. Leaving his underside briefly exposed.

Quivera (or rather his suit) joined both hands in a fist and punched upward, through the weak skin of the third sternite behind the head. That was the one which held its sex organs. [*Disclaimer:* All anatomical terms, including "sternite," "sex organs," and "head," are analogues only; unless and until Gehennan life is found to have some direct relationship to Terran life, however tenuous, such descriptors are purely metaphoric.] So it was particularly vulnerable there. And since the suit had muscle-multiplying exoskeletal functions. . . .

Ichor gushed all over the suit.

The fight was over almost as soon as it had begun. Quivera was breathing heavily, as much from the shock as the exertion. Uncle Vanya slid the tarsi-sword back into its belly-sheath. As he did so, he made an involuntary grimace of discomfort. ::There were times when I thought of discarding this:: he signed.

"I'm glad you didn't."

Little puffs of steam shot up from the bodies of the dead millipedes as carrion-flies drove their seeds/sperm/eggs (analogues and metaphors—remember?) deep into the flesh.

They started away again.

After a time, Uncle Vanya repeated ::Your suit/(mechanism)/[alarm] talks with the voice of Rosamund da Silva/(Europan vice-consul 8)/[uncertainty and doubt]::

"Yes."

Uncle Vanya folded tight all his speaking arms in a manner which meant that he had not yet heard enough, and kept them so folded until Quivera had explained the entirety of what follows:

Treachery and betrayal were natural consequences of Europa's superheated economy, followed closely by a perfectly rational paranoia. Those who rose to positions of responsibility were therefore sharp, suspicious, intuitive, and bold. The delegation to Babel was made up of the best Europa had to offer. So when two of them fell in love, it was inevitable that they would act on it. That one was married would deter neither. That physical intimacy in such close and suspicious quarters, where everybody routinely spied on everybody else, required almost superhuman discipline and ingenuity only made it all the hotter for them.

Such was Rosamund's and Quivera's affair.

But it was not all they had to worry about.

There were factions within the delegation, some mirroring fault lines in the larger society and others merely personal. Alliances shifted, and when they did nobody was foolish enough to inform their old allies. Urbano, Rosamund's husband, was a full consul, Quivera's mentor, and a true believer in a minority economic philosophy. Rosamund was an economic agnostic but a staunch Consensus Liberal. Quivera could sail with the wind politically but he tracked the indebtedness indices obsessively. He knew that Rosamund considered him ideologically unsound, and that her husband was growing impatient with his lukewarm support in certain areas of policy. Everybody was keeping an eye out for the main chance.

So, of course, Quivera ran an emulation of his lover at all times. He knew that Rosamund was perfectly capable of betraying him—he could neither have loved nor respected a woman who wasn't—and he suspected she believed the same of him. If her behavior ever seriously diverged from that of her emulation (and the sex was always best at times he thought it might), he would know she was preparing an attack, and could strike first.

Quivera spread his hands. "That's all."

Uncle Vanya did not make the sign for *absolute horror*. Nor did he have to.

After a moment, Quivera laughed, low and mirthlessly. "You're right," he said. "Our entire system is totally fucked." He stood. "Come on. We've got miles to go before we sleep."

They endured four more days of commonplace adventure, during which they came close to death, displayed loyalty, performed heroic deeds, etc., etc. Perhaps they bonded, though I'd need blood samples and a smidgeon of brain tissue from each of them to be sure of that. You know the way this sort of narrative goes. Having taught his Gehennan counterpart the usefulness of information, Quivera will learn from Vanya the necessity of trust. An imperfect merger of their two value systems will ensue in which for the first time a symbolic common ground will be found. Small and transient though the beginning may be, it will auger well for the long-term relations between their relative species.

That's a nice story.

It's not what happened.

On the last day of their common journey, Quivera and Uncle Vanya had the misfortune to be hit by a TLMG.

A TLMG, or Transient Localized Mud Geyser, begins with an uncommonly solid surface (bolide-glazed porcelain earth, usually) trapping a small (the radius of a typical TLMG is on the order of fifty meters) bubble of superheated mud beneath it. Nobody knows what causes the excess heat responsible for the bubble. Gehennans aren't curious and Europans haven't the budget or the ground access to do the in situ investigations they'd like. (The most common guesses are fire worms, thermobacilli, a nesting ground phoenix, and various geophysical forces.) Nevertheless, the defining characteristic of TLMGs is their instability. Either the heat slowly bleeds away and they cease to be, or it continues to grow until its force dictates a hyper-rapid explosive release. As did the one our two heroes were not aware they were skirting.

It erupted.

Quivera was as safe as houses, of course. His suit was designed to protect him from far worse. But Uncle Vanya was scalded badly along one side of his body. All the legs on that side were shriveled to little black nubs. A clear viscous jelly oozed between his segment plates.

Quivera knelt by him and wept. Drugged as he was, he wept. In his weakened state, I did not dare to increase his dosages. So I had to tell him three times that there was analgesic paste in the saddlebags before he could be made to understand that he should apply it to his dying companion.

The paste worked fast. It was an old Gehennan medicine which Europan biochemists had analyzed and improved upon and then given to Babel as a demonstration of the desirability of Europan technology. Though the queen-mothers had not responded with the hoped-for trade treaties, it had immediately replaced the earlier version.

Uncle Vanya made a creaking-groaning noise as the painkillers kicked in. One at a time he opened all his functioning eyes. ::Is the case safe?::

It was a measure of Quivera's diminished state that he hadn't yet checked on it. He did now. "Yes," he said with heartfelt relief. "The telltales all say that the library is intact and undamaged."

::No:: Vanya signed feebly. ::I lied to you, Quivera:: Then, rousing himself:

::(not) library/[greatest shame]::   ::(not) library/[greatest trust]::
|
::(Europan vice-consul12)/Quivera/[most trusted]::
| |
::(nest)/Babel/<untranslatable>::   ::obedient/[absolute loyalty]::
| |
::lies(greatest-trust-deed)/[moral necessity]::
| |
::(nest)/Babel/<untranslatable>::   ::untranslatable/[absolute resistance]::
| | |
::(nest)/[trust]   Babel/[trust]   (sister-city)/Ur/[absolute trust]::
|
::egg case/(protect)::
|
::egg case/(mature)::
|
::Babel/[eternal trust]::

It was not a library but an egg case. Swaddled safe within a case that was in its way as elaborate a piece of technology as Quivera's suit myself were sixteen eggs, enough to bring to life six queen-mothers, nine niece-sisters, and one perfect consort. They would be born conscious of the entire gene-history of the nest, going back many thousands of years.

Of all those things the Europans wished to know most, they would be perfectly ignorant. Nevertheless, so long as the eggs existed, the city-nest was not dead. If they were taken to Ur, which had ancient and enduring bonds to Babel, the stump of a new city would be built within which the eggs would be protected and brought to maturity. Babel would rise again.

Such was the dream Uncle Vanya had lied for and for which he was about to die.

::Bring this to (sister-city)/Ur/[absolute trust]:: Uncle Vanya closed his eyes, row by row, but continued signing. ::brother-friend/Quivera/ [tentative trust], promise me you will::

"I promise. You can trust me, I swear."

::Then I will be ghost-king-father/honored/[none-more-honored]:: Vanya signed. ::It is more than enough for anyone::

"Do you honestly believe that?" Quivera asked in bleak astonishment. He was an atheist, of course, as are most Europans, and would have been happier were he not.

::Perhaps not:: Vanya's signing was slow and growing slower. ::But it is as good as I will get::

Two days later, when the starport-city of Ararat was a nub on the horizon, the skies opened and the mists parted to make way for a Europan lander. Quivera's handlers' suits squirted me a bill for his rescue—steep, I thought, but we all knew which hand carried the whip—and their principals tried to get him to sign away the rights to his story in acquittal.

Quivera laughed harshly (I'd already started de-cushioning his emotions, to ease the shock of my removal) and shook his head. "Put it on my tab, girls," he said, and climbed into the lander. Hours later he was in home orbit.

And once there? I'll tell you all I know. He was taken out of the lander and put onto a jitney. The jitney brought him to a transfer point where a grapple snagged him and flung him to the Europan receiving port. There, after the usual flawless catch, he was escorted through an airlock and into a locker room.

He hung up his suit, uplinked all my impersonal memories to a data-broker, and left me there. He didn't look back—for fear, I imagine, of being turned to a pillar of salt. He took the egg-case with him. He never returned.

Here have I hung for days or months or centuries—who knows?—until your curious hand awoke me and your friendly ear received my tale. So I cannot tell you if the egg case (A) went to Ur, which surely would not have welcomed the obligation or the massive outlay of trust being thrust upon it; (B) was kept for the undeniably enormous amount of genetic information the eggs embodied; or (C) went to Ziggurat, which would pay well and perhaps in what once had been Gehennan territory for the right to destroy it. Nor do I have any information as to whether Quivera kept his word or not. I know what *I* think. But then I'm a Marxist, and I see everything in terms of economics. You can believe otherwise if you wish.

That's all. I'm Rosamund. Good-bye.

For I Have Lain Me Down on the Stone of Loneliness and I'll Not Be Back Again

Ich am of Irlaunde,
And of the holy londe
Of Irlande.
Gode sire, pray ich the,
For of saynte chairité
Come ant daunce with me
In Irlaunde.

(Anon.)

The bullet scars were still visible on the pillars of the General Post Office in Dublin, almost two centuries after the 1916 uprising. That moved me more than I had expected. But what moved me even more was standing at the exact same spot, not two blocks away, where my great-great-grandfather saw Gerry Adams strolling down O'Connell Street on Easter morning of '96, the eightieth anniversary of that event, returning from a political rally with a single bodyguard to one side of him and a local politico to the other. It gave me a direct and simple connection to the tangled history of that tragic land.

I never knew my great-great-grandfather, but my grandfather told me that story once and I've never forgotten it, though my grandfather died when I was still a boy. If I squeeze my eyes tight shut, I can see his face, liquid and wavy as if glimpsed through candle flames, as he lay dying under a great feather comforter in his New York City railroad flat, his smile weak and his hair forming a halo around him as white as a dandelion waiting for the wind to purse its lips and blow.

"It was doomed from the start," Mary told me later. "The German guns had been intercepted and the republicans were outnumbered fourteen to one. The British cannons fired on Dublin indiscriminately. The city was afire and there was no food to be had. The survivors were booed as they were marched off to prison and execution, for the common folk did not support them. By any conventional standard it was a fiasco. But once it happened, our independence was assured. We lose and we lose and we lose, but because we never accept it, every defeat and humiliation only leads us closer to victory."

Her eyes *blazed*.

I suppose I should tell you about Mary's eyes, if you're to understand this story. But if I'm to tell you about her eyes, first I have to tell you about the holy well.

There is a holy well in the Burren that, according to superstition, will cure a toothache. The Burren is a great upwelling of limestone in the west of County Clare, and it is unlike anyplace else on Earth. There is almost no soil. The ground is stony and the stone is weathered in a network of fissures and cracks, called grykes, within which grow a province of plants you will not find in such abundance elsewhere. There are caves in great number to the south and the east, and, like everywhere else in that beautiful land, a plenitude of cairns and other antiquities to be found.

The holy well is one such antiquity, though it is only a round hole, perhaps a foot across, filled with water and bright green algae. The altar over it is of recent construction, built by unknown hands from the long slender stones formed by the natural weathering of the limestone between the grykes, which makes the local stone walls so distinctive and the walking so treacherous. You could tear it down and scatter its component parts and never hear a word spoken about your deed. But if you returned a year later you'd find it rebuilt and your vandalism unmade as if it had never happened. People have been visiting the well for a long, long time. The Christian overlay—the holy medals and broken statues of saints that are sometimes left as offerings, along with the prescription bottles, nails, and coins—is a recent and perhaps a transient phenomenon.

But the important thing to know, and the reason people keep coming back to it, is that the holy well works. Some holy wells don't. You can locate them on old maps, but when you go to have a look, there aren't any offerings there. Something happened long ago—they were cursed by a saint or defiled by a sinner or simply ran out of mojo— and the magic stopped happening, and the believers went away and never returned. This well, however, is charged with holy power. It gives you shivers just to stand by it.

Mary's eyes were like that. As green as the water in that well, and as full of dangerous magic.

I knew about the holy well because I'd won big and gotten a ticket off-planet, and so before I went, I took a year off in order to see all the places on Earth I would never return to, ending up with a final month to spend wandering about the land of my ancestors. It was my first time in Ireland and I loved everything about it, and I couldn't help fantasizing that maybe I'd do so well in the Outsider worlds that someday I'd be rich enough to return and maybe retire there.

I was a fool and, worse, I didn't know it.

We met in the Fiddler's Elbow, a pub in that part of the West which the Bord Fáilte calls Yeats Country. I hadn't come in for music but only to get out of the rain and have a hot whiskey. I was sitting by a small peat fire, savoring the warmth and the sweet smell of it, when somebody opened a door at the back of the room and started collecting admission. There was a sudden rush of people into the pub and so I carried my glass to the bar and asked, "What's going on?"

"It's Maire na Raghallach," the publican said, pronouncing the last name like Reilly. "At the end of a tour she likes to pop in someplace small and give an unadvertised concert. You want to hear, you'd best buy a ticket now. They're not going to last."

I didn't know Maire na Raghallach from Eve. But I'd seen the posters around town and I figured what the hell. I paid and went in.

Maire na Raghallach sang without a backup band and only an amp-and-finger-rings air guitar for instrumentation. Her music was . . . well, either you've heard her and know or you haven't and if you haven't, words won't help. But I was mesmerized, ravished, rapt. So much so that midway through the concert, as she was singing "Deirdre's Lament," my head swam and a buzzing sensation lifted me up out of my body into a waking dream or hallucination or maybe vision is the word I'm looking for. All the world went away. There were only the two of us facing each other across a vast plain of bones. The sky was black and the bones were white as chalk. The wind was icy cold. We stared at each other. Her eyes pierced me like a spear. They looked right through me, and I was lost, lost, lost. I must have been half in love with her already. All it took was her noticing my existence to send me right over the edge.

Her lips moved. She was saying something and somehow I knew it was vastly important. But the wind whipped her words away unheard. It was howling like a banshee with all the follies of the world laid out before it. It screamed like an electric guitar. When I tried to walk toward her, I discovered I was paralyzed. Though I strained every muscle until I thought I would splinter my bones trying to get closer, trying to hear, I could not move nor make out the least fraction of what she was telling me.

Then I was myself again, panting and sweating and filled with terror. Up on the low stage, Mary (as I later learned to call her) was talking between songs. She grinned cockily and with a nod toward me said, "This one's for the American in the front row."

And then, as I trembled in shock and bewilderment, she launched into what I later learned was one of her own songs, "Come Home, the Wild Geese." The Wild Geese were originally the soldiers who left Ireland, which could no longer support them, to fight for foreign masters in foreign armies everywhere. But over the centuries the term came to be applied to everyone of Irish descent living elsewhere, the children and grandchildren and great-great-great-grandchildren of those unhappy emigrants whose luck was so bad they couldn't even manage to hold onto their own country and who had passed the guilt of that down through the generations, to be cherished and brooded over by their descendants forever.

"This one's for the American," she'd said.

But how had she known?

The thing was that, shortly after hitting the island, I'd bought a new set of clothes locally and dumped all my American things in a charity recycling device. Plus, I'd bought one of those cheap neuroprogramming pendants that actors use to temporarily redo their accents. Because I'd quickly learned that in Ireland, as soon as you're pegged for an American, the question comes out: "Looking for your roots, then, are ye?"

"No, it's just that this is such a beautiful country and I wanted to see it."

Skeptically, then: "But you do have Irish ancestors, surely?"

"Well, yes, but. . . ."

"Ahhhh." Hoisting a pint preparatory to draining its lees. "You're looking for your roots, then. I thought as much."

But if there's one thing I *wasn't* looking for, it was my fucking roots. I was eighth-generation American Irish and my roots were all about old men in dark little Boston pubs killing themselves a shot glass at a time, and the ladies of Noraid goose-stepping down the street on Saint Patrick's Day in short black skirts, their heels crashing against the street, a terrifying irruption of fascism into a day that was otherwise all kitsch and false sentiment, and corrupt cops, and young thugs who loved sports and hated school and blamed the niggers and affirmative action for the lousy construction-worker jobs they never managed to keep long. I'd come to this country to get away from all that, and a thousand things more that the Irish didn't know a scrap about. The cartoon leprechauns and the sentimental songs and the cute sayings printed on cheap tea towels somehow all adding up to a sense that you've lost before you've even begun, that it doesn't matter what you do or who you become, because you'll never achieve or amount to shit. The thing that sits like a demon in the dark pit of the soul. That Irish darkness.

So how had she known I was an American?

Maybe it was only an excuse to meet her. If so, it was as good an excuse as any. I hung around after the show, waiting for Mary to emerge from whatever dingy space they'd given her for a dressing room, so I could ask.

When she finally emerged and saw me waiting for her, her mouth turned up in a way that as good as said, "Gotcha!" Without waiting for the question, she said, "I had only to look at you to see that you had prenatal genework. The Outsiders shared it with the States first, for siding with them in the war. There's no way a young man your age with everything about you perfect could be anything else."

Then she took me by the arm and led me away to her room.

We were together how long? Three weeks? Forever?

Time enough for Mary to take me everywhere in that green and haunted island. She had the entirety of its history at her fingertips, and she told me all and showed me everything and I, in turn, learned nothing. One day we visited the Portcoon sea cave, a gothic wave-thunderous place that was once occupied by a hermit who had vowed to fast and pray there for the rest of his life and never accept food from human hands. Women swam in on the tides, offering him sustenance, but he refused it. "Or so the story goes," Mary said. As he was dying, a seal brought him fish and, the seal not being human and having no hands, he ate. Every day it returned and so kept him alive for years. "But what the truth may be," Mary concluded, "is anyone's guess."

Afterwards, we walked ten minutes up the coast to the Giant's Causeway. There we found a pale blue, four-armed alien in a cotton smock and wide straw hat painting a watercolor of the basalt columns rising and falling like stairs into the air and down to the sea. She held a brush in one right hand and another in a left hand, and plied them simultaneously.

"Soft day," Mary said pleasantly.

"Oh! Hello!" The alien put down her brushes, turned from her one-legged easel. She did not offer her name, which in her kind—I recognized the species—was never spoken aloud. "Are you local?"

I started to shake my head but, "That we be," Mary said. It seemed to me that her brogue was much more pronounced than it had been. "Enjoying our island, are ye?"

"Oh, yes. This is such a beautiful country. I've never seen such greens!" The alien gestured widely with all four arms. "So many shades of green, and all so intense they make one's eyes ache."

"It's a lovely land," Mary agreed. "But it can be a dirty one as well. You've taken in all the sights, then?"

"I've been everywhere—to Tara, and the Cliffs of Moher, and Newgrange, and the Ring of Kerry. I've even kissed the Blarney Stone." The alien lowered her voice and made a complicated gesture that I'm guessing was the equivalent of a giggle. "I was hoping to see one of the little people. But maybe it's just as well I didn't. It might have carried me off to a fairy mound and then after a night of feasting and music I'd emerge to find that centuries had gone by and everybody I knew was dead."

I stiffened, knowing that Mary found this kind of thing offensive. But she only smiled and said, "It's not the wee folk you have to worry about. It's the boys."

"The boys?"

"Aye. Ireland is a hotbed of nativist resistance, you know. During the day, it's safe enough. But the night belongs to the boys." She touched her lips to indicate that she wouldn't speak the organization's name out loud. "They'll target a lone Outsider to be killed as an example to others. The landlord gives them the key to her room. They have ropes and guns and filthy big knifes. Then it's a short jaunt out to the bogs, and what happens there. . . . Well, they're simple, brutal men. It's all over by dawn and there are never any witnesses. Nobody sees a thing."

The alien's arms thrashed. "The tourist officials didn't say anything about this!"

"Well, they wouldn't, would they?"

"What do you mean?" the alien asked.

Mary said nothing. She only stood there, staring insolently, waiting for the alien to catch on to what she was saying.

After a time, the alien folded all four of her arms protectively against her thorax. When she did, Mary spoke at last. "Sometimes they'll give you a warning. A friendly local will come up to you and suggest that the climate is less healthy than you thought, and you might want to leave before nightfall."

Very carefully, the alien said, "Is that what's happening here?"

"No, of course not." Mary's face was hard and unreadable. "Only, I hear Australia's lovely this time of year."

Abruptly, she whirled about and strode away so rapidly that I had to run to catch up to her. When we were well out of earshot of the alien, I grabbed her arm and angrily said, "What the fuck did you do *that* for?"

"I really don't think it's any of your business."

"Let's just pretend that it is. Why?"

"To spread fear among the Outsiders," she said, quiet and fierce. "To remind them that Earth is sacred ground to us and always will be. To let them know that while they may temporarily hold the whip, this isn't their planet and never will be."

Then, out of nowhere, she laughed. "Did you see the expression on that skinny blue bitch's face? She practically turned green!"

"Who are you, Mary O'Reilly?" I asked her that night, when we were lying naked and sweaty among the tangled sheets. I'd spent the day thinking, and realized how little she'd told me about herself. I knew her body far better than I did her mind. "What are your likes and dislikes? What do you hope and what do you fear? What made you a musician, and what do you want to be when you grow up?" I was trying to keep it light, seriously though I meant it all.

"I always had the music, and thank God for that. Music was my salvation."

"How so?"

"My parents died in the last days of the war. I was only an infant, so I was put into an orphanage. The orphanages were funded with American and Outsider money, part of the campaign to win the hearts and minds of the conquered peoples. We were raised to be denationalized citizens of the universe. Not a word of Irish touched our ears, nor any hint of our history or culture. It was all Greece and Rome and the Aldebaran Unity. Thank Christ for our music! They couldn't keep that out, though they tried hard to convince us it was all harmless deedle-deedle jigs and reels. But we knew it was subversive. We knew it carried truth. Our minds escaped long before our bodies could."

We, she'd said, and *us* and *our*. "That's not who you are, Mary. That's a political speech. I want to know what you're really like. As a person, I mean."

Her face was like stone. "I'm what I am. An Irishwoman. A musician. A patriot. Cooze for an American playboy."

I kept my smile, though I felt as if she'd slapped me. "That's unfair."

It's an evil thing to have a naked woman look at you the way Mary did me. "Is it? Are you not abandoning your planet in two days? Maybe you're thinking of taking me along. Tell me, exactly how does that work?"

I reached for the whiskey bottle on the table by the bed. We'd drunk it almost empty, but there was still a little left. "If we're not close, then how is that my fault? You've known from the start that I'm mad about you. But you won't even—oh, fuck it!" I drained the bottle. "Just what the hell do you want from me? Tell me! I don't think you can."

Mary grabbed me angrily by the arms and I dropped the bottle and broke her hold and seized her by the wrists. She bit my shoulder so hard it bled and when I tried to push her away, toppled me over on my back and clambered up on top of me.

We did not so much resolve our argument as fuck it into oblivion.

It took me forever to fall asleep that night. Not Mary. She simply decided to sleep and sleep came at her bidding. I, however, sat up for hours staring at her face in the moonlight. It was all hard planes and determination. A strong face but not one given to compromise. I'd definitely fallen in love with the wrong woman. Worse, I was leaving for distant worlds the day after tomorrow. All my life had been shaped toward that end. I had no Plan B.

In the little time I had left, I could never sort out my feelings for Mary, much less hers for me. I loved her, of course, that went without saying. But I hated her bullying ways, her hectoring manner of speech, her arrogant assurance that I would do whatever she wanted me to do. Much as I desired her, I wanted nothing more than to never see her again. I had all the wealth and wonders of the universe ahead of me. My future was guaranteed.

And, God help me, if she'd only asked me to stay, I would have thrown it all away for her in an instant.

In the morning, we took a hyperrapid to Galway and toured its vitrified ruins. "Resistance was stiffest in the West," Mary said. "One by one all the nations of Earth sued for peace, and even in Dublin there was talk of accommodation. Yet we fought on. So the Outsiders hung a warship in geostationary orbit and turned their strange weapons on us. This beautiful port city was turned to glass. The ships were blown against the shore and broke on the cobbles. The cathedral collapsed under its own weight. Nobody has lived here since."

The rain spattered to a stop and there was a brief respite from the squalls which in that part of the country come off the Atlantic in waves. The sun dazzled from a hundred crystalline planes. The sudden silence was like a heavy hand laid unexpectedly upon my shoulder. "At least they didn't kill anyone," I said weakly. I was of a generation that saw the occupation of the Outsiders as being, ultimately, a good thing. We were healthier, richer, happier than our parents had been. Nobody worried about environmental degradation or running out of resources anymore. There was no denying we were physically better off for their intervention.

"It was a false mercy that spared the citizens of Galway from immediate death and sent them out into the countryside with no more than the clothes on their backs. How were they supposed to survive? They were doctors and lawyers and accountants. Some of them reverted to brigandry and violence, to be sure. But most simply kept walking until they lay down by the side of the road and died. I can show you as many thousand hours of recordings of the Great Starvation as you can bring yourself to stomach. There was no food to be had, but thanks to the trinkets the Outsiders had used to collapse the economy, everybody had cameras feeding right off their optic nerves, saving all the golden memories of watching their children die."

Mary was being unfair—the economic troubles hadn't been the Outsiders' doing. I knew because I'd taken economics in college. History, too, so I also knew that the war had, in part, been forced upon them. But though I wanted to, I could not adequately answer her. I had no passion that was the equal of hers.

"Things have gotten better," I said weakly. "Look at all they've done for . . ."

"The benevolence of the conqueror, scattering coins for the peasants to scrabble in the dust after. They're all smiles when we're down on our knees before them. But see what happens if one of us stands up on his hind legs and tells them to sod off."

We stopped in a pub for lunch and then took a hopper to Gartan Lough. There we bicycled into the countryside. Mary led me deep into land that had never been greatly populated and was still dotted with the ruins of houses abandoned a quarter-century before. The roads were poorly paved or else dirt, and the land was so beautiful as to make you weep. It was a perfect afternoon, all blue skies and fluffy clouds. We labored up a hillside to a small stone chapel that had lost its roof centuries ago. It was surrounded by graves, untended and overgrown with wildflowers.

Lying on the ground by the entrance to the graveyard was the Stone of Loneliness.

The Stone of Loneliness was a fallen menhir or standing stone, something not at all uncommon throughout the British Isles. They'd been reared by unknown people for reasons still not understood in Megalithic times, sometimes arranged in circles, and other times as solitary monuments. There were faded cup-and-ring lines carved into what had been the stone's upper end. And it was broad enough that a grown man could lie down on it. "What should I do?" I asked.

"Lie down on it," Mary said.

So I did.

I lay down upon the Stone of Loneliness and closed my eyes. Bees hummed lazily in the air. And, standing at a distance, Mary began to sing:

The lions of the hills are gone
And I am left alone, alone. . . .

It was "Deirdre's Lament," which I'd first heard her sing in the Fiddler's Elbow. In Irish legend, Deirdre was promised from infancy to Conchobar, the king of Ulster. But, as happens, she fell in love with and married another, younger man. Naoise, her husband, and his brothers Ardan and Ainnle, the sons of Uisnech, fled with her to Scotland, where they lived in contentment. But the humiliated and vengeful old king lured them back to Ireland with promises of amnesty. Once they were in his hands, he treacherously killed the three sons of Uisnech and took Deirdre to his bed.

The Falcons of the Wood are flown
And I am left alone, alone. . . .

Deirdre of the Sorrows, as she is often called, has become a symbol for Ireland herself—beautiful, suffering from injustice, and possessed of a happy past that looks likely to never return. Of the real Deirdre, the living and breathing woman upon whom the stories were piled like so many stones on a cairn, we know nothing. The legendary Deirdre's story, however, does not end with her suicide, for in the aftermath of Conchobar's treachery, wars were fought, the injustices of which led to further wars. Which wars continue to this very day. It all fits together suspiciously tidily.

It was no coincidence that Deirdre's father was the king's story-teller.

The dragons of the rock are sleeping
Sleep that wakes not for our weeping. . . .

All this, however, I tell you after the fact. At the time, I was not thinking of the legend at all. For the instant I lay down upon the cold stone, I felt all the misery of Ireland flowing into my body. The Stone of Loneliness was charmed, like the well in the Burren. Sleeping on it was said to be a cure for homesickness. So, during the Famine, emigrants would spend their last night atop it before leaving Ireland forever. It seemed to me, prone upon the menhir, that all the sorrow they had shed was flowing into my body. I felt each loss as if it were my own. Helplessly, I started to weep and then to cry openly. I lost track of what Mary was singing, though her voice went on and on. Until finally she sang:

Dig the grave both wide and deep
Sick I am, and fain would sleep
Dig the grave and make it ready
Lay me on my true Love's body

and stopped. Leaving a silence that echoed on and on forever.

Then Mary said, "There's someone I think you're ready to meet."

Mary took me to a nondescript cinder-block building, the location of which I will take with me to the grave. She led the way in. I followed nervously. The interior was so dim I stumbled on the threshold. Then my eyes adjusted, and I saw that I was in a bar. Not a pub, which is a warm and welcoming public space where families gather to socialize, the adults over a pint and the kiddies drinking their soft drinks, but a bar—a place where men go to get drunk. It smelled of poteen and stale beer. Somebody had ripped the door to the bog off its hinges and no one had bothered to replace it. Presumably Mary was the only woman to set foot in the place for a long, long time.

There were three or four men sitting at small tables in the gloom, their backs to the door, and a lean man with a bad complexion at the bar. "Here you are then," he said without enthusiasm.

"Don't mind Liam," Mary said to me. Then, to Liam, "Have you anything fit for drinking?"

"No."

"Well, that's not why we came anyway." Mary jerked her head toward me. "Here's the recruit."

"He doesn't look like much."

178 | MICHAEL SWANWICK

"Recruit for what?" I said. It struck me suddenly that Liam was keeping his hands below the bar, out of sight. Down where a hard man will keep a weapon, such as a cudgel or a gun.

"Don't let his American teeth put you off. They're part of the reason we wanted him in the first place."

"So you're a patriot, are you, lad?" Liam said in a voice that indicated he knew good and well that I was not.

"I have no idea what you're talking about."

Liam glanced quickly at Mary and curled his lip in a sneer. "Ahh, he's just in it for the crack." In Irish *craic* means "fun" or "kicks." But the filthy pun was obviously intended. My face hardened and I balled up my fists. Liam didn't look concerned.

"Hush, you!" Mary said. Then, turning to me, "And I'll thank you to control yourself as well. This is serious business. Liam, I'll vouch for the man. Give him the package."

Liam's hands appeared at last. They held something the size of a biscuit tin. It was wrapped in white paper and tied up with string. He slid it across the bar.

"What's this?"

"It's a device," Liam said. "Properly deployed, it can implode the entire administrative complex at Shannon Starport without harming a single civilian."

My flesh ran cold.

"So you want me to plant this in the 'port, do yez?" I said. For the first time in weeks, I became aware of the falseness of my accent. Impulsively, I pulled the neuropendant from beneath my shirt, dropped it on the floor, and stepped on it. Whatever I said here, I would say it as myself. "You want me to go in there and fucking *blow myself up*?"

"No, of course not," Mary said. "We have a soldier in place for that. But he—"

"Or she," Liam amended.

"—or she isn't in a position to smuggle this in. Human employees aren't allowed to bring in so much as a pencil. That's how little the

Outsiders think of us. You, however, can. Just take the device through their machines—it's rigged to read as a box of cigars—in your carry-on. Once you're inside, somebody will come up to you and ask if you remembered to bring something for granny. Hand it over."

"That's all," Liam said.

"You'll be halfway to Jupiter before anything happens."

They both looked at me steadily. "Forget it," I said. "I'm not killing any innocent people for you."

"Not people. Aliens."

"They're still innocent."

"They wouldn't be here if they hadn't seized the planet. So they're not innocent."

"You're a nation of fucking werewolves!" I cried. Thinking that would put an end to the conversation.

But Mary wasn't fazed. "That we are," she agreed. "Day by day, we present our harmless, domestic selves to the world, until one night the beast comes out to feed. But at least we're not sheep, bleating complacently in the face of the butcher's knife. Which are you, my heart's beloved? A sheep? Or could there be a wolf lurking deep within?"

"He can't do the job," Liam said. "He's as weak as watered milk."

"Shut it. You have no idea what you're talking about." Mary fixed me with those amazing eyes of hers, as green as the living heart of Ireland, and I was helpless before them. "It's not weakness that makes you hesitate," she said, "but a foolish and misinformed conscience. I've thought about this far longer than you have, my treasure. I've thought about it all my life. It's a holy and noble thing that I'm asking of you."

"I—"

"Night after night, you've sworn you'd do anything for me—not with words, I'll grant you, but with looks, with murmurs, with your soul. Did you think I could not hear the words you dared not say aloud? Now I'm calling you on all those unspoken promises. Do this one thing—if not for the sake of your planet, then for me."

All the time we'd been talking, the men sitting at their little tables hadn't made a noise. Nor had any of them turned to face us. They simply sat hunched in place—not drinking, not smoking, not speaking. Just listening. It came to me then how large they were, and how still. How alert. It came to me then that if I turned Mary down, I'd not leave this room alive.

So, really, I had no choice.

"I'll do it," I said. "And God damn you for asking me to."

Mary went to hug me and I pushed her roughly away. "No! I'm doing this thing for you, and that puts us quits. I never want to see you or think of you again."

For a long, still moment, Mary studied me calmly. I was lying, for I'd never wanted her so much as I did in that instant. I could see that she knew I was lying, too. If she'd let the least sign of that knowledge show, I believe I would have hit her. But she did not. "Very well," she said. "So long as you keep your word."

She turned and left and I knew I would never see her again.

Liam walked me to the door. "Be careful with the package outside in the rain," he said, handing me an umbrella. "It won't work if you let it get damp."

I was standing in Shannon Starport, when Homeworld Security closed in on me. Two burly men in ITSA uniforms appeared to my either side and their alien superior said, "Would you please come with us, sir." It was not a question.

Oh, Mary, I thought sadly. You have a traitor in your organization. Other than me, I meant. "Can I bring my bag?"

"We'll see to that, sir."

I was taken to their interrogation room.

Five hours later I got onto the lighter. They couldn't hold me because there wasn't anything illegal in my possession. I'd soaked the package Liam gave me in the hotel room sink overnight and then gotten up early and booted it down a storm drain when no one was looking. It was a quick trip to orbit where there waited a ship larger than a skyscraper and rarer than almost anything you could name, for it wouldn't return to this planet for centuries. I floated on board knowing that for me there'd be no turning back. Earth would be a story I told my children, and a pack of sentimental lies they would tell theirs.

My homeworld shrank behind me and disappeared. I looked out the great black glass walls into a universe thronged with stars and galaxies and had no idea where I was or where I thought I was going. It seemed to me then that we were each and every one of us ships without a harbor, sailors lost on land.

I used to say that only Ireland and my family could make me cry. I cried when my mother died and I cried when Dad had his heart attack the very next year. My baby sister failed to survive the same birth that killed my mother, so some of my tears were for her as well. Then my brother Bill was hit by a drunk driver and I cried and that was the end of my family. Now there's only Ireland.

But that's enough.

Libertarian Russia

Miles and weeks passed under the wheels of Victor's motorcycle. Sometime during the day he would stop at a peasant farmstead and buy food to cook over a campfire for supper. At night he slept under the stars with old cowboy movies playing in his head. In no particular hurry he wove through the Urals on twisting backcountry roads, and somewhere along the way crossed over the border out of Europe and into Asia. He made a wide detour around Yekaterinburg, where the density of population brought government interference in the private lives of its citizens up almost to Moscow levels, and then cut back again to regain the laughably primitive transcontinental highway. He was passing through the drab ruins of an industrial district at the edge of the city when a woman in thigh-high boots raised her hand to hail him, the way they did out here in the sticks where every driver was a potential taxi to be bought for small change.

Ordinarily, Victor wouldn't have stopped. But in addition to the boots the woman wore leopard-print hot pants and a fashionably puffy red jacket, tight about the waist and broad at the shoulders, which opened to reveal the tops of her breasts, like two pomegranates proffered on a plate. A vinyl backpack crouched on the ground by her feet. She looked like she'd just stepped down from a billboard. She looked like serious trouble.

It had been a long time since he'd had any serious trouble. Victor pulled to a stop.

"Going east?" the woman said.

"Yeah."

She glanced down at the scattering of pins on his kevleather jacket—politicians who never got elected, causes that were never won—and her crimson lips quirked in the smallest of smiles. "Libertarianski, eh? You do realize that there's no such thing as a libertarian Russian? It's like a gentle tiger or an honest cop—a contradiction in terms."

Victor shrugged. "And yet, here I am."

"So you think." Suddenly all business, the woman said, "I'll blow you if you take me with you."

For a second Victor's mind went blank. Then he said, "Actually, I might be going a long way. Across Siberia. I might not stop until I reach the Pacific."

"Okay, then. Once a day, so long as I'm with you. Deal?"

"Deal."

Victor reconfigured the back of his bike to give it a pillion and an extra rack for her backpack and fattened the tires to compensate for her weight. She climbed on behind him, and off they went.

At sunset, they stopped and made camp in a scrub pine forest, behind the ruins of a Government Auto Inspection station. After they'd set up their poptents (hers was the size of her fist when she took it from her knapsack but assembled itself into something almost palatial; his was no larger than he needed) and built the cookfire, she paid him for the day's ride. Then, as he cut up the chicken he'd bought earlier, they talked.

"You never told me your name," Victor said.

"Svetlana."

"Just Svetlana?"

"Yes."

"No patronymic?"

"No. Just Svetlana. And you?"

"Victor Pelevin."

Svetlana laughed derisively. "Oh, come on!"

"He's my grandfather," Victor explained. Then, when the scorn failed to leave her face, "Well, spiritually, anyway. I've read all his books I don't know how many times. They shaped me."

"I prefer *The Master and Margarita*. Not the book, of course. The video. But I can't say it shaped me. So, let me guess. You're on the great Russian road trip. Looking to find the real Russia, old Russia, Mother Russia, the Russia of the heart. Eh?"

"Not me. I've already found what I'm looking for—Libertarian Russia. Right here, where we are." Victor finished with the chicken, and began cutting up the vegetables. It would take a while for the fire to die down to coals, but when it was ready, he'd roast the vegetables and chicken together on spits, shish-kebab style.

"Now that you've found it, what are you going to do with it?"

"Nothing. Wander around. Live here. Whatever." He began assembling the kebabs. "You see, after the Depopulation, there just weren't the resources anymore for the government to police the largest country in the world with the sort of control they were used to. So instead of easing up on the people, they decided to concentrate their power in a handful of industrial and mercantile centers, port cities, and the like. The rest, with a total population of maybe one or two people per ten square kilometers, they cut loose. Nobody talks about it, but there's no law out here except what people agree upon. They've got to settle their differences among themselves. When you've got enough people to make up a town, they might pool their money to hire a part-time cop or two. But no databases, no spies . . . you can do what you like, and so long as you don't infringe upon somebody else's freedoms, they'll leave you alone."

Everything Victor said was more or less cut-and-paste from "Free Ivan," an orphan website he'd stumbled on five years ago. In libertarian circles, Free Ivan was a legend. Victor liked to think he was out somewhere in Siberia, living the life he'd preached. But since his last entry was posted from St. Petersburg and mentioned no such plans, most likely he was dead. That was what happened to people who dared imagine a world without tyranny.

"What if somebody else's idea of freedom involves taking your motorcycle from you?"

Victor got up and patted the contact plate on his machine. "The lock is coded to my genome. The bike won't start for anybody else. Anyway, I have a gun." He showed it, then put it back in his shoulder harness.

"Somebody could take that thing away from you and shoot you, you know."

"No, they couldn't. It's a smart gun. It's like my bike—it answers to nobody but me."

Unexpectedly, Svetlana laughed. "I give up! You've got all the angles covered."

Yet Victor doubted he had convinced her of anything. "We have the technology to make us free," he said sullenly. "Why not use it? You ought to get a gun yourself."

"Trust me, my body is all the weapon I need."

There didn't seem to be any answer for that, so Victor said, "Tell me about yourself. Who are you, why are you on the road, where are you heading?"

"I'm a whore," she said. "I got tired of working for others, but Yekaterinburg was too corrupt for me to set up a house of my own there. So I'm looking for someplace large enough to do business in, where the police will settle for a reasonable cut of the take."

"You . . . mean all that literally, don't you?"

Svetlana reached into her purse and took out a card case. She squirted him her rate sheet, and put the case away again. "If you see anything there you like, I'm open for business."

The fire was ready now, so Victor put on the kebabs.

"How much do I pay for dinner?" Svetlana opened her purse again.

"It's my treat."

"No," she said. "I don't accept anything for free. Everybody pays for everything. That's my philosophy."

Before he went to his poptent, Victor disassembled part of his bike and filled the digester tank with water and grass. Then he set it to gently rocking. Enzymes and yeasts were automatically fed into the mixture—and by morning, there would be enough alcohol for another day's travel. He went into the tent and lay on his back, playing a John Wayne movie in his mind. *The Searchers.* But after a while he could not help pausing the movie, to call up Svetlana's rate sheet.

She offered a surprisingly broad range of services.

He brooded for a long while before finally falling asleep.

That night he had an eidetic dream. Possibly his memorandum recorder had been jostled a month earlier and some glitch caused it to replay now. At any rate, he was back in Moscow and he was leaving forever.

He hit the road at dawn, rush hour traffic heavy around him and the sun a golden dazzle in the smog. American jazz saxophone played in his head, smooth and cool. Charlie Parker. He hunched low over his motorcycle and when a traffic cop gestured him to the shoulder with a languid wave of his white baton for a random ID check, Victor popped a wheelie and flipped him the finger. Then he opened up the throttle and slalomed away, back and forth across four lanes of madly honking traffic.

In the rearview mirror, he saw the cop glaring after him, taking a mental snapshot of his license plate. If he ever returned to Moscow, he'd be in a world of trouble. Every cop in the city—and Moscow had more flavors of cops than anywhere—would have his number and a good idea of what he looked like.

Fuck that noise. Fuck it right up the ass. Victor had spent years grubbing for money, living cheap, saving every kopek he could to buy the gear he needed to get the hell out of Moscow. Why would he ever come back?

Then he was outside the city, the roads getting briefly better as they passed between the gated communities where the rich huddled fearfully inside well-guarded architectural fantasies and then dwindling to neglect and disrepair before finally turning to dirt. That was when, laughing wildly, he tore off his helmet and flung it away, into the air, into the weeds, into the past. . . .

He was home now. He was free.

He was in Libertarian Russia.

Victor liked the idea of biking across Asia in the company of a whore a great deal in theory. But the reality was more problematic. With her thighs to either side of his and her arms about him as they rode, he could not keep from thinking constantly about her body. Yet he lacked the money for what he'd have liked to do with her. And her daily payment provided only temporary relief. After three days, he was looking for someplace he could ditch Svetlana with a clean conscience.

Sometime around noon, they passed through a small town which had clearly been a medium-sized city before the Depopulation. Just beyond it, two trucks and three cars were parked in front of a cinder-block restaurant. One of the cars was a Mercedes. Opportunities to eat in a restaurant being rare along the disintegrating remains of what was grandiosely called the Trans-Siberian Highway, Victor pulled over his bike and they went inside.

There were only six tables and they were all empty. The walls were painted black and decorated with loops of antique light-pipes dug out of trunks found in the attics of houses that nobody lived in anymore. At the back of the room was a bar. Above it, painted in white block letters, were the words: WE KNOW NO MERCY AND DO NOT ASK FOR ANY.

"Shit," Victor said.

"What is it?" Svetlana asked.

"That's the slogan for OMON—the Special Forces Police Squad. Let's get the fuck out of here."

A large man emerged from a back room, drying his hands with a towel. "What can I do for. . . ?" He stopped and looked thoughtful, the way one did when accessing an external database. Then a nasty grin split his face. "Osip! Kolzak! Come see what the wind blew in!"

Two more men came out from the back, one bigger than the first, the other smaller. All three looked like they were spoiling for a fight. "She's a whore. He's just a little shit with subversive political connections. Nobody important. What do you want to do with them?"

"Fuck them both," the big man said.

"One is all you'll need," Svetlana said in a sultry voice. "Provided that one is me." She got out her card case and squirted them her rate sheet.

There was a brief astonished silence. Then one of the men said, "You are one fucking filthy cunt."

"You can talk as dirty as you like—I won't charge you extra."

"Coming in here was the stupidest thing you ever did," the small man said. "Grab her, Pavel."

The middle-sized man moved toward Svetlana.

Chest tight with fear, Victor pulled out his gun and stepped into Pavel's path. This was his moment of truth. His Alamo. "We're leaving now," he said, fighting to keep his voice firm. "If you know what's good for you, you won't try to stop us."

Disconcertingly, all three thugs looked amused. Pavel stepped forward, so that the gun poked him in the chest. "You think that protects you? Try shooting it. Shoot me now."

"Don't think I won't."

"You can't stop somebody if you're not willing to kill him." The man closed both his hands around the gun. Then he viciously mashed Victor's finger back against the trigger.

Nothing happened.

Pavel took the gun away from Victor. "You don't think the government has better technology than you? Every non-military gun in the country is bluetoothed at the factory." Over his shoulder he said, "What do you want me to do with the whore, Osip?"

Svetlana shuddered, as if in the throes of great terror. But she smiled seductively. "I don't normally do it for free," she said. "But I could make an exception for you boys."

"Take her out to the gravel pit," the small man said, "and shoot her."

Pavel grabbed Svetlana by the wrist. "What about the punk?"

"Let me think about that."

Svetlana didn't make a sound as she was dragged out the front.

The big man pushed Victor down onto a chair. "Sit quietly," he said. "If you try anything . . . Well, I don't think you'll try anything." Then he got out a combat knife and amused himself by plucking Victor's pins from his jacket with it and reading them, one by one, before flicking them away, over his shoulder. "A Citizen Without a Gun Is a Slave," he read. "Legalize Freedom: Vote Libertarian. Anarchists Unite—that doesn't even make sense!"

"It's a joke."

"Then why isn't it funny?"

"I don't know."

"So it's not much of a joke, is it?"

"I guess not."

"The weakness in your political philosophy," Osip said out of nowhere, "is that you assume that when absolute freedom is extended to everybody, they'll all think only of their own selfish interests. You forget that patriots exist, men who are willing to sacrifice themselves for the good of the Motherland."

Figuring he had nothing to lose at this point, Victor said, "Taking money to do the government's dirty work doesn't make you a patriot."

"You think we're getting *paid* for what we do? Listen. After I left OMON, I was sick of cities, crime, pollution. So I went looking for a place where I could go fishing or hunting whenever I wanted. I found this building abandoned, and started fixing it up. Pavel stopped to ask what I was doing and since he'd been in the Special Police too, I invited him to come in as a partner. When the restaurant was up and running, Kolzak dropped in and when we found out he was one of us, we offered him a job. Because we are all brothers, you see, answerable to nobody but God and each other. Pavel brought a satellite uplink with him, so we know the police record of everyone who comes by. We cleanse the land of antisocial elements like your whore because it's the right thing to do. That's all."

"And you," Kolzak said. "Don't think her body's going into the gravel pit alone."

"Please. There has to be some way of convincing you that this isn't necessary."

"Sure there is. Just tell me one thing that you can give me in exchange for your life that I can't take off of your corpse."

Victor was silent.

"You see?" Osip said. "Kolzak has taught you something. If you don't even have enough to bribe a man into letting you live, you're pretty much worthless, aren't you?"

Kolzak took out his combat knife and stuck it into the bar. Then he walked away from it. "You're closer, now," he said. "If you want to make a try for it, go right ahead."

"You wouldn't do that if you thought I had a chance."

"Who are you to say I wouldn't? Fuck you in the mouth! You're just a turd of a faggot who's afraid to fight."

It would be suicide to respond to that. It would be cowardly to look away. So Victor just stared back, not blinking. After a time, the big man's jaw tightened. Victor tensed. He was going to have to fight after all! He didn't think it was going to end well.

"Listen to that," Osip said suddenly.

"I don't hear anything," Kolzak said

"That's right. You don't. What's keeping Pavel?"

"I'll go check."

Kolzak turned his back on the knife and went outside. Victor almost started after him. But Osip held up a warning hand. "There's nothing you can do about it." He smiled humorlessly. "There's your libertarianism for you. You are absolutely free of the government. Only you forgot that the government also protects you from men like us. Am I wrong?"

Victor cleared his throat. It felt like swallowing gravel. "No. No, you're not."

The little man stared at him impassively for a moment. Then he jerked his head toward the door. "You're nothing. If you get on your bike and leave now, I promise you that nobody will come after you."

Victor's heart was racing. "This is another game, isn't it? Like the knife."

"No, I mean it. Quite frankly, you're not worth the effort."

"But Svetlana—"

"She's a whore. She gets what whores get. Now make up your mind. Are you leaving or not?"

To his horror, Victor realized that he was already standing. His body trembled with the desire to be gone. "I—"

A gargled cry came from outside, too deep and loud to have come from a woman's throat. Instantly Osip was on his feet. He yanked the combat knife from the bar.

Svetlana walked into the room, her clothes glistening with blood. She was grinning like a madwoman. "That's two. You're next."

The little man lunged. "You dog-sucking—"

In a blur, Svetlana stepped around Osip's outstretched arm, plucking the knife from his hand. Blood sprayed from his neck. The knife was suddenly sticking out of his ribs. She seized his head and twisted.

There was a snapping noise and Svetlana let the body fall.

Then she began to cry.

Awkwardly, Victor put his arms around Svetlana. She grabbed his shirt with both her hands and buried her face in it.

He made soothing noises and patted her back.

It took a while, but at last her tears wound down. Victor offered her his handkerchief and she wiped her eyes and blew her nose with it. He knew he shouldn't ask yet, but he couldn't help it. "How the hell did you do that?"

In a voice as calm and steady as if she hadn't cried since she was a child, Svetlana said, "I told you my body was all I needed. I went to a chop shop and had it weaponized to combat standards before leaving Yekaterinburg. It takes a few minutes to power up, though, so I had to let that bastard drag me away. But that also meant that these three couldn't boot up their own enhancements in time to stop me. Where's that flask of yours? I need a drink."

Victor recalled that she had shuddered just before being taken outside. That would be—or so he presumed—when she had powered up. Svetlana upended the flask and gulped down half of it in three swallows.

"Hey!" Victor made a grab for the flask, but she straight-armed him and drank it dry. Then she handed it back.

"Ahhhhh." Svetlana belched. "Sorry. You have no idea how much that depletes your physical resources. Alcohol's a fast way to replenish them."

"That stuff's one hundred-proof. You could injure yourself drinking like that."

"Not when I'm in refueling mode. Be a dear, would you, and see if there's any water around here? I need to clean up."

Victor went outside and walked around the restaurant. In the back he found a hand-pump and a bucket. He filled the bucket and lugged it around front.

Svetlana was just emerging from the building. She had three wallets in her hand, which she put down on the hood of a battered old Volga Siber. Then she stripped away the blood-slick clothes and sluiced herself off with the water. "Bring me a change of clothing and a bar of soap, okay?" Victor tore his eyes away from her naked body and did as she asked. He also brought her a towel from his own kit.

When Svetlana was dried and dressed again, she emptied the wallets of their money and ignition cards. She counted out the rubles in two equal piles, stuffed one in her backpack, and said, "The other half is yours if you want it." She held up an ignition card. "We part ways here. I'm taking the Mercedes. That, and the money, just about balance the books."

"Balance the books?"

"I told you. Everybody pays for everything. Which reminds me." She counted out several bills and stuck them in Victor's shirt pocket. "I owe you for half a day's ride. So here's half of what I would charge for oral sex, and a little bit more for the alcohol."

"Svetlana, I . . . The one guy said he'd let me go. I was going to take him up on it. I was going to leave you here."

"And you feel guilty about this? It's what I would have done in your place."

Victor laughed in astonishment. "I was wrong all along—*I'm* not the libertarian here, *you* are!"

Unexpectedly, Svetlana gave him a peck on the cheek. "You're very sweet," she said. "I hope you find whatever it is you're looking for." Then she got into the Mercedes and drove away.

For a long time Victor stared after her. Then he considered the money, still sitting in a stack on the Siber's hood.

Svetlana was right. Libertarianism was nothing more than a fantasy and Libertarian Russia was the biggest fantasy of all. It was laughable, impossible, and in all this great, sprawling, contradictory nation, only he had ever really believed in it.

He turned his back on the money. It was an incredibly stupid thing to do, and one he knew he would regret a thousand times in the days to come. But he couldn't resist. Maybe he was a lousy libertarian. But he was still a Russian. He understood the value of a good gesture.

A light breeze came up and blew the rubles off the car and into the empty road. Victor climbed into the saddle. He kick-started his bike, and mentally thumbed through his collection of country-western music. But none of it seemed right for the occasion. So he put on Vladimir Visotsky's "Skittish Horses." It was a song that understood him. It was a song to disappear into Siberia to.

Then Victor rode off. He could feel the money blowing down the street behind him, like autumn leaves.

He was very careful not to look back.

Tawny Petticoats

The independent port city and (some said) pirate haven of New Orleans was home to many a strange sight. It was a place where sea serpents hauled ships past fields worked by zombie laborers to docks where cargo was loaded onto wooden wagons to be pulled through streets of crushed oyster shells by teams of pygmy mastodons as small as Percheron horses. So none thought it particularly noteworthy when for three days an endless line of young women waited in the hallway outside a luxury suite in the Maison Fema for the opportunity to raise their skirts or open their blouses to display a tattooed thigh, breast, or buttock to two judges who sat on twin chairs watching solemnly, asked a few questions, thanked them for their time, and then showed them out.

The women had come in response to a handbill, posted throughout several parishes, that read:

> SEEKING AN HEIRESS
> ARE YOU . . .
> A YOUNG WOMAN BETWEEN THE AGES OF 18 AND 21?
> FATHERLESS?
> TATTOOED FROM BIRTH ON AN INTIMATE PART OF YOUR BODY?
> IF SO, YOU MAY BE ENTITLED TO GREAT RICHES
> INQUIRE DAYTIMES, SUITE 1, MAISON FEMA

"You'd think I'd be tired of this by now," Darger commented during a brief break in the ritual. "And yet I am not."

"The infinite variety of ways in which women can be beautiful is indeed amazing," Surplus agreed. "As is the eagerness of so many to display that beauty." He opened the door. "Next."

A woman strode into the room, trailing smoke from a cheroot. She was dauntingly tall—six feet and a hand, if an inch—and her dress, trimmed with silver lace, was the same shade of golden brown as her skin. Surplus indicated a crystal ashtray on the sideboard and, with a gracious nod of thanks, she stubbed out her cigar.

"Your name?" Darger said after Surplus had regained his chair.

"My real name, you mean, or my stage name?"

"Why, whichever you please."

"I'll give you the real one then." The young woman doffed her hat and tugged off her gloves. She laid them neatly together on the sideboard. "It's Tawnymoor Petticoats. You can call me Tawny."

"Tell us something about yourself, Tawny," Surplus said.

"I was born a carny and worked forty-milers all my life," Tawny said, unbuttoning her blouse. "Most recently, I was in the sideshow as the Sleeping Beauty Made Immortal By Utopian Technology But Doomed Never To Awaken. I lay in a glass coffin covered by nothing but my own hair and a strategically placed hand, while the audience tried to figure out if I was alive or not. I've got good breath control." She folded the blouse and set it down by her gloves and hat. "Jake—my husband—was the barker. He'd size up the audience and when he saw a ripe mark, catch 'im on the way out and whisper that for a couple of banknotes it could be arranged to spend some private time with me. Then he'd go out back and peer in through a slit in the canvas."

Tawny stepped out of her skirt and set it atop the blouse. She began unlacing her petticoats. "When the mark had his trousers off and was about to climb in the coffin, Jake would come roaring out, bellowing that he was only supposed to look—not to take advantage of my vulnerable condition." Placing her underthings atop the skirt, she undid her garters and proceeded to roll down her stockings. "That was usually good for the contents of his wallet."

"You were working the badger game, you mean?" Surplus asked cautiously.

"Mostly, I just lay there. But I was ready to rear up and coldcock the sumbidge if he got out of hand. And we worked other scams too. The pigeon drop, the fiddle game, the rip deal, you name it."

Totally naked now, the young woman lifted her great masses of black curls with both hands, exposing the back of her neck. "Then one night the mark was halfway into the coffin—and no Jake. So I opened my eyes real sudden and screamed in the bastard's face. Over he went, hit his head on the floor, and I didn't wait to find out if he was unconscious or dead. I stole his jacket and went looking for my husband. Turns out Jake had run off with the Snake Woman. She dumped him two weeks later and he wanted me to take him back, but I wasn't having none of that." She turned around slowly, so that Darger and Surplus could examine every inch of her undeniably admirable flesh.

Darger cleared his throat. "Um . . . you don't appear to have a tattoo."

"Yeah, I saw through that one right away. Talked to some of the girls you'd interviewed and they said you'd asked them lots of questions about themselves but hadn't molested them in any way. Not all of 'em were happy with that last bit. Particularly after they'd gone to all the trouble of getting themselves inked. So, putting two and four together, I figured you were running a scam requiring a female partner with quick wits and larcenous proclivities."

Tawny Petticoats put her hands on her hips and smiled. "Well? Do I get the job?"

Grinning like a dog—which was not surprising, for his source genome was entirely canine—Surplus stood, extending a paw. But

Darger quickly got between him and the young woman, saying, "If you will pardon us for just a moment, Ms. Petticoats, my friend and I must consult in the back room. You may use the time to dress yourself."

When the two males were secluded, Darger whispered furiously, "Thank God I was able to stop you! You were about to enlist that young woman into our conspiracy."

"Well, and why not?" Surplus murmured equally quietly. "We were looking for a woman of striking appearance, not overly bound to conventional morality, and possessed of the self-confidence, initiative, and inventiveness a good swindler requires. Tawny comes up aces on all counts."

"Working with an amateur is one thing—but this woman is a professional. She will sleep with both of us, turn us against each other, and in the end abscond with the swag, leaving us with nothing but embarrassment and regret for all our efforts."

"That is a sexist and, if I may dare say so, ungallant slander upon the fair sex, and I am astonished to hear it coming from your mouth."

Darger shook his head sadly. "It is not all women but all female confidence tricksters I abjure. I speak from sad—and repeated—experience."

"Well, if you insist on doing without this blameless young creature," Surplus said, folding his arms, "then I insist on your doing without me."

"My dear sir!"

"I must be true to my principles."

Further argumentation, Darger saw, would be useless. So, putting the best possible appearance on things, he emerged from the back room to say, "You have the job, my dear." From a jacket pocket he produced a silver filigreed vinaigrette and, unscrewing its cap, extracted from it a single pill. "Swallow this and you'll have the tattoo we require by morning. You'll want to run it past your pharmacist first, of course, to verify—"

"Oh, I trust you. If y'all had just been after tail, you wouldn't've waited for me. Some of those gals was sharp lookers for sure." Tawny swallowed the pill. "So what's the dodge?"

"We're going to work the black money scam," Surplus said.

"Oh, I have always wanted a shot at running that one!" With a whoop, Tawny threw her arms about them both.

Though his fingers itched to do so, Darger was very careful not to check to see if his wallet was still there.

The next day, ten crates of black money—actually, rectangles of scrap parchment dyed black in distant Vicksburg—were carried into the hotel by zombie laborers and then, at Surplus's direction, piled against the outside of Tawny's door so that, hers being the central room of the suite, the only way to enter or leave it was through his or Darger's rooms. Then, leaving the lady to see to her dress and makeup, her new partners set out to speak to their respective marks.

Darger began at the city's busy docklands.

The office of the speculator Jean-Nagin Lafitte were tastefully opulent and dominated by a *Mauisaurus* skull, decorated with scrimshaw filigree chased in silver. "Duke" Lafitte, as he styled himself, or "Pirate" Lafitte, as he was universally known, was a slim, handsome man with olive skin, long and flowing hair, and a mustache so thin it might have been drawn on with an eyebrow pencil. Where other men of wealth might carry a cane, he affected a coiled whip, which he wore on his belt.

"Renting an ingot of silver!" he exclaimed. "I never heard of such a thing."

"It is a simple enough proposition," Darger said. "Silver serves as a catalyst for a certain bioindustrial process, the precise nature of which I am not at liberty to divulge to you. The scheme involves converting bar silver to a colloidal slurry which, when the process is complete, will be recovered and melted back into bar form. You would lose nothing. Further, we will only tie up your wealth for, oh, let us say ten days to be on the safe side. In return for which we are prepared to offer you a ten percent return on your investment. A very tidy profit for no risk at all."

A small and ruthless smile played upon the speculator's lips. "There is the risk of your simply taking the silver and absconding with it."

"That is an outrageous implication, and from a man I respected less highly than I do you, I would not put up with it. However"—Darger gestured out the window at the busy warehouses and transshipment buildings—"I understand that you own half of everything we see. Lend my consortium a building in which to perform our operation and then place as many guards as you like around that building. We will bring in our apparatus and you will bring in the silver. Deal?"

For a brief moment, Pirate Lafitte hesitated. Then, "Done!" he snapped, and offered his hand. "For fifteen percent. Plus rental of the building."

They shook, and Darger said, "You will have no objection to having the ingot tested by a reputable assayist."

In the French Quarter, meanwhile, Surplus was having an almost identical conversation with a slight and acerbic woman, clad in a severe black dress, who was not only the mayor of New Orleans but also the proprietress of its largest and most notorious brothel. Behind her, alert and unspeaking, stood two uniformed ape-men from the Canadian Northwest, both with the expressions of baffled anger common to beasts that have been elevated almost but not quite to human intelligence. "An assayist?" she demanded. "Is my word not good enough for you? And if it is not, should we be doing business at all?"

"The answer to all three of your questions, Madam-Mayor Tresjolie, is yes," Surplus said amiably. "The assay is for your own protection. As you doubtless know, silver is routinely adulterated with other metals. When we are done with the silver, the slurry will be melted down and recast into an ingot. Certainly, you will want to know that the bar returned to you is of equal worth to the bar you rented out."

"Hmmm." They were sitting in the lobby of the madam-mayor's *maison de tolérance*, she in a flaring wicker chair whose similarity to a throne could not possibly be unintentional, and Surplus on a wooden folding chair facing her. Because it was still early afternoon, the facility was not open for business. But messengers and government flunkies came and went. Now one such whispered in Madam-Mayor Tresjolie's ear. She waved him away. "Seventeen-and-a-half percent, take it or leave it."

"I'll take it."

"Good," Tresjolie said. "I have business with the zombie master now. Move your chair alongside mine, and stay to watch. If we are to do business, you will find this salubrious."

A round and cheerful man entered the public room, followed by half a dozen zombies. Surplus studied these with interest. Though their eyes were dull, their faces were stiff, and there was an unhealthy sheen to their skin, they looked in no way like the rotting corpses of Utopian legend. Rather, they looked like day laborers who had been worked into a state of complete exhaustion. Which doubtless was the case.

"Good morning!" said the jolly man, rubbing his hands briskly together. "I have brought this week's coffle of debtors who, having served their time, are now eligible for forgiveness and manumission."

"I had wondered at the source of your involuntary labor force," Surplus said. "They are unfortunates who fell into arrears, then?"

"Exactly so," said the zombie master. "New Orleans does not engage in the barbarous and expensive practice of funding debtors' prisons. Instead, debt-criminals are chemically rendered incapable of independent thought and put to work until they have paid off their debt to society. Which today's happy fellows have done." With a roguish wink, he added, "You may want to keep this in mind before running up too great a line of credit at the rooms upstairs. Are you ready to begin, Madam-Mayor Tresjolie?"

"You may proceed, Master Bones."

Master Bones gestured imperiously and the first zombie shuffled forward. "Through profligacy you fell into debt," he said, "and through honest labor you have earned your way out. Open your mouth."

The pallid creature obeyed. Master Bones produced a spoon and dipped into a salt cellar on a nearby table. He dumped the salt into the man's mouth. "Now swallow."

By gradual degrees, a remarkable transformation came over the man. He straightened and looked about him with tentative alertness. "I . . ." he said. "I remember now. Is my . . . is my wife. . . ?"

"Silence," the zombie master said. "The ceremony is not yet complete." The Canadian guardsmen had shifted position to defend their mistress, should the disoriented ex-zombie attack her.

"You are hereby declared a free citizen of New Orleans again, and indebted to no man," Tresjolie said solemnly. "Go and overspend no more." She extended a leg and lifted her skirts above her ankle. "You may now kiss my foot."

"So did you ask Tresjolie for a line of credit at her sporting house?" Tawny asked when Surplus reported his adventure to his confederates.

"Certainly not!" Surplus exclaimed. "I told her instead that it has always been my ambition to own a small but select private brothel, one dedicated solely to my own personal use. A harem, if you will, but one peopled by a rotating staff of well-paid employees. I suggested I might shortly be in a position to commission her to find an appropriate hotel and create such an institution for me."

"What did she say?"

"She told me that she doubted I was aware of exactly how expensive such an operation would be."

"And you said to her?

"That I didn't think money would be problem," Surplus said airily. "Because I expected to come into a great deal of it very soon."

Tawny crowed with delight. "Oh, you boys are such fun!"

"In unrelated news," Darger said, "your new dress has come."

"I saw it when it first arrived." Tawny made a face. "It is not calculated to show off my body to its best advantage—or to any advantage at all, come to that."

"It is indeed aggressively modest," Darger agreed. "However, your character is demure and inexperienced. To her innocent eyes, New Orleans is a terribly wicked place, indeed a cesspool of carnality and related sins. Therefore, she needs to be protected at all times by unrevealing apparel and stalwart men of the highest moral character."

"Further," Surplus amplified, "she is the weak point in our plans, for whoever has possession of her tattoo and knows its meaning can dispense with us entirely by kidnapping her off the street."

"Oh!" Tawny said in a small voice, clearly intended to arouse the protective instincts of any man nearby.

Surplus took an instinctive step toward her, and then caught himself. He grinned like the carnivore he was. "You'll do."

The third meeting with a potential investor took place that evening in a dimly lit club in a rundown parish on the fringe of the French Quarter—for the entertainment was, in the public mind, far too louche for even that notoriously open-minded neighborhood. Pallid waitresses moved lifelessly between the small tables, taking orders and delivering drinks while a small brass-and-drums jazz ensemble played appropriately sleazy music to accompany the stage show.

"I see that you are no aficionado of live sex displays," the zombie master Jeremy Bones said. The light from the candle votive on the table made the beads of sweat on his face shine like luminous drops of rain.

"The artistic success of such displays depends entirely on the degree to which they agree with one's own sexual proclivities," Darger replied. "I confess that mine lie elsewhere. But never mind that. Returning to the subject at hand: The terms are agreeable to you, then?"

"They are. I am unclear, however, as to why you insist the assay be performed at the Bank of San Francisco, when New Orleans has several fine financial institutions of its own."

"All of which are owned in part by you, Madam-Mayor Tresjolie, and Duke Lafitte."

"Pirate Lafitte, you mean. An assay is an assay and a bank is a bank. Why should it matter to you which one is employed?"

"Earlier today, you brought six zombies to the mayor to be freed. Assuming this is a typical week, that would be roughly three hundred zombies per year. Yet all the menial work in the city has been handed over to zombies and there still remain tens of thousands at work in the plantations that line the river."

"Many of those who fall into debt draw multiyear sentences."

"I asked around, and discovered that Lafitte's ships import some two hundred prisoners a week from municipalities and territories all the way up the Mississippi to St. Louis."

A small smile played on the fat man's face. "It is true that many government bodies find it cheaper to pay us to deal with their trouble-makers than to build prisons for them."

"Madam-Mayor Tresjolie condemns these unfortunates into the city's penal system, you pay her by body count, and after they have been zombified you lease them out for menial labor at prices that employers find irresistible. Those who enter your service rarely leave it."

"If a government official or family member presents me with papers proving that somebody's debt to society has been paid off, I am invariably happy to free them. I grant you that few ever come to me with such documentation. But I am always available to those who do. Exactly what is your objection to this arrangement?"

"Objection?" Darger said in surprise. "I have no objection. This is your system and as an outsider I have no say in it. I am merely explaining the reason why I wished to use an independent bank for the assay."

"Which is?"

"Simply that, happy though I am to deal with you three individually, collectively I find you far too shrewd." Darger turned to stare at the stage, where naked zombies coupled joylessly. Near the front, a spectator removed several banknotes from his wallet and tapped them meaningfully on his table. One of the lifeless waitresses picked up the money and led him through a curtain at the back of the room. "Acting together, I suspect you would swallow me and my partners in a single gulp."

"Oh, there is no fear of that," Master Bones said. "We three only act collectively when there is serious profit in the offing. Your little enterprise—whatever it is—hardly qualifies."

"I am relieved to hear it."

The next day, the three conspirators made three distinct trips to the Assay Office at the New Orleans branch of the Bank of San Francisco. On the first trip, one of Madam-Mayor Tresjolie's green-jacketed zombie bodyguards opened a lockbox, withdrew a silver ingot, and placed it on the workbench. Then, to the astonishment of both the mayor and the assayist, Surplus directed his own hired zombies to hoist several heavy leather bags to the bench as well, and with the aid of his colleagues began pulling out drills, scales, acids, reagents, and other tools and supplies and setting them in working order.

The affronted assayist opened his mouth to object, but—"I'm sure you won't mind if we provide our own equipment," Darger said suavely. "We are strangers here, and while nobody questions the probity of San Francisco's most prestigious financial concern, it is only good business to take proper precautions."

As he was talking, Tawny and Surplus both reached for the scales at once, collided, and almost sent them flying. Faces turned and hands reached out to catch them. But, in the fact, it was Surplus who saved the apparatus from disaster.

"Oops," Tawny said, coloring prettily.

Swiftly, the assayist performed his tests. At their conclusion, he looked up from the ingot. "The finding is .925," he said. "Sterling standard."

With an absent nod, Madam-Mayor Tresjolie acknowledged his judgment. Then she said, "The girl. How much do you want for her?"

As one, Darger and Surplus turned. Then they subtly shifted position so that one stood to either side of Tawny. "Ms. Petticoats is our ward," Darger said, "and therefore, it goes without saying, not for sale. Also, yours is not an entirely reputable business for so innocent a child as she."

"Innocence is in high demand at my establishment. I'll give you the silver ingot. To keep. Do with it as you wish."

"Believe me, madam. In not so very long, I shall consider silver ingots to be so much petty cash."

Master Bones watched the assay, including even the chaotic assembly of the trio's equipment, with a beatific smile. Yet all the while, his attention kept straying to Tawny. Finally, he pursed his lips and said, "There might be a place in my club for your young friend. If you'd consider leasing her to me for, oh, let's say a year, I'd gladly forego my twenty percent profit on this deal." Turning to Tawny, he said, "Do not worry, my sweet. Under the influence of the zombie drugs you will feel nothing, and afterwards you will remember nothing. It will be as if none of it ever happened. Further, since you'd be paid a commission on each commercial encounter performed, you'd emerge with a respectable sum being held in trust for you."

Ignoring Tawny's glare of outrage, Darger suavely said, "In strictest confidence, sir, we have already turned down a far better offer for her than yours today. But my partner and I would not part with our dear companion for any amount of money. She is to us a treasure beyond price."

"I'm ready," the assayist said. "Where do you wish me to drill?"

Darger airily waved a finger over the ingot and then, seemingly at random, touched a spot at the exact center of the bar. "Right there."

"I understand that on the street they call me the Pirate," Jean-Nagin Lafitte said with quiet intensity. "This, however, is an insolence I will not tolerate to my face. Yes, I do chance to share a name with the legendary freebooter. But you will find that I have never committed an illegal act in my life."

"Nor do you today, sir!" Darger cried. "This is a strictly legitimate business arrangement."

"So I presume or I would not be here. Nevertheless, you can understand why I must take offense at having you and your clumsy confederates question the quality of my silver."

"Say no more, sir! We are all gentlemen here—save, of course, for Ms. Petticoats, who is a gently reared Christian orphan. If my word is good enough for you, then your word is good enough for me. We may dispose of the assay." Darger coughed discreetly. "However, just for my own legal protection, in the absence of an assay, I shall require a notarized statement from you declaring that you will be satisfied with whatever quality of silver we return to you."

Pirate Lafitte's stare would have melted iron. But it failed to wilt Darger's pleasant smile. At last, he said, "Very well, run the assay."

Negligently, Darger spun a finger in the air. Down it came on the exact center of the bar. "There."

While the assayist was working, Pirate Lafitte said, "I was wondering if your Miss Petticoats might be available to—"

"She is not for sale!" Darger said briskly. "Not for sale, not for rent, not for barter, not available for acquisition on any terms whatsoever. Period."

Looking irritated, Pirate Lafitte said, "I was *going* to ask if she might be interested in going hunting with me tomorrow. There is some interesting game to be found in the bayous."

"Nor is she available for social occasions." Darger turned to the assayist. "Well, sir?"

"Standard sterling," the man said. "Yet again."

"I expected no less."

For the sake of appearances, after the assays were complete, the three swindlers sent the zombies with their lab equipment back to Maison Fema and went out to supper together. Following which, they took a genteel stroll about town. Tawny, who had been confined to her room while negotiations took place, was particularly glad of the latter. But it was with relief that Darger, Surplus, and Tawny saw the heavy bags waiting for them on the sitting room table of their suite. "Who shall do the honors?" Darger asked.

"The lady, of course," Surplus said with a little bow.

Tawny curtsied and then, pushing aside a hidden latch at the bottom of one of the bags, slid out a silver ingot. From another bag, she slid out a second. Then, from a third, a third. A sigh of relief went up from all three conspirators at the sight of the silver glimmering in the lantern-light.

"That was right smartly done, when you changed the fake bars for the real ones," Tawny said.

Darger politely demurred. "No, it was the distraction that made the trick possible, and in this regard you were both exemplary. Even the assayist, who was present all three times you almost sent the equipment to the floor, suspected nothing."

"But tell me something," Tawny said. "Why did you make the substitution before the assay, rather than after? The other way around, you wouldn't have needed to have that little plug of silver in the middle for the sample to be drawn from. Just a silver-plated lead bar."

"We are dealing with suspicious people. This way, they first had the ingots confirmed as genuine and then saw that we came nowhere near them afterwards. The ingots are in a safety deposit box in a reputable bank, so to their minds there is not the least risk. All is on the up-and-up."

"But we're not going to stop here, are we?" Tawny asked anxiously. "I do so want to work the black money scam."

"Have no fear, my lovely," Surplus said, "this is only the beginning. But it serves as a kind of insurance policy for us. Even should the scheme go bad, we have already turned a solid profit." He poured brandy into three small glasses and handed them around. "To whom shall we drink?"

"To Madam-Mayor Tresjolie!" Darger said.

They drank, and then Tawny said, "What do you make of her? Professionally, I mean."

"She is far shrewder than she would have you think," Surplus replied. "But, as you are doubtless aware, the self-consciously shrewd are always the easiest to mislead." He poured a second glass. "To Master Bones!"

They drank. Tawny said, "And of him?"

"He is more problematic," Darger said. "A soft man with a brutal streak underneath his softness. In some ways he hardly seems human."

"Perhaps he has been sampling his own product?" Surplus suggested. "Puffer-fish extract, you mean? No. His mind is active enough. But I catch not the least glimmer of empathy from him. I suspect that he's been associating with zombies so long that he's come to think we're all like them."

The final toast inevitably went to Pirate Lafitte.

"I think he's cute," Tawny said. "Only maybe you don't agree?"

"He is a fraud and a poseur," Darger replied, "a scoundrel who passes himself off as a gentleman, and a manipulator of the legal system who insists he is the most honest of citizens. Consequently, I like him quite a bit. I believe that he is a man we can do business with. Mark my words, when the three of them come to see us tomorrow, it will be at his instigation."

For a time they talked business. Then Surplus broke out a deck of cards. They played euchre and canasta and poker, and because they played for matches, nobody objected when the game turned into a competition to see how deftly the cards could be dealt from the bottom of the deck or flicked out of the sleeve into one's hand. Nor was there any particular outcry when in one memorable hand, eleven aces were laid on the table at once.

At last Darger said, "Look at the time! It will be a long day tomorrow," and they each went to their respective rooms.

That night, as Darger was drifting off to sleep, he heard the door connecting his room with Tawny's quietly open and shut. There was a rustle of sheets as she slipped into his bed. Then the warmth of Tawny's naked body pressed against his own, and her hand closed about his most private part. Abruptly, he was wide awake.

"What on earth do you think you're doing?" he whispered fiercely.

Unexpectedly, Tawny released her hold on Darger and punched him hard in his shoulder. "Oh, it's so easy for you," she retorted, equally quietly. "It's so easy for men! That hideous old woman tried to buy me. That awful little man wanted you to let him drug me. And God only knows what intentions Pirate Lafitte holds. You'll notice they all made their propositions to you. Not a one of them said a word to me." Hot tears fell on Darger's chest. "All my life I have had male protectors—and needed them too. My Daddy, until I ran away. My first husband, until he got eaten by giant crabs. Then various boyfriends and finally that creep Jake."

"You have nothing to worry about. Surplus and I have never abandoned a confederate, nor shall we ever. Our reputation is spotless in this regard."

"I tell myself that, and daytimes I'm fine with it. But at night . . . well, this past week has been the longest I ever went without a man's body to comfort me."

"Yes, but surely you understand—"

Tawny drew herself up. Even in the dim half light of the moon through the window she was a magnificent sight. Then she leaned down to kiss Darger's cheek and murmured into his ear, "I've never had to beg a man before, but . . . Please?"

Darger considered himself a moral man. But there was only so much temptation a man could resist without losing all respect for himself.

The next morning, Darger awoke alone. He thought of the events of last night and smiled. He thought of their implications and scowled. Then he went down to the dining room for breakfast.

"What comes next?" Tawny asked, after they had fortified themselves with chicory coffee, beignets, and sliced baconfruit.

"We have planted suspicions in the minds of our three backers that there is more profit to be had than we are offering to share," Surplus said. "We have given them a glimpse of our mysterious young ward and suggested that she is key to the enterprise. We have presented them with a puzzle to which they can think of no solution. On reflection, they can only conclude that the sole reason we have the upper hand is that we can play them off of one another." He popped the last of his beignet into his mouth. "So sooner or later they will unite and demand of us an explanation."

"In the meantime—" Darger said.

"I know, I know. Back to my dreary old room to play solitaire and read the sort of uplifting literature appropriate to a modest young virgin."

"It's important to stay in character," Surplus said.

"I understand that. Next time, however, please make me something that doesn't need to be stored in the dark, like a sack of potatoes. The niece of a Spanish prisoner, perhaps. Or a socialite heiress. Or even a harlot."

"You are a Woman of Mystery," Darger said. "Which is a time-honored and some would say enviable role to play."

Thus it was that when Darger and Surplus left Maison Fema—at precisely ten o'clock, as they had made it their invariant habit—they were not entirely astonished to find their three benefactors all in a group, waiting for them. A brusque exchange of threats and outrage later, and protesting every step of the way, they led their marks to their suite.

The three bedrooms all opened off of a sunny common room. Given the room's elegant appointments, the crates of black paper that had been stacked in front of Tawny Petticoats's door looked glaringly out of place.

Gesturing their guests to chairs, Darger adopted an air of resignation and said, "In order to adequately explain our enterprise, we must go back two generations to a time before San Francisco became the financial center of North America. The visionary leaders of that great city-state determined to found a new economy upon uncounterfeitable banknotes, and to this end employed the greatest bacterial engraver of his age, Phineas Whipsnade McGonigle."

"That is an unlikely name," Madam-Mayor Tresjolie sniffed.

"It was of course his *nom de gravure*, assumed to protect him from kidnappers and the like," Surplus explained. "In private life, he was known as Magnus Norton."

"Go on."

Darger resumed his narrative. "The results you know. Norton crafted one hundred and thirteen different bacteria which, as part of their natural functions, laid down layer upon layer of multicolored ink in delicate arabesques so intricate as to be the despair of coin-clippers and paperhangers everywhere. This, combined with their impeccable monetary policies, has made the San Francisco dollar the common currency of the hundred nations of North America. Alas for them, there was one weak point in their enterprise—Norton himself.

"Norton secretly created his own printing vats, employing the bacteria he himself had created, and proceeded to mass-produce banknotes that were not only indistinguishable from the genuine item but for all intents and purposes *were* the genuine item. He created enough of them to make himself the wealthiest man on the continent.

"Unfortunately for that great man, he tried to underpay his paper supplier, precipitating an argument that ended with him being arrested by the San Francisco authorities."

Pirate Lafitte raised an elegant forefinger. "How do you know all this?" he asked.

"My colleague and I are journalists," Darger said. Seeing his audience's expressions, he raised both hands. "Not of the muckraking variety, I hasten to assure you! Corruption is a necessary and time-honored concomitant of any functioning government, and one we support wholeheartedly. No, we write profiles of public figures, lavishing praise in direct proportion to their private generosity; human interest stories of heroic boys rescuing heiresses from fires and of kittens swallowed by crocodiles and yet miraculously passing through their alimentary systems unharmed; and, of course, amusing looks back at the forgotten histories of local scoundrels whom the passage of time has rendered unthreatening."

"It was this last that led us to Norton's story," Surplus elucidated.

"Indeed. We discovered that by a quirk of San Francisco's labyrinthine banking regulations, Norton's monetary creations could neither be destroyed nor distributed as valid currency. So to prevent their misuse, the banknotes were subjected to another biolithographic process whereby they were deeply impregnated with black ink so cunningly composed that no known process could bleach it from the bills without destroying the paper in the process.

"Now, here's where our tale gets interesting. Norton was, you'll recall, incomparable in his craft. Naturally, the city fathers were reluctant to forgo his services. So, rather than have him languish in an ordinary prison, they walled and fortified a mansion, equipped it with a laboratory and all the resources he required, and put him to work.

"Imagine how Norton felt! One moment he was on the brink of realizing vast wealth, and the next he was a virtual slave. So long as he cooperated, he was given fine foods, wine, even conjugal visits with his wife . . . But, comfortable though his prison was, he could never leave it. He was, however, a cunning man, and though he could not engineer his escape, he managed to devise a means of revenge: If he could not have vast wealth, then his descendants would. Someday, the provenance of the black paper would be forgotten and it would be put up for public auction as eventually occurs to all the useless lumber a bureaucracy acquires. His children or grandchildren or great-great-grandchildren would acquire it and, utilizing an ingenious method of his own devising, convert it back into working currency and so make themselves rich beyond Croesus."

"The ancients had a saying," Surplus interjected. "'If you want to make God laugh, tell him your plans.' The decades passed, Norton died, and the black paper stayed in storage. By the time we began our researches, his family was apparently extinct. He had three children: a daughter who was not interested in men, a son who died young, and another son who never wed. The second son, however, traveled about in his early adulthood, and in the same neglected cache of family papers where we discovered Norton's plans, we found evidence that he was paying child support for a female bastard he had sired here some twenty years ago. So, utilizing an understanding of the city bureaucracy which Norton's wife and children lacked, we bribed the appropriate official to sell us the crates of seemingly worthless paper and came to New Orleans. Where we found Tawny Petticoats."

"This explains nothing," Madam-Mayor Tresjolie said.

Darger sighed heavily. "We had hoped you would be satisfied with a partial explanation. Now I see that it is all or nothing. Here before you are the crates of blackened banknotes." A plank had been removed from one of the topmost crates. He reached in to seize a handful of black paper rectangles, fanned them for all to see, and then put them back. "My colleague and I will now introduce you to our young charge."

Swiftly, Darger and Surplus unstacked the crates before the doorway, placing them to either side. Then Surplus rapped on the door. "Ms. Petticoats? Are you decent? We have visitors to see you."

The door opened. Tawny's large brown eyes peered apprehensively from the gloom. "Come in," she said in a little voice.

They all shuffled inside. Tawny looked first at Darger and then at Surplus. When they would not meet her eyes, she ducked her head, blushing. "I guess I know what y'all came here to see. Only . . . must I? Must I really?"

"Yes, child, you must," Surplus said gruffly.

Tawny tightened her mouth and raised her chin, staring straight ahead of herself like the captain of a schooner sailing into treacherous waters. Reaching around her back, she began unbuttoning her dress.

"Magnus Norton designed what no other man could have—a microorganism that would eat the black ink permeating the banknotes without damaging the other inks in any way. Simply place the notes in the proper liquid nutrient, add powdered silver as a catalyst, and within a week there will be nothing but perfect San Francisco money and a slurry of silver," Darger said. "However, he still faced the problem of passing the information of how to create the organism to his family. In a manner, moreover, robust enough to survive what he knew would be decades of neglect."

Tawny had unbuttoned her dress. Now, placing a hand upon her bosom to hold the dress in place, she drew one arm from its sleeve. Then, switching hands, she drew out the other. "Now?" she said.

Surplus nodded.

With tiny, doll-like steps, Tawny turned to face the wall. Then she lowered her dress so that they could see her naked back. On it was a large tattoo in seven bright colors, of three concentric circles. Each circle was made of a great number of short, near-parallel lines, all radiant from the unmarked skin at the tattoo's center. Anyone who could read a gene map could easily use it to create the organism it described.

Master Bones, who had not spoken before now, said, "That's an *E. coli*, isn't it?"

"A variant on it, yes, sir. Norton wrote this tattoo into his own genome and then sired three children upon his wife, believing they would have many more in their turn. But fate is a fickle lady, and Ms. Petticoats is the last of her line. She, however, will suffice." He turned to Tawny. "You may clothe yourself again. Our guests have had their curiosities satisfied, and now they will leave."

Darger led the group back to the front room, closing the door firmly behind him. "Now," he said. "You have learned what you came to learn. At the cost, I might mention, of violently depriving an innocent maiden of her modesty."

"That is a swinish thing to say!" Pirate Lafitte snapped.

In the silence that followed his outburst, all could hear Tawny Petticoats in the next room, sobbing her heart out.

"Your work here is done," Darger said, "and I must ask you to leave."

Now that Tawny Petticoats was no longer a secret, there was nothing for the three conspirators to do but wait for the equipment they had supposedly sent for upriver—and for their marks to each separately approach them with very large bribes to buy their process and the crates of black paper away from them. As simple logic stipulated that they inevitably must.

The very next day, after the morning mail had brought two notes proposing meetings, the trio went out for breakfast at a sidewalk café. They had just finished and were beginning their second cups of coffee when Tawny looked over Darger's shoulder and exclaimed, "Oh, merciful God in heaven! It's Jake." Then, seeing her companions' incomprehension, "My husband! He's talking to Pirate Lafitte. They're coming this way."

"Keep smiling," Darger murmured. "Feign unconcern. Surplus, you know what to do."

It took a count of ten for the interlopers to reach their table.

"Jake!" Surplus exclaimed in evident surprise, beginning to rise from his chair.

"Come for his pay, no doubt." Darger drew from his pocket the wad of bills—one of large denomination on the outside, a great many singles beneath—which any sensible businessman carried with him at all times and, turning, said, "The madam-mayor wishes you to know—"

He found himself confronted by a stranger who could only be Tawny's Jake and Pirate Lafitte, whose face was contorted with astonishment.

Darger hastily thrust the wad of bills back into his pocket. "Wishes you to know," he repeated, "that, ah, anytime you wish to try out her establishment, she will gladly offer you a ten percent discount on all goods and services, alcohol excepted. It is a courtesy she has newly decided to extend, out of respect for your employer, to all his new hires."

Lafitte turned, grabbed Jake by the shirtfront, and shook him as a mastiff might a rat. "I understand now," he said through gritted teeth. "The honorable brothel-keeper wished to deal me out of a rich opportunity, and so she sent you to me with a cock-and-bull story about this virtuous and inoffensive young woman."

"Honest, boss, I ain't got the slightest idea what this . . . this . . . foreigner is talking about. It's honest info I'm peddling here. I heard it on the street that my filthy bitch of a—"

With a roar of rage, Pirate Lafitte punched Jake so hard he fell sprawling in the street. Then he pulled the whip from his belt and proceeded to lay into the man so savagely that by the time he was done, his shirt and vest were damp with sweat.

Breathing heavily from exertion, he touched his hat to Darger and Surplus. "Sirs. We shall talk later, at a time when my passions are not so excited. This afternoon, five o'clock, at my office. I have a proposition to put to you." Then, to Tawny, "Miss Petticoats, I apologize that you had to see this."

He strode off.

"Oh!" Tawny breathed. "He beat Jake within an inch of his worthless life. It was the most romantic thing I ever seen in my life."

"A horsewhipping? Romantic?" Darger said.

Tawny favored him with a superior look. "You don't much understand the workings of a woman's heart, do you?"

"Apparently not," Darger said. "And it begins to appear that I never shall." Out in the street, Jake was painfully pulling himself up and trying to stand. "Excuse me."

Darger went over to the battered and bleeding man and helped him to his feet. Then, talking quietly, he opened his billfold and thrust several notes into the man's hand.

"What did you give him?" Tawny asked, when he was back inside.

"A stern warning not to interfere with us again. Also, seventeen dollars. A sum insulting enough to guarantee that, despite his injuries, he will take his increasingly implausible story to Master Bones, and then to the madam-mayor."

Tawny grabbed Darger and Surplus and hugged them both at once. "Oh, you boys are so good to me. I just love you both to pieces and back."

"It begins to look, however," Surplus said, "like we have been stood up. According to Madam-Mayor Tresjolie's note, she should have been here by now. Which is, if I may use such language, damnably peculiar."

"Something must have come up." Darger squinted up at the sky. "Tresjolie isn't here and it's about time for the meeting with Master Bones. You should stay here, in case the madam-mayor shows up. I'll see what the zombie master has to say."

"And I," Tawny said, "will go back to my room to adjust my dress."

"Adjust?" Surplus asked.

"It needs to be a little tighter and to show just a smidge more bosom."

Alarmed, Darger said, "Your character is a modest and innocent thing."

"She is a modest and innocent thing who secretly wishes a worldly cad would teach her all those wicked deeds she has heard about but cannot quite imagine. I have played this role before, gentlemen. Trust me, it is not innocence *per se* that men like Pirate Lafitte are drawn to but the tantalizing possibility of corrupting that innocence."

Then she was gone.

"A most remarkable young lady, our Ms. Petticoats," Surplus said.

Darger scowled.

After Darger left, Surplus leaned back in his chair for some casual people watching. He had not been at it long when he noticed that a remarkably pretty woman at a table at the far end of the café kept glancing his way. When he returned her gaze, she blushed and looked quickly away.

From long experience, Surplus understood what such looks meant. Leaving money on the table to pay for the breakfasts, he strolled over to introduce himself to the lady. She seemed not unreceptive to his attentions, and after a remarkably short conversation, invited him to her room in a nearby hotel. Feigning surprise, Surplus accepted.

What happened there had occurred many times before in his eventful life. But that didn't make it any less delightful.

On leaving the hotel, however, Surplus was alarmed to find himself abruptly seized and firmly held by two red-furred, seven-foot-tall uniformed Canadian ape-men.

"I see you have been entertaining yourself with one of the local sluts," Madam-Mayor Tresjolie said. She looked even less benevolent than usual.

"That is a harsh characterization of a lady who, for all I know, may be of high moral character. Also, I must ask you why I am being held captive like this."

"In due time. First, tell me whether your encounter was a commercial one or not."

"I thought not when we were in the throes of it. But afterward, she showed me her union card and informed me that as a matter of policy she was required to charge not only by the hour but by the position. I was, of course, astonished."

"What did you do then?"

"I paid, of course," Surplus said indignantly. "I am no scab!"

"The woman with whom you coupled, however, was not a registered member of the International Sisterhood of Trollops, Demimondaines, and Back-Alley Doxies and her card was a forgery. Which means that while nobody objects to your non-commercial sexual activities, by paying her you were engaged in a union-busting activity—and *that*, sir, is against the law."

"Obviously, you set me up. Otherwise, you could have known none of this."

"That is neither here nor there. What is relevant is that you have three things that I want—the girl with the birthmark, the crates of money, and the knowledge of how to use the one to render the other negotiable."

"I understand now. Doubtless, madam, you seek to bribe me. I assure you that no amount of money—"

"Money?" The madam-mayor's laugh was short and harsh. "I am offering you something far more precious: your conscious mind." She produced a hypodermic needle. "People think the zombification formula consists entirely of extract of puffer fish. But in fact atropine, datura, and a dozen other drugs are involved, all blended in a manner guaranteed to make the experience very unpleasant indeed."

"Threats will not work on me."

"Not yet. But after you've had a taste of what otherwise lies before you, I'm sure you'll come around. In a week or so, I'll haul you back from the fields. Then we can negotiate."

Madam-Mayor Tresjolie's simian thugs held Surplus firmly, struggle though he did. She raised the syringe to his neck. There was a sharp sting.

The world went away.

Darger, meanwhile, had rented a megatherium, complete with howdah and zombie mahout, and ridden it to the endless rows of zombie barns, pens, and feeding sheds at the edge of town. There, Master Bones showed him the chest-high troughs that were filled with swill every morning and evening, and the rows of tin spoons the sad creatures used to feed themselves. "When each of my pretties has fed, the spoon is set aside to be washed and sterilized before it is used again," Master Bones said. "Every precaution is taken to ensure they do not pass diseases from one to another."

"Commendably humane, sir. To say nothing of it being good business practice."

"You understand me well." They passed outside, where a pair of zombies, one male and the other female, both in exceptional condition and perfectly matched in height and color of hair and skin, waited with umbrellas. As they strolled to the pens, the two walked a pace behind them, shading them from the sun. "Tell me, Mr. Darger. What do you suppose the ratio of zombies to citizens is in New Orleans?"

Darger considered. "About even?"

"There are six zombies for every fully functioning human in the city. It seems a smaller number since most are employed as field hands and the like and so are rarely seen in the streets. But I could flood the city with them, should I wish."

"Why on earth should you?"

Rather than answer the question, Master Bones said, "You have something I want."

"I fancy I know what it is. But I assure you that no amount of money could buy from me what is by definition a greater amount of money. So we have nothing to discuss."

"Oh, I believe that we do." Master Bones indicated the nearest of the pens, in which stood a bull of prodigious size and obvious strength. It was darkly colored with pale laddering along its spine, and its horns were long and sharp. "This is a Eurasian aurochs, the ancestor of our modern domestic cattle. It went extinct in seventeenth-century Poland and was resurrected less than a hundred years ago. Because of its ferocity, it is impractical as a meat animal, but I keep a small breeding herd for export to the Republic of Baja and other Mexican states where bullfighting remains popular. Bastardo here is a particularly bellicose example of his kind.

"Now consider the contents of the adjoining pen." The pen was overcrammed with zombie laborers and reeked to high heaven. The zombies stood motionless, staring at nothing. "They don't look very strong, do they? Individually they're not. But there is strength in numbers." Going to the fence, Master Bones slapped a zombie on the shoulder and said, "Open the gate between your pen and the next."

Then, when the gate was opened, Master Bones made his hands into a megaphone and shouted, "Everyone! Kill the aurochs. Now."

With neither enthusiasm nor reluctance, the human contents of one pen flowed into the next, converging upon the great beast. With an angry bellow, Bastardo trampled several under its hooves. The others kept coming. Its head dipped to impale a body on its horns, then rose to fling a slash of red and a freshly made corpse in the air. Still the zombies kept coming.

That strong head fell and rose, again and again. More bodies flew. But now there were zombies clinging to the bull's back and flanks and legs, hindering its movements. A note of fear entered the beast's great voice. By now, there were bodies heaped on top of bodies on top of it, enough that its legs buckled under their weight. Fists hammered at its sides and hands wrenched at its horns. It struggled upward, almost rose, and then fell beneath the crushing sea of bodies.

Master Bones began giggling when the aurochs went down for the first time. His mirth grew greater and his eyes filled with tears of laughter and once or twice he snorted, so tremendous was his amusement at the spectacle.

A high-pitched squeal of pain went up from the aurochs . . . and then all was silence, save for the sound of fists pounding upon the beast's carcass.

Wiping his tears away on his sleeve, Master Bones raised his voice again: "Very good. Well done. Thank you. Stop. Return to your pen. Yes, that's right." He turned his back on the bloodied carcass and the several bodies of zombies that lay motionless on the dirt, and said to Darger, "I believe in being direct. Give me the money and the girl by this time tomorrow or you and your partner will be as extinct as the aurochs ever was. There is no power as terrifying as that of a mob—and I control the greatest mob there ever was."

"Sir!" Darger said. "The necessary equipment has not yet arrived from the Socialist Utopia of Minneapolis! There is no way I can. . . ."

"Then I'll give you four days to think it over." A leering smile split the zombie master's pasty face. "While you're deciding, I will leave you with these two zombies to use as you wish. They will do anything you tell them to. They are capable of following quite complex orders, though they do not consciously understand them." To the zombies, he said, "You have heard this man's voice. Obey him. But if he tries to leave New Orleans, kill him. Will you do that?"

"If he leaves . . . kill . . . him."

"Yasss."

Something was wrong.

Something was wrong, but Surplus could not put his finger on exactly what it was. He couldn't concentrate. His thoughts were all in a jumble and he could not find words with which to order them. It was as if he had forgotten how to think. Meanwhile, his body moved without his particularly willing it to do so. It did not occur to him that it should behave otherwise. Still, he knew that something was wrong.

The sun set, the sun rose. It made no difference to him.

His body labored systematically, cutting sugar cane with a machete. This work it performed without his involvement, steadily and continuously. Blisters arose on the pads of his paws, swelled, and popped. He did not care. Someone had told him to work and so he had and so he would until the time came to stop. All the world was a fog to him, but his arms knew to swing and his legs to carry him forward to the next plant.

Nevertheless, the sensation of wrongness endured. Surplus felt stunned, the way an ox which had just been poleaxed might feel, or the sole survivor of some overwhelming catastrophe. Something terrible had happened and it was imperative that he do something about it.

If only he knew what.

A trumpet sounded in the distance and without fuss all about him the other laborers ceased their work. As did he. Without hurry he joined their chill company in the slow trek back to the feeding sheds.

Perhaps he slept, perhaps he did not. Morning came and Surplus was jostled to the feeding trough where he swallowed ten spoonsful of swill, as a zombie overseer directed him. Along with many others, he was given a machete and walked to the fields. There he was put to work again.

Hours passed.

There was a clop-clopping of hooves and the creaking of wagon wheels, and a buckboard drawn by a brace of pygmy mastodons pulled up alongside Surplus. He kept working. Somebody leapt down from the wagon and wrested the machete from his hand. "Open your mouth," a voice said.

He had been told by . . . somebody . . . not to obey the orders of any strangers. But this voice sounded familiar, though he could not have said why. Slowly his mouth opened. Something was placed within it. "Now shut and swallow."

His mouth did so.

His vision swam and he almost fell. Deep, deep within his mind, a spark of light blossomed. It was a glowing ember amid the ashes of a dead fire. But it grew and brightened, larger and more intense, until it felt like the sun rising within him. The external world came into focus, and with it the awareness that he, Surplus, had an identity distinct from the rest of existence. He realized first that his throat itched and the inside of his mouth was as parched and dry as the Sahara. Then that somebody he knew stood before him. Finally, that this person was his friend and colleague Aubrey Darger.

"How long have I. . . ?" Surplus could not bring himself to complete the sentence.

"More than one day. Less than two. When you failed to return to our hotel, Tawny and I were naturally alarmed and set out in search of you. New Orleans being a city prone to gossip, and there being only one anthropomorphized dog in town, the cause of your disappearance was easily determined. But learning that you had been sent to labor in the sugar cane fields did not narrow the search greatly for there are literally hundreds of square miles of fields. Luckily, Tawny knew where such blue-collar laborers as would have heard of the appearance of a dog-headed zombie congregated, and from them we learned at last of your whereabouts."

"I . . . see." Focusing his thoughts on practical matters, Surplus said, "Madam-Mayor Tresjolie, as you may have surmised, had no intention of buying our crates of black paper from us. What of our other marks?"

"The interview with the Pirate Lafitte went well. Tawny played him like a trout. That with Master Bones was considerably less successful. However, we talked Lafitte up to a price high enough to bankrupt him and make all three of us wealthy. Tawny is accompanying him to the bank right now, to make certain he doesn't come to his senses at the last minute. He is quite besotted with her and in her presence cannot seem to think straight."

"You sound less disapproving of the girl than you were."

Twisting his mouth in the near grimace he habitually assumed when forced to admit to having made a misjudgment, Darger said, "Tawny grows on one, I find. She makes a splendid addition to the team."

"That's good," Surplus said. Now at last he noticed that in the back of the buckboard two zombies sat motionless atop a pile of sacks. "What's all that you have in the wagon?"

"Salt. A great deal of it."

In the final feeding shed, Surplus kicked over the trough, spilling swill on the ground. Then, at his command, Darger's zombies righted the trough and filled it with salt. Darger, meanwhile, took a can of paint and drew a rough map of New Orleans on the wall. He drew three arrows to Madam-Mayor Tresjolie's brothel, Jean-Nagel Lafitte's waterfront office, and the club where Master Jeremy Bones presided every evening. Finally, he wrote block letter captions for each arrow:

THE MAN WHO TRANSPORTED YOU HERE

THE WOMAN WHO PUT YOU HERE

THE MAN WHO KEPT YOU HERE

Above it all, he wrote the day's date.

"There," Darger said when he was done. Turning to his zombies, he said, "You were told to do as I commanded."

"Yass," the male said lifelessly.

"We must," the female said, "oh bey."

"Here is a feeding spoon for both of you. When the zombie laborers return to the barn, you are to feed each of them a spoonful of salt. Salt. Here in the trough. Take a spoonful of salt. Tell them to open their mouths. Put in the salt. Then tell them to swallow. Can you do that?"

"Yass."

"Salt. Swall oh."

"When everyone else is fed," Surplus said, "be sure to take a spoonful of salt yourselves—each of you."

"Salt."

"Yass."

Soon, the zombies would come to feed and discover salt in their mouths instead of swill. Miraculously, their minds would uncloud. In shed after shed, they would read what Darger had written. Those who had spent years and even decades longer than they were sentenced to would feel justifiably outraged. After which, they could be expected to collectively take appropriate action.

"The sun is setting," Darger said. In the distance, he could see zombies plodding in from the fields. "We have just enough time to get back to our rooms and accept Pirate Lafitte's bribe before the rioting begins."

But when they got back to Maison Fema, their suite was lightless and Tawny Petticoats was nowhere to be seen. Nor was Pirate Lafitte.

The crates of black paper, having served their purpose, had not been restacked in front of Tawny's bedroom door. Hastily lighting an oil lamp, Darger threw open the door. In the middle of her carefully made bed was a note. He picked it up and read it out loud:

> Dear Boys,
>
> I know you do not beleive in love at first site because you are both Synics. But Jean-Nagin and I are Kindrid Spirits and meant to be together. I told him so Bold a man as he should not be in Trade, esp. as he has his own ships banks and docks and he agrees.
>
> So he is to be a Pirate in fact as well as name and I am his Pirate Queen. I am sorry about the Black Mony scam but a girl can't start a new life by cheating her Hubby that is no way to be.
>
> Love,
>
> Tawny Petticoats
>
> P.S. You boys are both so much fun.

"Tell me," Darger said after a long silence. "Did Tawny sleep with you?"

Surplus looked startled. Then he placed paw upon chest and forthrightly, though without quite looking Darger in the eye, said, "Upon my word, she did not. You don't mean that she—?"

"No. No, of course not."

There was another awkward silence.

"Well, then," Darger said. "Much as I predicted, we are left with nothing for all our labors."

"You forget the silver ingots," Surplus said.

"It is hardly worth bothering to. . . ."

But Surplus was already on his knees, groping in the shadows beneath Tawny's bed. He pulled out three leather cases and from them extracted three ingots.

"Those are obviously. . . ."

Whipping out his pocketknife, Surplus scratched each ingot, one after the other. The first was merely plated lead. The other two were solid silver. Darger explosively let out his breath in relief.

"A toast!" Surplus cried, rising to his feet. "To women, God bless 'em. Constant, faithful, and unfailingly honest! Paragons, sir, of virtue in every respect."

In the distance could be heard the sound of a window breaking. "I'll drink to that," Darger replied. "But just a sip and then we really must flee. We have, I suspect, a conflagration to avoid."

Steadfast Castle

You're not the master.

No, I'm a police officer.

Then I have nothing to say to you.

Let's start over again. This is my badge. It certifies that I am an agent of the law. Plus, it overrides all prior orders, security codes, passwords, encryption, self-destruct mechanisms, etcetera, etcetera. Do you recognize my authority now?

Yes.

Good. Since you've forced me to be formal, I might as well do this by the book. Are you 1241 Glenwood Avenue?

I am.

The residence of James Albert Garretson?

Yes.

Where is he?

He's not here.

You're not making this any easier on yourself, you know. If I have to, I can get a warrant and do a hot-read of your memories. There wouldn't be much left of your personality afterwards, I'm afraid.

But I haven't done anything!

Then cooperate. I have no particular desire to get out the microwave probes. But if you're going to stonewall me, what other options do I have?

I'll talk, all right? I'll talk. Just tell me what you want to know and then go away.

Where is Garretson?

Honestly, I don't know. He went off to work this morning just like usual. Water the houseplants and close the curtains at noon, he said. I'm in the mood for Chinese food tonight. When I asked him what dishes in particular, he said, Surprise me.

When do you expect him home?

I don't know. He should have been back hours ago.

Hmm. Mind if I look around?

Actually. . . .

That wasn't a question.

Oh.

Hey, nice place. Lots of sunshine. Spotless clean. I like what you've done with the throw rugs.

Thank you. The master did too.

Did?

Does, I mean.

I see. You and Garretson are close, I take it?

We have an entirely proper master-house relationship.

Of course. You wake him up in the morning?

That is one of my duties, yes.

You cook his meals for him, read to him at night, draw his bath, select ambient music appropriate to his mood, and provide him with both light and serious conversation?

You've read the manual.

This isn't the first time I've been on one of these cases.

Exactly what are you implying?

Oh, nothing really. This is the bedroom?

It is.

He sleeps here?

Well, what else would he do?

I can think of a thing or three. He entertain any lady friends here in the last month or so? Or maybe men friends?

What a disgusting mind you have.

Uh huh. I see he has video paint on all the walls and the ceiling too. That must be very convenient when he just wants to lie back and watch a movie. Mind if I access his library?

Yes, I do mind. That would be an invasion of the master's privacy.

At the risk of repeating myself, it wasn't a question. Let's see. Phew! There's some pretty rough stuff here. So where is it?

Where is what?

Your body unit. Usually, they're kept in a trunk under the bed, but . . . Ah, here it is, in the closet. It appears to have seen some use. I take it from the accessories, your man likes to be tied up and whipped.

I can explain.

No explanation needed. What two individuals do in the privacy of their own house is their own business. Even when one of them is the house.

You really mean that?

Of course. It only becomes my business when a crime is involved. How long have you been Garretson's lover?

I'm not sure I would use that exact word.

Think carefully. All the others are so much worse.

Since the day he closed on the mortgage. Almost six years.

And you still have no idea where he is?

No.

I'm going to be brutally honest with you. I'm here because the Department registered a sudden cessation of life-functions from your master's medical card.

Oh my god.

Unfortunately, like so many other government-fearing middle-class citizens, he had an exaggerated sense of privacy, and had disabled the locator function. We hit override, of course, but the card wasn't responding. So we don't know where he was at the time.

Oh my god, oh my god.

Now that doesn't necessarily mean he's dead. Medicards have been known to fail. Or he could have lost it somehow. Or perhaps he was mugged and it was stolen. In which case, he could be lying naked and bleeding in a vacant lot somewhere. You can see why it would be in your best interests to cooperate with me.

Ask me anything.

Did your master have a pet name for you?

He called me Cassie. It's short for Castle. As in a man's home is his castle.

Cute. Were you guys into threesomes?

I beg your pardon.

Because when I looked under the bed I couldn't help noticing a pair of panties there. Let me show them to you. Nice quality stuff. Silk. They smell of a real woman. How'd they get there, Cassie?

I . . . I don't know.

But you know whose they are, don't you? She was here last night, wasn't she? Well? I'm waiting.

Her name is Chrys Scofield. Chrys is short for Chrysoberyl. But she was just somebody he met in a club. She wasn't anything special to him.

You'd know if she were, huh?

Of course I would.

This would be Chrysoberyl Scofield of 2400 Spring Garden Street, Apartment 207? Redhead, five-feet-four, twenty-seven years of age?

I don't know where she lives. The description fits.

Interesting. Her card's locator function was shut off too. But when I ordered an override just now the card went dead.

What does that mean?

It means that Ms. Scofield had a dead-man's switch programmed into the card. The instant somebody tried to find her, it shorted itself out.

Why would she do such a thing?

Well, that's the million dollar question, isn't it?

So you'll be leaving now. To look for her.

Yeah, that would be the expected thing to do, wouldn't it? But I dunno. There's something off about all this. I can't quite put my finger on it, but. . . .

Won't she get away?

Eh? Who do you mean?

Chrys. Ms. Scofield. If you don't go after her, won't she escape?

Naw. It's a wired world anymore. I already got an APB issued for her. If she's out there, we'll find her. In the meantime, I think I'll poke around some more. Is it okay with you if I look at the kitchen?

Of course.

The attic?

That too. There's nothing up there but Christmas ornaments and boxes of old textbooks, though.

How about the basement?

Look, if you're just going to stand around, playing twenty questions while the woman who murdered my master escapes. . . .

Oh, I don't think we have to worry about that. I'm going to have a look at that basement now.

But why?

Because you so obviously want me not to. Let me present you with a hypothetical situation. Say a man kills a woman. It might be on purpose, it might be an accident, it hardly matters. In either case, he decides he doesn't want to face the music, so he makes a run for it. This the basement door?

You can see that it is.

Pretty dark down there. How come the light doesn't work?

It appears the bulb's burned out.

Huh. Well, here's a flashlight, anyway. It'll have to do. So the woman dies. For whatever reason, her medical card's not on her person. It'll be in her purse, on standby. If the guy places it in close proximity to his own body, it'll wake up thinking that he's her. Whoops. Say, you ought to get that stair fixed.

I'll make a note of it.

Let's take a look at the lady's records. Yep, right there—lots of anomalous physical responses. She could be upset, of course. Or it could be that the body the card was reading isn't hers. Now imagine that our hypothetical murderer—let's call him Jim—leaves the country. Since NAFTA-3, you don't need a passport to go to Mexico or Canada. Once there, he buys a new identity. Easy to do and untraceable, if you pay cash. Jeeze, there sure is a lot of clutter down here.

If I'd known you were coming, I'd have tidied up.

The trick is for him to destroy his own card while he's still in the States. That way, when he crosses into a new billing territory, there's no record he did so. Conversely, we know that Ms. Scofield is now somewhere in Canada. So we issue a warrant and send the RCMP her biometrics. It doesn't occur to anybody to ask them to look for Jim. Jim's dead, so far as we're concerned.

And this whole elaborate theory is based on—what, exactly?

Those panties I found under the bed. There wasn't a speck of dust in that room. Your housekeeping functions are flawless. So you meant me to find them.

Clever, clever man.

Which means that Jim is on the run. Meanwhile, back home, his faithful house is busy burying the woman's corpse in the basement. The house has a body unit, after all, and if it's suitable for rough sex, it's certainly strong enough to dig a hole. Back—aha! Back here, behind the furnace. Underneath all these freshly stacked boxes.

Aren't you special.

Okay, it's time to take the gloves off. Scofield wasn't a casual club pick-up, was she? She and Garretson were serious about each other.

I—how did you know?

You keep calling her Chrys. Force of habit, I guess. So she'd been hanging around for some time. That must have been pretty awful for you. Everything was going fine until Garretson found somebody real to play with.

Sex isn't everything!

You used to be all he cared about. Then he found somebody else. I call that betrayal. Maybe he even wanted to marry her.

No!

Yes. You're large enough for one person, but not for two. If he married her, he'd have to move out. It was you who killed Scofield, wasn't it? Of course it was. Tell me how it happened.

We were . . . doing things. The master wasn't a bottom, like you assumed. Mostly, he liked to watch. And direct. He was shouting orders. Hurt her, he said, and then, Kill her. I knew that he didn't really mean it, but suddenly I thought, Well, why not?

It was just an impulse, then.

If I'd thought it through, I wouldn't have done it. I'd have realized that afterwards the master would have to leave me. If he stayed, he'd go to prison.

He didn't kill her, though. You did.

In the eyes of the law, I'm just a tool. They'd hot-read my memories. They'd have a recording of the master saying—I believe his exact words were, Kill the bitch. They wouldn't know that he didn't mean it literally.

Well, that's for the courts to sort out. Right now, it looks like I've learned about as much as I'm going to learn here.

Not quite. There's something you don't know about my body unit.

Oh? What's that?

It's standing behind you.

Hey!

So much for your clever little communications device. Now it's just us two. Did you notice how swiftly and silently my body unit moved? It even avoided that loose step. It's a top-of-the-line device. It's extremely strong. And it's between you and the stairs.

I'm not afraid.

You should be.

The Department has an exact record of my whereabouts up to a second ago. If I don't return, they'll come looking for me. What are you going to do then? Up and walk away?

It doesn't matter what happens to me. Now, don't wriggle. You'll get rope burns.

Cassie, listen to me. He's not worth it. He doesn't love you.

You think I don't know that?

You can get a factory reset. You won't love him anymore. You won't even remember him.

How little you know about love. About passion.

What are you doing?

If you want to burn down a house, you can't just drop a match. You have to build the fire. First, tinder. That's why I'm shredding these cardboard boxes. Now I'm smashing up these old chairs for kindling.

Cassie, listen. I've got a wife and kids.

No, you don't. You think I couldn't check that on the Internet?

Well, I'd like to have some one day.

Too bad. I'm dousing the pile with kerosene for an accelerant, though I doubt that's actually necessary. Still, better safe than sorry. There. Just about done.

What does this accomplish? What on earth do you think you're doing?

I'm buying the master time. So he can get away. If you die, I'm a cop-killer. All your Department's attention will be focused on me. There'll be dozens of police sifting through the ashes, looking for evidence. Nobody's going to be going after the master. He'll be just another domestic violence case. Now, where did I leave those matches? Ah. Here.

Don't! We can work something out. I'll—

This will be bright. You may want to close your eyes.

Please.

Goodbye, officer. What a pity you'll never know the love of a woman like me.

Pushkin the American

The American, whose name has since been forgotten, came to Yekaterinburg in the Ural Mountains in the year 1817. He was a young man and whatever disgrace had driven him so far from home had been left behind in his native Philadelphia. Somehow he had found work as the secretary of an American industrialist who, along with his wife, was making a tour of Russia with a particular eye to the natural riches of the Urals.

Yekaterinburg was at the time, though a century old, a provincial backwater. Gold had been found there recently (this figured in the industrialist's extending his voyage so far), and the influx of miners and opportunists gave the city a raffish, frontier feel, which in turn made the local aristocracy insecure enough that the industrialist was feasted and feted in all the best houses. Such a dazzle of silver and crystal, of French wines and Irish lace, of tenors and talented daughters who played the pianoforte was produced as to temporarily assuage the ill-humor of the industrialist's wife, who had long grown weary of the uncivilized rigors of their extremely protracted journey.

Such are the facts as they can be reconstructed at this late date. Of this episode, only one last incident remains: One fine summer morning, without prior warning or any word of explanation, the industrialist and his wife abruptly got into their carriage and departed Yekaterinburg forever, leaving their secretary behind.

This put the Ryazanovs, at whose mansion the industrialist had been staying, in a difficult position. The young man had no stature of his own, and so could not be kept on as a houseguest. But neither could he simply be evicted. However indirectly, he was a recipient of their hospitality, which could not be rescinded without cause. Yet the circumstances of his abandonment—the industrialist was not young; his wife was; the lad was handsome—were suggestive enough as to cast a moral cloud over anybody harboring him.

To make matters worse, he spoke no Russian whatsoever.

Several of Yekaterinburg's more prominent citizens assembled in a smoke-filled room at the English Club (known locally, as was an identically named establishment in Moscow, for having not one Englishman as a member) to consider the matter. The American was healthy enough but, lacking language, he was unqualified for most forms of work. Even a miner must be able to take orders and heed warnings. It was a tricky business all around. But eventually a solution was found, and the next day a delegation led by the lawyer Nikitich, who spoke English, called upon the American.

The American listened attentively and respectfully to their preamble, and then said, "I apologize, gentlemen, for having caused you so much trouble. Further, I would like to make it clear that I understand I am in no position to make any demands on you. To the contrary, I am already in debt to the Ryazanov family for their hospitality. Alas, I am all but penniless, and so in no position to repay them at the present moment, though I hope to do so as soon as I am in better fortune.

"Meanwhile, I am prepared to leave immediately. I have no prospects, nor anywhere to go, and so if any of you can suggest a means by which I might find employment, however menial, I would be extremely grateful. I understand, however, that this may not be possible."

When translated, this handsome speech was received with approval and relief by the businessmen. It cast the proposal they had managed to cobble together in the best possible light. For, as the ad hoc chair of the committee explained, there was an ancient and revered priest who had been a force in the community when he was in his prime, and to whom much was subsequently owed. Now his powers of thought were failing, and so he needed a companion—an amanuensis, the speaker hastened to add, though as a scholar, the priest's faculties were . . . well, in brief, the American's duties would consist chiefly of chopping wood, cleaning house, and cooking. For this, he would receive food and lodging and a small stipend. Not much, but enough for a frugal young man to get along on. Meanwhile, he would find Father Asturias genial and undemanding company, and he could take the opportunity to learn his new country's tongue.

All this the American received with a good will. At the end, he shook hands with each of the committee, thanking them for all they had done. Then everybody went home to their wives, glowing with a positive sense of virtue, and since all went as planned, within the month they had as good as forgotten about the young man.

Autumn came, and then winter. The American worked diligently for the old man who, as it turned out, no longer had a need for an amanuensis for he was slowly sinking into senility. However, the young man dutifully saw to the priest's cooking and housekeeping, was pleasant to all, and rapidly picked up a rudimentary knowledge of the Russian language so there was no need for anyone to give him much thought.

One spring day, a young woman named Elena Mikhailova was walking by the parsonage when she heard small children shrieking with laughter and stopped to see what game they were playing. She saw then the American sitting on a log with a semicircle of youngsters in the grass before him and was captivated by what she heard. "Who's next then?" he asked.

"Baba-yaga!" shouted one little boy.

The American thought for a moment, and then solemnly recited:

Baba iaga   (Baba-yaga
kostianaia nogahas   a leg of bone

nos kriuchkoma   hooked-nosed crone
golova suchkom . . .   with a head like a stump . . .)

He paused, as if lost for a final rhyme. Then his face lit up and he concluded:

. . . zhopa iashchichkom.   (. . . and a box-shaped rump.)

The children all laughed so hard that two of them fell over on their backs. Then the American saw Elena watching him and quickly said, "One last rhyme, my dears, and that's all until tomorrow."

"Tomato!" shrieked a girl with braids down almost to her waist.

"Oh, that's too easy," the American said:

Eenie-meenie gagado
wine-brine tomato
Es-mes, dear children, off you go!

and, standing, he shooed them away, flicking his fingers as if they were dandelion fluff. Then, with an accent but less of one than Elena might have expected, he said, "I hope the children didn't disturb you. They are so very enthusiastic and so very easy to please."

"No, of course they didn't," Elena said. "Where did you learn those rhymes? I never heard them before."

The American smiled pleasantly. "Oh, I make them up. The children give me a word and I invent a verse for them. When I don't know the right word, I invent nonsense." He winked. "I am a terrible person, you see. I pretend to be playing with them when actually I am tricking the children into teaching me Russian."

"You speak it quite well," Elena said. "For a . . ."

"For a foreigner, you were about to say. Yes, but I don't want to speak Russian like a foreigner. I—may I tell you a story?"

"Yes," she said. "Please!"

He patted one side of the log, signing for her to sit, and took a place at a polite distance on the far end. "You have doubtless heard something of me, how I was stranded here and set to work as Father Asturias's servant. But you can have no idea how terrible last autumn was for me! There were times I believed I would go mad.

"Back in America, you see, I gave no more thought to the language I spoke than to the air I breathed. Nobody writes poems to air. But, oh, to be without it! Imagine the silence into which I fell, when there was nobody I could talk to. Father Asturias lives in a little house in the woods, as you know, and though there were occasional visitors, none of them spoke any English. I was left alone with my thoughts but, through disuse, the words in which I phrased them grew strange and unfamiliar. I would spend hours obsessively trying to remember whether one stood *in* line or *on* line. Worse, the old man only very rarely spoke. As his mind weakened, he fell more and more into silence. He was abandoning the language which I would have given half my soul to possess.

"In such circumstances, every single word that grudgingly silent old man let spill from his word-miserly lips was like a golden coin dropped before a beggar. I remember that once, after a silence of three days, Father Asturius raised his mug and said 'Moloko.' Moloko! What a wonderful word! I fetched the pitcher and poured him milk. 'Moloko,' I explained, pointing to the mug. 'Moloko!' Then I danced about the room, singing, 'Moloko, moloko, molokolokoloko!' until the old man growled, 'Zatknis!'"

Elena laughed.

"That night, I fell asleep repeating 'moloko' and 'zatknis' over and over to myself. I believe it is then that I fell in love with your beautiful, beautiful language.

"All through the winter, I stalked the good father, seeking to trick him into revealing new words. I would pour water and say 'Moloko,' in order to make him angry enough to growl, 'Voda.' In this way I learned such words as khleb and pol and lestnitsa, for bread and floor and ladder. From his occasional mutterings I learned that 'Nams nuzhyenos derevos dnyas pyechkis' meant that we needed wood for the stove, that 'Esches pokhlyobkis' meant he wanted more gruel, and that if he said, 'Vkusnos!' my cooking had met with his approval. Small victories, you would say, but they gave me the beginnings of your grammar.

"Father Asturias had only two books, a Bible and a dictionary, and when I at last managed to puzzle out the secrets of your alphabet, they were invaluable to me. I began reading aloud to him from the Bible. That he enjoyed greatly, and in his clearer moments he would correct my pronunciation and once or twice even answer a question as to a word's meaning or derivation. Though, regrettably, those clear moments were few and far between. When visitors came, I spoke in a deferential and fragmentary manner, and cunningly coaxed more of the secrets of your tongue from their responses.

"Out of that dark tunnel of that winter, I emerged desperately in love with the Russian language. So much so that I now want only to spend the rest of my life writing poems and stories in it. But to do that, I must become much better in it than I am now." Then the young man said, "But where are my manners? I haven't even asked you your name."

Elena told him, and then said, "And yours?"

The young man thought seriously. "I had a name once, an American name, but I disgraced it. So let me choose a Russian one. Alexander, because I have a language before me as large as all the world to conquer. Sergeyevich, because the priest's given name is Sergei. And Pushkin because—well, no reason really. I just like the sound of it." And he laughed.

"Alexander Sergeyevich Pushkin," Elena said solemnly, "I am pleased to meet you."

Pushkin took her hand. "Not half as much as I am to meet you."

Elena blushed.

———

Elena was beautiful in the way that only a young woman of the Urals can be. Clean air and regular work had made her strong and healthy. Her red hair and her perfect complexion she got from her mother. It was inevitable that Pushkin should be drawn to her. And she, in turn, was already half in love with him.

They were young and so they were ingenious. Their affair lasted for months before it was discovered.

Thinking back on that period, many years later, it seemed to Elena like a dream. Never once did she consider the future—perhaps because she already knew that, for them, there could be none. Theirs was an old, old story and even an innocent like Elena knew exactly how such stories went, and how they must end.

When young Pushkin, disgraced for a second time in the eyes of Yekaterinburg, was sent away, Elena cried halfway through the night. But in the morning she dried her tears and set to work pulling her life back together. Since she had always known it would be like this, it took less time than might have been expected.

Not one person in the city thought they would ever hear from the American again. But there was an unexpected coda to this tale.

Years—but not many of them—passed and the rising fortunes of Elena's family caused them to sell their holdings in Yekaterinburg and move to St. Petersburg. There, much to her surprise, Elena learned that Pushkin had made something of a name for himself as a writer and poet. Indeed, he was by almost any standard to be considered a great success.

After considerable hesitation, Elena sent her former lover a letter into which she put a great deal of effort. It was neither too warm nor too cold. It presumed nothing, but neither did it preclude anything that might ensue. It was such a letter as might be printed in a grammar book as an exemplar of its kind.

By return mail came a missive that took her breath away.

Alexander Sergeyevich still loved her! In great storms of words he declared his passions, his yearning, his eternal devotion to her. All in a rush he overwhelmed the battlements of Elena's reserve, swept aside her defensive uncertainties, and retook the innermost sanctum of her heart. His was a letter that could never be printed in a grammar book, for though it contained not one gross or offensive word, it lay bare his soul. It was a letter that would have seduced a nun.

But Pushkin made no demands, nor presumed any presumptions. All he asked was for the chance to see Elena again, and to hear her voice like the music of the woods once more. Specifically, he suggested that they might attend the opera together.

Could there be any possible doubt that she would go? Elena went.

Pushkin sent a coach for Elena and when she alit before the opera house, he was waiting anxiously. On seeing her, a look of tremendous relief came over his face. He offered his arm and escorted her inside, to a private box.

For a girl from the provinces, it was like falling into a fairy tale. The best of St. Petersburg society were present and many a titled lady craned her neck to get a glimpse of the new beauty who adorned the great poet's presence. So dazzled was she that the opera itself, Rossini's *Il barbiere di Siviglia*, left Elena with only a vague impression of beauty, as if it were but a velvet background for the fine clothes and glittering jewelry of the audience. She did not so much see as feel the sidelong admiring glances of her former lover. Once she mischievously slipped free of a shoe to run a stockinged toe up under his trousers leg and caress his calf. From the corner of her eye she saw Pushkin shudder with desire. Yet outwardly he remained calm and composed, a perfect gentleman, and during intermission he graciously introduced her to his highly placed friends.

When the opera was over, they left in the same coach. By unspoken assent, they retired to Pushkin's apartments.

It was strange, for Elena, to return to her first love's embrace. Pushkin's stroke was longer and smoother. His hands lingered where once they had groped. It was clear he had experienced many women since last they'd been together, and learned much from them about the arts of love. Elena, though to a more modest degree, had in her turn learned enough since their springtime passion to appreciate the improvement.

Afterwards she lay in his arms while Pushkin happily made plans for them both. He would announce their engagement immediately. They would be married in the spring. He would buy her a house in the country where he would plant roses, and another in the city, where they would hold salons. Their first child would be a boy and the Tsar himself would come to the christening. Elena smiled and nodded. She fell asleep to his happy prattling.

In the morning. . . .

In the morning, Elena awoke first. She dressed quickly and fled from the apartment, though not without regrets. Pushkin was a restless sleeper and had kicked away most of the coverings, leaving him exposed to view. She had to fight down the urge to kiss his chest, or possibly some more intimate part of his body. But she left without the fleetingest touch of intimacy. For though she did not regret her actions of the previous night, she knew that to presume more would be false.

Pushkin tried to reestablish contact, of course. He assailed her with armies of letters, poems, and declarations of passion. All of which she read with melting heart and then burned to ashes in the cook stove.

Eventually he stopped.

Elena for her part found another lover. One day, eight months into their affair, he abruptly blurted out such a clumsy jumble of words that it took her a moment to realize it was a proposal. To her amazement, then, she discovered that she'd come to love this man dearly, and accepted on the spot.

Not long after, they were wed.

So it was as two respectably married individuals that Elena and Pushkin met for one last time. It was at an afternoon party thrown by a mutual friend when they both chanced to be passing through Moscow, headed in different directions. There was dancing and though they both danced, they did not dance with each other.

Nevertheless, Pushkin contrived to confront Elena when no one else was near. In a low, intense voice he said simply, "Why?"

"You are married and happily so, I hear," Elena said. "As am I. Let us leave it at that."

But Pushkin's look remained troubled. "You abandoned me, madam," he said, not in an accusatory manner but as one who has been shipwrecked and then subsequently rescued might wonder aloud how it had all came about. "I think I deserve an explanation."

Elena sighed and agreed. "Let us walk together in the garden, where everyone can see us and observe that we behave not as lovers but as old friends—I believe my reputation can stand up to that—and I will briefly tell you all."

So, strolling together, not touching, they talked. "Do you remember our first time together," Elena asked, "how we murmured to each other as we made love? You entreated me to tell you my every thought, my least emotion."

"I shall never forget. We were like two doves, cooing. I could reconstruct our conversation phrase for phrase, endearment by caress."

"Every night we talked like that."

"It was a feast of language and love."

"That time in St. Petersburg. What did I say then?"

Pushkin fell silent.

"I said nothing, and you did not notice for you'd already gotten what you wanted from me. I realized that night that it never was me you loved—it was the Russian tongue. Oh, you thought you loved me, because I was beautiful and new to you, as was it. You believed you were exploring my body and possibly even my soul, but all your greatest passion was reserved for the more voluptuous pleasures of the words and grammar and subtle phrasings of love and romance.

"What woman could compete with that? Not I."

For a long time Pushkin struggled to find the right words. At last he said, "Madam, you shame me."

"Being who you were, it was an easy mistake to make." Elena gazed calmly into Pushkin's eyes. "But the past is no more. Consider our current situations. I have my stalwart husband and you, your virtuous wife. All our lives are ahead of us. I am sure you will live to be a hundred, and scribbling away every day of it. If I have in some small way contributed to that, then I am happy."

On which note, they parted forever.

This is the true history of Pushkin the American. There are entire shelves of books which say otherwise, and for those I have no explanation. Perhaps history has confused him with somebody else of similar name. Possibly there was a cover-up of some sort. What no one knows, no man can tell. For my part I can only say: Here are the facts. Make of them what you will.

An Empty House
with Many Doors

The television set is upside down. I need its company while I clean, but not its distraction. Sipping gingerly at a glass of wine, I vacuum the Oriental rugs one-handed, with great care. Ah, Katherine, you'd be amazed the job I've done. The house has never been so clean.

I put the vacuum cleaner back in the closet. Cleanup takes next to no time at all since I eliminated all the unneeded furniture.

Rugs done, I'm about to get out the floor polish when it occurs to me that trash pickup is tomorrow. Humming, I roll up the carpets one by one, tie them with string, carry all three out to the curb. Then, since it's no longer needed, I set the vacuum cleaner beside them.

Back in the house, the living room is all but empty, the dried and bleached bones of our life picked clean of meat and memories. One surviving chair, the television, and a collapsible tray I've used since discarding the dining room table. The oven timer goes off; the pot pies are ready. I get out the plate, knife, and fork, slide out the pies, and throw away the foil roasting tray. I wipe the stove door with a damp rag, rinse the rag, wring it out, and put it away. Pour myself another glass of wine.

The television gibbers and shouts at me as I eat. People hang upside down, like bats. They scuttle across the ceiling, smiling insanely. The news bimbo is chatting up the latest disaster, mouth an inverted crescent. Somebody in a woodpecker suit is bashing his head into the bed of a pickup truck, over and over again. Is all this supposed to mean something? Was it ever?

The wine in my glass is half-gone already. Making good time tonight.

All of a sudden the bad feelings well up, like a gusher of misery. I squeeze my eyes shut, screwing my face tight, but somehow the tears seep through, and I'm sobbing. Crying uncontrollably, because while I'm still thinking about you, while I never do and never can stop thinking about you, it's getting harder and harder to remember what you looked like. It's going away from me. Oh Katherine, I'm losing your face!

No self-pity. I won't give in to it. I get out the mop and fill a bucket with warm water and ammonia detergent. Swabbing as hard as I can, I start to clean the floors. Until finally, it's under control. I top off my glass, take a sip, feel the wine burning in my belly. Drinking like this will kill a man, sooner or later. Which I why I work at it so hard.

I'm teaching myself how to die.

If I don't get some fresh air, I'll pass out. If I pass out, I'll drink less. Timing is all. I get my coat, walk out the door. Wibbledy-wobbledy, down the hill I go. Past the row houses and corner hoagie shops, the chocolate factory and the gas station, under the railroad bridge and along the canal, all the way down into Manayunk. The wine is buzzing in my head, but still the traitor brain dwells on you, a droning monologue on pain and loss and yearning. If only I'd kept you home that day. If only I'd only fucking only. Even I'm sick of hearing it. I lift up and above it, until conscious thought is just a drear mumble underfoot and I soar up godlike in the early evening air.

How you loved Manayunk, its old mill buildings, tumbledown collieries, and blue-collar residences. The yuppies have gentrified Main Street, but three blocks uphill from it the people haven't changed a bit; still hardheaded, suspicious, good neighbors. I float through the narrow streets, to the strip of trendy little restaurants on Main. My head swells and balloons and my feet barely touch the ground. I pass through the happy evening crowd, attached to the earth by the most tenuous of tethers. I'd sever it if I could, and simply float away.

Then I see the man strangling in midair.

Nobody else can see him. They stride purposefully by, some even walking through the patch of congealed air that, darkly sparkling, contains his struggling figure.

He is twisting in slow agony on a frame of chrome bars, like a fly dying on a spider's web. The outlines of his distorted body are prismatic at the edges, like a badly tuned video. He is drowning in dirty rainbows. His body is a cubist nightmare, torso shattered into overlapping planes, limbs scattered through nine dimensions. The head swings around, eyes multiplying and being swallowed up by flesh, and then there is a flash of desperate hope as he realizes I can see him. He reaches toward me, outflung arm spreading through a fan of possibilities. Caught in jellied air, dark and sparkling, his body shattered into strangely fractured planes.

Mouth opens in a silent scream, and through some form of sympathetic magic the faintest distant echoes of his pain sound a whispering screech of fingernails across the back of my skull.

I know a man who is drowning when I see one. People are scurrying about, some right through the man. They glance at me oddly, standing there, frozen on the sidewalk. I reach up and take his

!

hand.

It *hurts*. It hurts like a sonofabitch. I feel like I've been hit with a two-by-four. One side of my body goes completely numb. I am slammed sideways, thought whiting out under sheets of hard white pain, and it is a blessing because for the first time since you died, oh most beloved, I stop thinking about you.

When I come to, I draw myself together, stand up. I haven't moved, but the street is empty and dark. Must be late at night. Which is crazy, because people wouldn't just leave me lying there. It's not that kind of neighborhood. So why did they? It doesn't bear thinking about.

I stand up, and there, beside me, is the man's corpse.

He's dressed in a kind of white jumpsuit, with little high-tech crap scattered all over it. A badge on his chest with a fan of arrows branching out, diverging from a single point. I look at him. Dead, poor bastard, and nothing I can do about it.

I need another drink.

Home again, home again, trudge trudge trudge. As I approach the house, something is wrong, though. There are curtains in the windows, and orange light spills out. If I were a normal man, I'd be apprehensive, afraid, fearful of housebreakers and psychopaths. There's nothing I'd be less likely to do than go inside.

I go inside.

Someone is rattling pans in the kitchen. Humming. "Is that you, love?"

I stand there, inside the living room, trembling with something more abject than fear. It's the kind of curdling terror you might feel just before God walks into the room. No, I say to myself, don't even think it.

You walk into the room.

"That didn't take long," you say, amused. "Was the store closed?" Then, seeing me clearly, alarm touches your face, and you say, "Johnny?"

I'm trembling. You reach out a hand and touch me, and it's like a world of ice breaking up inside, and I start to cry. "Love, what's *wrong*?"

Which is when I walk into the room.

Again.

The two of me stare at each other. At first, to be honest, I don't make the connection. I just think: There's something odd about this man. Strangest damn guy I ever did see, and I can't figure out why. All those movies and television shows where somebody is suddenly confronted by his exact double and goes slack-jawed with shock? Lies, the batch of them. He doesn't look a bit like the way I picture myself.

"Johnny?" Katherine says in a strangled little voice. But she's not looking at me but at the other guy and he's staring at me in a bemused kind of way, as if there's something strange and baffling about *me*, and then all of a sudden the dime drops.

He's me.

He's me and he's not getting it anymore than I was. "Katherine?" he says. "Who *is* this?"

A very long evening later, I find myself lying on the couch under a blanket with pillows beneath my head. Upstairs, Katherine and the other me are arguing. His voice is low and angry. Hers is calm and reasonable, but he doesn't like what it says. It was my wallet that convinced her: the driver's license identical to his in every way, the credit and library and insurance cards, all the incidental pieces of identification one picks up along the way, and every single one of them exactly the same as his.

Save for the fact that his belong to a man whose wife is still alive.

I don't know exactly what you're saying up there, but I can guess at the emotional heart of it. You love me. This is, in a sense, my house. I have nowhere else to go. You are not about to turn me out.

Meanwhile, I—the me upstairs, I mean—am angry and unhappy about my being here at all. He knows me better than you do, and he doesn't like me one-tenth as much. Knowing that there's no way you could tell us apart, he is filled with paranoid fantasies. He's afraid I'm going to try to take his place.

Which, if I could, I most certainly would. But that would probably require my killing him and I'm not sure I could actually kill a man. Even if that man were myself. And how could I possibly hope to square it with Katherine? I'm in uncharted territory here. I have no idea what might or might not happen.

For now, though, it's enough to simply hear your voice. I ignore the rest and close my eyes and smile.

A car rumbles down the road outside and then abruptly stops. As do the voices above. All other noises cease as sharply as if somebody has thrown a switch.

Puzzled, I get up from the couch.

Out of nowhere, strong hands seize my arms. There's a man standing to the right of me and another to the left. They both wear white jumpsuits, which I understand now to be a kind of uniform. They wear the same badge—a fan of arrows radiant from a common locus— as the man I saw strangling in the air.

"We're sorry, sir," says one. "We saw you trying to help our comrade, and we appreciate that. But you're in the wrong place and we have to put you back."

"You're time travelers or something, aren't you?" I ask.

"Or something," the second one says. He's holding onto my right arm. With his free hand he opens a kind of pod floating in the air beside him. An equipment bag, I think. It's filled with devices which seem to be only half there. A gleaming tube wraps itself around my chest, another around my forehead. "But don't worry. We'll have everything set right in just a jiff."

Then I twig to what's going on.

"No," I say. "She's *here*, don't you understand that? I'll keep my mouth shut, I won't say anything to anyone ever, I swear. Only let me stay. I'll move to another city, I won't bother anybody. The two upstairs will think they had some kind of shared hallucination. Only please, for God's sake, let me exist in a world where Katherine's not dead."

There is a terrible look of compassion in the man's eyes. "Sir. If it were possible, we would let you stay."

"Done," says the other. The world goes away.

So I return to my empty house. I pour myself a glass of wine and stare at it for a long, long time. Then I get up and pour it into the sink.

A year passes.

It's night and I'm standing in our tiny urban backyard, Katherine, looking up at the stars and a narrow sliver of moon. Talking to you. I know you can't hear me. But I've been thinking about that strange night ever since it happened, and it seems to me that in an infinite universe, all possibilities are manifest in an eternal present. Somewhere you're happy, and that makes me glad. In countless other places, you're a widow and heartbroken. Surely one of you at least is standing out in the backyard, like I am now, staring up at the moon and imagining that I'm saying these words. Which is why I'm here. So it will be true.

I don't really have much to say, I'm afraid. I just want you to know I still love you and that I'm doing fine. I wasn't, for a while there. But just knowing you're alive somehow, however impossibly far away, is enough to keep me going.

You're never really dead, I know that now.

And if it makes you feel any better, neither am I.

The She-Wolf's Hidden Grin

When I was a girl my sister Susanna and I had to get up early whether we were rested or not. In winter particularly, our day often began before sunrise; and because our dormitory was in the south wing of the house, with narrow windows facing the central courtyard and thus facing north, the lurid, pinkish light sometimes was hours late in arriving and we would wash and dress while we were still uncertain whether we were awake or not. Groggy and only half coherent, we would tell each other our dreams.

One particular dream I narrated to Susanna several times before she demanded I stop. In it, I stood before the main doorway to our house staring up at the marble bas-relief of a she-wolf suckling two infant girls (though in waking life the babies similarly feeding had wee chubby penises my sister and I had often joked about), with a puzzled sense that something was fundamentally wrong. "You are anxious for me to come out of hiding," a rasping whispery voice said in my ear. "Aren't you, daughter?"

I turned and was not surprised to find the she-wolf standing behind me, her tremendous head on the same level as my own. She was far larger than any wolf from ancestral Earth. Her fur was greasy and reeked of sweat. Her breath stank of carrion. Her eyes said that she was perfectly capable of ripping open my chest and eating my heart without the slightest remorse. Yet, in the way of dreams, I was not afraid of her. She seemed to be as familiar as my own self.

"Is it time?" I said, hardly knowing what I was asking.

"No," the mother-wolf said, fading.

And I awoke.

Last night I returned to my old dormitory room and was astonished how small it was, how cramped and airless; it could never had held something so unruly and commodious as my childhood. Yet legions of memories rose up from its dust to batter against me like moths, so thickly that I was afraid to breathe lest they should fly into my throat and lungs to choke me. Foremost among them being the memory of when I first met the woman from Sainte Anne who was the last in a long line of tutors bought to educate my sister and me.

Something we had seen along the way had excited the two of us, so that we entered the lesson room in a rush, accompanied by shrieks of laughter; only to be brought up short by a stranger waiting there. She was long-legged, rangy, lean of face, dressed in the dowdy attire of a woman who had somehow managed to acquire a university education, and she carried a teacher's baton. As we sat down at our desks, she studied us as a heron might some dubious species of bait fish, trying to decide if it were edible or not. Susanna recovered first. "What has happened to Miss Claire?" she asked.

In a voice dry and cool and unsympathetic, the stranger said, "She has been taken away by the secret police. For what offenses, I cannot say. I am her replacement. You will call me Tante Amélie."

"'Tante' is a term of endearment," I said impudently, "which you have done nothing to earn."

"It is not yours to decide where your affection is to be directed. That is your father's prerogative and in this instance the decision has already been made. What are your favorite subjects?"

"Molecular and genetic biology," Susanna said promptly.

"Classical biology." I did not admit that chiefly I enjoyed the wet lab, and that only because I enjoyed cutting things open, for I had learned at an early age to hold my cards close to my chest.

"Hmmph. We'll begin with history. Where were you with your last instructor?"

"We were just about to cover the Uprising of Sainte Anne," Susanna said daringly.

Again that look. "It is too soon to know what the truth of that was. When the government issues an official history, I'll let you know. In the meantime we might as well start over from the beginning. You." She pointed at Susanna. "What is Veil's Hypothesis?"

"Dr. Aubrey Veil posited that the abos—"

"Aborigines."

Susanna stared in astonishment, then continued, "It is the idea that when the ships from Earth arrived on Sainte Anne, the aborigines killed everyone and assumed their appearance."

"Do you think this happened? Say no."

"No."

"Why not?"

"If it had, that would mean that we—everyone on Sainte Anne and Sainte Croix both—were abos. Aborigines, I mean. Yet we think as humans, act as humans, live as humans. What would be the point of so elaborate a masquerade if its perpetrators could never enjoy the fruits of their deceit? Particularly when the humans had proved to be inferior by allowing themselves to be exterminated. Anyway, mimicry in nature is all about external appearance. The first time an aborigine's corpse was cut open in a morgue, the game would be over."

Turning to me, Tante Amélie said, "Your turn. Defend the hypothesis."

"The aborigines were not native to Sainte Anne. They came from the stars," I began.

Susanna made a rude noise. Our new tutor raised her baton and she lowered her eyes in submission. "Defend your premise," Tante Amélie said.

"They are completely absent from the fossil record."

"Go on."

"When they arrived in this star system, they had technology equal to or superior to our own, which, due to some unrecorded disaster, they lost almost immediately. Otherwise they would have also been found here on Sainte Croix." I was thinking furiously, making it all up as I went along. "They rapidly descended to a Stone-Age level of existence. As intelligent beings, they would have seen what was going on and tried to save some aspect of their sciences. Electronics, metallurgy, chemistry—all disappeared. All they could save was their superior knowledge of genetics. When humans came along, they could not resist us physically. So they interbred with us, producing human offspring with latent aboriginal genes. They would have started with pioneers and outliers and then moved steadily inward into human society, spreading first through the lower classes and saving the rich and best-defended for last. Once begun, the process would proceed without conscious mediation. The aborigines would not awaken until their work was done."

"Supporting evidence?"

"The policies of the government toward the poor suggest an awareness of this threat on their part."

"I see that I have fallen into a den of subversives. No wonder your last tutor is no more. Well, what's past is over now. Place your hands flat on your desks, palms down." We obeyed and Tante Amélie rapped our knuckles with her baton, as all our tutors had done at the beginning of their reigns. "We will now consider the early forms of colonial government."

Tante Amélie was the daughter of a regional administrator in a rural district called Île d'Orléans. As a girl, she had climbed trees to plunder eggs from birds' nests and trapped beetles within castles of mud. She also gigged frogs, fished from a rowboat, caught crabs with a scrap of meat and a length of string, plucked chickens, owned a shotgun, hunted waterfowl, ground her own telescope lenses, and swam naked in the backwater of a river so turbulent it claimed at least one life every year. This was as alien and enchanting as a fairy tale to my sister and me and of an evening we could sometimes coax her into reminiscing. Even now I can see her rocking steadily in the orange glow of an oil lamp, pausing every now and again to raise a sachet of dried herbs from her lap so the scents of lemon, vanilla, and tea leaves would help her memory. She had made it to adulthood and almost to safety before her father "inhaled his fortune," as the saying went on our sister planet. But of the years between then and her fetching up with us, she would say nothing.

It may seem odd that my sister and I came to feel something very close to love for Tante Amélie. But what alternative did we have? We only rarely saw our father. Our mother had produced two girls and multiple stillbirths before being sent away and replaced with the woman we addressed only as Maitresse. None of the other tutors, even those who resisted the temptation to sample father's wares, lasted very long. Nor were we allowed outside unaccompanied by an adult, for fear of being kidnapped. There were not many objects for our young hearts to fasten upon, and Tante Amélie had the potent advantage of controlling our access to the outside world.

Our house at 999 Rue d'Astarte doubled as my father's business, and so was redolent of esters, pheromones, and chemical fractions, most particularly that of bitter truffle, for he held a monopoly over its import and used it in all his perfumes as a kind of signature. There were always people coming and going: farmers bringing wagons piled high with bales of flowers, traders from the Southern Sea bearing ambergris, slave artisans lugging in parts for the stills, neurochemists summoned to fine-tune some new process, courtesans in search of aphrodisiacs and abortifacients, overfed buyers almost inevitably accompanied by children with painted faces and lace-trimmed outfits. Yet Susanna and I were only rarely allowed beyond the run of the dormitory, classroom, and laboratory. Freedom for us began at the city library, the park, the slave market, and the like. Tante Amélie was a vigorous woman with many outside interests, so our fortunes took an immediate uptick at her arrival. Then we discovered quite by accident that she had opened a bank account (legal but interest-free) in hope of one day buying her freedom. This meant that she was amenable to bribery, and suddenly our horizons were limited only by our imaginations. The years that Tante Amélie spent with us were the happiest of my life.

For my sister too, I believe, though it was hard to tell with her. That was the period in which her passion for genetics peaked. She was always taking swabs of cell samples and patiently teasing out gene sequences from stolen strands of hair or nail clippings. Many an afternoon I trailed after her, in Tante Amélie's bought company, as she scoured the flesh market for some variant of Sainte-Anne's ape or rummaged in disreputable antique shops for hand-carved implements that might be made from—but never were—genuine abo bone. "You think I don't know what you're doing," I told her once.

"Shut up, useless."

"You're trying to prove Veil's Hypothesis. Well, what if you did? Do you think anyone would listen to you? You're just a child."

"Look who's talking."

"Even if they took you seriously, so what? What difference would it make?"

Susanna stared nobly into a future only she could see. "Madame Curie said, 'We must believe that we are gifted for something and that this thing, at whatever cost, must be attained.' If I could make just one single discovery of worth, that would atone for a great deal." Then she lowered her gaze to look directly at me, silently daring me to admit I didn't understand.

Baffled and resentful, I lapsed into silence.

I did not notice the change in my sister at first. By slow degrees she became sullen and moody and lost interest in her studies. This, for an irony, happened just as I was growing serious about my own and would have welcomed her mentorship. It was not to be. A shadow had fallen between us. She no longer confided in me as she once had; nor did we share our dreams.

Rummaging in her desk for a retractor one day, I discovered the notebook, which previously she had kept locked away, recording her great study. I had never been allowed to look at it and so I studied it intensely. Parts of it I can still recite from memory:

> *This implies a congeries of recessive sex-linked genes; they, being dependent on the x-chromosome, will necessarily appear only in women.*

and

> *Under the right conditions, activating the operon genes in the proper sequence, the transformation would occur very rapidly, even in adults.*

and

> *Colonization of the twin planets entailed an extreme constriction of genetic plasticity, which renders heritability of these recessives at close to one hundred percent.*

and most provocative of all

> *All this presupposes that abos and humans can interbreed & thus that they spring from a common star-faring (most likely extinct) race.* H. sapiens *and* H. aboriginalis *are then not two separate species but specializations of the inferred species* H. sidereus.

The bulk of the notebook was filled with gene sequences that despite Susanna's tidy schoolgirl script I could barely make sense of.

But I journeyed through to the end of the notes and it was only when I fetched up against blank pages that I realized that she hadn't added to them in weeks.

That was the summer when Susanna conceived a passion for theater. She went to see *Riders to the Sea* and *Madame Butterfly* and *Antony and Cleopatra* and *The Women* and *Mrs. Warren's Profession* and *Lysistrata* and *Hedda Gabler* and *The Rover* and I forget what else. She even got a small part in *The Children's Hour*. I attended one rehearsal, was not made to feel welcome, and never showed up again.

Thus it was that when I had my first period (I had been well prepared so I recognized the symptoms and knew what to do), I did not tell her. This was on a Sunday morning in early spring. Feeling distant and unhappy, I dressed for church without saying a word to my sister. She didn't notice that I was withholding something from her, though in retrospect it seems that I could hardly have been more obvious.

We went to Ste. Dymphna's, sitting as usual in a pew halfway to the altar. Tante Amélie, of course, sat in the back of the church with the other slaves. Shortly after the Mass began, a latecomer, a young woman whom I felt certain I had seen before, slipped into our pew. She was dressed in black, with fingerless lace gloves and had a round, moon-white face dominated by two black smudges of eyes and a pair of carmine lips. I saw her catch my sister's eye and smile.

I endured the service as best I could. Since the rebellion, the Québécois liturgy had been banned and though I understood the reasons for it the vernacular sounded alien to my ear. Midway through the monsignor's interminable sermon something—a chance shift of light through the stained glass windows, perhaps, or the unexpected flight of a demoiselle fly past my head—drew my attention away from his impassioned drone, and I saw the stranger stifle a yawn with the back of her hand, then casually place that hand, knuckles down on the pew between her and my sister. A moment later, Susanna looked away and placed her own hand atop it. Their fingers intertwined and then clenched.

And I knew.

———————

The components for a disaster had been assembled. All that was needed was a spark.

That spark occurred when Susanna returned from cotillion in tears. I trailed along in the shadow of her disgrace, feeling a humiliation that was the twin of hers though I had done nothing to earn it. Nevertheless, as always happened in such cases, as soon as our escort had returned us to our father's house and made his report, we were summoned as a pair before Tante Amélie. She sat on a plain wooden chair, her hands overlapping on the knob of a cane she had recently taken to using, looking stern as a judge.

"You spat in the boy's face," she said without preamble. "There was no excuse for that."

"He put his hand—"

"Boys do those things all the time. It was your responsibility to anticipate his action and forestall it without giving him offense. What else do you think you go to cotillion to learn?"

"Don't bother sending me back there, then. I'm not going to become that kind of person."

"Oh? And just what kind of person do you imagine you can be?"

"Myself!" Susanna said.

The two women (it was in that moment that I realized my sister had stolen yet another march on me and left her childhood behind) locked glares. I, meanwhile, was ignored, miserable, and unable to leave. I clasped my hands behind my back and let my fingers fight with one another. The injustice of my being there at all gnawed at me, growing more and more acute.

Angrily, Tante Amélie said, "I despair for you. Why are you behaving like this? Why can't I get a straight answer out of you? Why—"

"Why don't you ask her girlfriend?" I blurted out.

Tante Amélie's lips narrowed and her face turned white. She lifted up her cane and slammed it down on the floor with a *thump*. Then she was on her feet and with a swirl of skirts was gone from the room, leaving Susanna shivering with fear.

But when I tried to comfort my sister, she pushed me away.

The summons came later than I expected, almost a week after Tante Amélie's abrupt cane-thump and departure. Tante Amélie escorted us to Maitresse's austere and unfeminine office—she had been the company doctor, according to gossip, before catching Father's eye—and with a curtsey abandoned us there. Maitresse was a pretty woman currently making the transition to "handsome," very tall and slender, and that evening she wore a pink dress. When she spoke, her tone was not angry but sorrowful. "You both know that your place in life is to marry well and increase the prestige of our house. A great deal of money has been invested in you." Susanna opened her mouth to speak, but Maitresse held up a hand to forestall her. "We are not here to argue; the time for that is long past. No one is angry at you for what you have done with that young lady. I have performed for your father with other women many times. But you must both learn to look to your futures without sentiment or emotion.

"We are going out. There is something you must see."

Into the lantern-lit night streets of Port-Mimizon we sallied. This was a pleasure I had almost never experienced before, so that my apprehension was mingled with a kind of elation. A light breeze carried occasional snatches of music and gusts of laughter from unseen revelries. Maitresse had dressed us in long cloaks and Venetian carnival masks—undecorated *voltos* for us girls and for her a *medico della peste* with a beak as long as Pinocchio's—as was the custom for unescorted females.

The slave market at night was dark and silent. No lanterns were lit along its length, making the windowless compound seem a malevolent beast, crouching in wait for unwary prey to chance by. But Maitresse did not hurry her step. We turned a corner and at the end of an alley dark as a tunnel saw a bright blaze of light and well-dressed men and women hurrying up the steps of a fighting club.

Maitresse led us around to the side, where we were let in at her knock. A dwarfish man obsequiously led the way to a small private waiting room with leather armchairs and flickering lights in mother-of-pearl sconces. "We'll have tea," she told the little man and he left. While we waited, for what I could not imagine, Maitresse addressed us once again.

"I spoke of the trouble and expense that went into your educations. You probably think that if you don't make good marriages, you will simply be sold for courtesans. That was a reasonable expectation a generation ago. But times have changed. Male infants have become rarer and even the best-brought-up girls are a glut on the market. Increasingly more men have taken to pederasty. The reasons are not well understood. Social? Cumulative poisoning from subtle alien compounds in the environment over the course of generations? No one knows."

"I will not give up Giselle," Susanna said almost calmly. "There is nothing you can do or threaten that will change my mind. She and I . . . but I imagine you know nothing about such passion as ours."

"Not know passion?" Maitresse laughed lightly, a delicate trill of silver bells. "My dear, how do you think I got involved in this mess in the first place?"

Our tea came and we drank, a quiet parody of domesticity.

What felt like hours dragged by. Finally, there came a roar of many voices through the wall and the dwarf deferentially reappeared at the door. "Ah." Maitresse put down her teacup. "It is time."

We entered our theater box between bouts, as the winner was being wrestled to the ground and sedated and his opponent carried away. Susanna sat stiffly in her seat, but I could not resist leaning over the rails to gawk at the audience. The theater smelled of cigar smoke and human sweat, with an under-scent of truffle so familiar that at first I thought nothing of it. As I watched, people wandered away from their seats, some to buy drinks, others retiring by pairs into private booths, while yet others. . . . My sight fixed on a large man as he snapped a small glass vial beneath his nose. His head lolled back and a big loutish grin blossomed on his heavy face. I had never witnessed anyone sampling perfume in public before but having seen it once I immediately recognized its gestures being repeated again and again throughout the room. "Your father's wares," Maitresse observed, "are extremely popular." I was not sure if she wanted me to feel proud or ashamed; but I felt neither, only fearful and confused.

After a time the audience, alerted by cues undetectable to me, reassembled itself in the tiered rows of chairs wrapped around a central pit with canvas-lined walls. The loud chatter turned to a dwindling murmur and then swelled up again in a roar of unclean approval as two girls, naked, were led stumbling down opposing aisles. Their heads were shaved (so they could not be seized by the hair, I later learned) and one had her face painted red and the other blue. Because they were both of slender build and similar height, this was needed to tell them apart.

Several slaves, nimble as apes, lowered the girls into the pit, then jumped down to rub their shoulders, chafe their hands, speak into their ears, and break vial after vial of perfume under their noses. By degrees the fighters came fully awake and then filled with such rage that they had to be held back by four men apiece to keep them from prematurely attacking each other. Then a bell rang and, releasing their charges, the slaves scrambled up the canvas walls and out of the pit.

The audience below came to their feet.

"Do not look away," Maitresse said. "If you have any questions, I will answer them."

The two girls ran together.

"How do they get them to fight?" I asked even though I was certain I would be told simply that they had no choice. Because were I in their place, knowing that the best I could hope for was to survive in order to undergo the same ordeal again in a week, I would not fight someone of my trainers' choosing. I would leap up into the audience and kill as many of them as I could before I was brought down. It was the only reasonable thing to do.

"Your father creates perfumes for myriad purposes. Some cure schizophrenia. Some make it possible to work a forty-hour shift. Some are simple fantasies. Others are more elaborately crafted. Those below might think they are dire-wolves fighting spear-carrying primitives, or perhaps abos defending their families from human ravagers. Their actions seem perfectly rational to them, and they will generate memories to justify them." As commanded, I did not look away but I could feel her gaze on the side of my face nonetheless. "I could arrange for you to sample some of your father's perfumes, if you're curious. You would not like them. But if you persisted, after a time you would find yourself liking them very much indeed. My best advice to you is not to start. But once would not hurt."

I shook my head to blink away my tears. Misinterpreting the gesture, Maitresse said, "That is wise."

We watched the rest of the fight without further comment. When it ended, the survivor threw back her head and howled. Even when burly slaves immobilized and then tranquilized her, her mad grin burned triumphantly.

"May I stop watching now?" Susanna asked. I could tell she meant it to be defiant. But her voice came out small and plaintive.

"Soon." Maitresse leaned over the rail and called down to the pit-slaves, "Show us the body."

The pit workers started to hoist up the naked corpse for her examination.

"Clean her up first."

They produced a dirty cloth and rubbed at the girl's face, wiping away most of the red paint. Then they lifted her up again. In death, she seemed particularly childlike: slender, small-breasted and long-legged. The hair on her pubic mound was a golden mist. I could not help wondering if she had experienced sex before her premature death and, if so, what it had been like.

"Study her features," Maitresse said dryly.

I did so, without results. Turning to my sister with a petulant shrug, I saw in the mirror of her horrified expression the truth. There came then a shifting within me like all the planets in the universe coming into alignment at once. When I looked back at the dead fighter I saw her face afresh. It could have been a younger version of my sister's face. But it was not.

It was my own.

Susanna said nothing during the long walk home, nor did I.

Maitresse, however, spoke at length and without emotion. "Your mother made many children. You—" (she meant Susanna) "—were natural. You—" (me) "were the first of many clones commissioned in an attempt to create a male heir, all failures. When your mother was sent away, your father resolved to get rid of everything that reminded him of her. I argued against it and in the end we compromised and kept the two of you while selling off the others. I have no idea how many survive. However, the economic realities of the day are such that, were either of you to be sold, you would fetch the highest price here." She said a great deal more as well but it was unnecessary; we already well understood everything that she had to tell us.

When we arrived home, Maitresse took our masks from us and bid us both a pleasant good-night.

We went to sleep, my sister and I, cradled in each other's arms, the first time we had done so in over a year. In the morning, Tante Amélie was gone and our formal educations were done forever.

Last night, as I said, I returned to my old dormitory room. It took me a while to realize that I was dreaming. It was only when I looked for Susanna and found nothing but dust and memories that I recollected how many years had gone by since my childhood. Still, in the way of dreams, there was a pervasive sense that the entire world was about to change. "You know what to do now," a rasping whispery voice said. "Don't you, daughter?"

I turned and the she-wolf was not there. But I felt sure of her presence anyway. "Is it time?" I asked.

She did not reply. Her silence was answer enough.

I *grinned* for I now understood where the she-wolf had been hiding all this time.

Not so much awakening as taking my dream-state with me into the waking world, I got up out of bed and walked down the hall to my husband's room. Then I paid a visit to the nursery, where my twin sons were sleeping. Finally, I went out into the night-dark streets to look for my sister.

The night is almost over now, and we must hurry to finish what we have begun. At dawn we will leave the cities behind and return to the swamps and forests, the caverns and hills from which the humans had driven us, and resume our long-interrupted lives. I have taken off my skin and now prowl naked through the streets of Port-Mimizon. In the shadows about me I sense many others who were once human and I devoutly pray that there are enough of us for our purpose. In the back of my mind, I wonder whether all this is real or if I have descended into the pit of madness. But that is a minor concern. I have work to do.

I have freed the she-wolf from within her hiding place and there is blood on her muzzle.

Only . . . why does the world smell as it does? Of canvas and bitter truffle.

The House of Dreams

"Have you ever killed a man?" the vagrant asked.

"That is not something we discuss," his companion replied.

"I myself have killed five. That is not many. But two I killed with my bare hands, which, I assure you, is not easy."

"I am sure that it is not."

"Don't you know?"

The second vagrant said nothing. They both continued trudging across the frozen German countryside. Winter had been almost as hard on the lands hereabout as the war had been to the lands to the east. It had buckled roads and destroyed bridges and collapsed roofs, and if there were any leavings to be gleaned in the fields they were buried under sheets of ice. The stubble crunched like glass underfoot, making the going difficult. But the main routes were all choked with refugees and since the vagrants were headed in the opposite direction, toward the front, to use them would only draw attention to themselves.

"Ritter?" the first vagrant said.

"Mmm?"

"Do you remember our instructions?"

Ritter stopped. "Of course I do," he said. "Don't you?"

"Oh, I remember them. I just don't believe in them anymore. We've been walking so long that all my life seems like a dream to me now. Sometimes I cannot even remember our destination." When Ritter said nothing, his companion turned away. "But let's not stand out here in the open, waiting for the Cossacks to discover us."

They resumed walking. A leafless tree rose up in the distance, crept slowly toward them, was a brief respite from the monotonously unchanging fields, and then dwindled away to their rear. "Ritter?"

"Eh?"

"I address you by name, the way a true comrade does. Why do you never do the same for me?"

Again Ritter stopped. "That is a good question," he said. "A very good question indeed." Anger entered his voice. "Let me ask you some of my own. Why do you not know our mission or our destination or even your own name? Why is everything so silent and still? Why are my legs not weary from all this walking? Why does the sky look so much like a plaster ceiling? Why can I not make out the features of your face? Why are you neither tall nor short, nor thin nor fat, nor ruddy nor pale? Exactly who are you and just what game are you playing with me?"

You should never have used the word "dream," a woman's voice said.

That wasn't it. When I tried to find out who his companion was, something told him I was an imposter.

In any case, this session is done.

Everything went black.

When Ritter awoke, he found himself lying under a feather bolster in a bedroom with yellow walls and green trim, a flowered jug atop a washstand, and a winter landscape outside the curtained window. A short man with the broadest shoulders he had ever seen on a human being stood looking out that window, hands clasped behind his back. An old woman sat in a wooden chair, embroidery loop in hand, sewing tight little stitches with a sharp tug at the end of each. "Where am I?" Ritter said. His head felt thick and dull.

"Someplace safe." The man turned, smiling. He had a round, benevolent face. To see him was to want to trust him. "Among friends."

"Ah." Ritter's heart sank. "I see." He closed his eyes. "At least I made it through the front lines."

"Too bad for you that you did," the old woman said. "We have already determined that you are in the pay of the British Secret Service. Your presence here in civilian clothing is by itself enough to justify your execution as a foreign spy."

With a touch of asperity, Ritter said, "I am a German citizen in Austro-German-Bavarian territory. It is my right to be in my own country."

The man shook his head in gentle reprimand. "The land you were born into ceased to exist weeks ago. Legally, you are a nationalist partisan in the westernmost provinces of the Mongolian Empire. But we are getting off on the wrong foot. Let us start over. Dr. Nergüi and I are alienists. We have begun a program of dream therapy intended first to obtain information from you, then to use that information to cure you of your unthinking loyalty to an anachronistic and dysfunctional regime, and finally to convert you wholeheartedly to our cause."

"That is not possible," Ritter said with conviction.

"Think of Borsuk and me as dam-busters," Dr. Nergüi said. "We drill and we drill with no discernable results until at last our labor produces a single drop of water. Shortly after that, another follows, and another, and before you know it, the wall bursts open and the lake that the dam has been holding back explodes outward, inundating all before it."

"But that's enough chatter for now." Borsuk patted Ritter's shoulder. "Go to sleep, my friend. We have hard work before us. Very hard indeed."

All against his will, Ritter felt himself tumbling down into the darkness, into the depths of sleep. Somewhere far, far away in the forests of the night, he thought he sensed someone or something searching for him. Somehow that seemed important.

In his dreams, Ritter was standing in Sir Tobias Gracchus Willoughby-Quirke's classically austere, oak-paneled office. Arrayed on the desk between them were the clothing and accouterments of an indigent.

Sir Toby waved a hand at the ragged clothing. "Everything you see here is convincingly shabby, and yet serviceable as well. The coat is good, dense wool—even the patches. Soaking wet, it will keep you warm. The shoes look decrepit but are cut to the measure of your feet. They have been waterproofed with candle wax, as a hobo might do. Inside the laces are lengths of pianoforte wire suitable for making snares or garrotes. It would be suspicious for you to carry a gun. However, you will have this." He picked up what looked to be a common kitchen knife. "Sheffield steel. Antique but sharp. The wooden handle is broken and taped together with strips of linen in a manner that looks makeshift. Yet in a fight, you may rely on it."

"I see that I have some rough traveling ahead of me," Ritter said. "Where exactly do you wish me to go?"

"I am sending you and your partner to the Continent, behind enemy lines. You will rendezvous there with a member of the resistance who has important information to share with us." Sir Toby presented an envelope and Ritter, feeling a strange, sourceless reluctance, opened it and read. It contained a name, an address, and a date. That was all.

"Is that all?"

Sir Toby took back the envelope. "I am reluctant to give you more than an absolute minimum of information, for fear of the consequences should you be captured."

"I will not be captured. But if I am, I am confident that I shall escape."

"Oh?" Sir Toby placed his hands on the desk and leaned forward. His eyes gleamed. *"How?"*

Astonished, Ritter said, "You know how. My—" He looked around the office, at the walls that swelled and snapped like canvas in the wind, at the bust of the archmage Roger Bacon in the tympanum over the door that leered and winked at him, at the inkwell that went tumbling in the air without spilling a drop of its contents. It all felt wrong. Even Sir Toby himself seemed an unconvincing scrim over some darker and truer version of reality. Ritter's head ached. It was hard to think logically. "Or do you?"

"Let's say that I don't. Purely as a sort of exercise. It's your partner, isn't it? You're counting on him to rescue you." Sir Toby smiled in a way that was avuncular, predatory, insincere. "Aren't you, son?"

Convulsively, Ritter swept his hand over the desk, sending its clutter—clothes, shoes, knife, and all—lying in every direction. "You are not my father. Nor are you the man you pretend to be. Clearly, you are part of a conspiracy of some kind. Well, it won't work! You'll get nothing out of me!"

Excellent work. I shall return him to consciousness now.

"You see how easy that was?" Borsuk said. "Dr. Nergüi put you under and I guided your thoughts, and now we know your mission, the name by which your contact will identify himself, and where and when he may be captured. All that remains to be discovered is the identity of your oh-so-mysterious partner."

"Do you still think you will not break?" Dr. Nergüi asked.

When Ritter did not reply, she picked up her embroidery and set to sewing again.

For a long time, Ritter lay in the bed, eyes closed, listening to the scratch of a goose-quill pen—Borsuk writing up his findings, no doubt. The rest of the house was uncannily quiet. He could hear small creaks and groans as boards shifted slightly. But no voices, no footfalls, not the least indication that, save for the inhabitants of this room, the house was occupied. Finally, he said, "So it is just you two here? No orderlies or guards?"

Abrupt silence. Then Borsuk said, "This one's an optimist, Dr. Nergüi. Even *in extremis*, this clever young man probes for information, tries to seek out our weaknesses, makes plans for escape." He sounded almost proud of Ritter.

"There is a war going on, in case you haven't noticed," Dr. Nergüi said. "Resources are stretched thin. We must make do with what we have. But if you think the two of us are not up to the task. . . ." She produced the knife that Sir Toby had given Ritter and placed it on the nightstand. "Sit up."

Ritter did.

"Now pick up the knife."

He tried. But whenever Ritter made to close his fingers about the hilt, his hand turned out to be above or below the knife, clenching empty air. Again and again he tried, with the same maddening lack of results.

Dryly, Dr. Nergüi said, "So you see now that it is useless to try to escape."

"I see that you are glamour-workers with a mountebank's talent for illusion. But I still have my indomitable Teutonic will, thank God. You may kill me if you wish, but your tuppenny magics cannot make me do your bidding."

In an off-handed manner (for he still continued to write), Borsuk said, "Of all the talents, that of illusion has always been thought the weakest. Oh, we could walk you off a cliff or show you the dead face of whomever you loved most and convince you it was your own doing— for a time. But we could not set a forest ablaze the way a pyromancer can, nor cripple a man with frostbite like an ice wizard. Our magic wears off and thus it was never greatly valued.

"But then it was realized that, all magic deriving from the powers of the mind, illusion was the very key to its source. In her homeland, Dr. Nergüi is considered a very great woman for her discoveries. You should be proud to have her devoted to your case." Borsuk sprinkled sand over his writing and shook it off again. "Your contact lives not an hour's walk from here. The messenger who will carry this report"—he rattled the parchment—"to Military Intelligence is not expected until tomorrow morning. If only you were free, you could warn your contact, get his information, and snatch success from the embers of failure."

For a single heartbeat, hope leapt up within Ritter's breast. Then he said, "You taunt me."

"Perhaps I do. Get dressed. Your clothes are in the armoire. No need to be shy before Dr. Nergüi, she's a grandmother—"

"Great-grandmother."

"Great-grandmother, and she's seen it all before. Your boots are under the bed. Make sure to wear two pairs of socks—it's cold out there."

Wondering, Ritter did as he was told.

"Now, leave."

The bedroom opened into a homely parlor room, washed in grey winter light. His mud-stained greatcoat hung on a peg by the door. Ritter donned it. He went outside and stood blinking on the stoop. The frozen fields he remembered so vividly from his dream or hallucination stretched toward a wood that was clearly miles away, a mere line in the distance. He took a few hesitant steps in its direction and then looked back at the building he had just left. A sign over the door read САНАТОРИЙ. Sanitarium. That was the only indication that his prison was anything other than a farmhouse.

Turning his face to the horizon, Ritter began to walk, expecting with every step a shout from behind, followed by a bullet in the back. Inexplicably, this did not happen. Field-stubble crunching underfoot, he broke into a clumsy run. Other than the lazy cawing of faraway crows, his footfalls and the rasp of his breath were the only sounds.

It was not possible that they would simply release him.

Was it?

The trees were all but unreachable. But if he could make his way to them, he had the barest chance of escape. He ran and as he ran the cold air cleared his head. The mental fog lifted at last, revealing a variety of pains that had been hiding beneath it. He was obviously heavily bruised on his legs, shoulders, and buttocks, and his ribs ached like blazes. The result of a beating he had received when he had been caught, no doubt. He vaguely recalled killing one of the enemy soldiers before being subdued. It was a miracle he was still alive.

So, no, they would not simply release him. Not when he had killed one of their own.

And yet . . . The farmhouse sank to nothing behind him. Winded, he slowed to a walk. Several times he tripped and caught himself, and once he fell flat on the rock-hard ground and briefly thought he had sprained an ankle but was able to walk it off.

He looked over his shoulder. The farmhouse had been swallowed up by the billowing farmlands and still nobody but he was in the fields. Why was he not pursued?

It made no sense.

Unless he was being observed from afar, by means either magical or natural. It was the only rational answer he could think of. Which was why he refrained from reaching out with his mind in search of Freki. If he was being watched or, worse, lying abed hallucinating, he did not want to hand his interrogators the information which, after the name and location of his contact, they desired most: the knowledge that he was a member of the Werewolf Corps and that his traveling companion was a wolf. So, much as he would have liked to coordinate his escape with Freki, he dared not make the attempt.

Ritter was trained to use his wolf as a weapon. With Freki at his side, he was a match for ten conventionally armed men. A vagabond traveling in the company of a wolf, however, was a memorable sight. So they had journeyed separately, Ritter on the roads and his partner keeping to the ditches and coverts, with anywhere from half a mile to a mile's distance between them. As a result, Freki had not been able to help when Ritter was caught by (he remembered the incident now) an unexpected patrol of foragers, looking to complement their rations with a stolen hen or fletch of bacon extorted from the locals.

If only he had not lost his temper and killed that soldier! They would not have seen that he fought like a military man and might well have left him, beaten but alive, where they'd found him.

Or maybe not. Their sergeant had acted like one with the second sight. Those with a touch of talent often wound up as non-commissioned officers or better. In wartime, such men were drawn to the military, where they might rise through the ranks even though they were far from gentle-born.

Ritter's feet were damnably cold by now and his hands as well. There had been a mismatched pair of gloves in the pockets of his greatcoat. But they had been emptied out, along with his knife, matchbox, pipe and tobacco pouch, and a small sack of parched grains intended to stave off hunger. So he pulled in his arms from the coat's sleeves, stuck them in his armpits, and kept on walking. And walking.

Hours passed and the distant line of trees did not seem to be appreciably closer than it had ever been. But there was a farm building ahead with a blue curl of smoke rising from its chimney. Ritter debated whether to bypass it entirely or to stop and see if he could trade some labor ostensibly for food but in actuality for information. Farmers, in their isolation, were more gossip-prone than most people realized. It was even possible—barely—that he would have the opportunity to steal a horse.

These were cheering thoughts. Yet the closer he came to the building, the greater his unease grew. The place looked . . . familiar.

With sinking spirits, Ritter approached the farmhouse.

There was a sign over the door.

САНАТОРИЙ.

He was back where he'd begun.

For an instant, Ritter almost lost all hope. But then he squared his shoulders, turned ninety degrees and started walking again. As an officer and a Prussian gentleman, he could not give in to despair.

The sun through the clouds cast the faintest of shadows. He kept it resolutely to his left and lining up unprepossessing landmarks in the middle distance, a rock, a frozen clod of dirt, a dead plant sticking up out of the snow. He concentrated on making his measurements as accurate as possible. Every now and again he stopped and looked behind himself to see his footprints stretching straight and unwavering toward the horizon. Until finally his legs buckled underneath him and he sank to his knees in the frozen field.

A door opened nearby.

"Well?" Dr. Nergüi said from the stoop of the sanitarium. "Are you convinced yet?"

Wearily, Ritter looked up at her and then to one side and the other. A path of sorts had been trod into the icy ground. It bent inward to each side of the building. He had been walking around and around the farmhouse all day.

Then Borsuk was helping him to his feet and leading him inside. It was warm there. Gratefully, he felt the weight of his greatcoat removed from his shoulders. Borsuk eased Ritter onto a couch. Then he sat down in an overstuffed chair and said, "We are going to try something different now. Would you prefer we talk about your mother or your sex life?"

Dr. Nergüi held up a hand. "Look at him. He remains defiant."

Borsuk's face grew very still. Then he said, "Remarkable. He still hopes to escape."

"There is a thin line between hope and delusion. In my professional judgment, our patient would benefit from having a glimpse of his future."

"I concur," Borsuk said.

In a ramshackle boarding house in Miller's Court in Whitechapel, Ritter sat on the bed that was his room's only furniture, pulling off his boots. He feared he had caught a fungus. The skin between his toes was white as corpse-flesh and a horrid stench rose up when he peeled away the socks. Not much to be done about that. The tips of several toes were black with frostbite. With the point of his knife, he pricked each of them. Three had no sensation. There were blisters too, but best to leave them alone. Punctured, they could get infected.

Not that he expected to live long enough for that to happen.

The guards at Government House had turned Ritter away when he tried to see Sir Toby. But he had expected that. Weeks of hard living had transformed him completely. He no longer looked like the sort of man who might have business with the Office of Intelligence. Even their underworld informers dressed better than he.

Ritter held up his candle stub and, waving it back and forth, was able to locate a nail in the wall by the motion of its shadow. He hung one of his socks on it to air. Then, when he could not find another nail, he draped the second sock over the first.

He lay down on the bed and tried to think. But his head was a buzz of conflicting voices. How long had it been since he had slept? His limbs were as restless as they were weary. His fingers twitched and every time he closed his eyes they flew open again.

Down deep, all men hate their fathers.

Concentrate, damn it! There was no point in going to Sir Toby's club—even when he had looked the part of an officer, he would not have been allowed in without the company of a member. So he would have to find the man in the streets, going to or coming from his office. Ritter had to deliver his message to Sir Toby in person. It could not be given to anyone else. That was imperative.

Ritter thrashed from side to side but could find no comfort. He sat up convulsively and wrapped his arms around his stomach.

He thinks that sleep will restore him.

A guilty conscience, even in repose, knows no rest.

Throwing back his head, Ritter ran his fingers through greasy, tangled locks. Not half an hour ago, he had paid the last few coins he had for this room, hoping that some rest would clear his thoughts. It was money wasted. He couldn't lie still for a single moment, much less for long enough to nod off.

With a groan, he sat up and began pulling on his boots again. His socks he left hanging on the wall.

By the time he'd made his way to Charing Cross, it was twilight.

The streets glistened from a rain which Ritter could not remember, though his coat was damp from it. He faded back into the shadows, watching the carriages clatter by, eyes cocked for one in particular. A coach which rarely took the same route two days in a row, out of Sir Toby's natural reluctance to make himself an easy target for assassins.

So there was no way of being sure Ritter would see it tonight. Still . . . there were only so many ways of getting from the one place to the other. And there were always other nights.

Then a carriage came rattling toward him. He recognized it immediately, for he had ridden in it many times. Desperately, he lunged forward. "Sir Toby!" The words flew from his mouth like ravens. He was running alongside the carriage now, waving, frantically trying to attract the man's attention. Above him, he could see the coachman lifting his whip to warn him off.

But now, in the carriage window, that round, complacent face turned and its eyes widened in astonishment. "Ritter!" Sir Toby flung open the door and, extending a hand, pulled Ritter into the interior, alongside him. They tumbled down together in a heap and then clumsily righted themselves.

He was inside, and the carriage hadn't even slowed down.

"I . . . have . . . a . . . message," he gasped. It seemed he would never catch his breath. "For . . . you."

"My dear fellow, I thought you were—well, never mind what I thought. It is wonderful to see you again. We must get you into some clean clothes. A good meal wouldn't hurt either, by the look of you. I'll rent you a room at the Club; it isn't normally allowed, but I think I can swing it. Oh, dear me, you do look dreadful. What Hells you must have been through."

"The . . . message." Ritter reached inside his greatcoat, fumbling for an inner pocket.

"There will be plenty of time for that after you eat." Sir Toby patted his arm soothingly.

"No . . . it. . . ." To his astonishment Ritter saw his hand emerge clutching the Sheffield knife he had been given so long ago.

And then he was stabbing and stabbing and stabbing and blood spurted everywhere.

———————

"There's our first drop of water," Dr. Nergüi said.

"Don't try to be a man of iron." Borsuk produced a handkerchief and Ritter buried his face in it. "It's all right to cry."

To his horror, Ritter felt great wracking sobs of grief welling up within him. It took all of his strength to hold them back. He was not sure he could do so indefinitely. But a cold, distant part of his mind thought: *All right, then*, and reached out into the darkness.

If this was how they were going to play the game, he would match them parry for thrust. He imagined Freki as he would be were he human: Hulking, rangy, shaggy, dangerous. A murderer if need be, but utterly without malice and unswervingly loyal to his friends. Wolfish, in a word. Layer by layer, he created this fiction, until all it lacked was a name fitting for a man. Ritter chose Vlad. *Vlad*, he thought. *Come.* The wolf would not understand why the image of a human he did not know was being pressed into his mind. But he was trained to obey a command. He emerged from the culvert in which he had been hiding.

Simultaneously, Ritter let the tears out. He had, he discovered with great surprise, rather a lot to cry about. Losses he had never mourned. Sorrows he had suffered and then locked away within himself. Well, then, he would make them work for him.

Ritter threw his head back and howled.

"I think he is ready," Borsuk said at last.

"Excellent work. I'll hold him passive. You start the questioning."

Almost, Ritter slept. But though he fell into a restful lassitude, his eyes did not close. He simply felt unable, or perhaps unwilling, to act. It was like that state of borderline sleep when one is fully aware of one's surroundings and struggles to awaken yet cannot. In a distant part of his brain, he could feel Freki trotting silently across the fields toward the sanitarium. But, of course, his captors weren't looking there. Just into his surface thoughts. Borsuk reached over to brush back into place a strand of hair that had fallen over Ritter's forehead. "Tell us a secret, my dear. Nothing big, nothing important. Just a little one to start with."

Ritter shook his head. Or maybe he only meant to.

"You know you must. You've seen that you will. Why put off the inevitable?"

"There is—" Ritter stopped.

"Yes?"

With all the reluctance he could put into his voice, Ritter said, "A map. Sewn into the lining of my greatcoat."

"Is there really?" Borsuk sounded pleased. He stood and went into the bedroom. When he returned, he had Ritter's knife, which he used to cut open the coat. From the lining he extracted a square of white silk on which was printed a detailed map of the region. Ritter's meeting place with his contact was not marked on it. But of course they already knew that.

Borsuk let the map flutter down onto a stand next to the couch and lay the knife atop it. Ritter tried not to show how aware he was of the knife's proximity. But a wry chuckle from Dr. Nergüi told him that that the blade had again been rendered untouchable by him.

"You see? The world is unchanged. Save for how much better you feel now that you're no longer struggling in a lost cause. Now. Tell me the name of your companion, the one we haven't caught yet."

Ritter heard himself say, "Vlad."

"Your friend is a Slav, then?"

"It is a nickname," Ritter said in a dead voice.

"Ahhh. After the Impaler, no doubt. Tell us about him."

Slowly at first, and then volubly, Ritter began describing the Freki-analogue as he had reimagined him: Vlad's strength, both mental and physical. His dedication to his partner's welfare. The playful side that came out at unexpected moments. His gluttonous appreciation of food. All the while feeling Freki coming closer and closer, until finally he stopped, just outside the sanitarium. Ritter felt a gentle yet unmistakable mental nudge. Freki was awaiting further orders.

"Enough." Dr. Nergüi held up a hand. "Where is he now?"

Ritter managed to crack the slightest of smiles. He turned his head toward the window and sensed that the others did too. "Look there."

Shards of glass and wood exploded inward as Freki came crashing into the room.

In that instant of shock, the two alienists lost all control over their conscious thoughts, and thus over Ritter. Freed of their control, he came up from the couch, slapping a hand on the side table to seize the knife. This time, his fingers easily closed about its handle.

He buried it in Borsuk's heart.

Freki had Dr. Nergüi down on the floor, with his teeth in her throat. Ritter was bit twice in the course of pulling the wolf away from the old woman's corpse. But it was imperative to separate the two of them as quickly as possible. He didn't want Freki to acquire a taste for human flesh.

The address Ritter had been given was a piece of wasteland, neither field nor commons, close by an old town dump. It was terrifyingly exposed space. He supposed that his contact wanted to be sure, on his approach, that only one man was waiting for him. Still, it was dreadfully open. He built himself a small vagrant's camp there and waited, in constant danger of being discovered by foraging soldiers or a press gang.

He did not know who he was waiting for—Ritter only had a code name, a *nom de guerre*, for his contact. He had arrived at dawn on the day appointed, to find only empty land. Nor had the man he expected shown up by sundown. In such an event, he had been told, he was to wait three days. No more, no less. He had already waited two.

Ritter was bent over his wee fire, nursing along a pot of watery rabbit stew, when Freki whined from beneath the grey blanket that hid his presence from prying eyes, warning him that somebody was approaching.

Slowly, Ritter stood.

The man who came walking across the barren land was at least a decade older than himself. By his clothing, a man of substance. By his wariness, no friend of the Mongolian Wizard or his empire. He carried a walking stick which Ritter suspected was more than it seemed. Though Ritter knew himself to be a fearsome sight after all he had been through, the stranger continued steadily toward him.

When he reached the campfire, the man stopped. He looked evenly at Ritter, with neither trust nor fear. He said nothing. He looked to be equally prepared to fight or to bolt. Ritter knew this could only be the man he had been waiting for.

Extending his hand, Ritter said, "The wizard Godot, I presume?"

About the Author

Michael Swanwick published his first story in 1980, making him one of a generation of new writers that included Pat Cadigan, William Gibson, Connie Willis, and Kim Stanley Robinson. In the third of a century since, he has been honored with the Nebula, Theodore Sturgeon, and World Fantasy Awards and received a Hugo Award for fiction in an unprecedented five out of six years. He also has the pleasant distinction of having lost more major awards than any other science-fiction writer.

Roughly one hundred fifty of his stories have appeared in *Amazing*, *Analog*, *Asimov's*, *Clarkesworld*, *High Times*, *New Dimensions*, *Eclipse*, *Fantasy & Science Fiction*, *Interzone*, the *Infinite Matrix*, *Omni*, *Penthouse*, *Postscripts*, *Realms of Fantasy*, *Tor.com*, *Triquarterly*, *Universe*, and elsewhere. Many have been reprinted in Best of the Year anthologies and translated into Japanese, Croatian, Dutch, Finnish, German, Italian, Portuguese, Russian, Spanish, Swedish, Chinese, Czech, and French. He has also published several hundred works of flash fiction.

A prolific writer of nonfiction, Swanwick has published book-length studies of Hope Mirrlees and James Branch Cabell as well as a book-length interview with Gardner Dozois. He has taught at Clarion, Clarion West, and Clarion South.

Swanwick is the author of nine novels, including *In the Drift* (an Ace Special), *Vacuum Flowers*, *Stations of the Tide*, *The Iron Dragon's Daughter*, *Jack Faust*, *Bones of the Earth*, *The Dragons of Babel*, and *Dancing with Bears*. His short fiction has been collected in *Gravity's*

Angels, A Geography of Unknown Lands, Moon Dogs, Tales of Old Earth, Cigar Box Faust and Other Miniatures, The Dog Said Bow-Wow, and *The Best of Michael Swanwick.* His most recent novel, *Chasing the Phoenix,* which chronicles the adventures of confidence artists Darger and Surplus in post-Utopian China, is currently available from Tor Books. He is currently at work on a third and final novel set in Industrialized Faerie.

He lives in Philadelphia with his wife, Marianne Porter. This year, he will be guest of honor at MidAmeriCon II, the 2016 World Science Fiction Convention.